Books By Chris Broyhill

Fiction
<u>The Colin Pearce Series</u>
The Viper Contract
The Cabo Contract
The Satan Contract
The Shadow Contract
The Bronco Contract
The Enteron Contract

Non-Fiction
Business Aviation Leadership:
From the Traits to the Trenches

The Enteron Contract

Colin Pearce Series VI

Chris Broyhill

Published by
**Citadel Publishing LLC
Dover, Delaware, USA
2020**

ISBN-13: 978-1-7345196-1-7
ISBN-10: 1-7345196-1-4

Paperback

Cover Design and Text Formatting By:
Welhaven and Associates

This is a work of fiction.
The characters in this book are fictitious and the
creation of the author's imagination. Any resemblance to
other characters or to persons living or
dead is purely coincidental.

Dedication

To My Loyal Fans. You Continue to Inspire Me.

Acknowledgements

The Enteron Contract is Colin Pearce's sixth adventure, and it is about seven months late.

When I published The Bronco Contract in December 2018, I already had Enteron outlined and had planned to release it a year later. But life intervened. In February of 2019, I undertook the project of writing a leadership book for the business aviation industry that had a hard delivery date of the following February. While I was able to get some of the writing for Enteron completed during 2019, the year was primarily occupied with the interviews, research, and eventually the writing tasks for the leadership book, as well as working at my day job as a senior executive for an aircraft management company. Once the book, Business Aviation Leadership: From the Traits to the Trenches, had been published in early February of this year, I finally had the time to complete Enteron. Hence, it's late arrival.

I must thank you, my loyal fans, for your continued notes and questions about the status of Enteron. During the fall of 2019 and early 2020, I have been deluged with texts, emails, and Facebook messages regarding the status of the book. While the wording in the messages varied, the gist was the same – "really eager for your next book, when will it be available?" Your continued enthusiasm for a book you hadn't seen yet warmed my heart and inspired me. I hope the finished product lives up to your expectations.

Some may see parallels in the locales and organizations in this book to events from my career. I would advise caution with those comparisons. Like most writers, I am a professional observer of human beings and human nature. Regardless of where I am or what I'm doing, I'm always watching people. I regularly make notes about what I observe, whether I'm in an office or a bar. Sometimes, these observations become fodder for main characters or elements of richness for minor ones, as well as plot elements. In all cases, what winds up in the story are amalgams of many different observations, and never built on one or a few. I have a small sign that hangs from a lamp in my home that says: "Careful, you'll wind up in my novel!" Maybe I should start wearing it around my neck.

I need to express a grateful acknowledgment to my wife, Denise Broyhill, for her editing inputs in the final stages of this book. She's been my editor for all books in the Colin Pearce series, and her contributions have, without fail, made the books much better. Sometimes, I go too far in making Colin Pearce edgy. Denise knows right where that edge is and provides the right perspective to allow me to take Pearce right up to the edge but not go over; to enable Pearce to stay redeemable. Thank you, Denise.

Finally, again, to you, my loyal fans, thank you for your patience and even your impatience, as you've waited for this book. I hope it was worth the wait!

Tailwinds Always,

Chris Broyhill
Arlington, Texas
June 2020

Prologue

"Tango Charlie, Kunsan Tower, Runway 36, line up and wait." The controller's voice was tense. I couldn't blame him. He knew the stakes were impossibly high tonight. We all did.

I toggled the mic switch on the F-16's throttle to the UHF position. "Tango Charlie copies line up and wait, Runway 36."

I released the pressure on the Viper's brake pedals and eased the throttle forward. At first, the heavily loaded Block 40 machine seemed anchored to the concrete, unwilling to move. But as I continued to apply power, the jet began to creep toward the runway boundary, slowly and sluggishly, plodding through the pouring rain and howling wind that surrounded it.

I glanced beneath the left and right wings of my jet as it rolled forward. Under each wing, on the pylons just outboard of the external fuel tanks, three stubby incendiary bombs rested securely against a standard USAF triple ejector rack. The bombs were Russian-made, and they were attached to the racks through an improvised mounting system. God only knew if they'd come off when I pushed the pickle button.

The target was a truck carrying a load of nuclear material that would change the balance of power on the Korean peninsula. The truck was 150 miles away, behind the most sophisticated air defense network in the world. I had to get through those defenses, find a moving vehicle in heavy rain under a low overcast, and put six bombs on it, with no ballistics data for the weapons I was expending. And do it all without getting blown out of the sky.

I was on my own. There would be no support from my service or my country. My actions had to be deniable and disavowable. Even though the President himself had approved them.

If I failed, war on the Korean Peninsula was a likely outcome, and with that conflict came the high probability of a war that would engage the most powerful nations on earth.

"Jesus," I said to myself as I stopped the Viper on the centerline of Runway 36. "You've really done it this time, Pearce."

"Tango Charlie, Kunsan Tower. You are released. God speed, sir."

I nodded as I pushed the Viper's throttle up to 90% RPM and waited for the engine instruments to stabilize. The tower controller couldn't clear me for takeoff – that would indicate official approval for the mission.

"Tango Charlie, roger," I said.

I released the brakes and pushed the throttle over the detent into MAX AB. I felt the usual kick in the middle of my back as afterburner lit, and the nozzle gauge swung to 50-85% open. The sheets of rain began to part in front of me as the sleek jet and its cumbersome cargo accelerated down the runway. Mere moments later, I applied backpressure to the sidestick, rotating the jet's nose skyward. Then, after lingering in the takeoff attitude for a few seconds – a few seconds that seemed to last an eternity – the Viper lifted off into the tempestuous night.

The target was 40 minutes away.

CHAPTER ONE

Monday, January 4th
1900 Hours Local Time
St. Charles Place Restaurant
St. Charles, Illinois, USA

I was seated in a comfortable chair and nursing my second martini when she walked into the bar. For a moment, I thought I was hallucinating. The last time we had seen each other was just a few weeks ago, and I had thought about her since – wondering where she was and what she was doing. Perhaps even obsessing a little. When she materialized here, unexpectedly, I first thought she was an illusion generated by alcohol and wishful thinking.

But there she was. She looked at me, smiled radiantly, and walked over to me. I couldn't help smiling in return.

She was dressed for the Chicagoland weather, with a long black overcoat and a scarf that had black and lavender in it. She stopped next to my chair, put her arms around me, and raised her mouth to mine. I shook off my surprise and kissed her. Our lips lingered just a moment or two longer than the standard 'friends' kiss. Then, she stepped back and began to unbutton her coat. After a moment, she turned around and spoke to me over her shoulder.

"Would you help me with this?" she asked.

I nodded and helped her remove the jacket. When she was completely out of it, I draped it over the chair to my left and turned back to her. She had slipped into the chair to my right and was now facing me with her right arm resting on the bar's padded edge. She wore a black sweater with a scoop neck, black tights, and boots with spiked heels. The outfit accentuated her superb figure and cappuccino skin perfectly. I could see an ornate gold chain hanging from her neck. At the end of the chain, just above her décolletage, there were several golden charms, grouped together. I didn't take the time to stare at them, but I had a feeling they told some kind of story.

The bartender walked over just then. His name was Chad, and he was thin and fit and had very precisely cut brown hair. He had been stealing glances at me since I had entered the bar an hour ago. He seemed to have a disappointed expression on his face now.

"I'll have what he's having," Sharona Brown said without looking at him. Sharona Brown wasn't her real name. She had told me her real name many years ago, but she had gone by a few different ones in our meetings since then and had used several in her career. Sharona happened to be the name I liked best.

Chad nodded and set about the martini-making chores.

"I think he has the hots for you," she whispered when Chad was out of earshot.

"Lucky me," I said. But then I thought for a moment. "Actually, I guess I am lucky if you're here."

Sharona smiled and nodded. "That's nice of you to say. But you might not think so after we're finished talking."

I nodded. "Kind of figured this might not be a personal visit." I looked around the room for a moment, then returned my gaze to her. "I'll ask the obvious question even though I think I already know the answer. How did you find me?"

She started to open her mouth, but before she could speak, I interrupted her.

"And don't say that thing that Smith always says: 'We're the CIA, it's what we do.'" Dave Smith was my usual handler from the Agency.

"Damn," Sharona said, smiling. "You took the words right out of my mouth."

"You're the one that told me I needed to come to Chicago," I said. "I have the address, and I'm going to knock on that door tomorrow, although I have absolutely no idea what I'm going to say if she opens it."

"She'll open it," Sharona said. "She's expecting you."

That was a bit of a shock to me, but it shouldn't have been. Sarah Morton, the woman I had loved and nearly married six years ago, was less than a mile from where we were sitting, living in a condominium the CIA and I had bought for her. Of course the CIA would have told her I was coming.

"How's she doing?" I asked after a long moment.

"Great," Sharona said. "But her name is Sarah Connor now. She's working part-time as a scheduler in a local flight department at the DuPaul airport."

I laughed softly. "We have aliases in common," I said. "My assumed first name and her assumed last name. Too bad she doesn't have a son named John. Like the movies."

Sharona smiled and opened her mouth to say something, but then seemed to think better of it. "It seems to suit her," she said at last.

Chad arrived with Sharona's martini and set it in front of her. "Anything to eat?" he asked.

I glanced at the menu I had been perusing earlier. "How's the shrimp de jonghe?" I asked.

"A best-seller," he said. "But it's really garlicky. It might… interfere…if you have plans…" his voice trailed off when he realized what he was implying.

"No worries there, Chad," I said, laughing. "I have a distinct feeling that my lovely companion is here on business." I looked over at her. "As much as I'd like to believe otherwise."

"So, an appetizer helping of the de jonghe?" he asked.

I looked at Sharona and she nodded.

I turned my head back to our bartender. "You bet, Chad. Thank you."

He nodded and turned away.

I picked up my glass and offered a toast to Sharona. "Cheers, ma'am," I said. We clinked glasses and drank.

"Not as good as Plymouth, is it?" she said after sipping.

I shook my head. "Bombay is good," I said. "But nothing is as smooth as Plymouth." I took another sip and looked across the top of my glass at her. "You knew I'd eventually come here, obviously. And you were waiting for the moment. Now I'm here and you're here. The question is: why?"

Sharona looked around the room. "What kind of look do you think they were going for here?" she asked, ignoring the question.

I smiled to myself. I was used to this tactic. Sharona provided information on her schedule or the Agency's. Sometimes the two aligned. Other times they did not.

I gestured to the room as I faced the bar and allowed my eyes to roam the area again. "I've been wondering that same thing since I sat down here. The décor is kind of eclectic. We have the big artificial oak tree with the lights hanging from it, a mountain cabin motif in the next room, and the bar area here looks like it could have come from a Chinese restaurant.

Sharona nodded as she continued to take in the space around us. Then she returned her eyes to me. "Does your boss know where you are?" she asked.

I nodded as I turned to her. "Yes. But he's not technically my boss anymore since he gave me control of the company. I did tell him all about Sarah and our daughter and told him I needed to see them. He didn't have a problem with me being gone a few days to spend some time with them."

"Well, you are the president of Brooks Air Service now," Sharona said. "As the owner, I'm sure he'd be concerned about your absence."

"Co-owner," I said, correcting her.

"Oh yes," she said after a moment. "That's right. He gave you some equity in the company."

"Not some," I said. "Forty-nine percent. It was very generous of him." Brooks Air Service was based in Sedona, Arizona, and sported a fleet of five OV-10A Broncos that we used for sightseeing and acrobatic flights. I had worked there for the past five years before Ian Brooks, the owner, had promoted me to President and given me equity in the company. I might have earned his generosity to some extent. I did save his life.

"You might be gone more than a few days," Sharona said. "We've got something we need you to look into. Something that could be very serious."

I sat back in my chair and took another sip of my martini. "I should have known," I said.

CHAPTER TWO

Tuesday, January 5th
0730 Hours Local Time
1721 Stuarts Drive
St. Charles, Illinois, USA

I was parked at the curb across the street from the address I had been given. It was a condominium that looked like a townhouse. There were four condos in each cluster, two end units, and two in the middle. The address was the one on the far right of its cluster. I sat in the car and tried to gather my wits and my courage. I hadn't seen Sarah or our daughter, Colleen, for over five years. Part of the reason had to do with the ten-million-dollar contract on my head. I didn't want to put them into any danger. But the real reason, the main reason, was I just thought they were better off without me.

"It's not going to get any easier, the longer you sit here," I said to myself.

But I didn't get out of the car. I looked into the vanity mirror above my seat and straightened my tie for the fifth or sixth time. I had decided to wear a suit today for reasons I didn't understand. I peered at my face in the small mirror. My brown hair had more gray in it than it did when I had seen Sarah last, and my face had more lines. The hazel eyes that stared back at me were colder and wearier. I was in considerably better shape these days, but sometimes, as one gets older, less weight and less fat can make one look gaunt, not younger.

"Goddamn it," I said to myself. "Enough is enough. Get your ass out of the car."

I exited the rented Cadillac ATS and locked it. I strode across the street and up the short walk to the front door. There was a fine layer of snow on the ground, and it coated the grass and the flowerbeds on either side of the walk. The cement looked like it had been freshly shoveled and swept. To my right was a side yard of sorts that separated Sarah's condo with the end unit on the next cluster. I looked through the yard to the street than ran behind the development. It was called Kirk Road, and it seemed busy that morning. Even though Sarah's condo backed up to the road, it was separated from the thoroughfare by a man-made lake that was about fifty yards wide, providing at least some distance from the noise. I wondered what the view of the lake looked like from inside.

I stepped to the door and inhaled deeply to steady my nerves. Then, I rang the bell.

I heard footsteps on some sort of hard flooring behind the door and heard the sound of the deadbolt turning in the doorframe. I caught my breath as the door opened.

Sarah Morton had been an accomplished business jet pilot. But she was also a Monthly Mistress for Bachelor Magazine, and her issue of the magazine had sold over a million copies. The red hair still looked like silk, and the green eyes were still warm and affectionate. She was wearing jeans and a sweater that flattered her figure without drawing obvious attention to the physical attributes of her body that had made her magazine a bestseller.

She smiled at me across the three feet or so that separated

us. The expression on her face communicated so many things that I had trouble taking them all in at once. She motioned for me to enter.

"Get out of the cold, Colin," she said. "Fifteen degrees is cold even for Chicago."

I walked through the door, and she shut it behind me. Then we turned to face each other. Six years ago, we would have been in each other's arms in seconds. But six years was a long time, and we had both endured a lot of mileage since then. She stood there, looking beautiful and searching my face with those deep green eyes.

"It's good to see you again," she said after a long moment.

I nodded at her. "It's fantastic to see you. You look incredible. You haven't aged a day."

"I've missed you," she said.

"I've missed you as well." I looked away from her for a moment. "I'm sorry I've been out of touch."

Sarah stepped forward and took my hands in hers. "The lady from the CIA was here," she said, still looking up at me. "She explained it. She said the contract was still in place. She said you were trying to protect us."

I flashed back to a month ago. The tattooed face of a Mexican assassin appeared in my mind's eye. He was looking at the short-barreled shotgun in my hand. A second later, I had pulled the trigger and blown a hole in his chest the size of a dinner plate. He was one of four that had died trying to kill me that week. I involuntarily squeezed Sarah's hands as I forced the image from my mind.

"What name did she give you?" I asked as I found my way back into the moment.

"Sharona Brown," Sarah replied. She searched my face and must have seen some pain there. She stepped closer to me and put her arms around me and her head on my chest. "She said you two knew each other."

Sarah felt good against me, and I relished the warmth that emanated from her. I felt a lump seize the back of my throat. "We've been on a few operations together," I said when I could trust my voice. "Sharona, which isn't her real name, might be the deadliest human being I've ever met." I didn't mention that I had slept with Sharona once. The circumstances were complicated, and I still couldn't decide how I felt about it.

"Let's go sit down," Sarah said after we had held each other for a while. "We have some things to talk about before... everyone gets here."

"Everyone?" I asked.

She nodded against me. "You'll see." Then she pushed back and looked up at me. "Do you want the tour?" she asked.

"Sure," I said.

"You ought to see it," she replied as she released me and took my hand. "You're paying for it."

I nodded. "The least I could do."

Sarah looked up at me and smiled. "And we're very grateful. You didn't have to do anything. Sharona was very clear about that. The CIA would have paid for everything."

"I needed to do something," I said, more to myself than to Sarah. "I needed to participate."

Sarah led me upstairs. We stopped at the top of the landing. "There are two bedrooms up here," she said. "The master and the kids' room. And two bathrooms."

I noticed a loft area at the top of the staircase that had been converted to a small office with several bookcases and a desk.

"Nice," I said. "What do you do here?"

"I'm working on my MBA," she said. "I needed a place I could do that and be close to the kids. They can play in their room, and I can do my homework."

It was the second time she had used the plural for children. She and I had one daughter, named Colleen. I didn't know where the other kid came from and decided to keep my questions to myself for the time being.

We descended the stairs to the main level, where I had come in, and then went into the basement. The central area was L-shaped and open, with a separate room in one corner. Exercise equipment was set-up in the open part. I could see a smith machine, an elliptical trainer and a rowing machine as well as a set of dumbbells. The door was open to the separate room, and I could see various toys scattered about the carpeted floor.

"So, you come down here to work out, and the kids play in there?" I asked.

Sarah nodded. "Yep. Keeps them out of my hair when I'm trying to stay in shape."

"Awesome," I said. "This is a perfect set-up. I'm envious. I have to go to a gym to exercise."

We went back upstairs to the main level. Sarah led me into a cozy area that was a combination of living room and dining room. There was a gas fireplace in one corner. On the opposite wall there was a sliding glass door that looked out onto the lake behind the property. Sarah and I sat on a leather sofa facing the fireplace.

"Do you want anything to drink?" she asked.

I would have killed for a shot of scotch at that moment, but I shook my head. "No, thank you," I said. "I think I'm good."

Sarah nodded and leaned back against the cushions of the sofa. She was facing me and had one leg bent on the sofa while the other stayed on the floor. There was a moment of awkward silence. I could tell she had something important to say to me but was having difficulty finding the right words. I decided to make it easy for her.

"Six years is a long time," I said. "And however well-intentioned the reasons for the separation, life has to go on, Sarah."

Sarah wasn't looking at me. She was looking down at her

hands. After several seconds, she spoke. "Has life gone on for you?"

I chuckled and shook my head. "No. Not really. In fact, I've spent the last five years of my life in Sedona, Arizona, trying to stay off the grid and find myself."

"What happened?"

I looked at her and cocked my head. "What do you mean?"

"Why are you here? Now?"

I had to think about that one. I wanted to tell her everything, but I wasn't sure about what I could or should share. After a few moments, it occurred to me that the truth was the best answer.

"About five years ago," I began. "I was tracking an assassin that was killing people all over the world. This assassin killed a close friend," I made eye contact with Sarah, "a close female friend."

Sarah nodded but said nothing.

"Sharona was wounded during that same operation and almost died."

I rose from the sofa without willing it and walked over to the sliding glass door next to the dining table. The vertical blinds had been retracted, and the view out of the door was peaceful and relaxing. The layer of snow surrounded the small lake behind the condo. The surface of the lake was mostly frozen, but there were a few spots where the water was visible. A small family of ducks was making their way across one of the larger open spots, a green-tinted male, a brown female, and three yellow and brown-colored ducklings. I wondered why they hadn't flown south and fled the Chicago winter.

"I buried my friend in the cemetery at the Air Force Academy," I continued, looking out at the lake. "She was the fourth woman to die because she had known me or been around me."

I looked over at Sarah. She was still sitting on the sofa.

She wasn't looking at me. It was like she was trying to take in what I was saying without being distracted.

"I couldn't take the death anymore," I said, returning my gaze to the lake. The duck family had reached the far side of the lake and were climbing the bank on the other side. "And I was scared shitless that somehow you and Colleen might get caught up in all of it." I paused for a few seconds and swallowed. "So, I went off the grid. I changed my name and found a new job in Sedona, flying OV-10s for tourists." I glanced over at Sarah. "You'd love it."

Sarah nodded in my peripheral vision. She was still looking down.

"Then, about a month ago, I got caught up in another CIA operation. I didn't realize it at first, but it soon became evident. Sharona was part of that operation. She told me where you were living and that I should visit you."

I looked down at the deck on the other side of the glass. There was a compact gas grill, two chairs, and a small table, all covered with a thin white blanket of snow. I felt a flash of longing to be part of a couple or a family where I could sit in one of those chairs with a good drink and watch the world go by.

"Anyway," I concluded, as I watched the ducks find a place to sit together in the snow, "after the operation was finished, she encouraged me to make the journey. Here I am."

I saw Sarah nod again out of the corner of my eye. She rose from the sofa and walked to my side. She put her arm around my waist and her head on my shoulder.

"I love you," she said, her voice barely a whisper. "And I always will."

Her words lightened my heart, but I knew there was more to follow, and I prepared myself for it.

"You're the man who taught me how to love," she continued, "and you're the one who rescued me from a fate that would have been worse than death."

"Right place. Right time," I said, without thinking. "I'd rather be lucky than good."

Sarah abruptly turned me towards her and raised her hands to my face. "You can be such an idiot at times," she said as she looked into my eyes and shook her head.

I nodded in response.

"You *are* good," Sarah whispered to me. "It's who you are. That's one of the things I love about you."

I looked down into those bottomless green eyes. They glowed with the love and tenderness I remembered, an intensity of feeling that had left me in awe when I had first experienced it years ago.

An emotional key turned inside of my carefully locked and compartmented psyche. Doors that had been sealed and barred for six years were flung open, and a flood of sentiment and passion came forth. In that moment, I realized how closely I had held her to me during these years of separation and how much her love had kept me going through my darkest hours. Even though I had repeatedly chosen not to acknowledge it.

And now, as I continued to search her eyes, I felt a sense of profound loss inside myself, for in those eyes, while I saw that love and tenderness I cherished, I also saw a difference in the character of those emotions. Where there was once passion, there was now affection – platonic affection. Part of me was grateful for the change in her feelings, thankful for the freedom the change would give her. But another part felt like it had been ripped in two.

The sound of the front door opening tore me from the moment. I spun to the sound and reached under my jacket for the .45 Colt Commander on my right hip.

Sarah stayed my hand. "Relax," she whispered.

One man and two children came down the hallway and entered the living room a few seconds later. The man was shorter than I was. He had a closely trimmed beard, brown hair that was receding, and a friendly face with an easy smile. As soon as he saw Sarah, his eyes sparkled, and all was clear.

The dichotomy of emotion rose inside me again. I felt an intense sensation of happiness for Sarah and for this young man, whoever he was. Yet, with the happiness, I also felt a sense of profound pain and loss.

I didn't have time to dwell on the feelings. The two children stopped at the end of the hallway and looked at me. There was a girl who appeared to be about six years old and a slightly younger boy. The little girl had Sarah's silken red hair and my hazel eyes. The boy had Sarah's deep green eyes and brown hair, the same color as mine. The boy had detached himself from the man and the girl. He looked at me across the carpet with his arms crossed and a skeptical expression on his little face.

Suddenly, I felt my head spinning. I was looking at a five-year-old version of myself.

"How?" I said without thinking.

"You and I were together, just the once," Sarah whispered. "After we found out we couldn't get married. The night before you left."

I nodded dumbly. I remembered the interlude clearly. There had been more than a few sexual interactions with other women since then, but none had been as powerful as the evening with Sarah.

"What's his name?" I asked, my voice barely audible.

"Christopher," Sarah said, matching my tone and volume. "I was going to name him Colin, but I thought it might be too obvious." Then she spoke in a normal tone of voice. "Kids," she said. "Come over here and meet your father."

CHAPTER THREE

Tuesday, January 5th
0845 Hours Local Time
1721 Stuarts Drive
St. Charles, Illinois, USA

"I imagine it's a little hard to take in," Sarah's friend said. I could hear him in the kitchen, mixing some kind of drink. Sarah had introduced him as Brett Zeigler. They worked together at the local airport.

I nodded in response, staring at the fireplace in front of me, not looking at him. I was still seated on the sofa, where the kids had been with me until a few moments ago when Sarah had left to take them to school. I felt a swell of sentiment inside of me that I didn't know I possessed. It had been difficult for me to talk to the kids. Not because I didn't know what to say, although that was part of it. It was more because I was in awe at the sight of them. In my mind's eye, I could still visualize the two small faces, innocent faces that looked like mine, each in their own way. Emotions were careening off the walls of my psyche like bumper cars in a carnival midway.

Brett walked over to me, retrieved a coaster from a pile of them on the coffee table, and set a red-colored drink in a glass on top of the coaster.

I nodded at him and reflexively reached for the glass. I took a long sip of it without asking him what it was. The drink turned out to be an excellent bloody mary, spicy and well-proportioned with vodka.

"Thanks," I said as I lowered it from my mouth. "I needed that."

"Figured you might," he said with a good-natured tone in his voice. "I'm not sure what how I would react if I just met two kids I didn't know I had."

"One kid," I said as I took another swig of the bloody mary. "I knew about Colleen. I just didn't know about the little boy."

"Oh, that's right," Brett said, shaking his head at himself. "I knew that."

Brett sat down on the love seat that was adjacent to the sofa. He leaned forward slightly. His knee was bouncing up and down with nervous energy. He was apprehensive about something. Maybe it was me.

"What else do you know?" I asked, turning my head to look at him.

He shrugged. "As much as she was willing to tell me," he said. "We're pretty good friends."

I felt my face change expressions without my willing it, and he must have seen something threatening in my visage.

"Just friends," he said, anxiously, raising his two hands, palms up towards me in a gesture of surrender. "Just friends."

"Sorry," I said. "I guess I'm a little protective." I raised my glass towards him and nodded. "This is a good bloody mary."

Brett smiled. "My personal hangover cure. Half a glass of vodka, half a glass of Zing Zang mix, a few splashes of Tabasco, and some ground pepper on top of it."

"Well done," I said as I took another sip of it. The glass was now half empty, and I could feel the soothing warmth of the alcohol inside me. I was grateful for it. "Tell me about you and Sarah. Did you meet at work?"

Brett shook his head and motioned over his shoulder with his left hand. "I live about three doors down. She was struggling to get her trash out one winter morning last year while I was on my way to work. I stopped and helped her."

I nodded as he spoke. The scenario sounded plausible, but it also sounded like it could have been a set up if someone had wanted to get close to Sarah to get at me. But, according to Sharona, Sarah had dutifully reported the contact to the Agency, and a full background check had been run on the young man. Other than a few speeding tickets, he was clean.

"We kept seeing each other around the neighborhood and became friends. One day, she asked if I could babysit for her when she went to the doctor's office." He shrugged in a self-deprecating way. "I'm the youngest of five, and all my brothers and sisters have small kids. I enjoy being around them and I'm good with them."

I smiled at him. "So, you were qualified for the task."

He nodded and smiled back. "Coll and Chris are great kids too. Sarah has raised them very well."

I looked across the room at the studio portrait of Sarah and the two kids on the fireplace. Typically, studio-generated photographs can look forced and artificial. The expressions in the picture on the mantle looked happy and genuine. The eyes seemed to sparkle with love and warmth. There was only one thing wrong with the photo – I wasn't in it. I forced the thought aside. "I'm sure she has," I said at last.

The conversation lapsed into silence. I took another sip of the bloody mary and gazed around me. The room was very tastefully decorated. The sofa, loveseat, end table, and coffee table showed none of the typical damage that small children can cause. There were no gashes in the wood and no stains or tears in the leather. I smiled to myself. My mom had not fared so well. My two brothers and I had caused some significant damage when we were young, to the point that we were banned from certain rooms in the house.

There was some artwork on the walls, a few landscapes, and artistic photos. But the center point of the room was a low shelving unit to the left of the kitchen bar area that featured pictures of the kids at various ages in their short lives. There were holiday photos and birthday photos as well as pictures with no occasion at all, just moments that Sarah wanted to capture and savor. I rose from the sofa, walked to the unit and looked at each photo, one by one, willing each image to imprint itself on my brain.

On the middle shelf, at the far right, was a photo of an older man and woman in full ski gear. I detected a resemblance to Sarah. It occurred to me that the two had to be her mother and father. As I scanned the other photos, I didn't see them in any of the images with the kids.

"They haven't seen the kids," Sarah said from beside me. I had heard her come in, so her voice didn't startle me. She spoke very softly. I could hear the regret in her words. She didn't need to explain. She couldn't contact her parents because that would violate the rules of her CIA protection program and expose her. She had to deprive her parents of the joy of grandkids to keep those kids safe.

"That sucks," I said.

"It does," she replied. She reached for the bloody mary glass, and I handed it to her. She took a long sip of the drink and looked at me over the glass. "What did you think of them?" she asked after a moment.

I was still staring at the pictures of the kids on the shelf in front of me. "I think they're the most amazing things I've ever seen," I said. I turned my gaze to her and smiled. "Present company notwithstanding."

Sarah smiled back at me and motioned towards Brett with the glass in her hand. "He makes a mean bloody, doesn't he?"

I nodded. "That he does."

"Hey Brett-ster," Sarah said, glancing over at him. "Can you scare up a round of these for all of us."

"You bet!" he said.

***

A few minutes later, we were seated around Sarah's dining table with full drinks in front of us. There was an expectant silence in the air. As I looked between the two faces at the table with me, I could see anticipation and affection pass between them. Brett and Sarah obviously cared for one another, but there was a distance between them, and that distance seemed to affirm Brett's assertion that the two of them were just friends. Something told me that it was a distance that Sarah insisted upon, and at that moment, one of the reasons for this meeting became clear: they wanted my blessing.

Jesus, I thought. The juxtaposed feelings of both happiness and loss flooded through me again. I took a long sip of my drink to mask the conflict occurring inside of me.

I looked across the table at Brett as I lowered my glass. "What do you do at the airport, Brett? I don't think we got around to that."

"I'm a business analyst for a flight department there," he said. "It's a company you've probably never heard of," he continued. "Unless you're from around here. It's called Enteron. It's an energy company."

I nodded at him to encourage him to keep talking. I did know of Enteron. In addition to the briefing I had received from Sharona the night before, I had saved the CEO's life at Lake Tahoe five years ago.

"We're one of the largest nuclear power plant operators in the United States. We have a business presence in almost every state."

"What kind of jets do you fly?" I asked.

Brett beamed with pride. "We have two Falcon 7Xs and two Falcon 2000 LXS's. We also have a Sikorsky S-76, but it's based at our eastern location, at the Baltimore-Washington Airport."

I nodded again. The CIA's reason for my involvement was becoming clearer. I was typed in both Falcons and had experience in the 7X.

"That's a big fleet," I said. I looked at Sarah. "Do you work there too, Sarah?"

She nodded. "Part-time," she answered. "Brett got me the job. I do scheduling for them. I work with the admin assistants for the execs and schedule the jets and crew to support the execs' travel schedules. It's a pretty cool job, and they're very flexible with me since I'm a single mom."

"She's working on her dispatch certificate!" Brett broke in excitedly. "She'll have it in about another month!"

"Nice!" I said. "Congratulations, Sarah."

Sarah looked away for a moment. Understandably, Brett didn't have the full story of her past. Sarah had several thousand hours of flight time to her credit. Getting a dispatcher's license would be child's play for her. As an experienced pilot, she already had the knowledge base required.

"She's helping us work these real complicated trips!" Brett continued, bubbling with enthusiasm. "Enteron has been chosen by the U.S. Government to help the North Korean Government stabilize its nuclear power program. We're actually flying into North Korea all the time now! We're the only operator in the U.S. allowed to do that!"

Sharona's words from the briefing last night were ringing in my ears. *"They fly in and out of Pyongyang about twice a month,"* she had said. *"Ostensibly to help the NK nuke industry improve its safety standards. But we think they might be up to something else. We recruited your buddy Mark Hill to look into it."*

"The trips require a ton of planning," Sarah said, putting a hand on his arm to slow him down. "The political and diplomatic clearances are extensive. I do a lot of my work from home since Korea is twelve hours ahead of us."

"We even have a dedicated representative at the U.S. State Department!" Brett said, not taking the hint. "Sarah talks to him all the time!" His pride in her tasks brought a smile to my lips.

"That's pretty cool," I said. "I might have to drop in on the department and say hello to the director. He and I were classmates at the Air Force Academy."

In an instant, both faces transformed from animation into shock. A line of worry knit its way into Brett's forehead, just above his dark eyebrows. Sarah's eyes took on a knowing, haunted look. A glance passed between the two of them.

"You mean Mark Hill?" Brett asked after several seconds had passed.

I nodded. "We called him Hill-man when we were in the service together."

A look of realization entered Sarah's eyes. "You won't be able to see him, but you should still go by the department," she said.

I went hollow inside as I remembered the last words from Sharona's briefing last night. *"Hill's gone silent. We need you to find out why."*

"Why can't I see him?" I asked, knowing the answer as I uttered the words.

"He's dead," Brett said, his eyes welling with tears. "The Saint Charles Police found him in his townhouse yesterday morning. The company told us about it yesterday afternoon."

"How?" I asked.

"Self-inflicted gun-shot wound," Sarah said in a tone of angry skepticism. "They ruled it a suicide."

Well, that's fucking handy, I thought. I felt a flash of anger.

The CIA had known about Hill and, as usual, hadn't bothered to provide all the relevant information in the briefing. But their real intentions for my visit to Enteron now became clear.

The Agency didn't want me to find out why Hill had gone silent. They wanted me to find out why someone had killed him.

But I knew that wasn't all.

The Agency's agenda included more than discovery. The 'why' behind Hill's death wouldn't be enough. Behind the 'why' would be a 'who.' And the 'who' would need to be dealt with. My way.

The old blood lust, the Darkness, stirred inside of me, roused from a slumber that had lasted just over a month. I could feel it smile.

CHAPTER FOUR

Tuesday, January 5th
1000 Hours Local Time
Main Street
St. Charles, Illinois, USA

"You could have told me he was actually dead," I said into the car's interior as I guided the Cadillac down Main Street and into the heart of downtown St. Charles.

"Well, that wouldn't have been any fun," Sharona replied over the car's Bluetooth phone connection. "It's always so much better when you discover these little details yourself, Colin."

I was enjoying my surroundings as I drove. Well-maintained stores, bars, and restaurants lined both sides of the street, making the area look quaint, tidy, and unpresumptuous. The place had a nice, homey feel.

"The fact that he was dead isn't exactly a little detail," I responded.

"No, it isn't," she said. "But I know after working with you and hearing about you from Bart and Bruiser that when you dig the facts up yourself, it gets you more invested. And it makes things more...dynamic."

Bart was the nickname for John Amrine, a senior CIA

operations officer who was often in charge of the scenarios where my talent was necessary. He was built like a powerlifter and had a mop of blond hair, hence the name, linked to Bart Simpson of television fame. Bruiser was Dave Smith, my usual handler, who was slightly shorter than I was, with brown hair and jade green eyes. His ability to damage people was legendary in the CIA and had generated his moniker.

"Dynamic, my ass," I said.

She laughed. "As I recall, your ass can be a bit dynamic when it needs to be."

I didn't know whether she was referring to my tactical exploits or the brief intimate interlude that she and I had shared several weeks ago, and I had no intention of finding out. I was still a little pissed about how the interlude itself had occurred.

"What's your play with the cops?" Sharona asked, neatly changing the subject. She had a habit of doing that when it suited her.

"I'm going to flash that NSA ID you guys gave me at the front desk and see if I can get them to show me the case file," I said. "With a bit of luck, I might even get to talk to the detective who is working the case."

"What makes you so sure it wasn't a suicide?"

"Jesus," I said. "Why are you asking me that? I know you don't believe that."

"I know why we don't believe it. I want to hear why you don't."

"Easy." I hit the right turn signal and eased the Cadillac off of Main Street and onto North Riverside Avenue. "Hill's family lives in Maryland. He was taking vacation time. Brett and Sarah told me he was called back to fly a trip that is leaving for Korea this evening. Pilots don't commit suicide when they're scheduled to fly. They don't commit suicide when people are counting on them. It's not in the DNA."

"Makes sense," Sharona said.

I drove past a building that looked like a fire station on the right and then saw the sign for the police headquarters ahead and to my left. I crossed State Street, made a left turn into the parking lot, and pulled into a spot.

"What makes it more suspicious is the fact that he had no plans to be in Saint Charles yesterday, and they called him back to be here. That sounds a lot like a set up to me."

"We agree," Sharona said. "Did Sarah or this guy Brett tell you who told Hill to come back?"

"They did," I said. "It was his boss. The executive in charge of the department. Some woman named Brenda Rowe."

Sharona didn't respond.

I smiled to myself and shook my head. "But...you already knew that."

"She's on our radar," Sharona said. "We knew she was Hill's boss. We didn't know she was the one who called him back, but it makes sense."

"Anything else you'd like to share?"

"Maybe. When the time is right."

"Nice," I said, shutting the car off. "Well, time to go talk to the cops."

"So, this is you doing your standard thing, right?"

"Excuse me?"

"Rattling things around until something happens?"

I nodded, even though I knew she couldn't see me. "That would be it," I said. "It's all I know how to do."

I ended the call and put the phone in an inside coat pocket. I was about to exit the car, but I remembered the gun on my right hip. Probably not the best move to enter a strange police station armed, even if I did have a government ID. I removed the pistol and its holster, as well as the two magazines on my left hip and locked them all in the Cadillac's center console.

I left the car and walked toward the two buildings that

comprised the Saint Charles Police Department Headquarters. The first one was on my right, a plain two-story building with a red brick façade. It looked institutional and uninspiring. Ahead of me, there was a white brick half-wall with one word, POLICE, etched on the stone. It seemed to be directing me to the second unit in the complex, a one-story building with glass doors and a blue metal roof. As I stepped to the doors, the green waters of the Fox River were visible just beyond the building. I looked down to my left and could see the white arches of the main street bridge spanning the river to the western section of the downtown area. I could even hear the sounds of a small waterfall near the bridge. I smiled to myself. Saint Charles seemed like a peaceful place.

But a friend of mine had been killed here.

I opened the glass door and walked through a waiting area with several empty chairs to the front desk. A woman in civilian clothes sat at the reception desk. She appeared to be a few years older than I was, wore her gray hair in an untidy bun on the top of her head, and had heavy framed metal glasses suspended on a bulbous nose. The placard on the counter said PHYLLIS BLANCHARD. I stopped in front of her, and she looked up at me with a neutral expression on her face.

"May I help you?" she asked, in a tone of voice that clearly indicated she wasn't eager about the task.

"I hope so, Ms. Blanchard," I said. I removed a credential wallet from my inner coat pocket and presented it to her. "I'm Special Agent Connor Price from the National Security Agency. I need to speak to the detective in charge of the Mark Hill Case, please."

The credentials were inscribed with the pseudonym I had been using for the last five years, and it rolled off my tongue easily. I had no idea if the credentials were valid or even if the NSA actually had agents, but I was about to find out. I wondered if the CIA would rescue me if I was arrested for impersonating a federal officer.

Phyllis scrutinized the ID card and accompanying badge closely. She looked up at me several times as she examined the document. I didn't see a scanner on her desk. I breathed a small sigh of relief. Visual scanning was increasingly used for identification, and I had no idea how many databases had my ugly mug loaded in them. After a few more moments, Phyllis nodded to herself and seemed satisfied. She handed me the wallet and gave me a courteous smile. I seemed to have passed muster.

"What case did you say you were here about?" she asked.

"Mark Hill. He was found dead yesterday morning, I believe."

"Oh yes," Phyllis said as she typed into the keyboard in front of her and regarded a monitor I couldn't see. "That would be Detective Jarvis's case." She inclined her chin toward the chairs in the waiting area behind me. "If you'll have a seat, I'll page her for you."

"Thank you," I said.

I turned from the counter, and instead of sitting, I walked over to the glass window facing the Fox River. It was a sunny winter day in Chicagoland. A few wisps of stratus clouds moved lazily across the sky above, casting narrow shadows on the green water of the river. To my left was the bridge I had seen earlier. Where it met the western shore, there was a brownish brick building with the words *Hotel Baker* inscribed near the roof of the building. The hotel looked posh and inviting. A great hotel usually meant a great bar. I made a mental note to stop into the bar before I left the city.

"Agent Price?" A nasal female voice asked from behind me.

I turned to find a stocky woman with blonde hair and dark eyebrows standing there. She was about five feet five inches tall and was carrying a good thirty pounds she didn't need, forced into black knit pants and a white blouse, both of which seemed to be straining at the seams. She extended her right arm and forced her face into a professional smile.

"I'm Detective Jarvis," she said. "Betty Jarvis. I'm the lead detective on the Mark Hill Case."

I shook her hand. Her grip was limp and unenthusiastic. I didn't know if that was as a statement about her job, her circumstances, or her life.

"Special Agent Connor Price," I said. "Pleased to meet you."

Jarvis motioned back over her shoulder. "Would you care to come with me? I've got the case file on my desk. We can go to an interview room and you can look it over."

"Sounds good."

Jarvis led me into the back of the building. We went to the right of the reception desk and down a hallway that had cubicles on the left side and doors to various rooms on the right side. I didn't pass through any metal detectors or x-ray machines. Either the Saint Charles Police didn't think they were vulnerable to a random shooting attack or they had very sophisticated scanning technology. I was betting on the former. Suddenly, my right hip felt very light without the .45 Commander riding there.

Jarvis motioned me into the last open door on the right. I had been in a few interview rooms in my life and knew the typical layout. Like others I had seen, this room was very spartan, with two chairs on one side of a worn rectangular metal table, for the accused and his or her lawyer and the two chairs on the other side for the interviewing officers. I was wondering which side of the table would be allocated to me. On the wall to my left was a large mirror. I was sure it was composed of two-way glass. There was a room on the other side in which observers could watch or record the proceedings. It occurred to me that I might be playing to two audiences now, Jarvis, and whoever was on the other side of the glass.

"Have a seat," Jarvis said. "I'll get the file. Would you care for any coffee?"

I nodded. "With cream and sugar, please."

She smiled – another forced expression on her tight face. "Same as me," she said. "I'll get it."

Again, I chose not to sit. I roamed the room purposefully. I spent a fair amount of time staring into the mirror. I wanted the observers behind the glass to know I was aware of their presence. Assuming there was anyone behind the glass in the first place.

As I looked into the mirror, I was also forced to regard my own reflection, something I didn't care for. I've never understood how people can look into a mirror at themselves for long periods. I hate looking at myself. It's not that I'm bad looking. I've got hazel eyes, brown hair with a lot of gray specks in it, and a warm face, or so I've been told. But the eyes can go cold when the Darkness rises, and they can emanate a degree of iciness that can chill those looking back at them. I've seen my face in the mirror every morning for the last 56 years, and I'm sick of it. Stature wise, though, things could be worse. I'm six feet two inches tall and a muscular 210 pounds, thanks to lots of time spent in the gym. Even though I'm in my mid-fifties, I can bench nearly 300 pounds and squat and deadlift more than that. The combination of these attributes has a tendency to threaten some of the people I meet. It's a condition I've learned to live with.

"Here we are," said Jarvis from behind me.

I turned to find her with a dark brown file folder under her arm and two cups of coffee in her hands. She offered me the cup in her right hand, and I accepted it. I took a cautious sip. The coffee wasn't what I was expecting from a police station. It was rich and flavorful.

"Wow," I said. "That's good. Better than what we get back in D.C."

Jarvis shot me a suspicious look. "I thought the NSA was headquartered in Fort Meade, Maryland," she said.

I narrowed my eyes at her. "How often do you get out that way?" I asked.

Her face reddened. "Not much," she said after a moment.

"The DC area is a metroplex," I said. I motioned to the area around us with my coffee cup. "Like Chicagoland. And we have offices in many places in the area. You get to think of the whole place as 'DC' after a while."

Jarvis nodded and gestured for me to join her at the table. We both sat on the same side, nearest the door, the "cop" side. I found I was relieved at that. She put the file on the table in front of her and turned to me.

"Not that I have an issue with interagency cooperation and all that, but why would the NSA be interested in a local murder?"

I was expecting this question.

"How much do you know about Hill's background?" I asked.

Jarvis shrugged. "Not much. He was a pilot for Enteron, and he worked over at the local airport. We're still putting together information to round out the file."

And yet you've already ruled it a suicide, I thought. *Interesting.*

"Hill was a USAF veteran and had access to classified information at the Top-Secret level when he was in the service," I said. "Beyond that, I'm not at liberty to discuss the reasons for our interest."

Jarvis seemed to accept my explanation. She pushed the file over to me and opened it.

I had never seen a police file before, so I didn't know what to expect. On the left side of the file jacket was a police report form. At the top of the form, the information for the reporting officer was listed. The officer here was a Sergeant Phillip Graham. I skimmed over the rest of the standard language until I got to the narrative section. Sergeant Graham was a man of few words.

> NARRATIVE: I received a call from central dispatch at 0733 AM on Monday, January 4th. I was instructed to proceed to 1381 Brownstone Drive in St Charles to investigate an apparent break-in or burglary. I arrived at the residence at 0741 AM and found the door to the residence unlocked and ajar. I discovered the victim, a white male in his mid-fifties, seated in a leather recliner in the living room. The victim had a single gunshot wound to the right side of his head. I discovered a 9mm Glock Model 17 pistol on the floor near the victim's chair. An empty bottle of whiskey and a note were discovered on the table next to the victim's chair. I called for detectives and the medical examiner and explored the residence to ensure there were no other victims or signs of forced entry. I found nothing suspicious. I waited at the residence until Det. Jarvis arrived at 0830 AM. I then gave her control of the scene and returned to patrol duty.

Crime scene photos were in an envelope on the right side of the folder. I opened the envelope and began to go through them.

"We take hundreds of photos at a scene like this," Jarvis said. "They're all digital. We only print the photos that we think are most relevant for the folder."

I nodded. There were about 20 8 x 10 photos, some close-ups, and some taken from further away. It's one thing to see photos of random dead people. It's another when you know the person in the photo. You remember who they were in life and what they looked like with the fire of their personality inside them. I had known Mark Hill for over 30 years. In addition to attending the Air Force Academy together, we had both flown A-10s and F-16s at similar times. I had last seen him in the cockpit of one of Enteron's Falcon 2000s five years ago, at Truckee airport near Lake Tahoe. He had been the same boisterous and friendly soul I had known when we served together.

The body in the photo hardly looked like Mark Hill. The energy, the soul of the man, had been forcibly removed, and now, all that remained was a hollow, skin-covered shell.

Damn it, Hill-Man, I thought. *You didn't deserve this.*

"What was the time of death?" I asked, forcing my mind back into the moment.

"Hard for the M.E. To pinpoint," Jarvis said. "Sometime between the previous night and before we got the call the following morning."

Hill was dressed in a pink, button-down shirt, charcoal gray slacks, and a pair of black dress shoes. A black computer bag sat on the sofa, nearest the front door.

"It looks like he was on his way to work," I said. "Did you find any breakfast dishes or coffee cups or anything like that?"

"No," Jarvis said. "We did find a wet towel in the kitchen though, like a gym towel."

"A gym towel?"

"He has a lot of workout gear in his basement. It seems he had a workout that morning before..." her voice trailed off.

I shook my head and continued to look at the photos. Two pictures featured Hill's right hand. One of them was the hand itself, lying on the armrest of the chair. The other showed the hand with a plastic evidence bag secured around it.

"Preserving GSR?" I asked. "Gunshot residue?"

Jarvis nodded. "I swabbed it at the scene. It tested positive."

I looked over at her and raised my eyebrows.

"I used to be a CSI," Jarvis said. "In a previous job. I always carry a small kit with me when I go to scenes in this job. Saves the city a little money."

I picked up the last photo, the one of the empty bottle of whiskey. The label was clearly discernible. It was the Glenlivet Nadurra 15-Year Old, a rich, oaky single-malt scotch that I enjoyed. "Did he smell like he had been drinking?"

Jarvis nodded again. "Like he had been drinking a lot."

I sat back in my chair. "So, he wakes up, works out, gets dressed for work, then sits down in a chair in his living room, pours a bottle of whiskey down his throat, and blows his brains out?"

Jarvis shrugged. "Seems to fit the evidence. The coroner ruled it a suicide yesterday afternoon. We didn't contest it."

"They did the post-mortem yesterday afternoon?" I asked. "That was quick."

Jarvis allowed herself a grim smile. "This is Saint Charles, not Chicago. We don't get that many homicides out here."

It's all a little too tidy, I thought to myself. I looked through the photos again. When I got to one that showed the entire scene, with Hill, the gun and the whiskey bottle, I saw something that triggered a bell in my head.

I went through the rest of the photos and found what I was looking for. There was a sideboard, across from Hill in the living room, where several bottles of whiskey were arrayed. There were also several crystal glasses next to the bottles. I nodded to myself. There had been no glass next to the bottle. Hill appeared to be a whiskey aficionado like me. There was no way he would have consumed good scotch without a glass. I wouldn't have.

"What are you thinking?" Jarvis asked. I could feel her eyes on me, watching me.

I shook my head. "Probably nothing," I said. "Like you said, pretty clear that it's a suicide."

CHAPTER FIVE

Tuesday, January 5th
1130 Hours Local Time
DuPaul Airport (KDPL)
West Chicago, Illinois, USA

The drive from Saint Charles Police Headquarters to the address Sarah had given me for Enteron's flight department took about 15 minutes. After making my way back up Main Street, I turned south onto Smith Road, and then east onto National Drive a few minutes later. National Drive divided shortly after I entered the airport, with two lanes into the airport, two lanes out, and a loop in front of the DuPaul Flight Center, the marble-like edifice that dominated the west side of the airport. The lanes in and out of the airport were separated by a wide median with rows of trees lining the roads. Between the blanket of snow on the median and the small piles of the white precipitation resting on the tree branches, the scene looked quite idyllic.

I followed the guidance on my phone and made a right turn near the end of the inbound stretch of road and found myself next to a glass-fronted building, attached to a large hangar complex. I parked the car, turned it off, and then spent a few moments staring through the windshield at the building's front entrance. Mark Hill, my classmate, had run this department. According to Brett and Sarah, he had built it from scratch, many years ago, when Enteron's senior executives had decided they wanted to stop using charter services and have their own in-house flight department. He had acquired the aircraft, hired the people, and led the operation's growth.

And now he was dead.

"Why?" I asked myself in the rental car's rapidly chilling interior. "Why?"

I exited the car and cinched my overcoat around me as I walked across the plowed parking lot to the entry door. A gust of wind came across the snow to my left and went through me like a series of icy needles.

"Jesus," I muttered to myself. "It's fucking cold here."

I walked beneath the overhang that protected the entry door from the elements. It extended from the building across the portion of the drive directly in front of the door, obviously intended to protect passengers from the elements as they boarded or exited their vehicles.

"Nice setup," I said underneath my freezing breath.

I walked to the entry door and looked through the vestibule into the lobby beyond. The space was large and well-appointed. On the left side was a spacious waiting area, for passengers or visitors, with a large LCD TV, a comfortable sofa, and several plush-looking chairs. On the right, there was a series of desks. Sarah and Brett sat at the last two desks in the row, looking down at their work surfaces and intent on ignoring my approach, as we had agreed they would do. At the second desk in line sat an attractive blonde who had a phone to her ear and was inspecting me with curiosity. The person at the front desk was Asian, and she was eying me with an intense expression on her face. She pushed a button on a panel in front of her.

"May we help you?" She asked.

I looked to my right and saw a small speaker next to the doorframe.

"I hope so," I answered. "My name is Colin Pearce. I'm a friend of your director, Mark Hill. We were classmates at the Air Force Academy. I just dropped by to pay him a visit."

The Asian woman looked back at the blonde, and a conversation I couldn't hear took place behind the glass. After a moment, the Asian woman rose from her desk, came through the inner doors, opened the outer door, and allowed me to enter.

"Thanks," I said.

I stepped inside the lobby. It was well heated, and I could feel the Chicago cold dissipating.

"Welcome to Enteron's Aviation Department," the Asian woman said. "I'm Rose Santilong. I run our scheduling function."

"Glad to be here," I responded. "Seems like you have quite the setup."

Rose shrugged. "We like it." She gestured to the attractive blonde. "This is Julie Wegner; she's a full-time scheduler."

Julie nodded at me.

"Pleased to meet you," I said.

Rose motioned to Sarah and Brett. "Sarah Connor is a part-time scheduler and Brett Zeigler is our business analyst."

Both nodded in my direction, Brett somewhat nervously and Sarah with a thin smile on her lips.

"Would you care for something to drink?" Rose asked. "We have coffee, soft drinks, and water."

"I think I'm good for now," I answered. "But thank you."

Rose nodded at me, and her face took on a pained and hesitant expression. I saw her blink away a tear in one eye. A few awkward seconds passed. It became obvious that she was at a loss for words. I had unwittingly put her on the spot, even though I had full knowledge of the situation. She would now have to tell me that my friend was dead. That was a hard reality for anyone to communicate. Her visible discomfort over the situation spoke of her feelings for her former boss. I liked her for that. I decided to divert the conversation and relieve her anxiety.

"Of course, if he's not around, I can come back later," I said.

She nodded eagerly. "He's not," she said. "But I can take you someone who can...explain. Would that work?"

I kept my expression neutral. "Sounds good," I said.

Rose went to her phone, lifted the handset, and punched a few numbers into the keypad. A quick and intense conversation followed, most of which was in whispered tones. Finally, I heard an exasperated man's voice say. "Whatever. Bring him back."

I could see Rose stiffen a bit as the conversation ended. She hung the phone up and turned to me with a miffed expression on her face.

"He'll see you," she said, painting a pleasant but insincere smile on her face. "I'll take you back to his office."

Rose led me through the lobby and down a hallway that occupied the left side of a long room with a wall on the left and a row of several cubicles on the right.

"This is where the pilots sit," Rose said, "when they're not flying."

I nodded. The room was open and expansive. The cubicles were high end and well equipped. Some of the cubicles had personnel working at them; others were vacant.

"This is our kitchen and break room area," Rose said, motioning to the left as we stopped at an open door for a moment. The area had two refrigerators, a stove, an oven, a table, and expansive counters. Beyond the room was another area that had cartons of water, soft drinks, cookies, and potato chips. It was obviously a stock room that held supplies for the jets. Just to the left of the door to the room was a sign that was taped to the wall.

STOCK ROOM SUPPLIES ARE FOR AIRCRAFT ONLY, it said. The implication was obvious. Employees were not allowed to help themselves to anything in there.

Rose saw where I was looking.

"That's a new sign," she said with notes of both sadness and exasperation in her voice. "Just went up this morning."

I shook my head. "Someone thinks that employees are eating too much of the plane stock?"

Rose's face tightened. "Not just any someone," she said. "A new someone." She turned to me. "Mark Hill isn't here any longer. I'm not allowed to say anything else. I wish I could. We all loved him." Her voice cracked just slightly as she finished the sentence.

Rose led me further down the path. The room channeled into a hallway, and there were three office doors to the right and another corridor to the left. We stopped outside the last door on the right, and Rose knocked on the closed door.

"Enter," said an impatient voice.

Rose turned the knob and opened the door. The office inside featured a large wall unit/desk combination and a small conference table. There were boxes on the floor that were sealed and taped and other boxes on a credenza that were not. I could see a camouflaged airplane model protruding from one of them, the barrels of a GAU-8 30mm cannon clearly visible.

I swallowed hard and hoped that Rose and the guy behind the desk didn't notice. Someone was packing up Hill's office. Like anyone who had made a career in aviation, Hill had tokens and reminders of his previous positions. There would be certificates, pictures, and of course, the inevitable airplane models. Hill and I had both flown the A-10 while we were on active duty, and my latest adventure of a few weeks ago had renewed my love and respect for the aircraft. I hoped Hill's articles would be packed with the right amount of care and respect.

"Rose, you need to tell those guys to finish packing this sh.., er, stuff, up as soon as possible," said the voice behind the desk. "I can't work in here with all this clutter."

I turned my eyes to the voice. The man with the voice was perhaps the most unimpressive physical specimen of the male gender I had ever seen. He was about five feet eight, had a sunken chest, and might have weighed 150 pounds soaking wet. He had thin, oily hair that was plastered to his scalp with some kind of product and a pasty white complexion as if he had spent all of his life indoors. He extended a skinny arm towards me.

"William Darnell," he said. "I'm the director here."

"Interim Director," Rose said.

I feigned confusion as I looked back and forth between the two of them. Rose was looking at him with a distasteful expression on her face, and Darnell was looking back at her with one of haughty superiority.

I took Darnell's hand and shook it briefly. His grip was weak, and his hand was cold and clammy. He attempted a cordial smile. "Interim Director for now," he said. He looked at Rose and waved his hand dismissively. "That will be all, Rose."

Rose inclined her head in acknowledgment and exited the room, giving me a look of warning as she shut the door.

Darnell motioned to the chairs around the conference table as he sat down behind his desk.

Strike one, I thought to myself. If Darnell had cared about the sensitively of the news he was going to deliver, he would have joined me at the conference table and removed the desk as a barrier between us. But it was apparent that he needed the physical reinforcement of a piece of furniture to bolster his position of authority. I found that I disliked him intensely.

I sat in one of the chairs and kept a confused expression on my face. "I don't understand," I said. "I was expecting to see Mark Hill. He and I were classmates at the Air Force Academy. We served in the Air Force together. Last I heard he was running this place."

The haughty expression on Darnell's face took on an element of affected sympathy. I wanted to smack it off of him.

"Not anymore," Darnell said. "Sorry to be the one to tell you, but Mr. Hill is no longer with us. He committed suicide yesterday."

I've long since passed the point in my life where I need difficult news 'packaged' so that I can process it, but the lack of tact and sensitivity in Darnell's delivery was astounding. The Darkness was triggered inside of me and it rose to the surface in milliseconds.

I want him.

I shook my head slightly to ward it off. "Wow," I said, continuing the charade, "I didn't see that coming. What happened?"

Darnell shrugged. "Who knows. It doesn't matter. The company sent me here to mind the store and to clean things up. Hill wasn't doing things the Enteron way. I'm going to change that."

The Darkness flashed again. I bit my tongue for a few seconds and took a few deep breaths. "I've known Mark Hill for over thirty years," I said at last. "He was always a decent guy who seemed to have good reasons for the things he did."

The smart thing for Darnell to have done would have been to channel the conversation into a sympathetic and conciliatory place. But his ego wouldn't allow him. "Maybe. Maybe not," he said. "We hired a consultant team from a company called Vandelay, and they told us that a lot of the stuff he was doing was wrong."

I sat back in my chair, shocked at the direction the conversation was going. I was familiar with Vandelay. According to what I had gleaned from the business aviation industry grapevine, Vandelay specialized in working with corporate executives to undermine directors of aviation and get the directors fired. Until now, I hadn't known how much of what I had heard was gossip and how much of it was the truth. Now, the reality was staring me in the face. Hill had been targeted and probably never even suspected it.

It was time to go on the offensive.

"And who paid them?" I asked.

Darnell's eyebrows raised in surprise. "I beg your pardon?"

"When you hire a hitman, it's the person who pays them who is actually responsible for the deed," I said. "Who hired Vandelay? Since they specialize in taking down directors of aviation, they're known throughout the industry as the consultant equivalent of paid hitmen."

Darnell's face went through a series of expressions as he decided how to answer the question. He had the distinct look of someone who had realized he had revealed too much.

"It's not a difficult question, *Willy*," I said, accenting his name in an uncomplimentary way. "Who paid to have him set up by Vandelay?" I wanted to ask who paid to have him killed as well, but I managed to restrain myself.

At the mention of the words 'set up,' Darnell's face went pale.

Damn, I thought. *You know the answers to both questions, don't you?*

Darnell found his voice after a long moment. "I think you need to leave," he said.

CHAPTER SIX

Tuesday, January 5th
1330 Hours Local Time
Chili's Restaurant
St. Charles, Illinois, USA

"Oh my God," Brett said as he took another drink of his iced tea. "Did he throw a shit fit after you left!"

Brett, Sarah, and I were sitting at a secluded table in a local chain restaurant eating a late lunch. In our conversation earlier that day, we had prearranged a lunch meeting to debrief the effect of my visit to the Enteron Flight Department. It had taken them longer to get away from their desks than they had anticipated.

"I can have that effect on people sometimes," I said between the last few bites of my salad. I caught Sarah's eye, and she gave me a quick, knowing smile. "What did he do and say, exactly?"

"Well, first of all, you're banned from the premises," Brett said. "Darnell even made me call security and tell them all about you. They might have even been able to pull some video from one of our internal surveillance cameras."

Shit, I thought to myself. I hadn't counted on that. If they did facial recognition on the image and they were working with the police, they could find out that Connor Price, the NSA agent, and Colin Pearce were the same person. I had to hope they wouldn't make that link. At least not immediately.

"What else?"

"He came into the lobby and ranted at us for like 15 minutes. He accused us of giving out information about confidential Enteron business and told us that if he found out where the leak was, he'd have that person terminated, or worse! I mean, who says that?"

"For the record," I said, looking between Sarah and Brett, "I didn't betray any information you two gave me. I even acted surprised when he told me Hill was dead."

"Why was he so freaked out?" Brett asked.

"Because he told me something he shouldn't have," I said.

"About what?" Sarah asked.

"How long were the Vandelay folks around?" I asked in response.

Sarah and Brett looked at each other and shrugged.

"About a month or so," Sarah answered. "They finished up about three weeks ago."

"Did they generate a report?"

Brett nodded. "We were supposed to get debriefed on it, but we couldn't get it scheduled. Then yesterday happened...," his voice trailed off.

"The Vandelay report was going to be the excuse to fire Hill," I said, looking between the two of them. "That's what Vandelay does. They go to the executive in charge of the flight department and say they're going to provide 'benchmarking' data on the department. Their real goal is to unseat the flight department leader so they can earn a fee to replace him or her and sell other services to the company. They've got one of the worst reputations in the industry. I thought a lot of that was myth. Until today."

Brett sat up abruptly. "Do you think they told Mark? Do

you think that's why he killed himself?"

I shot a glance at Sarah and shook my head slightly. Then I shrugged. "I don't know," I said. "It doesn't sound like the Mark Hill I knew, but anything's possible."

A sudden thought occurred to me. *He wouldn't go quietly. That's why they killed him. Holy shit.*

"Darnell knew the intent of the Vandelay report all along," Sarah said.

I nodded. "And he was waiting in the wings to take over the department, thinking that he, with his extensive corporate knowledge, could run the department better than someone who had been in aviation leadership for over thirty years."

Brett looked between Sarah and me. "But isn't leadership... leadership?" he asked. "Don't get me wrong. I'm not taking his side, but when I got my business degree, they taught me that skill set was basically interchangeable."

"Yet another confirmation that most college professors don't live in the real world," I said. "The basic concepts of leadership might work in any scenario, but people follow people, not concepts. The person in charge has to be credible and proficient in the area he or she is trying to lead or they won't get the respect necessary to lead their team. Twenty years in the Air Force taught me that. The best leaders were those you would follow into combat, not those who would sit behind a desk and tell you how to get there."

The table was silent for a few moments.

When the waitress brought our check, I spoke. "Of course, after spending some time with Willy, I realized that none of these concepts apply."

"Why?" Brett asked.

"Because that man couldn't lead anyone out of a flaming paper bag filled with dog shit," I said. "I've seen the type before. They're products of a politically correct system that teaches that anyone can be a leader."

"And not everyone can?" Brett asked.

I shook my head. "Not in my experience. There's a basic element of DNA you have to have to be a leader. If you don't have it, no amount of training can make you one."

"What DNA is that?" Sarah asked, smiling at me. She knew what I was going to say.

"You have to care about your team and the mission more than you care about yourself," I said. "It's that simple. It can't be about you."

A few moments later, Sarah turned to me as she and I were waiting by the front door of the restaurant while Brett made a trip to the restroom.

"Colin, what's really going on?" she asked.

I raised my eyebrows are her. "Are you sure you want to know? It might tarnish your opinion of your current workplace."

She nodded.

"Mark Hill didn't commit suicide," I said. "He was killed. And unless I miss my guess, that bozo I spoke to earlier and Hill's boss were in on it."

CHAPTER SEVEN

Tuesday, January 5th
1500 Hours Local Time
Pursuit Bank Building
Chicago, Illinois, USA

The security guard at the desk in the lobby of the Pursuit Bank building took my driver's license and stared down at a printout in front of him. He was a middle-aged gentleman of color with close-cropped hair, and he had the no-nonsense look of 'former cop' about him.

"What is your business here, sir?" he asked in a polite, respectful tone.

"I'm on my way up to meet with Mark Lane, your CEO."

The guard tilted his head in understanding and nodded at me. Then he looked down at his computer screen and frowned at what he saw there. He looked back up at me and studied my face. Then he picked up a phone and made a call.

"I have a Mr. Colin Pearce here who says he's on his way to see the CEO, but there's a security alert in the system about him." The guard listened to the response for a few seconds and then nodded. "I understand," he said. "I'll tell him." He hung up the phone and looked back at me. "We can't let you up, Mr. Pearce. You've been designated a security risk."

I smiled at him and pulled my phone from my pocket. Then, I dialed the same number I had called as I had driven into downtown Chicago from St. Charles. I put the phone on speaker. After two rings, the line was answered.

"Colin? Pearce? Where the hell are you?" The voice was gruff and impatient. I could see the guard's eyes widen as he heard it.

"I'm in the lobby of the building, and they're not going to let me come up and see you," I replied. "Apparently, they think I'm a security risk."

"Jesus Christ!" said Mark Lane, the CEO of Enteron. "Let me talk with the guard."

"You're on speaker, Mark."

"Who's there? Joshua?"

"Yes, Mr. Lane," the guard replied. "This is Joshua."

"What the fuck is going on down there?"

"Mr. Pearce has been designated a security threat, sir. We're not permitted to let him into the building."

An impatient exhalation came out of the phone. "Joshua, do you remember when I was shot five years ago?"

"Yes sir," Joshua said. "We were all worried about whether you would recover."

"Well, the man you think is a security risk is the reason I'm not dead. Now let him the fuck into the building, please."

A few moments later, I was alone in a fast-moving elevator that was taking me to the 60th floor of the building. The elevator was paneled with rich, dark wood and was climbing so rapidly that my ears popped during the ascent.

In a minute's time, I was exiting into the foyer of the 60th floor. To my right was a wall of glass that looked out over the Chicago Lakeshore and Navy Pier. Lake Michigan lay beyond, its dark blue surface alive with white caps as the waters were stirred by the wind. Across the expanse of the lake, the western shore of the state of Michigan was barely visible.

"Are you Mr. Pearce?" an impatient female voice asked from behind me.

I turned to find a woman in a black business suit. Her auburn hair was pulled back into a severe ponytail, and she had the pale complexion of someone who rarely saw the sun.

I nodded at her. "I am."

"I'm Susan Greystone, Mr. Lane's assistant." She didn't offer her hand. "Come with me." She turned and stepped toward the glass doors in front of us without waiting to see if I was going to follow her.

I fell into trail behind her. We entered a reception area with a long desk made of light-colored, highly polished wood. Enteron's multi-colored logo was displayed prominently behind the desk, and several sofas, chairs, and tables were all neatly arranged in front of it. Two attendants stood behind the desk and watched me as I walked by, eying me with a wary curiosity that I had seen from onlookers peering into the lion cage at the zoo. I smiled to myself and wondered how Darnell had worded his alert message about me.

Susan led me out of the reception area and down a long hallway with no doors on either side. The walls featured a series of photographs of nuclear power plants, each with its own label. I counted fifteen of them.

Damn, I thought to myself. *This company is into nukes. Holy shit.*

Then I remembered the event where Lane had been shot, where I had barely saved him over five years ago, had been a worldwide meeting of nuclear operators, and Lane had been the star speaker. That bespoke a great deal about both the man and the company. As Susan led me around a corner and toward a set of wooden doors, I wondered how much I could tell Lane about why I was here.

We went through the doors and into a vast outer office with a large workstation in the center of it that featured several desks and was shaped liked a large square. Two other women were busily clicking away on their computers, but they too watched me walk with the same look of wariness. I wondered what they'd think if they got a look at the .45 on my right hip.

Susan led me to another set of doors, knocked twice, opened one of them, and held it open to allow me to walk through.

I had never been in the office of a Fortune 100 CEO before. It was lavishly furnished with a large wooden desk, matching bookshelves on the interior walls, and a conversation group with a circular coffee table and several chairs. The exterior wall was entirely made of glass, and it commanded a spectacular view of the northern end of downtown Chicago and the lakeshore.

Lane was seated in the conversation area with a file folder in his hand. He rose as I entered. The woman he was talking to rose with him. Lane was slightly shorter than I was, maybe about six feet tall. He looked just as trim and fit as he had five years ago and had the same full head of flowing gray hair.

"I want the details on the next visit on my email by tomorrow night," he said. "I need to brief the board and the Department of State."

"But William just got down there," said the woman. "This isn't really his area of expertise. It may take him a little longer."

"You've been pushing for him to take over flight operations since those consultants gave us the report. I don't want to hear any excuses."

The woman nodded and some kind of unspoken conversation took place between them.

Then, Lane turned and gestured to me. "This is Colin Pearce. He's the one who saved my life in Tahoe five years ago."

I walked over to the two of them and offered Lane my hand. He shook it vigorously and smiled at me. "Great to see you, Colin! Glad you could swing by!"

I returned the handshake and the smile. "Well, it wasn't'

the finest piece of work I've done," I said. "But I'm glad you lived through it, Mark. None the worse for wear?"

Lane shrugged. "That damn rifle put a big hole on both sides of me, but the wounds healed well. The muscles ached for a while, but that passed a few years ago." He grinned at me. "It's all good, though. My wife thinks the scars are sexy."

I nodded. "I'll bet she does."

The woman Lane had been talking to was standing behind him and she tensed slightly at Lane's mention of his wife. Thanks to the photo Sharona had sent me while I was in the car, I knew who the woman was. I could feel her staring at me. I raised my eyes to meet hers. I expected her gaze to be hostile, especially after the interaction I had with her subordinate at the DuPaul airport.

But the look on her face surprised me. Her eyes were keenly observational and devoid of emotion. Like those of a professional poker player. She nodded slightly as our eyes met, and I saw the edges of her mouth turn upward, just barely, in a smile of anticipation.

I felt a slight chill run up my spine.

She was painfully thin, almost gaunt, and her complexion was ashen. Her black hair was stringy and hung in lifeless strands around her plain face. She wore no makeup and was dressed in a drab business suit that hung on her skinny frame without accenting any of the characteristics of her body. I was reminded of a bedsheet draped from a clothesline.

"This is Brenda Rowe," Lane said. "She's my Chief Corporate Operations Officer."

Rowe silently offered her bony hand, and I shook it somewhat reluctantly. Her grip was surprisingly strong.

"Ms. Rowe," I said. "Pleased to meet you."

Rowe responded with a curt nod and left the room. Lane and I watched her go, and then he turned to me. "I wonder what's up her ass?" he asked.

I looked at him. "I might have an idea," I said.

A few moments later, we were sitting around the circular table with glasses of scotch at our sides. Lane had produced the whiskey and the glasses after Rowe departed, and he had poured liberal portions of the spirit into both of them.

"To life and living it," Lane had said.

We had clinked glasses and then taken our seats.

"I always said that if I ever saw you again, we'd enjoy a drink together," Lane said. "I owe you everything."

I shook my head. "I damn near got you killed, Mark. If I had been more on my game, you wouldn't have been hit. If I had been a fraction of a second later…"

"But you weren't," Lane said with enthusiasm. "And nearly being killed has done wonders for my life, believe it or not. It taught me that life is a gift and not to take things for granted. My relationships with my wife and kids are better, and I'm taking the company in a new direction. I want to use Enteron to make the world a better place."

"Too bad Mark Hill won't have a similar opportunity," I said without thinking.

Lane looked down at the table. "Yes, it is," he said. "We were going to move him out of his position. Maybe he heard, and that's why he killed himself."

"Why were you going to move him out?"

Lane shrugged. "The consultant group we hired said he was screwing up."

I sighed. "And who hired them in the first place? That Rowe woman?"

Lane looked back at me, thoughtfully. Then he looked down at his glass of scotch and seemed to ponder the amber liquid. I could almost see the cogs in his brain turning as he made the connections in his mind. He looked up at me. "I never told you she was Hill's boss," Lane said. "This isn't a social call, is it?"

I shook my head.

"Are you working with the same people you were working with in Tahoe?"

I nodded.

Lane's eyes grew wide. "Jesus," he said. "Maybe you should tell me why you're here."

"I'm afraid that I can't," I said. "But I can tell you it's serious and it threatens this company that you very nearly died for. And I...I mean we...need your help."

"Anything," Lane said without hesitation. "I owe that to you, the folks you work with, and to this company. What do you need?"

I nodded at him. "Well, it's obvious that this Willy guy running your flight operations doesn't know what the fuck he's doing, and you need someone who does so these flights to North Korea can continue."

His eyes narrowed. "You know, he's a nuke guy, and I usually love those guys because that's where I came from." Lane said. He sighed and took a sip of his scotch as he gathered his thoughts for a few moments.

I watched him and remained silent, taking a sip of my own drink. I was betting it was the Macallan 15-year-old, but I kept my mouth shut.

"Willy may be a nuke guy, but he's a tool. He's also very really close to retirement. But he's loyal to Brenda, and that's what she values."

I nodded and said nothing.

Lane looked over at me with his eyes set in determination. "What do you need me to do?"

"You're the CEO," I said. "Kick his ass out of there and let me run the place for a little while and get to the bottom of this."

Lane nodded back at me. "Let me make some phone calls," he said.

CHAPTER EIGHT

Tuesday, January 5th
1730 Hours Local Time
Enteron Flight Department
DuPaul Airport (KDPL)
West Chicago, Illinois, USA

I made it back to Enteron's spaces on the DuPaul airport in record time, given the usual mass exodus from the Chicago downtown area at rush hour. Along the way, I received a text message from Lane telling me the entire Enteron flight department would be assembled for a meeting as soon as I got back to their office. I smiled as I read the text while stopped at an intersection. Mark Lane was good to his word. Somehow, that didn't surprise me.

I parked my car in the same space I had vacated earlier and made my way across the parking lot and toward the office doors. Through the glass front of the building, I could see several men and women congregating in the waiting area, obviously waiting for the departure of an aircraft.

I nodded to myself. There was a flight to North Korea tonight, the flight that Hill was supposed to have been on. These were some of the passengers. I was surprised to see that Rowe wasn't among them.

As I approached the doors, many of the faces turned to me and eyed me with hostile suspicion. Word had gotten around. Darnell was a nuclear power guy, as were all the people waiting to depart on the jet. Some outsider was displacing one of their own. That probably didn't go over well.

Rose held the two sets of doors open and looked at me with a wry smile on her face.

"What did you do?" she whispered as I stepped up on the sidewalk. "Willy ran out of here like he had a swarm of bees chasing him."

I shrugged. "I might know some people," I said.

I walked into the office area and found Julie, Sarah, and Brett, all standing behind their desks. I doffed my jacket as the doors closed behind me, and Rose took it from me before I could protest.

"I'll just put it over here for you," she said, motioning to the area where her desk was.

I nodded at her. "Thanks," I said.

"They're waiting for you in the conference room," she said. "Around the corner there towards the left."

I nodded again and began to walk in that direction.

"So, who the hell are you?" a voice said from behind me. "And why did they kick Willy out of here and put *you* in charge?"

I froze and took a breath. Then, I turned to face the voice.

One of the men in the group of passengers was standing next to his chair with his hands on his hips. He had dark brown hair and a heavily pockmarked face. His eyes blazed with anger, and his mouth was set in an expression of distaste and displeasure. His colleagues were eyeing me with equally grim countenances.

"My name is Colin Pearce," I said. "Mark Lane sent me down here to run things for a while."

"Why would he do that?" the man replied impatiently.

"Willy was one of us. He was Enteron. What are you? Some aviation type? What the hell do you know about our company?"

I could feel the weight of the .45 on my hip, and the thought of pulling it from its holster for the shock effect played with my mind for a moment. But instead, I merely smiled at the man with the brown hair and his colleagues.

"You'll have to ask the CEO about why I'm here," I said. "But let me clue you in on one thing. Aviation people need to be led by aviation leaders. Not by corporate...types. Or nuclear types."

The man's face darkened as a series of emotions ran across it. "You can't talk to me like that," he said, his voice barely under control.

I stepped towards him. He was shorter than I was and trying desperately to look taller. I stopped about two feet from him and looked down at his enraged face.

"I can talk to you any way I want," I said. "I'm not an employee of this company, and I have no ambitions to remain and climb the food chain. But for the time being, I am in charge of this department and the jet you're going to fly on and the personnel who will be operating it, belong to me, not to you. So, unless you want me to kick your ass off the upcoming flight for being unruly, I suggest you have a seat and wait patiently for your crew to give you permission to board."

The man bristled with anger and took a step towards me, raising his hands into something resembling an offensive posture. He made a deliberate effort to assume some sort of stance. I didn't know what martial art he was taking in his off time, but he seemed to think he was pretty intimidating.

"Derek," one of the other passengers said. "Don't be stupid. Sit down and wait for the jet."

"That's good advice," I said, tilting my head toward the speaker. "You should take it, Derek. Unless you want to stay here when the jet leaves."

Derek's face contorted into an expression of disbelief. "You wouldn't dare!"

I leaned forward and looked him dead in the eyes. "Try me," I said.

A few moments later, I entered the flight department's conference room. It was impressive. Two walls were glass, and the other two were framed with rich woodwork. There was a long wooden table that looked like it could have come out of a boardroom. The room was packed to capacity with personnel, some sitting at the table, others standing around it. In addition to the schedulers and Brett from the outer office, there were several people in business casual attire, a few wearing neckties. I assumed these were the pilots. Intermingled with the pilots were people in work pants and work shirts, some with parka-like jackets on. These were the maintenance technicians. On a screen at the far end of the room, a video feed was displayed, and I could see another smaller conference room with about ten people sitting around a table. They stared through the screen with eager expressions on their faces.

"That's our location in Baltimore," Rose said in explanation as she closed the conference room door.

I stopped at the head of the table and remained standing, slowly scanning the room and looking into every face and every set of eyes. While the room was tense with expectation, no eyes avoided mine, and none of the faces showed angst or emotion. These men and women were professionals. All they wanted was to be led by someone who knew what he was doing.

"Ladies and gentlemen, my name is Colin Pearce," I began. "My apologies for the dramatic entrance. I didn't start my day expecting to be here. I came to the Chicago area to visit some people that are important to me, Mark Hill among them. Mark and I were classmates at the Air Force Academy, and we flew together in the USAF. Most recently, he and I met up in Lake Tahoe about five years ago when Mark Lane, your CEO, was nearly killed by a deranged sniper."

I could see eyes widening around the table, and I could feel an undercurrent of excitement pass through the room. They were doing the math. Hill had mentioned me to them. I had expected he would. Establishing trust as the leader of a new group is difficult. I was hoping that by linking myself to their previous leader and his account of my actions, I could start to build a foundation of credibility. Hopefully, trust would soon follow.

"You're the one who saved the CEO's life," Rose said from behind me.

I shrugged as I turned to her. "I pushed him out of the way before a .50 caliber bullet almost hit him dead center in the chest. If I had been faster, he wouldn't have been hit at all."

There was a rustle of whispered conversation in the room, and I quieted it by raising my hands as I turned back to the table.

"So, imagine my surprise when I discovered Mark Hill died yesterday. It was quite a shock for me. I'm sure it was for you as well."

The room was utterly silent. Every eye was locked on me. I briefly reviewed what I was going to say before I spoke again. Most of the time, it isn't wise to reveal one's objective to the very people that might end up being obstacles or enemies. But I had a feeling about this group. If Hill had led them well, and I was sure he had, they'd remain loyal, and they'd help me do what needed to be done. I knew there'd be a few rats in the group, but the best way to smoke them out would be to let them know I was coming.

"The problem is that we're being told Hill killed himself." I shook my head. "I don't believe that. I knew the man too well. And I've had access to some other...information that leads me to believe that he didn't commit suicide. In fact, I'm convinced he was murdered."

A collective gasp went up from the assembled personnel. I didn't give them time to recover before I threw down the gauntlet.

"And ladies and gentlemen, that's why I'm here, and the dweeb who left earlier is not. The answer to Mark Hill's death lies in this department," I said, swirling my right index finger in a circle. "And it lies in this company. I'm going to find out what that answer is. It's what I do."

Heads were nodding around the table and on the screen at the far end of the room. I could see respect in the eyes that looked back at me. I scanned their faces again and tried to find some sets of eyes that looked away or were evasive. For the moment, there weren't any.

"In the meantime, I expect you to run this department like the professionals you are, and in the manner Mark Hill would have wanted you to."

"But what about all the directives that Willy came out with yesterday?" a voice asked from the TV screen.

"Disregard them," I said, leaning forward for emphasis. "All of them. This is our show, and it's going to be run by aviation people who know what the hell they're doing, not by corporate types who can't even spell airplane."

Heads were nodding vigorously now. Faces were smiling. People were nudging each other, and the energy in the room was palpable. If I had done nothing else, I had given them their purpose back.

I raised my arms to still the motion. "I know we've got a jet to launch tonight, and I want you to get to the mission and perform it well. I'll give Rose my contact information. If any of you have concerns or you just want to talk about the department, feel free to call me, day or night. If I'm going to lead you, I need to know what you're thinking." I didn't add that I was going to pick their brains about the last few weeks of Mark Hill's life as part of that process. I knew that's where the specifics of the answer were. "But before we dismiss," I continued, "let me issue my first directive as your new leader."

I turned to my right, where the schedulers were standing. "Rose, go to the door of the stockroom and tear down that fucking sign."

A collective cheer went up from the assembled personnel and room erupted in relieved laughter. Rose was out the door like a flash, and a group of people went with her.

The personnel who remained in the room filed by me to shake my hand and introduce themselves. I greeted each one warmly as I made a mental note to get with Rose and get names and pictures of all the personnel so I could memorize their details. I didn't want to be the new boss who didn't remember names.

As the people continued by, I noticed something that I hadn't before. The glass rear wall of the conference room, the wall it shared with the lobby, was actually two panels of glass with a very small gap between the panes. The folks in the lobby would have overheard my entire spiel to the department. Even now, I was sure phones were alive with text messages and emails about what I had said.

I smiled to myself. *Fight's on, fuckers.*

CHAPTER NINE

Friday, January 8th
1915 Hours Local Time
Pappas Brothers Steak House
Dallas, Texas, USA

The martini appeared on the bar in front of me, the glass opaque with condensation and the contents frosty with ice crystals. I could see the wedge of lime resting on the bottom of the glass, barely visible through the icy liquid. The bartender, an attractive blonde thirty-something, was watching me expectantly out of the corner of her eye as she attended to another patron. The instructions I had given her were precise. She seemed anxious to see if she had executed them well.

I could have continued looking at my phone and kept her in suspense, but the truth was that I was longing for the taste of fine gin on my tongue. I deliberately put my iPhone down on the surface of the bar and lifted the glass to my lips, taking great care not to spill any of the liquid as I raised it. Then, I took a sip and let the first wave of ice-cold Plymouth race over my tongue and down my throat.

"Ahh," I said. The word slipped out of my mouth without me willing it. I realized that my eyes had been closed as I drank, and I opened them slowly.

"Well damn," the Bartender said as she turned to me and gave me an impossibly white smile. "You could do a commercial for that gin!"

'They wouldn't even have to pay me," I said, smiling and nodding at her. "I'd do it for the free drinks."

"Are you waiting on a table, Mister...?"

"Pearce," I said. "Colin Pearce. Call me Colin."

She extended her hand. "Candice," she said, deliberately leaving off her last name and repeating the name etched into the badge above her left breast. "Pleased to meet you."

"Pleased to meet you as well," I said, shaking her hand.

"Are you waiting for a table, Colin?"

I shook my head. "I'm going to have dinner here at the bar."

She nodded at me. "Bar menu or dinner menu?"

"Dinner menu, please."

Candice handed me a menu. "Have you been here before?"

I looked around the room and nodded. The Pappas Brothers Steak House was one of my favorite places on earth. It was a total sensory experience. The décor was elegant but not overdone, the drinks were good and the food, particularly the steaks, were positively succulent. I had always thought that if heaven could be a restaurant, it would be the Pappas Brothers Steak House. I had discovered the place in the early 2000s and came here every time I was in town. Given the fact that the two largest business jet training centers in the United States happened to be at the DFW airport, I had been in the metroplex very frequently indeed.

"Many times," I said at last.

"Welcome back!" Candice said. "Let me know when you're ready to order."

"Will do, Candice. It won't be for a while. I just want to sit here and enjoy this excellent martini."

She smiled in satisfaction and set about her work behind

the bar.

I sat back on the plush bar stool and took another sip of the ultra-smooth gin as some of the aircraft limitations numbers for the Falcon 7X flashed through my mind. I reviewed the weight limitations, slat/flat and landing gear speeds, maneuvering speed, and minimum control speeds and satisfied myself that the numbers were all locked into my brain and recallable on demand.

Enteron's training captain, a good-natured Wisconsinite named Brian Fuhrman, had worked some magic with FlightSafety's DFW Learning Center. Thanks to a last-minute cancellation from another operator, he was able to get me a slot in a 7X recurrent class that started yesterday at 0800. Yesterday and today had been nine hours of ground school each day, culminating in a written test this afternoon. Tomorrow and Sunday would be spent in the flight simulator. Fuhrman had managed to talk the Center into condensing the course from three simulator sessions to two sessions through the use of a dedicated right-seater who would play first-officer for me through both sessions and relieve me of the need to sit in the right seat for another client. The only downside was that the simulator sessions would take place late in the evening, from 7 pm to 1230 am, but that was a small price to pay given the timeline I was on.

I needed to get back to Chicago as soon as possible. There was another flight to North Korea in the upcoming week, and I needed to be part of the crew.

"Have you decided on anything?" Candice appeared in front of me with an order pad in her hands.

"I haven't looked at the menu yet, but I think I know what I want," I said.

Candice put pen to paper and waited.

"Do you have any of that awesome lobster bisque this evening?" I asked

Candice smiled and nodded.

"I'll start with a cup of that. I'll follow with the 12-ounce bone-in filet with skillet potatoes and grilled asparagus on the side."

"Great choices," Candice said as she finished writing.

"No hurry on any of this stuff, Candice," I said. "I'd like to linger here for a while."

"How about this," she said. "I'll put in the order for the bisque immediately, and you tell me when to put the order in for the steak and sides?"

I nodded at her. "That will work," I said.

As Candice turned back to her work, I took another sip of my martini and glanced down the bar at my fellow patrons. The bar wasn't nearly as crowded as I had seen it on previous Friday nights when I had been here. A few of the bar tables were occupied with couples, and there were five other people at the bar, all seated at the main span of it, perpendicular to the side span where I was. Nearest to me sat a smartly dressed couple about my age. They were laughing at a story he had just told. I heard the words 'naked' and 'chocolate' in his narrative and smiled to myself at the possible combinations. One seat down from the couple sat a man and woman of color, both in business clothes. There were arguing the merits of two college football teams, The University of Texas and Texas A & M University, which had a fierce rivalry. It quickly became apparent that the man had attended A & M, and the woman had attended UT.

"Damn," I said to myself. "That relationship probably won't last long."

The last person seated at the bar was another man who sat by himself. He was a young man, mid-thirties tops, with brown hair and a precisely trimmed beard. He wore a white dress shirt and sported a heavy-looking watch on his left wrist. He had a bottle of Shiner Bock beer in front of him that looked nearly untouched. He was drumming his fingers on the bar as he stared down at his beer bottle.

He's nervous, I thought. *What is he nervous about?*

The man's fingers settled on his phone, and he tilted the device on its side. Then he slowly pivoted the phone so that the backside of it, with the camera, was pointed down the bar.

At me.

I shook my head. *You were too impatient, pal,* I thought. *If you had waited until my food came, you could have taken the picture, and I probably wouldn't have even noticed you. Are you on a timeline, or are you just sloppy?*

I had my answer a second later when the man fumbled with the phone as he tried to push the button to take the picture. I could have found a way to threaten him and take the phone from him, but I decided to let the scenario play out. As the man aligned the phone for the picture once again, I raised my martini glass to my lips with my right hand and rotated my left-hand palm upward on the bar surface. Then I extended my middle finger.

The man was concentrating so hard on taking the picture unobtrusively that he didn't focus on the actual image he was photographing. He snapped the picture and then turned the phone screen towards him to examine his handiwork. His eyes grew wide as he looked down at the image, and his head slowly pivoted to me. He raised his eyes to mine, and I could see shock and surprise in his young face.

I lowered my glass to the bar and waved to him. Then I formed a pistol with my hand and 'shot' him with it.

The man stood up like a needle had come through the cushion of his chair and poked him in the ass. He grabbed his phone, threw some bills on the bar, and power-walked out of the bar, almost knocking a waitress over in the process.

I sighed and looked down at my phone. "Time to notify the cavalry," I said to myself. I opened the messaging app and texted a group message to Sharona, Smith, and Amrine.

THEY KNOW I'M HERE, I wrote. THEY'RE FOLLOWING ME.

MAKES SENSE, Smith replied after a few moments. DO YOU NEED BACKUP?

I thought about that for a moment or two and then shook my head to myself.

DON'T THINK SO, I typed. BUT YOU'LL NEED TO KEEP A SANITATION CREW NEARBY. WHEN THESE GUYS COME AFTER ME, I'M GOING TO MAKE IT MESSY.

Smith responded with a winking face and Amrine with a thumbs up, indicating his approval.

"Ready for your bisque?" Candice asked as she stood in front of me with a steaming cup of the rich soup.

I nodded and moved my arms aside so she could place the cup on the bar in front of me. I drained the last liquid from the martini and shook the glass slightly as Candice deployed my silverware and soup spoon. "And could you scare up another one of these? I think I'm going to need a few of them before the night is over."

She smiled and gave me a playful wink before she set about her task.

I placed my napkin in my lap and took the first spoonful of the luscious bisque. The soup made its way down my throat, creating a swath of warmth as it made the journey to my stomach.

As the evening went on, there was more warmth from additional martinis and the superb steak that followed. But there was another source of warmth that became increasingly present as well. The Darkness was wide awake, and it was hungry. It wanted blood. And after what the Enteron crew had done to Mark Hill, so did I.

CHAPTER TEN

Sunday, January 10th
0045 Hours Local Time
Flight Safety International, DFW Learning Center
Dallas-Fort Worth Airport (KDFW)
Irving, Texas USA

They came after me the next night, and I was ready.

Years of living with a multi-million-dollar pricetag on my head and continually looking over my shoulder had created a kind of sixth sense inside me - a sense triggered by coincidences, anomalies, and inconsistent situations. It was in high alert mode.

I felt them before I saw them.

I exited the north door of the FlightSafety building into a nearly vacant parking lot. The vast building was rectangular in shape, and the north side was one of the short sides of the rectangle. Since the FlightSafety building was situated on the DFW Airport grounds, an active taxiway lay about three hundred meters north of the building, elevated on a berm of earth that allowed the taxiway to pass over South Airfield Drive, the main road traversing the front side of the building. The parking lot itself was somewhat enclosed on three sides, by the building on the south side, the taxiway berm to the north, and by another berm of earth to the west.

I had purposefully chosen this parking lot because it would look like the perfect place for an ambush, deserted, somewhat isolated, and largely shielded from public view. The bad guys would think they had the edge.

But they were wrong.

Thanks to the many trips I had made to this training center over my business aviation career, it felt like familiar turf to me. Even more so because I had walked the ground thoroughly before my simulator session tonight. I knew every square inch of it.

I was making a few assumptions. I expected my pursuers to be sloppy. Odds were high they were mob hitmen from Chicago. They would presume I would be easy prey. I also expected them to get close. They'd have instructions to tell me who had sent them before they pulled the trigger. I was pretty confident that Rowe would want me to know she had won.

I sighed as I looked out into the parking lot and saw the few cars parked there. There were two sedans, the inevitable pick-up truck, and a panel van with no windows on the sides. The van was backed into a parking slot to my right, and the front of the vehicle was facing me. Because the nearest overhead lights in the parking lot were behind the van, the front seat was in shadow, and I couldn't tell if anyone was sitting there. But I was pretty sure that I could hear the engine idling.

I turned to my left and walked to my rental car, a Chevrolet Malibu, parked about fifty feet away, towards the rear of the FlightSafety building. I kept my pace steady. I needed them to think that I was unaware and vulnerable. But I also needed to use my car for cover if they had the chance to open fire before I did.

Forty feet to the car. I ensured the backpack hanging from my left shoulder was optimally positioned and glanced down at the main compartment's zipper to make sure it was open for easy access. I could have used the .45 on my right hip to engage these guys, but I wanted to make a statement as well as to contain the amount of lead flying through the air in a parking lot next to an airport taxiway.

Thirty feet to the car. From behind me, a telltale sound came through the still, night air – a dull, barely audible, mechanical thump.

I nodded to myself. They had put the van in gear. They'd be rolling any second. My heart rate began to increase slightly, and I could feel the blood warming inside of me.

Twenty feet to the car. I kept my eyes focused on my vehicle. The lighting poles above the lot were well spaced, and I had been very deliberate in the placement of my car. Between the glass windows and highly polished paint and lighting, the side of my car acted like a perfect mirror of the world behind me.

Ten feet to the car, and I could see the van's reflection begin to roll. It was moving slowly, and the sound of the tires on the pavement was soft and steady, almost indistinguishable from the white noise of the night.

I reached my car, and I could hear the van speeding up behind me. They wanted to catch me just as I was entering my car when I'd be distracted and vulnerable.

At that moment, the loud whine of jet engines broke the near silence of the evening. American Airlines Flight 4482 had just landed on runway 17L at DFW and was turning down taxiway ER, the one on the top of the berm just to the north. I had timed my exit from the building to take advantage of the noise and the distraction. The arrangement of the trees and buildings on this part of the airfield kept the noise of passing jets muted until they emerged onto the taxiway just behind us. I was ready for the sudden blast. The guys in the van wouldn't be and they reacted to the jet noise as I thought they might. The vehicle stopped.

In milliseconds, the Darkness came alive inside of me, propelling me into action against my attackers, like a cat that had been patiently waiting for exactly the right moment to pounce.

But the sensation was different this time. Instead of the normal bloodlust and frenzy that I felt with its presence, the Darkness brought on a feeling of icy and methodical control. It turned me into a coldly calculating machine of death. I almost found myself removed from my body and placed into an observation mode as the Darkness went about its business.

I pulled my weapon from the backpack, quickly stepped to my left, and pivoted 180 degrees. The van was just a few feet away. The driver, a middle-aged man with a swarthy complexion and a full black beard, had a confused look on his face. He was half looking over his left shoulder as if talking to someone behind him.

Then he saw the gun in my hands, and his eyes grew wide.

I had a shortened version of the venerable Remington 870 12-gauge shotgun. It was just 26 inches long and sported a 13-inch barrel with an open choke. I had it loaded with 5 rounds of magnum 00 buckshot.

Before the driver could react, the Darkness smiled at him and fired a round through his door. At this range, the nine .30 caliber lead pellets penetrated the thin steel of the door easily, and the driver screamed and slumped over. I sidestepped to my right and fired four rounds into the van's side door as quickly as I could cycle the gun's pump action. Then I put the weapon back into my pack, dropped the pack on the ground, and drew the .45, cycling the thumb safety to the off position as I raised the weapon. I threw the van's door open and leveled the .45.

Inside, one man lay dying in a rapidly expanding pool of blood. He was dressed in black slacks and a black turtlenecked sweater straight out of gangster wardrobe. The sweater had several ragged holes in the chest and stomach area, and the pants had a few holes below the belt line as well. The man's eyes were blinking rapidly, and he was struggling to breathe. A Glock pistol with a suppressor was in his right hand, loosely gripped by his limp fingers. I glanced around the interior of the van to make sure he was alone and relieved him of his weapon. Then, I walked around the van and scanned the parking lot, looking for possible reinforcements.

There were none.

The American Airlines 737 taxied off into the vast expanse of the DFW airport, and the silence of the night re-enveloped the parking lot. I returned to the driver's side of the van.

"You know guys, I think I'm a little insulted," I said as I holstered my weapon. "There were only two of you."

I stepped into the vehicle and pulled the driver through the opening between the seats and into the back of the van, a task made easier by the fact that his seatbelt was unbuckled. Clearly, he had thought he might have to exit the van and help out at some point. The driver landed on the van's metal floor next to his companion. The driver was in bad shape. He had been closer to the shotgun, and the pellets that had struck him had been more tightly grouped. His left arm was hanging by shreds of flesh, and his left side was torn open. But he was still alive. At least for the moment.

And a moment was all I needed.

"You two are going to send a message for me," the Darkness said in a voice that dripped with ice.

The two dying men looked at me, blankly.

I pulled my iPhone from my pocket and took a photo of the two of them, ensuring that I zoomed in on the two heads and faces.

Then, as they watched, I retrieved the shotgun from my bag, reloaded it with two more rounds, and returned to the open doorway of the vehicle's rear compartment.

"And the message needs to be a statement," I continued. "Kind of a bold statement, actually."

The Darkness charged the shotgun and blew the driver's head off, keeping the weapon at arm's length to avoid the inevitable spatter. Then I cycled the action and did the same to the other guy.

I photographed the two of them again, zooming in as I had before, this time to accentuate the lack of heads and faces.

As I replaced my phone in my pocket and felt the adrenaline begin to subside, I heard the buzzing of another phone coming from the front of the van. I reached through the opening between the front seats and found the phone in a cupholder on the front console. A call was coming through from a 312 area code. Downtown Chicago. What a surprise.

I answered the phone and waited for the caller to speak. After a moment, I heard a female voice, but it wasn't the one I was expecting.

"Is it done?" asked Detective Betty Jarvis.

For a moment, I was stunned. But then my brain began running with the implications of Jarvis being in charge of this hit.

Holy shit, I thought. *She must have been in on the Mark Hill hit as well.*

My few seconds of hesitation must have made Detective Jarvis impatient.

"Well?" she said, this time with a tinge of anger in her voice. "Is it? Is that asshole dead?"

And it was then that the Darkness spoke, in a voice so cold it could have come from the depths of the Arctic. "It certainly is done, Betty," I said. "But probably not the way you expected."

"Who is this?"

I clicked off the call and used the driver's thumb on the phone's home button to unlock the screen. I airdropped my recent photos onto the driver's phone and texted them to the number that had just called. Once I could tell that the images had been delivered, I tossed the phone back into the van and closed the side door.

A few moments later, I had the van parked in a remote corner of the parking lot with the perforated door facing a row of bushes that made it difficult for passersby to see the damage. I returned to my car and pulled off the coveralls I had donned to avoid getting blood on my clothes as I drove the van. I bagged the coveralls and removed my phone from my pocket, hitting Dave Smith's mobile number in the process.

Smith answered immediately. "I was wondering when I'd hear from you tonight. I take it everything went according to plan?" he asked.

I smiled as I recalled the earlier conversation with Jarvis. "They only sent two guys," I said. "It wasn't even exciting."

I heard Smith's low laugh over the airwaves. "We all get lucky sometimes." He paused for a second and then added, "They won't underestimate you the next time."

I shook my head. "No. They won't."

"You can't trust anyone," he said. "They have someone feeding them information from inside the department. They knew where you'd be and when. They even knew your simulator schedule, and you didn't even know that yourself until Thursday morning."

I nodded. "I thought they might," I said. "I was actually testing that hypothesis with this business tonight. They showed me their cards. They just didn't count on me surviving to use the knowledge. And they didn't count on me learning that Betty Jarvis was in charge. She called to check up on the boys in the van after I dealt with them. I sent her a few pictures from one of their phones that she might find disturbing."

Smith whistled. 'Wow," he said. "That was unexpected. But I guess they had to have someone in the local PD to keep a lid on Hill's death."

I nodded to myself. "I made the same connection."

"So, back to Chicago?"

"Yes," I responded. "After I finish my simulator tomorrow night. There's another flight to North Korea next week. I'm going to fly it. I think Rowe will be on it too."

"That would be handy," Smith said. "We flushed a few things out into the open tonight. Good job. Anything you might need help with?"

I sighed. "Yeah, there is," I said. "Can you send someone down here to help me with the trash?"

CHAPTER ELEVEN

Tuesday, January 12th
1100 Hours Local Time
Enteron Flight Department
DuPaul Airport (KDPA)
West Chicago, Illinois, USA

I returned to Enteron's flight department just about a week after I had made my initial, surprise entry. I was greeted by smiles from Rose, Julie, and Brett. Sarah smiled as well, but her eyes looked into me and saw something there that changed the expression on her face. Her eyes widened a bit, and she looked away quickly.

"Where can I sit so I won't be in the way?" I asked.

"You should use the office at the end of the hall!" Brett said with gusto in his voice. "That's where the Boss is supposed to sit."

I looked at the other faces as he spoke and didn't see a lot of enthusiasm for his idea. For my own part, I wasn't keen on occupying the same space that Mark Hill had made his own, let alone the space used by the weasel who had replaced him.

"Can I just sit in the conference room? As long as no one else needs to use it."

Brett shrugged but the rest of heads were nodding.

"Sounds good," Rose said. "The only event we have scheduled for that room is the NK trip briefing at 4 this afternoon. But you'll want to sit in on that anyway."

"When does that flight depart?"

Sarah looked down at her computer. "We've been doing this with both 7Xs to make sure we don't lose the flight to a mechanical issue," she said. "The first jet will depart tomorrow morning at 0900 with crew members only. The crew flying that jet will take it to Anchorage where they'll remain overnight and get crew rest. The second jet will leave on Thursday and take the passengers to Anchorage where the first crew will have the first jet fueled and ready as a spare aircraft. The second aircraft will land and get fuel. The crews will swap and if all is good with the second jet, the first crew will take the second jet to North Korea. If the second jet breaks, everyone switches to the first jet and they launch in that aircraft." She smiled. "I know that sounds complicated, but it seems to work."

I smiled back at her. "Sounds like a great plan," I said. "Put me on the first jet, please."

Sarah nodded. "We thought that might be the case. I've got you loaded as pilot-in-command."

I shook my head. "I appreciate that, but I haven't been there before. I assume the person you're pairing me with has been?"

She nodded again.

"Make him or her the PIC please."

"It's a him. His name is Rick Wilson."

"Is he around today?"

"Not quite yet," Rose said. "But he will be in later."

I nodded. "Great. I'll link up with him then."

I made my way into the conference room and set my briefcase on the table. Then I removed my coat and turned for the door. Rose was standing in the door, watching me.

"How do you intend to do this?" she asked.

I raised my eyebrows at her. "Do what?"

"Find out who killed Mark Hill."

For a moment, I was tempted to tell her that I thought I already knew the answer, but I didn't. Rose seemed to be well intentioned and loyal but giving her information might put her in jeopardy. I didn't want to do that.

I shrugged. "I have this way of just talking to people and moving things around until something happens," I said. "It's worked pretty well for me in the past."

She nodded and eyed me appraisingly.

"And I'm going to start the talking part immediately. Right after I get some coffee."

Rose motioned to the hall behind her and towards the kitchen area I had seen on my last visit. "I'll show you the way."

I followed her down the hall and we turned into the kitchen. She motioned toward the Bunn coffeemaker on the counter to the right. There was a stack of paper cups next to the machine.

"Coffee's there, cream is in the fridge and sweeteners are in the drawer under the coffeemaker."

I nodded and set about the coffee tasks. Rose stood at the door of the room and watched me as I poured myself a cup, put a healthy dose of cream into it and finished it with an envelope of stevia sweetener.

"Who are you going to start with?" she asked at last.

I shrugged. "Whoever is here," I said. "I'll just wander around, introduce myself and get people to talk to me."

"What about the people in Baltimore? How are you going to talk to them?"

"I don't think I need to," I said, as I raised the cup to my lips. "The people who did Mark Hill are local."

"How do you know that?"

"Let's just say I have...information to that effect."

She nodded slowly, keeping her eyes on me.

"Do you want to start with me and the people in the outer office?"

I shook my head. "Nope. It's not any one of you."

"How can you know that? You just met us!"

I shrugged. "Instinct. I just do."

Rose squinted her eyes at me, like she was trying to see through me. "I guess I thought you would be more..." she waved her hand in a circular motion, like she was trying to draw more words out of her brain, "more systematic."

I shrugged again and walked to the door. "It's easy for me to find killers, Rose. Always has been."

"Why?"

I looked down at her as I passed her. "Because they remind me of me."

I left the kitchen and turned left down the hall. In my last visit, I had passed the Director of Maintenance's office on my way to see Darnell, so I knew where it was. The lead maintainer in an organization like this one would have a lot on his plate, but he'd also be the one who knew a lot of the dirt. Technicians overhear a lot of conversations, and sometimes there was no love lost between technicians and pilots.

The DOM's door was down on the right, just prior to office at the end of the hall. It was closed but it had a glass panel down the right side. I could see a man sitting at the lone desk inside. I knocked on the door.

"Yeah? Who is it?" said a gruff voice from inside.

I opened the door and stuck my head inside. "Colin Pearce," I said. "Do you have a few minutes to talk?"

The man behind the desk rose begrudgingly and offered his hand. I had met him during my introduction to the department a week ago and his appearance was as I remembered. He was much shorter than I was and had a bald head. I knew that he was in his early forties, but his face was heavily lined, making him look older. He had blue eyes that darted about the room without seeming to focus on anything.

"Dave Gardner," he said.

I shook his hand and then sank into a chair opposite him as he seated himself at his desk.

"Please to see you again, Dave."

"Likewise," he said, in a tone that clearly indicated he wasn't. "What can I do ya for?"

I smiled dutifully at the attempt at humor. "I'm trying to understand the culture of the department. I thought I'd start with you."

He shrugged. "Not sure what to say about that," he said.

"How long have you been here? At Enteron?"

Gardner rolled his eyes to the ceiling as he thought about the question. "Not quite from the beginning," he said. "But soon after that. Maybe since 2008?"

"So, you've been here about eight years?"

He nodded. "I guess so."

"Was the department always this big? Four jets and a helicopter and two locations?"

"When I was hired, the department already had a Falcon 2000," he said. "We had just bought the first 7X, and we were in a hangar on the other side of National Drive. The Baltimore location didn't exist then."

I nodded. "I see. When did the other jets and people get added?"

"We bought the other 2000 next," he said. "In 2009. Then, in 2010, we moved the operation from the hangar across the road to this one. In 2011, we bought the helicopter and opened up the other location in Baltimore since the helicopter was going to operate on the east coast. In 2012, we bought the second 7X and moved one of the 2000s to join the helicopter at Baltimore. And here we are."

"How many technicians do you have working for you?"

"Eight," he said. "Four here to look after three jets and three in Baltimore to look after a jet and a helicopter. And I'm not sure it's enough."

"How much do you guys fly?"

"Each jet does about 400 hours per year and the helo does about same."

"Wow," I said. "That's a lot of flying. Not much time to work in the calendar and hourly inspection items I bet."

"You bet right. We have to do progressive inspections to the max extent possible, just hit a few items on the work-cards when the jets are idle."

I nodded. "Makes sense. I bet that keeps your dispatch reliability numbers pretty high."

There was silence for a moment and then Gardner leaned forward across his desk. "Why are you here, Mister Pearce?" he asked.

I looked into his eyes and tried to diagnose possible motives for the question. Was he suspicious? Afraid? Of just weary of different supervisors trying to get in the way of him doing his job.

"Not to change anything you're doing, for starters," I said. I watched him closely to see how he responded to my answer. He seemed to relax a bit.

But his eyes were still fixed on me as he waited for an additional answer. I decided to sidestep the question. For now.

"How did you like working for Mark Hill?" I asked.

Gardner leaned back in his chair and shrugged. "He was a decent boss, I guess. He took care of me, allowed me to take care of my folks, and stayed out of my way."

"In other words, he let you do your things, your way."

Gardner nodded, almost begrudgingly. "Yes," he said, after thinking about the question for several moments. "I guess he did."

"Why would someone want to kill him?"

Gardner looked at me blankly. "No idea," he said. "I thought he was okay."

A thought popped into my head then, startling me with its sudden intrusion into my brain.

"Did Hill make any requests concerning the airplanes that seemed...odd to you?"

Gardner opened his mouth to answer but seemed to think better of it. He looked at the ceiling for a few moments as he re-considered the question. Then he lowered his gaze to me.

"Shortly after we started this North Korean business, he asked me to install radiation detectors in the baggage compartments of the 7Xs," he said. "I thought it was odd because we weren't transporting any of that stuff, but he insisted."

"Did you tell anyone outside of the department?"

Gardner nodded. "I had to. I had to get the purchase approved by Rowe's office. Those things were expensive."

"Did she approve them?"

Gardner shook his head. "No. She said they were expensive and unnecessary."

And that's how she knew Hill was onto her, I thought. "One more question and then, if you don't mind, I'd like to get a tour of the hangar from you and meet your technicians who are here."

Gardner nodded. "No problem. What's your question?"

"Do you remember when Hill made that request?"

Gardner smiled grimly and shook his head. "I can't forget it. It was one month to the day before those damn consultants showed up and tried to tell me how to run my maintenance shop."

I spent most of the next hour touring the hangar and talking to the maintenance technicians who were on duty. The hangar was an impressive facility. In addition to the spaces I had already seen, there was an office for the maintenance technicians, a parts storage area, a battery workshop, and the hangar area itself, an expansive floor that was probably close to 40,000 square feet. Both Falcon 7Xs and one of the Falcon 2000s were parked on the floor and there was room left over. After showing me around, Gardner aimed me toward one of the 7Xs where two of the technicians were at work and returned to his office.

As I walked up to the side of the large business jet, I took some time to admire it. The sleek 7X was 76 feet long and sported an 86-foot wingspan. It was powered by three Pratt and Whitney PW307A engines and featured an elegant and sophisticated wing designed by engineers who also produced fighter aircraft. The jet had a digital flight control system similar that the one I had flown with in the F-16, the first business jet to utilize that modern technology. I had flown the 7X all over Europe in a previous adventure and taken it into some demanding airports. The aircraft had performed superbly. I was looking forward to flying it again.

"Hello Mr. Pearce," said a tall, sandy-haired man standing next to the jet. "What can we do for you?"

I reached out to shake his hand and my face must have communicated the fact that I couldn't remember his name.

"Joe Bernstein," he said. "I enjoyed meeting you last week. I think we're all glad you're here."

I nodded to him as I shook his hand. "I'm glad to be here as well," I said. "What are you guys up to?"

Bernstein shrugged. "We're changing the inflight internet router," he said. "There were issues during the last NK flight. God forbid if the passengers can't get online."

I nodded at him and smiled. "You can lose an engine and that's ok, but if you lose internet, the flight's a failure."

Bernstein laughed and revealed a toothy grin. "Ain't that

the truth!"

A shorter man with a broad face, dark hair and the swarthy complexion of Mediterranean heritage emerged from the door of the 7X with a metallic black component in his hand, about the size and shape of a small shoe box. He saw me and smiled.

"Pete Carlone," he said as he descended the airstair.

I shook his hand. "Glad to see you again, Pete." I looked between the two of them and allowed a wry smile to etch its way into my features. "So, Pete, you get to do all the work and Joe gets to stand out here and do what, exactly?"

"Supervise," Joe said, smiling back at me. "Just supervise. I am the senior guy after all!"

"Great work if you can get it, I think," I said.

"You bet!" Joe responded.

"Actually, Joe is minding the power cart for me and bringing me the tools I need," Pete said. "I'm actually keeping him pretty busy."

"I expected no less," I said. "When do you think you'll have the new router installed?"

Joe shrugged. "As soon as FEDEX delivers it. We've been told it's on the truck and headed our way."

I nodded. "Has the internet thing been the most significant issue you've had on these flights or have there been others?"

Pete and Joe looked at each other for a few moments and then Joe spoke.

"The 7X is a pretty reliable jet when it's maintained well," he said. "And we work on them and fuss over them all the time. The only other real issue we've had is a FADEC dispatch message on a return flight about two weeks ago on the other 7X. We swapped the pax onto the spare jet in Anchorage, had a spare FADEC flown into Anchorage and installed it on the broken jet when it arrived. The jet was back here about a day after the issue occurred and the only reason we had to wait that long was because the pilots were out of rest."

I nodded as he talked. FADEC stood for full authority digital engine controller. There were three of them installed in the aft equipment bay, and they controlled every aspect of operation for their associated engines.

"You had a technician based in Anchorage to deal with issues during the tech stop?"

Pete shook his head. "No. For overseas flights, we have a technician with each crew to deal with any anomalies or issues that might come up during the flight. Hill insisted on that."

I nodded in agreement. "Smart plan."

"It's saved our bacon a few times," Joe said. "Minor things have come up that pilots couldn't deal with and the technician on board either fixed it or signed off the MEL deferment."

The MEL was the aircraft's minimum equipment list. It provided guidance on which equipment items could be broken and still allow the aircraft to fly. Using the MEL often required a technician to inspect the broken item, take some kind of action, and make the associated logbook entry. Sometimes, depending on where the aircraft was when MEL use was required, technicians could be hard to come by. Hill's policy ensured the flights wouldn't be delayed.

"What did you guys think of your ex-boss?" I asked.

"Darnell?" Joe asked, his eyes flashing. "Utterly clueless. I have no idea whose idea it was to put some non-aviation corporate type down here, but it was the wrong answer."

I smiled at him but shook my head. "Not Darnell, Mark Hill."

Joe's eye's softened and he smiled sadly. "He was a good man and he took care of us on the floor," he said. "All the techs liked him."

"Except for Moore maybe," Pete said.

Joe nodded. "Yeah. You're right. Dylan Moore thinks he knows more than anyone."

"Who's he?"

"One of the other techs," Pete said. "Both he and Jake Barnhouse are on the late shift today so they can do the preflight inspections for their respective jets. They'll be the technicians on the upcoming flights."

"Jake's a good guy," Joe said. "But Dylan is a piece of work. Seems like he's always stirring the shit." He shook his head. "You know, I've always been one to believe if you don't have nothing good to say, then don't say nothing. But Dylan seems to look for reasons to bad mouth people, even the Boss."

I nodded slowly. Moore sounded a like a malcontent. It seemed like there was always at least one, even in the best organizations. I made a mental note to get him assigned to my crew so that I could spend some time talking to him and get inside his head. His attitude didn't necessarily make him an accomplice in Hill's murder, but it did raise him higher on the list.

"Well guys," I said. "I guess I should leave you to it. It's been great talking to you. I probably need to get inside and see if there are any fires that require my attention."

They nodded.

"Are you coming to the trip briefing this afternoon?" Joe asked.

"Trip briefing?"

"The one at 1600 local," Pete said. "For the NK trip."

I smacked myself in the forehead as I remembered Rose's words from earlier. I nodded and raised my cup at them. "Apparently I need more coffee," I said. "See you guys around."

I left them at the side of the 7X and departed the hangar area through the center door, thinking it might lead me to the kitchen area. I wasn't disappointed. The door led to the stock room and beyond it was the kitchen. As I walked into the kitchen, I saw Darnell's old sign on the floor with the words "Get a grip, DICK," scrawled on it in bold, black ink. I smiled to myself. Pilots and their senses of humor.

I recharged my coffee cup and made my way into the pilot office beyond. Directly in front of me, I saw two pilots at their desks. One was Brian Fuhrman, the Director of Training. He had his back to me and was typing something into a computer keyboard. I walked up and moved to his side so that he could see me standing there.

"Colin!" he said as his eyes lifted up. "How was the training?"

"Awesome," I replied. "I wanted to thank you for making it happen. It's been a few years since I've been in a 7X. I enjoyed getting reacquainted with the jet."

"They do a good job there. Who was your sim instructor?"

"Allen Dodson."

Fuhrman nodded. "He's good. Did he give you the Amsterdam to Le Bourget double rat's ass on cold weather day?"

I smiled, recalling the complicated profile. "Yes, he did. Pretty challenging scenario."

"Makes it real though. Right?"

I nodded. "Yes, it does."

Fuhrman looked back at his computer screen. "I just got the email that told me you completed the online international procedures course as well, so that's good."

"I needed that review. I've been flying domestically for the last few years."

"All that remains is for you and me to get together and get you some Ops Manual training. Will you have a few hours this afternoon?"

"You bet," I said. "Right up until the NK flight briefing at 1600."

Fuhrman looked at his watch. "About four hours," he said. "That should be enough time."

"Can we get some lunch brought in?"

He smiled at me. "That's up to you...Boss!"

I smiled back. "I guess it is. Let's do that."

"I'll go get the conference room set up," he said as he stood up. "We'll start as soon as you're ready."

"Sounds good."

I turned to the other pilot who was seated in the group of cubicles. He had a spreadsheet open on his computer screen. I could see airport identifiers down the left side of the screen and date intervals at the top.

"Fuel prices?" I asked.

The pilot turned to me. I remembered him from my introductory meeting a week ago. He was one of the only people in the room that didn't make an effort to introduce himself and shake my hand. He was short, had medium-colored curly hair and a bit of a pug nose. I extended my hand to him.

"I don't think we've met yet," I said. "I'm Colin Pearce."

The pilot didn't rise from his chair and he didn't make eye contact. Instead, he raised a skinny arm towards me and fixed his eyes on a point across the room.

"Allen Macy," he said in a flat voice.

"Are you the guy who tries to get the department the best fuel deals?" I asked in a conversational tone.

He shook his head and raised his eyes to mine. His face was etched into an expression of exasperation or impatience. "I'm responsible for the department's fuel strategy," he said, emphasizing the last word. "I try to build a consolidated program of pricing, budgeting and tankering to maximize our savings. I've got an MBA from the business school at SMU. I'm trying to put it to good use."

"Excellent," I said. "How much did you save the department last year?"

Macy sighed and turned to his computer. He hunted for another spreadsheet in his file listing and opened it. Then he turned the monitor toward me so I could see it more easily.

"Four hundred twenty five thousand over retail prices," he said, with a just a hint of smugness.

"That's pretty good," I replied. I could have left the conversation there, but I wanted to press the guy a little more. I didn't really know why. "What contract fuel purchase programs do you use?"

"Contract programs?" He shrugged. "The standard ones, Colt, CAA, World Fuel, AV Fuel and a few others."

"Do the airports you guys fly to allow you to make use of the contracts regularly?"

I could see Macy's jaw tense for a moment, as if he was going to make some kind of snappy comeback. But he managed to catch himself, and he shook his head. "Not often enough," he said. "At some of the destinations we go to a lot, like Baltimore, we have to buy fuel from the FBO and it's expensive."

I nodded. I remembered from my business jet contract days that some FBOs, particularly if they were part of a large chain and were the only facility on the field, refused to honor contract fuel programs in the name of more profit. But there was a way around that. I had been privy to the fuel purchase program my boss, Ian Brooks, had arranged and seen the effect of volume buying power on fuel prices. Brooks had teamed up with an aircraft management company to take advantage of their fuel pricing. It had lowered Brooks' operations fuel cost substantially.

"I might have an idea or two to fix that," I said. "We'll talk later."

Macy shrugged and returned to his computer screen, effectively dismissing me. I stood there for a moment, dumbfounded at his rudeness. Back in my days in the USAF, I would have stood him up against the wall, told him to get his chin in and chewed his ass royally. But it was a kinder, gentler world now. Sadly.

I brushed by him and made my way to the conference room. Fuhrman was sitting at the end of the table nearest the projection screen and looking at me with a bemused expression on his face.

"How did you like little Sir Allen?" he asked.

I raised my eyebrows at him.

"He sees himself as aviation nobility so that's what we call him. The little part is self-explanatory. He's so short we should get diversity credit for him."

I grinned at him. "The arrogance does show through," I said.

"He comes from a wealthy family in Dallas and has always gotten anything he's ever wanted. Did he tell you he has an MBA from SMU?"

"Yep. Within the first thirty seconds of the conversation."

"If he had spoken to you longer, you'd learn that he's a CAM, a certified aviation manager. He usually works that into the conversation within five minutes or so."

"Oh," I said. "We didn't talk that long. I told him I had an idea that might help with the fuel program and he didn't seem interested."

"Well you obviously didn't get it," Fuhrman said, smiling and shaking his head. "He's the only one that has good ideas. Anyone else's ideas are...inferior."

"I've encountered that before," I said. "I don't do well with those types of people. He and I are going to have to talk."

"Well, don't piss him off too much."

"Why?"

"He didn't tell you? He usually brags about it. He works financial projects for the executive in charge of the department, Brenda Rowe. He's down at her office at least once or twice per week. He's got her ear."

I felt a gear click into place in the back of my brain.

"Does he now?" I asked.

Fuhrman nodded. "Absolutely. And a lot of the financial shit she tries to do within our department has his fingerprints on it."

I cocked my head. "That's fucked up."

"You're telling me. We have an aggressive training program here and Hill had us signed up with an upset recovery training provider in California. The course was taught by test pilots and was the best upset recovery training out there. It was a three-ride course. One ride was flown in a Sabreliner and the other two were flown in a military trainer aircraft with an ejection seat. You got to experience the full gamut of possible upset events. But…"

"It was expensive," I said.

Fuhrman nodded. "Not only that, it made little Allen uncomfortable. It seems that he didn't like flying with people who knew so much more about aviation than he did. He also didn't like strapping into an ejection seat and getting turned upside down. He was airsick on both of his trainer rides and he got embarrassed. He started talking bad about the training and Hill cut him off and said that as long as he was in charge of the department, not only would everyone go to initial upset training, they would go to recurrent upset training, every two years. That didn't make Sir Allen happy."

"So, he fought it," I said, shaking my head. "And he used his connection with Rowe to do it. Jesus."

"Not only that, when those damn consultants came in, he gave them an earful."

"I bet he did," I said, thinking aloud.

"He and Rowe were trying to ambush Hill over this training. Hill saw it coming and scheduled a meeting with both Rowe and Allen about it."

I shot a glance at Fuhrman and he shrugged.

"I'm the training guy," he said. "Hill kept me in the loop about this stuff. Anyway, shortly after the meeting was scheduled, Hill was...." His voice trailed off.

I sank into the comfortable chair at the far end of the conference table and tried to halt the wheels that were spinning in my head. "Damn," I said, the word popping out of my mouth involuntarily.

Fuhrman nodded and there was silence for several seconds.

I finally pulled myself back into the moment and looked at him. "I guess we should get started with this training," I said. "Shall we get some lunch ordered?"

"Already done," Fuhrman said. "Rose took care of it. I hope you like Thai food."

"Love it," I said.

Fuhrman stood and called up the first slide in his presentation. Then he began to speak.

CHAPTER TWELVE

Tuesday, January 12th
1600 Hours Local Time
Enteron Flight Department
DuPaul Airport (KDPA)
West Chicago, Illinois, USA

"Ladies and gentlemen, welcome to the trip briefing for our upcoming flight to North Korea. You can consult the electronic trip packets I emailed earlier as we go through the briefing. If you have questions, please hold them until I get to the end of each segment. I'll ask for them then."

The speaker was my co-captain for the trip, Rick Wilson. He was a tall, thin man with graying hair and an easy smile. He had just a hint of an impish smirk on his features nearly all the time, and it made me wonder if there was some sort of humorous dialogue continually going on in his head.

I glanced down at the iPad in front of me. Before the briefing had started, I had tabbed through the trip package and been impressed at the thoroughness of the documentation there. While usual material: flight plans, weather depictions and forecasts, NOTAM printouts, customs forms, and manifests were included, there was also additional paperwork addressing accommodations, security issues, ground transportation, handling arrangements, and passenger itinerary. These folks knew what they were doing.

I raised my eyes from the iPad to see Sarah looking at me expectantly. The last time she and I had flown together, years ago, had been on international trips between Burbank, California and Cabo San Lucas, Mexico. The fingerprints of her experience were all over the paperwork in front of me. I nodded in deference to her and gave her a satisfied smile. She smiled back at me with a knowing sparkle in her eyes. Then we both turned our attention to Wilson's first slide.

An itinerary for the trip appeared on the screen along with a listing of the crew members for each of the two jets.

"The backup jet, N613CB, will be crewed by the new Boss and me," Wilson said. "I'll be trip captain. Our planned departure time is 0900 hours tomorrow morning. Arrival time in Anchorage will be approximately 1100 hours local time. The primary jet, N622CB, will be crewed by Gordon and Gutierrez. Gordon will be the trip captain. They'll depart at 0900 hours on Thursday and arrive at Anchorage at approximately 1100 hours local time on Thursday."

I recognized the two other crew members from my initial meeting, but I made sure I re-introduced myself to them before the briefing. Marty Gordon was the younger of the two. He was in his thirties, with an athletic build – like a runner. I learned he still flew C-17s in the USAF reserves. He was based in the Baltimore location but had been brought in for this trip. Jose Gutierrez, the other crew member, had a distinct Hispanic look about him, complete with jet black hair and dark eyes. As I had shaken his hand earlier, I had felt a vibe from him that was unsettling but couldn't put my finger on it. Then, as I saw he and Gordon sitting side by side at the table and Gordon's name announced as trip captain, I understood. Gutierrez obviously thought he should be in charge of the flight, not the younger man. I could almost see the waves of resentment emanating from him as he sat there, eyeing the screen with an expression that was a mixture of disdain and impatience. I made a mental note to ask the Chief Pilot about it later.

'The flight technicians will be Barnhouse and Moore," Wilson continued. "Moore will be aboard the backup jet, N613CB, and Barnhouse will be aboard the primary jet, N622CB."

The technicians were the two men Joe Bernstein had mentioned earlier, Jake Barnhouse and Dylan Moore. Barnhouse was a big, stocky guy with a self-deprecating smile and a relaxed manner. He had spoken with me for several moments at our initial meeting, and I had enjoyed meeting him. He and I had shaken hands warmly before the briefing. I remembered Moore as soon as I saw him again. I had met him at the initial meeting as well, but his glance had been furtive, and his handshake almost slimy, like that of a used-car salesman. As I greeted him before the briefing this afternoon, his eyes held mine for a few moments, like he was trying to gauge my resolve or something. I had made a mental note to keep a close eye on him, but since he had been assigned as the technician for my jet, that task seemed to have taken care of itself.

"As we've done in the past, the backup jet will be fueled, programmed, and ready by 1045 hours on Thursday," Wilson said. "Dylan, the Boss and I will have our bags on the ramp, ready to transfer. The primary jet will land, and while it is being refueled, the crews will transfer between aircraft. If no maintenance issues occur with the primary jet, it will launch with the passengers, Dylan, the Boss, and I, at approximately 1130 hours local time. If maintenance issues do occur, we'll move the passengers and their baggage to the backup jet, and we'll launch with the same personnel at about 1145." Wilson nodded at the three schedulers, Sarah, Julie, and Rose. "And you three will have to let everyone know of the tail change. Hopefully, the NK's will still let us into their airspace."

"Have you had to use the backup jet in any of these trips so far?" I asked.

Wilson shook his head. "No, we haven't," he said. "We've been lucky."

He advanced to the next slide in his presentation. A graphic depiction of a route of flight across the north Pacific appeared.

"The route is standard per our previous trips. I won't bore everyone here with the airways and control agencies. The pilots will brief that when we get together later." I noted that the route avoided flying into Russian airspace and instead skirted the Aleutian Islands, went south of the Kuril Islands, over the northernmost Japanese Island, Hokkaido, then over the Sea of Japan to Seoul, South Korea, before heading north to Pyongyang.

"Quick question?" I asked.

Wilson nodded at me.

"I understand why you're avoiding Russian airspace since they tend to make US aircraft fly lower and slower, but why aren't we going directly into North Korea instead of into South Korea first and then north."

"That's the way it was negotiated," Sarah said. "On the messages we get from the State Department we are given a very narrow airspace corridor that starts directly over the Inchon Airport and then heads north to Pyongyang. That's the route specifically negotiated with North Korea. Apparently, the North Koreans insisted upon it."

I nodded as she spoke.

"Something about us coming in from their sister country instead of the outside world," Sarah continued.

I smiled at her grimly and shook my head. "More like us flying over the border area where their air defense is the thickest," I said. "If we stray, it's easier to shoot us down."

Several of the heads at the table nodded at that. Gutierrez shrugged as if it didn't matter. I checked the anger that flashed inside of me and kept my mouth shut.

Wilson looked at me and raised his eyebrows. Then he glanced at Gutierrez. I could see the ever-present smirk etch its way deeper into Wilson's features.

"Care to elaborate, Boss?"

"Not much to say, really. I flew Vipers in that area of the world for a while, and the border is lined with anti-aircraft artillery pieces and surface-to-air missile sites, all coordinated by a central air defense radar system. It's probably some of the most heavily defended airspace in the world. We used to fly simulated close air support sorties in support of some Army units near the border in a piece of airspace called P-518, a prohibited area that overlies the DMZ and the terrain to the south. While we were flying, our jets were repeatedly locked up and tracked by surface-to-air missile radars."

Gutierrez quietly snorted and shook his head as he kept his eyes fixed on the screen.

I felt the anger flash inside of me again. I was about to ask him what his problem was when Sarah spoke.

"How did you know you were locked up?" she asked.

She already knew the answer to the question from our time together, years ago. It had been one of the many conversations we had horizontally, late into the evening. A smile crept onto my face, and I felt the ire in me washed away by a mental flood of pleasant memories.

"Radar homing and warning gear," I said when I was sure I could trust my voice. "It's a little like TCAS in the jets these days. We could see what types of radars were locked onto us and what their azimuth was. We could even tell if they launched a missile, which, fortunately, they didn't. It wasn't unusual to have an SA-2 site and an SA-3 site locked onto us at the same time. Oddly enough, you got used to it."

Gutierrez's posture changed slightly. He must have sensed that his display of disbelief wasn't affecting anyone.

"Rick, continue, please," I said. "I'm sorry to interrupt."

"No problem," he said, grinning. "But actually, I'm going to turn the show over to Mr. Gardner so he can talk to us about the jets."

Dave Gardner had come into the room while Wilson was discussing the crews and itinerary and had quietly taken a seat on the wall by the door. As the Director of Maintenance, he was ultimately responsible for the jets' maintenance status, and it seemed that he took the responsibility personally. I respected that.

Gardner rose from his seat as the slide for the first jet came up on the screen. It showed a side view picture of N613CB in the upper left corner with the jet's current hours and cycles to the right of the picture. On the bottom part of the slide, there were rows and columns for upcoming inspections and open discrepancies.

Gardner glanced at his clipboard and spoke. "Joe and Pete replaced the router on 613 this afternoon and reprogrammed it. The jet was towed out onto the ramp, and the satellite connection was ops checked. The jet's good on inspections until it hits another 100 hours or the end of the month, whichever occurs first."

He nodded at Wilson, and a similar slide for N622CB appeared on the screen.

"No further issues with the number two FADEC on 622 since we replaced it a few weeks ago. No other discrepancies. This jet is good on inspections for about 75 hours or three months." He raised his eyes from his clipboard and looked around the room. "Any questions?"

There were none.

Gardner nodded and turned to go.

"Thanks, Dave," Wilson said.

He advanced to the next slide. There was no title on the slide, but in its center, three words were displayed: THE BIG PICTURE.

"This is where the Boss... ahem," he paused and cleared his throat. "Where Mark Hill used to tell us his thoughts for each flight."

I nodded and took a sip from the bottle of water in front of me. I hadn't expected to have a formal speaking role in the briefing. I remembered Hill as a smart and inspirational guy. He had gone back to school for a Ph.D. and had an extensive vocabulary. I didn't think there was anything I could say that could inspire these people like he had.

But they wanted me to say something. Maybe they needed me to say something. Even Gutierrez was leaning forward in his seat, with an expectant look on his face.

I swallowed hard. "I'm not the orator your former boss was, so I guess I'll just keep it simple. The most important thing we can do over the next few days is to keep our eye on the ball." I looked around the room. "This organization, and with it all of you, have undergone a huge amount of change, particularly changes in leadership, over the last few weeks. When so much change happens in so little time, it's easy to get distracted. We obviously can't afford that. We're flying into the most reclusive country in the world through some of the most heavily defended airspace in the world. Everything needs to be right. It needs to be more than right. It needs to be perfect." I moved my eyes around the table and engaged every set of eyes that looked back at me. "It's times like these that the word 'professionalism' takes on new meaning," I continued. "True professionals put all of the shit aside, and they do their jobs. They focus, and they execute. No matter what else is going on around them."

I leaned back in my chair. "If your former boss was here, I think that's what he'd ask of you. It's what I'm asking of you. That's the big picture. Keep your eye on the ball. Focus. Execute. Be the professionals that Mark Hill knew you are."

There was a pregnant pause as my words settled in the room.

Rick Wilson broke the silence. "It'd be helpful if we knew why we're going there," he said, almost apologetically. "It's a pretty scary place. Even though we only drop the pax off and leave, there are a lot of military vehicles and guns. We've been intercepted twice on our way in there."

I leaned forward, and my jaw dropped involuntarily. "They've never told you the reasons for the flights?"

Wilson shook his head. "Not really," he said. "They've told us we're helping NK with its nuclear power generation. Nothing more than that."

I looked at the empty chair next to me, the chair designated for Brenda Rowe. She had made it known that she wanted to attend today's briefing but had not made the 1600 start time. I had directed Wilson to start without her. This would have been a question for her.

"That's because you don't need to know anything else," said a cold female voice. It came from the lobby side of the conference room's glass wall.

"Speak of the devil," I said to myself.

Brenda Rowe appeared in the doorway of the conference room a few moments later. She wore a unremarkable gray business suit that hung loosely on her frame, and her dark hair fell to her shoulders in an array of disheveled strings. She marched into the room like she owned the place and took the seat to my left. She removed a small notebook from a leather Tumi briefcase and opened the notebook on the table in front of her. Then she looked down the table at Rose.

"I believe I gave specific instructions about delaying the start of the briefing until I arrived," she said, in a quietly menacing voice.

"You weren't here on time," I said. "I directed that we start without you."

Rowe turned her gaze to me, rotating her head in what seemed like an exaggerated slow motion. She fixed her eyes on me, and her face took on an expression of surprised disbelief. She sat back in her chair and stared at me as she crossed her arms. Her dark eyes glowered like she was trying to bore holes through me.

This was a woman who demanded unconditional obedience. And I had challenged her. *How dare you!* the dark eyes seemed to be saying.

The atmosphere in the room became heavy with anticipation. It seemed that everyone here had been expecting a showdown of sorts, and that moment had arrived. All eyes in the room were fixed on me, but there was only one person present who had a clue about the things I had done in past adventures and what I was capable of. I felt Sarah's gaze on me, and I could feel her apprehension.

A thousand things went through my mind as I stared back at Rowe. *Does this shit actually work in the corporate world?* popped into my head. Suddenly, I felt an overwhelming urge to laugh in her face. But I fought to keep my face impassive and my voice even.

I motioned to the rest of the room. "Most of these people have a long, full day tomorrow, Ms. Rowe. I didn't want to keep them here one moment longer than necessary. We had no idea when you'd arrive, and Chicago traffic can be unpredictable. No offense to you was intended."

The tension in the room lessened a bit and Rowe's mouth turned up in a small smile of satisfaction.

"But," I continued. "Your arrival was very well-timed. We were all wondering about the purposes of these flights. Perhaps you'd care to enlighten us."

Rowe's smile vanished, and the dark eyes became hard,

almost lifeless.

"That's on a need to know basis," she said, the words leaving her mouth in a measured, deliberate tone. "And this department doesn't need to know. The only information you need is our destination and timetable."

It was my turn to sit back in my chair. I kept my eyes on hers and motioned to the room again. "For the past several weeks, you've asked several of the people in this department to risk their lives flying an aircraft into one of the most dangerous places in the world, and you don't think the company owes them an explanation?"

Rowe's eyes stayed fixed on mine. A line from the movie Jaws shot into my brain, and I could almost hear the crusty fisherman Quint whispering in my ear. *Sometimes that shark, he looks right into ya. Right into your eyes. And, you know, the thing about a shark... he's got lifeless eyes. Black eyes. Like a doll's eyes. When he comes at ya, doesn't seem to be living... until he bites ya.*

Rowe was a predator. And I was her prey. Or at least, that's what she thought.

"No," she said, with defiant tone in her voice. "I don't."

I nodded. "I see." I raised my hands in front of me and began slowly rubbing my palms together as I looked back at her. "But there's a problem with that line of thought," I said. "Sometimes, when you don't understand why you're doing what you're doing, or you don't understand exactly what you're up against, you can lose your *head*." I pronounced the last word distinctly, and paused for a moment, to let it sink in. "And that's really the last thing we need – to lose our *heads* as part of this process."

Rowe's face stayed impassive, but a glimpse of realization dawned in the dark eyes as she made the connection between my words and the events of a few nights ago. Until now, her knowledge had been theoretical, but now as she looked at me, she saw something she hadn't seen before. She wasn't looking at the eyes of a mere predator, she was looking into the eyes of a killer. My eyes. Suddenly the photos she'd seen, the photos that Jarvis undoubtedly sent her, became real. The threat became real.

And then, just for a moment, I saw something else in those dark lifeless eyes hers. A tinge of fear. I gave her a smile of my own and turned my head toward the far end of the room.

"Mr. Wilson," I said, "it seems an explanation will not be forthcoming. Please continue your briefing."

CHAPTER THIRTEEN

Tuesday, January 12th
2030 Hours Local Time
1721 Stuarts Drive
St. Charles, Illinois, USA

I leaned against the door frame of the kids' bedroom as Sarah tucked Colleen and Christopher into their beds. We had all eaten dinner together earlier, and I had offered to do the post-dinner cleanup while Sarah bathed the two kids and got them into their pajamas. I had just made it to their bedroom when I overheard the three of them.

"Tell us a story, Mommy!" little Colleen insisted.

"But I already read you a bedtime story," Sarah said. "You two will keep me up all night if I let you."

"Just one more, Mommy, please," said Christopher. "Just one."

"A short one," Colleen said. "Just a little one." I could see her holding her finger and her thumb up with a sliver of space in between.

The room was awash in the glow of a dim nightlight. Sarah was sitting on Colleen's bed with her back to me. Colleen's face was hidden from my sight by the corner of the room's closet wall, and Christopher was on the other bed, his face blocked by Sarah's body. I was content to stay just out of sight and listen to them.

"Okay," Sarah said, sighing and laughing at the same time, "just a little one. Which story do you want to hear?"

"A Brave Pilot story, Mommy!" Christopher said. "Those are the best."

"But tell the one with the good girl, not the one about the bad girl," Colleen insisted. "I don't like that bad girl."

"Okay. The one with the good girl," Sarah said. She cleared her throat. "Once upon a time, there were two very bad kings who wanted to hurt a lot of people and kill the two good kings," Sarah began.

I smiled to myself as she told a kid-friendly version of the adventure she and I had shared six years ago. Her version was much more interesting than the real story had been. Instead of a Saudi Arabian terrorist-prince and a Mexican drug lord, there were two bad kings, and instead of saving the presidents of the U.S and Mexico, the two good kings were saved. The heroes of the story were the brave pilots, a prince and princess who loved each other very much, and they flew in magical airplanes, side by side.

"And then one of the bad kings kidnapped the princess pilot and tried to take her away and hurt her," Sarah continued. "The brave boy pilot had to get into a small plane that was very fast and go save her."

"And he was shot!" Christopher interrupted. "You forgot that part, Mommy!"

I smiled to myself and looked down at my right leg. The gunshot wounds had long since healed, but sometimes they still ached in the middle of the night.

"You're right!" Sarah said. "He was shot! And that's what made him extra brave. But he jumped into that plane and took off to save the brave girl pilot."

"In afterburner!" Colleen said. "He lit the wick!"

The two kids giggled at the expression, and I smiled at their amusement. Sarah had obviously enhanced the story with some of the phrases she had heard me use.

"That's right," Sarah said. "And he chased the bad king in the plane up and down the valleys of the kingdom." Sarah was using her hands as the two airplanes, with one behind the other and making the two hands move from side to side as she described the chase. "Then the brave boy pilot got so close to the bad king's airplane that he scared the bad king so bad the bad king jumped out of the airplane!"

"Yay!" said Christopher.

"And he saved the brave girl pilot." Colleen said. "And she flew the airplane home!"

Sarah laughed. "I don't know why you two want me to tell you this story! You already know it!"

"But the boy pilot wasn't finished, was he Mommy?" Christopher asked.

"No, he wasn't," Sarah said. "He had to save the good kings from the other bad king. So, he flew his airplane very high and very fast to the south part of the kingdom."

"Faster than the speed of sound, right, Mommy?" Colleen asked.

"That's right, honey. But the brave boy pilot was in trouble because his airplane was almost out of gas and he didn't have any weapons. The bad king had a boat with big guns on it, and he was shooting at another boat with the good kings on it. The brave boy pilot thought and thought and then he knew there was only one thing he could do."

Sarah turned one of her hands into a boat, flat on the surface of the water. The other hand was an airplane high above the boat, and she moved the high hand into a dive aimed at the low hand.

"He had to ram the bad king's boat with his plane. So, he dived down, aiming his airplane at the bad king's boat. Faster and faster he got, and lower and lower. Then, when he was sure his plane would hit the bad king's boat, he jumped out of the plane."

"He eject-a-ted, Mommy!" Christopher said, struggling with the world. "He was going too fast. He couldn't jump out!"

"You're right, honey, he ejected. And he made it just in time and he was saved, but he was hurt really bad. But the brave girl pilot took care of him, and they got married and lived happily ever after."

"And they had two babies, right, Mommy?" Colleen asked.

"They sure did, honey. A girl and a boy. I think their names were Sue and Barney or something like that."

"No!" Christopher said. "Those weren't the names, Mommy!"

"Hmmm," Sarah said like she was thinking. "Maybe the two kids were named Patty and Bill."

"Mommy!" Colleen said. "Tell the story right!"

"Now that you mention it, maybe the kids' names were Colleen and Christopher."

"Well, of course!" Christopher said in an exasperated voice.

"Okay, that's enough, you two. It's time for bed. I'm going to go find your dad so he can kiss you good night."

"I'm right here," I said, stepping further into the room.

Sarah turned to me with a slight look of embarrassment on her face. "How long have you been standing there?" she asked.

"Long enough to hear that excellent story," I said, smiling at her. "But you know something kids, your mom forgot an important part of the story. The brave girl pilot actually saved the brave boy pilot's life!"

The two kids looked up at me with enthralled expressions.

"Remember when the boy pilot was diving his airplane down to crash into the bad king's boat?"

They nodded.

"Well, the boy pilot was very sad because he thought the girl pilot had died. So, he was going to crash his airplane into the bad king's boat and not get out of it."

"No!" said the two voices almost as one.

"But that didn't happen," I said. "You know why?"

The two kids shook their heads. I glanced at Sarah. I could see her eyes glistening in the dim light of the bedroom.

"Because the girl pilot was magic! And she put her voice inside the boy pilot's brain and told him to get out of the airplane. And the boy pilot loved her and trusted her, so that's what he did!"

"Is that really what happened, Mommy?" Colleen asked.

Sarah nodded and hugged her. "That's what happened, honey," Sarah said, with a slight crack in her voice. "Now why don't you two get some sleep. Tomorrow's another day."

Sarah crossed the aisle to Christopher's bed and gave him a kiss on the forehead and hugged him. "Good night, little man. Sleep tight."

She rose and motioned to me. "Do you want to give your dad a hug and a kiss?" she asked.

Colleen nodded shyly. I went to her bed, and she raised her little arms around my neck and kissed me on the check with tiny lips. "Good night," she said.

"Good night, little one," I responded.

I went to Christopher, and his arms went around my neck. He hugged me hard, almost clinging to me for a moment. Then he gave me a light kiss on the check. "Goodnight, Daddy," he said in a sleepy voice.

"Goodnight, little guy," I said, swallowing hard to force down all the emotion that had suddenly risen inside of me. "Sleep well."

I rose and went to the door of the room, where Sarah was standing. She slipped her hand into mine, and we stood there silently for a moment, gazing in on the kids. The two little faces were embedded into their pillows, and the eyelids were already drooping.

"Aren't they great?" Sarah whispered. "There are some nights when I'll stand here and look at them, and I totally lose track of time."

I nodded. "They're amazing," I said. "And you know what else?"

"What?" Sarah said.

I turned to her. "If the purpose of my entire miserable life was to give life to them, it was more than worth it."

She squeezed my hand, and we left the room, closing the door behind us.

A few minutes later, I was seated on Sarah's sofa with a glass of the Macallan 18 in my hand. Sarah had changed into sweatpants and a t-shirt and was curled up on the couch next to me but a discrete distance away. She was nursing a glass of Macallan as well. We both sat there silently, gazing into her gas fireplace.

I had no intention of staying for the evening. I had a room booked at the Marriott Courtyard hotel down the street, and I knew I needed to leave soon, so both of us could get some rest. But now that the time for my departure was imminent, I found myself reluctant to leave.

"I have to tell you something," Sarah said, her voice barely audible. "And I'm not sure how you're going to take it."

I sighed. "Well," I said. "You know how I feel about getting things out in the open." I turned to her. "Say what you have to say."

She nodded, still looking at the fire. She took a deep sip of her scotch. After a long moment, she spoke. "You scared the shit out of me today."

I nodded and waited for her to finish, although I was pretty sure I knew where she was headed.

"When you were having your standoff with Rowe," she

said. "You sounded so cold. Like ice. It was like I didn't know who you were." She turned to me and looked directly into my eyes. "Did it work? Did you scare her?"

I nodded again. "I think so."

"Why did you need to do that? She's a horrible person already. This will make her even more horrible."

"We don't have a lot of time to see what she's up to," I said. "I needed to force either action or error out of her. Hopefully, both."

"But how does scaring her...?"

"Brenda Rowe is a bully and a coward," I said, interrupting her. "She's used to having all the power and having people be afraid of her. She's not used to being scared. So, by scaring her, I put her on the defensive. If I read her correctly, she'll act hastily in response. I'm hoping that will force an error that I can exploit."

"What did you say specifically to make her afraid?"

I sighed and looked away. "I made reference to something that happened over the weekend. She sent a pair of hitmen to kill me while I was training in Dallas." I took a long, slow sip of my scotch. "They obviously weren't successful."

"Did you kill them?" Sarah asked. The apprehension in her voice was palpable.

I nodded.

"How?"

I looked over at her. "Are you sure you want to hear this?"

"Not really," she said. "But I think I need to."

I looked away again, suddenly ashamed of my actions. "With a sawed-off shotgun," I said, quietly. "At very close range."

I saw her nod in my peripheral vision. "Why?"

"Because I wanted to send a particular message," I said as I raised the whiskey glass to my lips. "And apparently, I succeeded."

She nodded again and took a sip of her own whiskey.

There was silence for a few moments. I was waiting for the next question. The inevitable next question. The question I didn't want her to ask but knew that she would.

She didn't make me wait long.

"Colin, how many people have you killed since we were together?"

I sighed again and looked down into my glass, wishing there was more of the amber nectar inside.

"I'm not sure, Sarah," I said.

She raised her eyebrows. "You're not sure?" She sounded incredulous. "There have been so many that you're not sure?"

I nodded. I had never tried to count them. I could have tried to differentiate between those I killed at long range with an aircraft and those I had killed up close and personal, but there didn't seem to be a point.

"How do you feel about that?" she asked.

I shrugged. "I try not to feel anything," I said. "I'm not always successful." I looked over at her. "You know when I told you I took five years off, to 'find myself?'"

She nodded.

"The truth is that I was tired of the killing," I said. "And I was tired of getting people killed who were around me. I wanted to see who I was without all the violence."

"How'd that work out?"

I shook my head. "I was fucking miserable. But as a result of this most recent business with the CIA, I learned something important. I wasn't miserable because I missed the violence. I was miserable because I missed doing something that mattered. I was miserable because I needed to make a difference. And I wasn't."

Sarah leaned forward with an earnest look on her face. There was something she needed to hear, and I wasn't sure what it was. "How does the violence work into that?" she asked. "How does the killing work into that?"

I shrugged. "It's a necessary part of it, I guess," I said. "It's like going into max AB in a dogfight. You don't want to spend all that fuel to get more thrust, but you have to do it if you want to win. If you want to live."

"You always said going to full afterburner in the F-16 was a rush. Like a high. Does it feel that way when you kill someone?"

I sank into the cushion behind me and scoured my brain for the right words to express my feelings adequately. Sarah didn't know about the Darkness. In our time together, we had never discussed it. She'd seen glimpses of it in action, but she didn't know about the full force of it or my struggle with it. I didn't know how to broach that subject with her, and given the direction of the conversation, I wasn't sure I wanted to.

"You know, I had almost forgotten about that morning in Malibu," she said quietly. "The morning Adam and Damian tried to kidnap Colleen and me. The morning you saved us. But I remembered it today."

Sarah took another long drink of her scotch and looked off into the fire. Her eyes grew distant, and I could tell she was pulling up the memories from six years ago in her brain.

"You had tossed Colleen to me, and I was running away with her, trying to find somewhere to hide. There were these two gunshots, and I stopped running and turned to see if you were hit. But when I looked, you were still standing, and the two guards were down. You were standing there with that sword of yours and swinging away at Adam and Damian. They were injured, but you kept swinging the sword. You had this look on your face. This weird, twisted smile. It was like you were a different person. Like you enjoyed the killing. That's the same look I saw you give Rowe today."

She turned back to me and motioned toward the bottle of Macallan on the coffee table in front of us. I retrieved the bottle and poured some more into her glass before replenishing my own. Sarah raised her glass and downed a healthy swallow of the liquid.

"Colin, I need you to look me in the eyes and tell me that you don't enjoy the killing. I need to know that the father of my kids isn't a killer." With the last word, her voice cracked, and tears began to roll down her cheeks. But she kept her gaze on me and she stared deep into my eyes. "I need to know that my kids...our kids...aren't going to be killers."

"You're not going to want to hear this," I said, my mouth uttered the words before my brain could catch up. "And I wasn't going to tell you. But it seems like the time has come."

I took a long drink of my scotch, using the alcohol to summon the courage to tell her all of it. I exhaled slowly and spoke without looking at her. "There's this...feeling...this Darkness...that lives inside of me. It's like," I searched my mind to find precise words to describe the Darkness, but they eluded me. I felt a small itch on the side of my forehead, and I scratched it unconsciously. Then I nodded to myself as I realized that I had found the description I needed. "It's like a terrible itch in my mind."

As I spoke, several thoughts collided inside my brain and a flash of epiphany occurred like the fusion of a thermonuclear reaction. I didn't know whether it was Sarah's angst about what she had seen or the emotion I had experienced in the kids' room upstairs or the tension of the situation at Enteron. It could have been all of the above combined with the general pattern of shit that had characterized my life. But in a moment. In a flash, I suddenly understood one of the great mysteries of my life.

I came back into the moment to find Sarah staring at me. Expectantly. She needed more. I put my glass on the table and took her free hand in both of mine. She didn't resist me.

"The only thing that satisfies the Darkness is killing. It has led me to do some horrific things. For a long time, I used to think it was random. But this last business in Arizona showed me it isn't." I felt a surge of emotion, a surge of gratitude, well up in my throat. I fought it down and continued. "It's not random at all. It's revenge. It's triggered by things and people who hurt others. When that happens, God help those who did the triggering."

I looked down at her hand in mine, and I gently massaged her hand with my thumbs. Then I looked back up at her.

"I am a killer," I said, looking her in the eyes. "But only when circumstances require it. The important thing is I'm not a murderer. And isn't that what you really want to know?"

Sarah searched my eyes with hers for several long moments, but my gaze didn't waver. More tears ran down her cheeks. She placed her glass on the table beside mine and took both of my hands in hers. After several more moments, she spoke with apprehension in her voice.

"Aren't you afraid the killing will make you cold inside?"

I smiled at her as I felt tears of my own well up in my eyes. "It's funny. I was afraid of that. I was terrified of it. But I experienced something that changed that forever."

"What was that?" she asked, with an intent expression on her beautiful features.

"I saw my kids' mother telling them a bedtime story," I said. "And then I watched them go to sleep." I squeezed her hands with mine. "My life will never be the same."

Sarah smiled through her tears and nodded at me. She raised her lips to mine, and I kissed her, my lips remaining on hers for several, poignant seconds. After our lips parted, she retrieved our glasses from the table and snuggled up next to me on the sofa, encircling my arm with hers. We sat there for several minutes, gazing at the fire, sipping whiskey, and enjoying the warmth of one another.

"So, you think you scared Rowe?" Sarah asked, her

question breaking the silence of the moment.

I nodded. "I saw it in her eyes."

"And you think she'll make a mistake because of that?"

I nodded again. "I hope so."

I could feel Sarah shaking her head against my shoulder. "That's not my read on her. I don't think she'll panic, and I don't think she'll make a mistake."

"Really? We'll you've known her longer than I have. What do you think she'll do?"

Sarah exhaled loudly and took another sip of her whiskey. "What does any animal do when it's backed into a corner?"

I nodded in realization as she finished the question. "It will lash out," I said. "It will attack."

"Exactly. And that's my read on Rowe's personality. She's a predator. She's an animal. She won't sit back. She'll lash out. She'll attack." Sarah raised her free hand to my cheek and turned my face to hers. "You need to be careful, Colin. Really careful."

I nodded back at her and gave her a confident smile. "I always am, and I will be."

Sarah shook her head at me and stroked my cheek with her hand.

"I think she might be different than some of the other people you've dealt with, Colin. You need to keep your guard up. I don't know what she'll try to do, but it will be something you don't expect. She's really focused on building her power inside the company. In the short time I've been here, she's gotten three senior executives fired, and she's taken over their departments. None of them saw it coming. Now, the only person keeping her in her place is the CEO, Mark Lane."

I flashed back to Lane and Rowe's interaction in Lane's office, and I realized there was something I had missed.

"Damn," I said unconsciously.

"What?" Sarah asked.

I shook my head. "Probably nothing," I said. "At least nothing I can talk about. For now, anyway."

I looked over at the clock on the fireplace. It read 10:00. I put my glass down on the table. "Sarah, I've got to get out of here so you can get some sleep."

Her eyes sparkled in the light of the fireplace, and she shook her head. "Not until you've finished your scotch," she said.

She tucked herself back into my side, and we sat next to each other, gazed at the fireplace and sipped our scotch. Before long, I could feel her breathing becoming more even. A few moments later, I heard her soft snores above the mild sound of the fireplace. I took her glass from her hand and placed it on the table alongside my own. Then, I slid my hands under her knees and her shoulders and carried her upstairs to her bedroom, careful to keep her head or her feet from snagging the walls on the way up. I entered the bedroom to find her covers turned down and was grateful to not have to balance her in my arms while I performed the task. I gently put her down in the bed, tucked her feet under the covers, and pulled them up to her face. Then I kissed her gently on the forehead, turned out the light, and closed her bedroom door behind me.

I went downstairs, returned the Macallan to her bar area, washed the glasses, and tidied up. Then, I retrieved an extra key I had seen on the key rack by the back door and went out of the front door, locking it behind me. She had a security system keypad by the door, but I didn't know the code, and I wasn't going to wake her. I figured that leaving it disarmed, just the one night, wouldn't make a difference.

As it turned out, I was wrong.

CHAPTER FOURTEEN

Wednesday, January 13th
1000 Hours Local Time
FL400 and Mach .85
Over the Northern Territories, Canada

I was back in the cockpit of a business jet at high-altitude and relishing the view from 40,000 feet. The Canadian sky was crystal clear, and the atmosphere surrounded us with that slightly darker shade of blue found only at high altitude. Below us, the northern Canadian Rocky Mountains dotted the landscape below, stretching into the distance, their gray, craggy peaks contrasting sharply with the snow-covered terrain below and around them.

"Been a while since you've been up this high?"

I looked to my right to find Rick Wilson looking at me through mirrored sunglasses, with the usual bemused expression on his face.

I nodded in reply. "Most of the flying I've been doing for the last several years has been at low altitude," I said. "I forgot how amazing the world looks from up here."

It was Wilson's turn to nod. "I never get tired of it." He turned his head to look through the windscreen in front of him and then pivoted to look through the side windows.

"Something about the perspective you get from up here." He reached up to adjust the left earpiece of his headset as he spoke. "Helps me to remember my place in the universe."

I smiled. "I feel that way every time I fly over Sedona," I said. "Something about those timeless red rocks." I gestured to the view in front of me. "Thanks for letting me fly in the left seat," I said. "It's great to get some stick time. Very generous of you."

Wilson turned to face me, and the smirk on his face grew. "It was generous in more ways than stick time," he said, motioning to the worktable in front of him, where charts and a flight log were neatly placed. "It's the record-keeping piece of these ocean-crossing flights that's the real work. And I wasn't going to ask you to jump feet first into that business without seeing it a few times."

I nodded. Because ocean-crossing flights took place mostly outside of radar coverage and far from alternate airfields, the flights required meticulous attention to navigational position, speed, altitude, and fuel consumption. Positions were plotted and verified on paper charts, height-keeping equipment was checked hourly, and fuel flow was continually compared against the computed flight-plan. The right-seater's job was to perform the monitoring and annotate it all on the flightplan. I was familiar with the workload, having performed it several times during contract flights back in the day.

"I'm grateful," I said. "I'm so rusty I'd probably screw it up anyway."

Wilson shrugged. "It's actually not so bad. Especially since CPDLC takes care of the position reports. That's a lot of radio calls we don't have to make anymore. It also keeps you from having to spend the brain bytes trying to decipher foreign-accented English."

CPDLC was controller-pilot data link, one of the more important changes to business jets since I had previously flown them. It was essentially a mechanism through which air traffic controllers and pilots could send text messages, but it also allowed the aircraft to automatically report its position to controlling agencies through the data link. The automatic reports took the place of position-reporting radio calls, using the archaic HF radio, which took several minutes and often required transmissions to be repeated due to the poor quality of communication.

"Quite the workload saver," I said.

"It is," Wilson agreed.

"I admire your diligence," I said. "You've been studying those charts and the flight plan for nearly the entire flight except when you were eating breakfast. And we're not going to actually fly it until tomorrow."

"Never too early to get ahead of the airplane," Wilson said. "I like having some extra time to study the paperwork. These flights are complicated enough, but the North Korean piece adds another layer of complication to it. It's like you said yesterday. We can't just be good. We have to be perfect."

I nodded. "How many flights into North Korea have you done?"

"Me personally or the whole department?"

"Both."

Wilson shrugged. "Let me think about that." He glanced over at me. "You can have one of the schedulers pull a report out of the operations software if you want an exact count."

I made a mental note to do that and nodded at him to continue.

"We started them last fall. At the beginning of October. It took three months before that to get all the diplomatic clearances. We started off slow, like maybe one every two weeks. We did two in October and two in November. At first, the Boss or the Chief Pilot had to be on every flight. But in December, we started flying one per week, and the pace got too high for one of those two to be on every flight." Wilson sat back in his seat and tilted his head upward, lost in thought. "This flight is my third one," he said after a long moment. "But the department has done nine of them before this one. This one is number ten."

"Was Mark Hill on those first two flights?"

Wilson thought for a second, then nodded. "But he only went on one of the two in November because he had to deal with those damn consultants. Tom Barrington, the Chief Pilot, took the second one. But Tom had been with the Boss on one of the flights in October, so he knew the drill."

The conversation I had with Gardner ran through my mind. *After the first two flights, Hill wanted to order the radiation detector. What did he see? Or hear?*

Then another thought occurred to me. "Speaking of Tom," I said. "It was kind of surprising to not see him around during the briefing yesterday. I would have thought as the Chief Pilot, he'd want to be there." I didn't mention that I was disappointed in not having the opportunity to get Barrington's thoughts about the individual pilots.

Wilson opened his mouth to speak but then closed it. A few moments elapsed as he seemed to consider what he wanted to say. When he finally spoke, his voice was tight and controlled.

"Tom and I go back a long way," he said. "But I wouldn't have selected him for the Chief Pilot job. Tom is about one thing above all others. And that would be Tom." He glanced over at me and rolled his eyes to emphasize the point. "He likes to compete in Ironman Triathlons, so he is always training. You rarely see him around if he's not scheduled to fly. Not the most engaged Chief Pilot I've worked with."

"I see."

"I mean, don't get me wrong, Tom's a decent enough guy. But he doesn't control the pilot group at all. He lets all of us do our own thing. For some of the older guys, like me and Phil

Janis, that's no big deal. But for some of the younger ones, like Allen, he doesn't give them any boundaries at all. And they often behave like spoiled brats."

"Why didn't Hill fire him?" I asked. "Tom, I mean."

"I think he tried to, but our HR folks wouldn't let him."

I raised my eyebrows in astonishment. "Seriously?"

Wilson shrugged. "Did you meet Annie First, the VP of HR?"

I shook my head. "I'm not sure."

He looked across the cockpit at me. "You'd remember if you did. She's hot and stacked and dresses to the nines."

I nodded. "You're right. I would have remembered that."

"Well, she has the HR disease."

I sighed. "Let me guess. There are no lost causes. Everyone can be better. Everyone can be a leader."

Wilson was nodding as I talked. "You're familiar with the syndrome."

"I haven't personally experienced it. Fortunately. But I've read about it. What utter nonsense."

"I agree. But apparently, she wouldn't allow Hill to make any of the changes in the department he wanted to."

"How could she have that kind of authority over the department? Hill wasn't reporting to her. He was reporting to Rowe."

"Only as of about six months ago," Wilson said. "Until then, we were under First. After we were approved by the State Department to do the NK thing, there was some kind of shakeup in the C-suite, and Rowe was given the department."

Yet another gear clicked into place in my head. It was getting to be a familiar feeling.

"November 613 Charlie Bravo," the radio blared in our headsets, "Edmonton center. Contact Anchorage Center on 143.5."

Wilson keyed the mic switch on his sidestick as he punched

the frequency into the keypad on his side of the pedestal. "613 Charlie Bravo, Anchorage on 143.5." He switched the frequency and checked us in with Anchorage.

I typed ATIS PANC into my keypad and transmitted a request on our SATCOM for the latest air terminal information at Anchorage.

"Guess we should get an approach loaded and get it briefed soon," I said. "As I recall from the last time I was here, they don't waste much time before they start you down on the descent into Anchorage."

Wilson nodded and began calling the terminal arrival and approach charts up in the lower, center display.

"Hey, did you guys get the revised trip paperwork?" Dylan Moore slid into the cockpit and sat on the jump seat. He had a clear plastic envelope in his hands.

"What revised paperwork?" Wilson asked. He looked over at me. "They're landing on the 25s down there. You okay with the ILS to 25 right?"

I nodded.

"Oh, it's not that big a deal, I guess," Moore continued. "I had a change in catering for the next leg. I texted it to Sarah last night and I didn't get a response, but I just figured she'd get to it this morning. But when I got in, there wasn't any new paperwork. She's usually really good about making those changes."

I felt a long and excruciating chill work its way up the center of my spine. I hadn't seen Sarah in the office this morning before we departed. I had just assumed she was coming in late.

"Does she usually come into the office when we launch these trips?" I asked, trying to keep my voice impassive.

Wilson shrugged. "Sometimes. But not always."

"She doesn't need to come in to change the paperwork," Moore said with an exasperated tone. "She can do it on her laptop and send the revised paperwork to the printer in the office. That's what she's done every time before."

"But not this morning?" I asked.

Moore shook his head.

"When did you send the text?"

Moore thought for a second. "About eleven o'clock last night. But Sarah is really good about checking her emails before we do these trips. If she gets up in the middle of the night, she responds. At the very least, she'd answer first thing in the morning."

Unless she couldn't, I thought. *Jesus.* A wave of raw panic and fear shot through me like several thousand volts of electric current.

"The WIFI is working, isn't it?" I asked.

Moore nodded. "Yep. I was just dealing with some emails in the back."

"Email the office and ask them if Sarah has come in."

"I don't have to," Moore said. "Brett and I have been texting each other and he told me she hadn't. He said he was worried about her and was going to swing by her house at lunchtime."

"Did he?" I asked.

Moore shrugged and looked at me. His face looked impassive, but there was a glow of malicious, secret knowledge in his eyes. And in that moment, I knew I had underestimated him.

Shit, I thought.

I pulled my iPhone off of the side console and turned it on. As I waited for it to power up, Sarah's words about Rowe rang in my ears.

She's a predator. She's an animal. She won't sit back. She'll lash out. She'll attack.

The screen of my phone flashed as it came to life. I connected it to the jet's WiFi system and opened up the running group chat to Smith, Amrine, and Sharona.

FIND SARAH AND THE KIDS, I typed. I THINK ROWE HAS TAKEN THEM.

CHAPTER FIFTEEN

Wednesday, January 13th
1500 Hours Local Time
Hotel Gym
Marriott Downtown
Anchorage, Alaska, USA

It wasn't the best hotel gym I'd seen, but it sufficed for the moment. I was alternating sets between the treadmill and dumbbells; thirty seconds sprinting, three minutes jogging, twelve reps of hammer curls, twelve reps of two-armed overhead triceps presses, and repeat. I was covered in sweat, and my heart was racing. I had no idea how many sets I had done, and I didn't care. I needed the physical exertion to distract me from the growing sensation of helplessness creeping over me.

The texts from my CIA crew had not been encouraging.

Sharona's reply to my text had come after we had landed at Ted Stevens airport and were post-flighting the aircraft.

THEY'RE NOT AT THE CONDO.

SARAH ISN'T AT WORK, I had replied, angry that I hadn't included that information earlier.

WE KNOW, Sharona's text read. AND KIDS NOT AT SCHOOL.

A fiery stream of expletives left my mouth before I even knew I was speaking. Fortunately, the noise of the 7X's auxiliary power unit concealed my outburst from nearby ears.

ENTRY TEAM ENROUTE TO CONDO, Sharona had texted a few minutes later. WILL KNOW MORE SOON.

It took me a moment to realize that she had known no one was home. Without eyes on the ground, there was only one feasible explanation. The condo was under electronic surveillance. I made a mental note to speak to them about that when something else occurred to me.

Shit, I thought.

I typed another text message into my phone and waited for a reply.

GOT IT, came back a few seconds later.

Two agonizing hours later, when my phone finally buzzed, I was in the gym, forcing my screaming biceps to knock out another set of hammer curls. I threw the 50-pound dumbbells down on the matted floor and tore the phone from my pocket.

"Talk to me," I said, barely able to get the words out between breaths.

There was a sigh on the other end of the line. "I wish I had better news," Sharona said.

I felt the air leave my lungs. I sank down onto a nearby bench.

"They were definitely taken. And it was a smooth snatch and grab job. No signs of a struggle. All the beds are made. The bathrooms have been wiped down. All the dishes have been put away. The place is fucking immaculate."

"Like they left on purpose," I said.

"But they didn't," Sharona countered. "No suitcases are gone. The clothes in the closets and drawers seem to be normally arranged. No packing took place."

"Jesus," I said.

"We found the listening devices you told us to look for,"

Sharona said. "That's how they found out how important she was to you."

"They must not review the tapes very often," I said. "Last night wasn't the first time I was there."

"They probably became more diligent after the interaction with Rowe that you told me about."

I nodded to myself. "Probably," I said. I ran my fingers through my sweaty hair as I exhaled in disgust. "What an idiot I was. Here I was thinking I was going to force Rowe's hand. I sure as shit did. But not in a good way."

"Don't be too hard on yourself," Sharona said. "I thought it was a good idea when you told me about it. We needed to get out in front of this."

"But now, if we do, we're fucked. They've got hostages to threaten us."

Sharona was silent. I knew exactly what she was thinking, and it infuriated me. She had nearly died in my arms to ensure the success of a mission five years ago. She would offer no quarter to others if the mission was at stake.

But then she surprised me.

"We'll figure it out," she said, with a soft tone in her voice. "I don't want anything to happen to Sarah and the kids either."

"But…what about…the mission," I stammered, barely able to get the words out.

She laughed lightly and it was music to my ears.

"I've gotten attached to them too," she said. "Who do you think has been looking out for them these last five years while you were on your self-imposed exile in Sedona?"

I shook my head in wonder. "I'll be damned."

"Anyway, like I said, we'll figure it out."

"I don't suppose you can consult the logs from your own listening devices there and gather some intel?"

There was a pregnant silence, and I realized my earlier assumption was wrong.

"You don't have her under surveillance. Do you?"

I could almost see Sharona shaking her head in denial. "It's easy to distance yourself from people you watch or listen to," she said. "Not so easy when you get to know them. I've been in that condo many times since I recovered from my wounds in Russia. I spoke to Smith and Amrine, and we agreed to allow her as much privacy as possible." She paused for a moment. "I actually wish we did have her under some kind of surveillance. We might know who took her. We know she and the kids never left the house because we have a GPS tracker on her car. It never left the garage after she got home last night."

"Damn," I said.

"But she might have left us a sign," Sharona said. "You know that alcove next to the front door where she had a lot of pictures?"

"Yes. It's where she had pics of some of the people she had flown when she was a charter pilot."

"The glass on one of the pictures was cracked. She must have tipped it over when they took her out the door."

"How do you know it wasn't broken from before?"

Sharona sighed again and then spoke like she was talking to a child. "Because I notice these things, Colin. It was obvious the pictures had been rearranged. I also found several glass particles on the shelf area among the pictures in the front row, but none in the second row. But the picture with the broken glass was in the back row. Interesting that, considering it was her with a former president. You'd think she'd have that upfront."

I replayed the tour of the condo in my mind and stopped the memory at the front entrance to the place. "Is that the one of her with Bill Clinton?" I asked.

"Yep," Sharona replied. "Kind of ironic now that I think about it. That guy has probably had several pictures of him broken, trashed, or otherwise defaced."

"She told me about the flight," I said, my mind drifting back into the past. "She said he came up to the cockpit of the Learjet she was flying and suggested they meet for a drink later. While Hilary was in the back of the jet."

"Why am I not surprised?" Sharona replied. "What a horndog." She paused for a moment. I could also hear her turning the incident over in her mind. After a long moment, she spoke. "Any idea at all what the broken picture could mean?"

I was shaking my head in mute response as my brain retrieved the picture and displayed it in my mind. Sarah had been dressed in a polo shirt and khaki pants. The picture had been taken shortly before her issue of Bachelor Magazine had been published, and the casual outfit hugged her magnificent figure like a second skin. The former president was wearing a suit and displaying the smile that won him two elections. He had his arm around Sarah's shoulders, and he was pulling her against him. I could still see the gleam in his eyes.

Then the memory of Moore's eyes from a few hours ago appeared before me.

"Huh," I said to myself.

"What does that mean?" Sharona asked.

"I just might know someone to ask."

CHAPTER SIXTEEN

Wednesday, January 13th
2000 Hours Local Time
Simon and Seafort's Saloon and Grill
Anchorage, Alaska, USA

We were seated at a table in Simon and Seafort's Saloon and grill, lingering over the last bit of wine that we had ordered with our dinner. The restaurant overlooked the Knik Arm of the Gompertz Channel – the inlet that led to Anchorage's harbor from the Pacific Ocean. The view would have been spectacular if we had been here at a different time of year. But the sun had set three hours ago, and the night beyond the window glass was dark and cold. The restaurant was an Alaskan landmark and had become a regular stop for Enteron's crews on their frequent stops in Anchorage over the last several months. It was located only a few blocks from the hotel, and despite the frigid temperature outside, we had walked the distance from the Marriott.

The walk had been Dylan Moore's idea. "C'mon!" He had said. "The walk will do us all some good! We need the exercise, and it will help us work up an appetite."

I could have made the argument that my hours in the gym had provided all the exercise I needed, but time was short. I wanted to gather as much intelligence as I could from both Wilson and Moore, and figure out a way to get Moore alone for some intense questioning.

"Will there be anything else?" our waiter asked. He was a young, dark-haired guy with an impressive array of tattoos on his forearms that were distinctly visible through the sleeves of his white dress shirt.

Wilson looked around the table. Moore and I both shook our heads.

"No," Wilson said. "That will be all. We'll take the check whenever you're ready."

The waiter immediately produced a black restaurant bill portfolio and handed it to Wilson. "There's no hurry on that," he said. "Stay as long as you like." He left us and walked to another table across the narrow dining room.

Wilson opened the portfolio and looked at the bill. "No problem with the meal limits tonight," he muttered as he retrieved a credit card from his wallet and placed it the appropriate slot on the back of the portfolio.

"Excuse me?" I asked. "Meal limits?"

Wilson nodded. "According to the company travel policy, we're limited to $75 per day for dining expenses in the US, like everyone else in the company. Mark Hill tried to get that restriction lifted because of the places we travel to, but Rowe and team weren't buying it. In fact, she went ballistic about it. She has her chief of staff review all of our expense reports and give her a list of all meal limit violators. Anyone spending over $75 per day has to reimburse the company, and their pay is docked for the funds on the next paycheck."

I leaned forward as my jaw dropped. "You're kidding," I said.

Wilson shook his head. "Wish I was."

"Well, we should abide by the same limits as the rest of the company," Moore said, with a tone of self-righteousness in his voice. "It's only fair. We're all Enteron employees."

Wilson bit his lip and looked away. It seemed he had this conversation before. There were many perspectives on the subject of meal allowances for flight crew, and in my contract pilot career, I had seen all of them firsthand. I decided to stay silent on the subject. At least for now. I looked across the table at Wilson.

"Did you do any transpacific flights before Enteron, Rick?"

He shook his head. "I was a sim instructor at FlightSafety when I was hired by Enteron," he said. "Before that, I flew an old Challenger 601 out of Dallas Love, and that was nearly all domestic flying, with an occasional trip to the Islands or to Europe."

I nodded in understanding.

"What about you?" he asked.

"I did a few Pacific trips in both the Falcon 900EX and the G-IV," I said, "and almost always through Anchorage. I've been to Tokyo, Seoul, Hong Kong, and Taiwan."

"You've been to Seoul in a business jet?" he asked. "Where'd you land?"

"At what used to be Seoul's main airport, Kimpo. When they switched the commercial traffic to Inchon, they changed the name of Kimpo to Gimpo for some reason. It was odd landing there the few times I went. When I was stationed in Korea, years ago, Kimpo was the major commercial airport."

"Then this trip will be like old home week for you. You probably saw on the trip paperwork that after we drop the execs off in Pyongyang, we reposition the jet to Gimpo. We stay at the JW Marriott downtown." He looked over at me. "Where were you stationed in Korea?"

"Kunsan Air Base," I said, smiling at him. "It's not the end of the world, but you can see it from there."

He laughed. "Well, I might have been at the end of the world. I was in the Army. I commanded a company of infantry at Camp Casey."

My eyes widened. "Wow," I said. "How far is it to the DMZ from there?"

"About a 20-minute drive," Wilson said. "We used to go up there periodically and look at the other side. One of the times we went up there, we saw the North Koreans actually shoot a few guys trying to escape to the south."

"That sucks," I said absently.

"Sure did for them," he said.

I thought for a second and then asked a question that had popped into my mind. "How do you feel about Enteron helping North Korea?"

Wilson shrugged. "Kinder, gentler world, I guess. Besides, I just go where they tell me. That's what this job is about, right?"

Moore seemed annoyed by my question. His expression tightened up, and he fidgeted in his seat. He glanced down at his watch. Then he motioned to the waiter to retrieve the portfolio with Wilson's credit card. The waiter saw him, hurried over to our table, and scooped up the portfolio.

"I guess," I said. "But back in the day, both of us were paid to risk our lives. That's supposedly not the case when you fly a business jet."

Wilson seemed to consider this for a few seconds. "They haven't shot at us yet," he said. "And the company did increase our life insurance, which is helpful."

"Too bad they didn't add hazardous duty pay," I said, grinning at him.

"That'll be the day," Wilson said, rolling his eyes. "Especially with the wicked witch of the west in charge. I think she's Ebenezer Scrooge's great-granddaughter or something. One of the things we get bitched at about is the amount we tip service staff." He shook his head in disgust. "Can you believe that?"

The waiter returned with the check and Wilson's credit card. As he signed the bill and did the math, I saw Moore glance at his watch again.

Hmm, I thought. *Apparently, we're on some kind of timeline.*

I looked at Moore and his eyes met mine. For the second time that day, he tried to keep his face impassive, but his eyes gave him away. He had the same sparkle of secret knowledge in his eyes; only this time, there was a touch of glee there as well.

I mentally nodded to myself. I had a pretty good idea of what might be in store.

"Well fuck her," Wilson said as he folded his copy of the receipt and put it into his wallet, along with his credit card. "This guy did a damn good job and he gets twenty percent. I don't give a shit what she says."

Moore looked over at him. "Shall we go?" he said in a stiff tone.

We rose to our feet and donned our coats. Then we made our way out of the restaurant's main entrance.

"Can you guys excuse me for just a second?" I asked. "I need to make a quick pit stop."

I darted into the nearby restroom and into one of the stalls. There, I made some adjustments to my wardrobe. Then I flushed the toilet, ran the water, and turned on the electronic hand dryer. Satisfied that the auditory illusion was complete, I exited the restaurant and re-joined my two fellow crew members. Together, we went through the doors and into the cold Alaskan winter.

There's something about intense cold that energizes the body. The temperature was about 10 degrees below zero, and I felt the hairs in my nose stiffen immediately as the trace amounts of mucus on them froze. The skin on my face stung with the frigid air, and I tightened my shoulders against the chill. I also buried my hands deep into my jacket pockets to keep them as warm as possible.

We walked quickly to the nearest corner and then turned right, down L street, the road that we would follow south to our hotel. Moore had done the navigation on the trip to the restaurant and he seemed to have assumed that role again, stepping along in front of Wilson and me at a brisk pace. I looked around as we walked. Anchorage wasn't a huge city, but the streets were well lit, and we had no difficulty seeing our surroundings.

Abruptly, Moore turned to his left and crossed the street to a darkened by-way between a house and a long rectangular building.

"Follow me!" he said. "I think I know a shortcut!" He turned his back on us and walked between the buildings.

Wilson looked at me, shrugged, and turned to follow him.

I put my left hand on his arm and stopped him. "Go back to the restaurant," I said. "If I don't come and join you in ten minutes, call the police."

He froze in his tracks, and his eyes widened.

"Do it," I said. "Do it now."

He nodded and turned back to the restaurant.

I crossed the street and entered the darkened area, removing my right hand from my jacket pocket and allowing the object in my sleeve to fall into my hand.

"Where's Wilson?" Moore asked, his silhouette visible at the end of the short street.

"He left something at the restaurant," I said. But it shouldn't matter to you. I'm pretty sure I'm the one you want."

"That's true," Moore said, laughing. "But I was still looking forward to seeing someone beat that damn smug expression off his face."

On cue, two large silhouettes appeared, one on either side of him. The two large figures began to move down the street towards me. Moore stayed where he was.

"That's your plan?" I asked. "Beat us up? Seriously? That's what you're going with?"

I saw him shrug in response. "That's where it will start," he said. "Until you tell us what we want to know."

The two figures were about twenty feet away from me. They were becoming more visible. I saw two hard faces with cruel eyes. Both men were dressed in biker-like apparel, complete with jeans, boots, and leather jackets. Both had heavy black gloves on, but their hands were empty. I heard the scuffing sound of leather soles on the pavement behind me and realized there was a third member of the team.

"Well, there's a problem with that plan," I said as I brought the object in my right hand up to chest level and thumbed back the hammer. "Your brought bare hands to a gunfight."

I leveled the suppressed .45 Colt commander at the dark figure on the right and trained the laser sight on the middle of his chest. I squeezed the trigger twice in quick succession and repeated the process with the figure on the left. The gun was loaded with subsonic ammunition, and the shots sounded like shoes stomping on the pavement. Both men shuddered with the impact of the bullets and sank to their knees.

I dropped down and pivoted 180 degrees. The man who was behind me had paused in his tracks about five feet away. I didn't give him time to reconsider. I shot him twice in the center of the chest, stepped forward and shot him once in the center of the forehead for good measure. I turned back to the first two men as I changed magazines and shot each of them in the head as well.

The suppressed reports briefly echoed in the confined space. Then the night was silent except for the sounds of cars in the distance.

Less than five seconds had elapsed.

I walked toward Dylan Moore with the gun at my side. His

silhouette was frozen, and as I approached him and his face became visible, I could see that his eyes were wide, and his mouth was agape. There was no gleam in the eyes this time. Instead, there was a mixture of fear, horror, and disbelief.

"This little episode you tried to arrange has worked out quite well for me," I said. "I usually have to threaten people and even hurt them a little to show them I'm serious. But now, I think you probably get that."

I raised the pistol and centered it on his forehead.

"Sarah and her kids were taken from their home earlier today. What do you know about that?"

"Oh my god," he said, his voice sputtering. "Oh my God. Please don't kill me."

"Dylan, I'm trying to be patient. But you're making it difficult. Sarah and her kids were taken from their home earlier today. What do you about that?"

He blinked his eyes like he was pulling himself back into the moment. "Not much. One of the guys who took her called me from their car or van or whatever to get her address. I could hear other guys talking in the background. I heard something about a nuke plant. That's all I know, I swear. Please don't kill me."

I pressed the muzzle of the silenced pistol against his forehead. Ordinarily, this would have burned him, but the frigid air had brought the hot metal down to a reasonable temperature. I heard the sound of liquid trickling onto the pavement and saw a puddle of steaming urine forming at the base of Moore's right foot. Almost as soon as the steam rose off the liquid, it began to freeze.

I ignored it.

"A nuke plant?" I asked. "Why would they be talking about a nuke plant?"

Moore tried to shake his head, but the pressure of the gun to his forehead dissuaded him from the motion. "I don't know!" he said. "I think they were talking about where they were going to take them."

"Where were they taking Sarah and the kids?"

Moore nodded against the suppressor, his head moving several times in small, frantic motions of agreement.

"Why would they take them to a nuke plant?"

Moore shrugged. "I don't know. Maybe because cops can't go there?"

I looked at him hard. "What do you mean, cops can't go there?"

"Nuke plants...highly...restricted," Moore said. "Protected by federal law. Very hard for anyone to get in."

"Damn," I said to myself, oblivious to him for the moment. "It's fucking genius. They'll be out of circulation and shielded from prying eyes. They won't get stumbled upon by nosy neighbors, passersby, or patrolling policemen. It's fucking genius."

"Rowe called me!" Moore volunteered. "I remember it now."

'What?"

"She called me yesterday to tell me to expect a call from one of the nuke security teams and give them the address."

"She used nuke security guys...company employees...to kidnap Sarah and her kids? Why the hell would she do that?"

"Standard company policy is only employees can get through the gate of the plants or any company facility," Moore said.

"Damn," I said, shaking my head. Sarah and her kids were being held in a nuke plant defended by security guards who were probably pros. Even the CIA might not be able to get them out of a place like that. Worse yet, Enteron was one of the largest nuclear power generators in the U.S. and had several plants. That realization spurred the obvious question in my mind.

"Which plant, Dylan?"

He shook his head in a tight, fearful motion. "I don't know. I swear. I didn't ask, and they didn't tell me."

I stared at him for a few, pregnant seconds, trying to gauge the truthfulness of his answer. His expression remained wild and fearful, and I couldn't detect a hint of reservation in his eyes. He was telling the truth.

Shit.

"Okay," I said. "Let's switch topics, Dylan. What's Rowe up to?"

"No," he said, shaking his head frantically, "I can't tell you. She said not to tell anybody anything. She'll kill me. She'll kill anyone who gets in her way."

I pushed the suppressor into his forehead more forcefully.

"You need to think about me, Dylan," I said in as menacing a tone as I could manage. I motioned to the alley behind me where three men lay dead. "And you need to think about them."

"Okay. Okay. Okay," he said, raising his hands in a gesture of both surrender and supplication. "I don't know much. All I know is that she needed me to modify the baggage area in both jets."

"Modify the baggage area? How?"

"I pulled up the carpet in both baggage areas and put a piece of sheet metal down to better distribute the weight for some of the stuff that they're taking to North Korea."

"What are they taking, Dylan?"

He shook his head again. "I don't know what's in the crates. They're small, and they're really heavy. But I don't know what's in them."

Nuclear material, I thought. *It has to be. No wonder Hill wanted to put a detector back there. And Rowe wouldn't let him. Jesus.*

I made a mental note to text the CIA about my discoveries.

There was one final order of business.

"Who else has she killed, Dylan?"

Moore's body twitched in a spasm of impatience and frustration. I pulled the gun back from his head and then pushed it into his skin, hard.

"Who else has she killed?"

He shrugged his shoulders nervously. "Hill was the only one I knew about."

I knew the answer to the next question, but I asked it anyway. "And how do you know that?"

"Because some woman called me and asked me to confirm his address."

"And the next thing you knew, he was dead."

Moore nodded against the gun.

"So, you provide the address for Hill, and he dies. You provide the address for Sarah, and she and her kids are kidnapped. You're quite the address boy."

"I was just doing what I was told to do," he said. "I was just doing what she wanted me to do." His voice had transitioned from a fearful tone to a whiny one. I found that I was getting annoyed with him.

"Do you have any kids, Dylan?"

"No," he said, shaking his head against the muzzle of the suppressor again.

"Good," I said. "Then I won't feel bad about this."

I squeezed the .45's trigger and put a half-inch hole in the center of his forehead.

The ability of the human brain to process death is morbidly fascinating. Sometimes, when death is instantaneous, the brain doesn't have time to react, and the dead person's eyes go sightless immediately. Other times, when death is protracted, you can see the life slowly ebb out of the eyes, like an image fading on a video screen.

But tonight was different.

As the Colt recoiled in my hand, Moore took an abrupt step backward. His eyes opened wide as he recognized what had happened, and he also realized that he would die. For a moment, I saw shock and surprise in his eyes. His jaw dropped open in disbelief, and his face took on a perplexed expression, like he had been cheated.

"Not fair," he said, "Not...fair."

But the hydrostatic shock of 230 grains of lead passing through his brain was taking its toll. His mouth stopped moving, his eyes slowly glazed over, and he crumpled to the cold Alaskan pavement.

"It wasn't fair for Mark Hill either," I said.

I stowed the .45 inside my coat and pulled out my phone. There was an anonymously labeled app on the third screen. I tapped on it.

CONFIRM LOCATION? it asked.

I confirmed the location the app displayed on the map it provided.

NUMBER?

I selected 4 from the drop-down menu.

METHOD?

I selected GUNSHOT, PISTOL, CLOSE RANGE from the menu of available options.

CL? The app wanted to know the carnage level, how much blood and gore would have to be cleaned up.

I looked around me and selected 3 on the 1 – 10 scale provided.

RECEIVED, the app responded. CREW ON SCENE IN 30 MINUTES. LEAVE THE AREA NOW.

I nodded to myself and retreated back to the restaurant, avoiding the bodies in the roadway as I made my way to the street. I was going to need both Rick Wilson's silence and his cooperation to finish this mission. The restaurant's bar had a fine selection of single malt. I decided that I would talk him through a few of the whiskey regions of Scotland. And perhaps, in the process, give him a glimpse of the world I occupied.

CHAPTER SEVENTEEN

Thursday, January 14th
1110 Hours Local Time
Ross Aviation
Ted Stevens Anchorage International Airport (PANC)
Anchorage, Alaska, USA

It was a crisp and cold morning in Anchorage. As Wilson and I sat in the cockpit of our jet, waiting for the other 7X to arrive, I tried to quell the tension inside me by allowing my eyes to wander over the imposing terrain that surrounded us.

The Anchorage International airport was situated on the water of the Gompertz channel – the large natural bay that led to the northern Pacific Ocean. Since the airport was only about 150 feet above sea level, it sat in a low area surrounded by mountains to the north, east, south, and west across the channel. North of us, the majestic peak of Denali loomed against the horizon, its snow-covered crags sparking in the morning sunlight, making its features clearly visible even though it was over 100 miles away. The peak recently had its name formally changed from Mount McKinley and was the highest mountain in the United States and the third highest in the world at 20,310 feet.

Looking at the magnificent mountain from ground level

on the tarmac of an airport and from the cockpit of a man-made machine that would reach heights far above that of the mountain, I felt a flash of my own mortality. *You may be able to fly higher*, the mountain seemed to be saying, *but I've been here far longer than you have and will be here long after you're gone.*

I nodded unconsciously at the thought. *And that might be sooner rather than later.*

Then my mind turned to Sarah and the kids. *Speaking of limited mortality.* I thought. *Damn.*

***

The CIA had found no trace of them, even after I had provided Sharona, Smith, and Amrine the intel I had gleaned from Moore last evening.

"Enteron operates fifteen nuclear plants, Colin," Sharona had said. "Seven in Illinois alone. And even if we knew which one they went to, we couldn't get inside without authorization from people way up on the food chain and a lot of cross-agency coordination that would blow any chance of us finding out what Rowe and the gang are up to. Or stopping it."

"I know," I had said, feeling the helplessness and the frustration well up inside of me. "I know."

"Look at the bright side," Sharona had said. "If they had wanted to kill her and the kids, they would have just done it. The bad guys obviously need them alive for leverage. That gives us time to find them."

***

"I'm not sure I can do this," Rick Wilson said, snapping me back into the moment. His voice was tight. "If these people were responsible for killing Hill and kidnapping Sarah, and they're smuggling nuclear material into North Korea, they're dangerous. We should tell the cops or something."

In front of us, the other 7X had just touched down on Runway 7R and deployed its thrust reverser to decelerate. They had a long way to roll until they reached the turnoff to the general aviation ramp, where we were. I watched the sleek jet roll down the concrete and didn't look at him.

"First of all, we don't really have anything substantive we can tell them. The only real intelligence we have came from a dead man."

"And again, why did you have to kill him?"

"Tactical expedience," I said, flatly. "If I had left him alive, he would have continued to make things difficult, and I didn't care to keep looking over my shoulder for him."

And also because that asshole needed to die, said the Darkness. I nodded to myself. *Yes,* I replied. *He did.*

I tilted my head toward the other 7X, now turning off the runway and onto the taxiway that led to the ramp. "It also takes another one of their pieces off the board. They were counting on having Moore around to watch us and report what he saw. Now we've removed that option. They're going to have to change their game plan a bit."

"It just doesn't seem real," Wilson said. "They're committing treason. And I've been helping them. We've all been helping them. Good God."

I raised my hand gently in a gesture to silence him.

"We don't know that," I said. "Although it seems likely." I looked across the cockpit at him. "On how many flights have you seen the crates loaded?"

Wilson shrugged. "All the flights that I've been on," he said. "We only carry one or two of them at a time. They're really heavy – about 250 pounds each. It takes four guys to raise them up to a level to get them into the jet and two guys inside to position them."

I nodded to myself as he talked. Sharona had given me a brief primer on nuclear materials transport when we had spoken last night.

"If they're using crates," she had said, "that means they have lead-lined cylinders inside the crates, with packaging on all sides so the cylinder will be protected in the event the crate is compromised."

"How big are the cylinders?" I had asked.

"They'll be almost as tall as the crate is high," she answered. "But substantially slimmer in diameter than the crate is wide. They have to allow for the packaging material."

"Is there any scenario you can think of where Enteron would be providing North Korea nuclear materials with the approval of our N.R.C. or Department of State?"

Sharona had paused. "Doesn't seem likely," she said after a long moment. "The problem is that we can't get access to the paperwork without tipping our hand. Enteron has to have someone helping them in D.C. Nuclear material has to be accounted for. The N.R.C. requires operators to maintain detailed records which can be spot-checked at any time. Rowe and the gang couldn't be moving the stuff out of their inventory to N.K. without someone knowing or eventually finding out."

"Unless they had help," I had said. "Jesus."

"The big question is, what the hell are they doing with the stuff?"

"Well, hopefully, I can get some answers to that question," I had said. "Without getting Sarah and the kids killed in the process."

"What about getting yourself killed?" Sharona asked. The timbre of her voice had changed. It wasn't businesslike or even playful. Instead, it was soft. Almost tender. "There are some people who might get upset if something happened to you."

I had shrugged at the words, even though I had been

astounded by them.

"My life is optional," I had said. "Always has been. Always will be."

I snapped back into the moment for the second time that morning as I watched the other 7X pull into the parking spot next to us, on the far north end of Ross Aviation's ramp. The jet was being directed by a ground crewman dressed in a bulky parka that made him resemble the Michelin Man. He looked almost comical as he clumsily tried to move the orange marshaling wands in the appropriate directions to command the pilot to turn and then stop the aircraft. I looked over at the other aircraft and saw Jose Gutierrez in the left seat.

"Of course," I said to myself.

The jet moved forward until the Michelin Man directed it to stop, and shortly afterward, I heard the sound of the engines winding down.

I looked over at Wilson. "You remember the script?"

He looked back at me and nodded slowly. Then he forced a few coughs and sniffled twice. "I guess," he said.

"Don't fuck up," I warned him. "Rowe is already going to smell a rat when she realizes Moore is out of the picture. If she doesn't know already. We have to play it straight. And she has to play it straight as well – at least as long as she's in front of the rest of the passengers."

Wilson looked at me apprehensively. "Do you think they're all in on it?"

I shrugged. "No idea. But for now, we need to assume that."

I exited the cockpit, leaving Wilson to monitor the APU. I collected my coat from the closet, donned it, and walked down the steps and into the frigid air. Our luggage was neatly arranged at the base of the airstair. I rolled the bags over to the baggage compartment access door underneath the other 7X's left engine.

Marty Gordon met me there.

"Joe's finishing the checklist," he said. "I'll just get our bags off, and you guys can load yours up."

"Just get his off," I said. "You're coming with us."

"But…"

I cut him off. "Rick is fighting a cold and if he goes down, we'll need you as a backup pilot. Besides, our jet has a FADEC issue and can't fly anyway. We can leave Gutierrez with it until Dassault can get a new FADEC here. In the meantime, the department can send another pilot up here to keep him company."

I didn't tell him that the FADEC failure had been created when I had disconnected one of the cables from the unit in the rear service compartment.

Gordon nodded. "Okay," he said. "But are you sure you don't want to take Joe with you?" he said, rolling his eyes. "After all, he is the more *experienced* captain."

I shook my head. "Not this time," I said. "I don't have the patience to deal with that kind of arrogance."

He nodded again. "Sounds good."

Gordon pulled the latch to unlock the baggage compartment. As he swung the door open, I could see two plain wooden crates, carefully arranged in the cozy space. Crew and passenger luggage, rollerboards, duffel bags, and garment bags, were stowed in between and on top of the crates. The crates themselves had a series of numbers on the outside, but none of the D.O.T.-required hazardous material markings.

The sight of the crates gave me a moment's pause. It was one thing to talk about smuggling nuclear material into North Korea. It was another to actually see the stuff in person.

Treason is a difficult thing to process. It's one thing to disagree with your country's actions or take issue with the vacuous idiots who seem to find their way into elected office with disappointing regularity. It's quite another thing to take action that betrays your country, actions that give another country the ability to injure yours, actions that could place your fellow countrymen in harm's way.

Purely for the sake of money. Or ego. Or both.

I had seen treason once before, six years ago, in the person of a former boss of mine who had tried to steal F-35s and sell them to China. He had died in a hail of my 20mm cannon bullets over the desert of Arizona. With him, it had been as much about ego as payment, and that had made him irrational and easy to predict.

But Rowe and crew were different. They were planners. They were coldly calculating. And that made them far more dangerous than my encounter in the past.

"Here's Joe's bag," Gordon said, handing me a rollerboard that had been lying on top of one of the two crates in the back of the compartment. He was standing on the top rung of the baggage compartment's ladder, about two feet off of the airport tarmac.

I took the bag from him and placed it on the ground, apart from the other bags. I grabbed the handle on the top of Wilson's bag and lifted it up to Gordon. He took it from me and placed it in the same spot he had taken Gutierrez's bag from. I handed him the remainder of the bags. After Gordon dismounted from the ladder and folded it a few moments later, I reached into the compartment and placed my hand next to the crate nearest to me and watched the face of the CIA-provided Apple watch on my left wrist. The dial of the Geiger counter app appeared on the face of the small screen immediately. After taking a moment or two to settle, the needle deflected to the right, registering a level of airborne radiation far above normal ambient levels.

I shook my head as I stepped back and watched Gordon secure the compartment. If I had any doubts about the intentions of Rowe and the gang, those doubts were gone. People who were transporting nuclear materials in good faith would have the containers properly marked in accordance with U.S. D.O.T. HAZMAT guidance. It was obvious that they were trying to conceal what was inside them.

"Damn," Gordon said. "I guess I need to open that thing back up. I forgot to stow Dylan Moore's luggage in there."

"No need," I said. "He had a family emergency. We put him on a jet for Chicago about two hours ago. We'll be taking Jake with us to Korea."

Gordon's eyes widened. "Wow!" he said. "I hope everything will be ok for him."

"We'll see," I said.

***

Jose Gutierrez was not happy about being left behind alone but, to his credit, he didn't whine about it. He nodded in acceptance of his fate and went down the stairs to replace Wilson in the other jet without another word. I slid into the captain's seat in the cockpit with the flight plan that Wilson had been making notes on yesterday and began to cross-check the waypoint coordinates loaded into the navigation system with the coordinates on the flight plan. As part of the aircraft turn process, Gutierrez should have downloaded the flight plan for the next leg from ARINC, Enteron's flight planning service, and loaded it into the 7X's flight management system. It looked like he had done just that. I nodded to myself as I verified the last set of coordinates. He may have been an arrogant ass, but at least he was a professional arrogant ass.

I called up the fuel system synoptic page on the 7X's lower display unit. The active depiction of the jet's fuel tanks and pumps indicated that fuel levels were rising. The refueling operation was proceeding smoothly. On the jet's EICAS display, the warning messages for the lavatory compartment doors had extinguished as well. Apparently, Gutierrez had ordered the forward and aft lavatories to be serviced and that servicing had been completed.

"What are *you* doing here?" asked a cold female voice from behind me.

I turned in my seat to find Brenda Rowe glaring down at me with dark, beady eyes that were icier than the polar caps. She was bundled up in a thick overcoat, which probably meant she had gone into Ross Aviation's terminal to go to the restroom or for some other purpose.

"I'm here to fly you to North Korea, Brenda," I said, with as flat a tone as I could muster. "That's what I was scheduled to do." I looked up at her and gestured with my hands. "Is there a problem?"

She stared back at me for a long moment, with a gaze that could have generated a stream of deadly icicles. Finally, she nodded at me, very slightly, the kind of nod you give to an opponent who had momentarily gotten the better of you. Then she retreated towards the back of the aircraft. She had almost made it through the galley when she turned back to me.

"Where's Moore?" she asked.

"He had a personal issue," I said without looking at her. I was trying to get through the POWER-ON checklist before Wilson joined me in the cockpit.

"What?" she demanded. "What kind of personal issue?"

I sighed and turned around as I raised my gaze to hers. "Something about a *death* in the family."

She looked back at me and gave me another small nod of acceptance. But there was a glow of secret knowledge and haughty superiority in those dark eyes.

"I hope deaths in families don't become a trend," she said. "Especially deaths in missing families."

The blood in my veins went from tepid to boiling in

milliseconds, as the Darkness sprang to life inside of me. My muscles tensed like they were preparing to spring, to leap at her, and break her flimsy body into multiple pieces. Gone was the cold, calculating entity that had been with me in the parking lot at FlightSafety. In its place was the raving monster that I had succumbed to on many occasions in the past. It was awake. It was hungry. It wanted blood. Her blood. And it wanted to make her pay for killing Mark Hill and make her suffer the anguish she had inflicted on Sarah and the kids. I forced myself to stay in my seat, and I clenched my fists tightly, feeling my body tremble in imposed restraint.

Rowe watched me closely, almost like a voyeur, as I struggled to keep myself in check. Then, a small smile etched itself onto her face.

"Interesting," she said.

After a long moment, she turned and exited the galley into the passenger area.

CHAPTER EIGHTEEN

Friday, January 15th
1240 Hours Local Time
FL 400 and .85 Mach
On NOPAC Route R220
Just South of the Kamchatka Peninsula

We had been airborne for about 3.6 hours and were just past the halfway point of the journey to Pyongyang. An hour or so ago, we had crossed the International Date Line and had been catapulted 21 hours forward in local time. With about 3.4 hours remaining in our flight, we were on schedule to make our arrival window in North Korea in the prescribed time slot.

The Falcon 7X was performing with its usual reliability and grace, the three Pratt and Whitney PW307A engines pushing the sleek jet through the atmosphere at 85% of the speed of sound while sipping gas at less than 3,000 pounds per hour of total fuel flow. The fuel totalizer on the pilot's flight display or PFD showed our current fuel weight at 18,070 pounds, well ahead of the predicted amount for this time in the flight. The FMS showed us landing in Pyongyang with 8,500 pounds of gas, plenty to make the short flight back across the border to Gimpo without refueling.

I nodded to myself and glanced down at the iPhone on the tray table in front of me. The screen remained stubbornly blank. I had texted Sharona, Smith, and Amrine the radiation readings I had taken from the crates in the back of the aircraft as well as the details Wilson had conveyed about the previous trips to North Korea with the crates aboard. That had been three hours ago and there had been no response. I wasn't sure what I was expecting to hear from them, but the silence was making me uneasy for reasons I couldn't understand.

'The tables are nice, aren't they?" Wilson said from across the cockpit. He had his own table deployed with an iPad on one side of the small surface, and a precisely-folded paper navigation chart on the other side. He was staring down at the chart and making an annotation with a pen on one side of it.

"They are," I replied. "They make things very civilized. Yet another benefit of a sidestick versus a yoke."

He nodded and finished writing. Then he sat up and yawned as he looked out of his side of the aircraft. The sky was abnormally clear, and the foreboding terrain of the Kamchatka Peninsula was clearly visible out of the right side of the aircraft. "Have you ever landed at Petropavlovsk?" he asked.

I shook my head and looked past him to the expanse of tundra-green earth and mountains that extended far to the north. "Nope. I've flown over the peninsula on a few trips, but never landed at the airfield there. Never wanted to. The Russians can be...difficult."

"We can't even go into their airspace while we're doing these missions," Wilson said, still looking out of the side window. "Something about the relationship between North Korea, Russia, and the United States. If we go into their airspace with Pyongyang as a destination, they have to intercept us and force us to land for inspection." He shrugged. "Not sure of the reason for that."

I nodded and allowed a wry smile to etch its way onto my face as I remembered my own adventure in St. Petersburgh five years ago. "They're Russians," I said after a moment. "They don't need a reason to do anything."

Wilson slowly turned his head to look at me. "What are we going to do when we get to North Korea?" he asked.

I looked back at him. "What normally happens after you arrive?"

He thought for a moment. "After we land, a vehicle meets us where we clear the runway. It leads us to the main ramp, and we shut down the engines. After we shut down, other vehicles pull up to the jet, and a squad of soldiers surrounds the aircraft. Then, an officer who speaks English comes aboard, checks passports, and inspects the aircraft."

"They inspect the aircraft?" I asked.

"I get the idea that it's some kind of formality. He looks at passports and not much else."

"What about unloading the crates and baggage?"

"After the passports are inspected, the passengers deplane and get into the vehicles. While that's happening, the cargo is unloaded."

"Do we get out and help?"

"The maintenance tech, Jake in this case, is allowed to go down and open the baggage the door, but then he has to stand out of the way while the crates and bags are unloaded. Two of us, probably Marty since he's already in the back and either you or me, will assist with the bags from inside the aircraft."

"And once everything is unloaded?"

"Baggage door is shut; the tech comes back aboard, and we're on our way. We barely spend twenty minutes in the chocks. Sometimes even less than that."

"What about brake energy limits for the takeoff after you unload?" During quick turns between landing and takeoff, aircraft brakes typically need cooling time to function with maximum efficiency in the event they would be required for a high-speed abort on the next takeoff.

Wilson shrugged. "They won't let us stay in the chocks long enough to allow the brakes to cool," he said. He smiled at me with his usual impish expression. "You'll just need to take it easy on them when we land."

I nodded. "I'll do my best."

I turned my head and looked out of my side window. The Pacific Ocean looked like an infinite, dark blue carpet that stretched to the horizon, the vastness of it difficult to comprehend.

"How many times have you crossed the Atlantic?" I asked Wilson as I stared out the window.

"Maybe ten times or so," he replied. "We fly to Europe a fair amount, but I seem to miss a lot of those trips."

"It's interesting that when you cross the Atlantic, which is a much smaller ocean, you seem to stay out of the sight of land for much longer periods of time than when you cross the Pacific, at least if you fly the NOPAC routes, like we are."

"I never really thought about that," he said. "But you're right. Have you ever crossed the Pacific via the southern route?"

I nodded without looking at him. "Once or twice, on contract trips. We were going to Hong Kong or Taiwan. I can't remember. We were in a G-IV which doesn't have the legs this jet has, and we had to make two fuel stops to avoid having a wet footprint." I turned to look at him. "That's when you get a sense of how big this ocean is. I remember being out of sight of land for nearly the entire length of all three legs and landing on islands each time. It was a little disconcerting."

"I bet," he said. Wilson's eyes darted to the center display and then over to the EICAS window on his PDU.

"You've been stealing glances at the EICAS for the whole flight," I said. "At first, I thought it was about you being thorough, but now I'm wondering if it's paranoia. What warning message are you looking for?"

He looked over at me and smiled apologetically. "That obvious, huh?"

I nodded at him. "What are you not telling me?"

"On one of our earlier flights, the crew got a BAG SMOKE warning message in the descent into Pyongyang."

I felt my eyes widen. Smoke in the aft baggage compartment usually meant there was a fire back there. The baggage compartment sat in front of the aft service compartment where the hydraulic reservoirs and pumps were installed. Fires in aircraft were never good, but a fire near flammable hydraulic fluid could be catastrophic.

"What did they do?" I asked.

"They had already crossed the border and were being escorted by North Korean fighters, so they couldn't turn around. And the North Koreans don't handle changes very well. They had to stay on the flight plan until they got to Pyongyang International. The guy in the right seat did what the guidance says. He left his seat, got a fire extinguisher, and went back to fight the fire."

"How bad was it?"

"It turns out that those crates have little refrigeration units installed in them. A unit in one of the crates burnt out. That's what was smoking."

"I see. At least it was easy to deal with."

"So, you would think," Wilson said. "But it didn't turn out that way. The guy who went back there emptied the extinguisher, but the damn smoke didn't stop. The crew had to open the bag vent valves during the descent and everything. The smoke persisted until they were on the ground."

"Did they do an emergency evac after they landed?"

Wilson shook his head. "No, they didn't."

My jaw dropped involuntarily. "With a possible fire in the

airplane? Jesus. Why not?"

He held up two fingers. "First, they were in North Korea and they didn't want to activate the engine and APU fire extinguishers and strand themselves there."

"But there was a fire!"

"Let me finish. Second, when they told the passengers what the issue was, the passengers didn't seem that concerned about it. One of them made a call on the sat phone. As soon as the plane stopped, guys in radiation suits approached the jet. A guy came on board the jet who spoke perfect English and asked the tech on the flight how to open the compartment. The North Korean crew opened the compartment themselves, got that crate out, and put it in a separate truck. Then they got the other crate into a different truck, and the passengers got off like they usually did. The crew went back and inspected the compartment, and everything was normal. They restarted the jet and got out of there."

I sat back in my seat and exhaled. "Wow," I said. "That could have been a mess." Then a thought occurred to me. "How far out from landing were they when the passengers made that call?"

Wilson shrugged. "I wasn't there, so I don't know. But I got the idea it was maybe 10-15 minutes from the runway."

I nodded. "The North Koreans were prepared for that contingency," I said. "That's why they were able to respond so well."

"What does that mean?"

I shook my head. "I don't know," I said, reaching for my iPhone. "But I might know someone who does."

I typed a text to the CIA group briefly describing the incident and emphasizing the installation of cooling units in the crates. I finished the text with a question. WHAT IN THE HELL ARE THEY CARRYING THAT THEY NEED TO KEEP COOL?

When I was finished typing, I put the phone back on the table and pushed it away from me, like it was contaminated from the subject of the text messages. I didn't know enough about nuclear material to put this new information into context, but the knot in my gut told me it wasn't good. I drummed my fingers on my knee and tapped the heel of my right foot against the floor.

The phone buzzed on the table's metal surface a few moments later. I reached for it with a mixture of anticipation and dread. I entered the code to view the screen.

Smith was the one who had replied. CONSENSUS HERE IS THAT YOU'RE CARRYING NUCLEAR WASTE, his message said. THAT'S WHY THE NRC HASN'T NOTICED IT. PROBABLY STRONTIUM 90 OR CESIUM 137. VERY DIRTY STUFF. IT CAN GET WARM. THAT'S WHY THEY USE THE COOLERS. DOESN'T MAKE SENSE THOUGH. NO GOOD FOR ENERGY OR BOMBS.

I sat back in my chair and sighed, aware that Wilson was staring at me as I looked down at the screen.

"No good for reactors or weapons," I said over the intercom. "Then what the fuck are they using it for?"

CHAPTER NINETEEN

Friday, January 15th
1255 Hours Local Time
Descending through FL250 at 300 KIAS
Crossing the 38th Parallel into North Korea

Three more hours of flight time and another three hours of time zone change, and we were descending into the bleak airspace of North Korea. We had made the turn northbound over South Korea's Inchon International Airport and followed the instructions for entry into the North very precisely, ensuring we crossed the border on the centerline of the track, below 25,000 feet and at precisely 300 knots true airspeed.

"I don't know why they make us get so low when we're over a hundred miles to the airport," Wilson muttered under his breath. "Uses up a lot of extra gas."

"Because we're easier to intercept," I said, looking down at the paper copy of the flight plan, where the instructions were printed. "We're supposed to level at 20,000 feet and 300 knots. That makes us the perfect 'duck' target for an intercept. When I was teaching Viper babies to fly intercepts at Luke, I'd almost always have the target aircraft at 20,000 feet and 300 knots."

"I guess I figured it had to be something like that," Wilson said. "I've been intercepted once flying into here, and it was a few minutes after we had stabilized at 20,000."

"What type of airplane intercepted you?" I asked. "Did you recognize it?"

Wilson shot me a wry glance. "I may have started life in the Army as an infantry officer, but I finished my career flying helicopters. My aircraft ID skills might not be as good as yours, Mister Fighter Pilot, but they're passable."

I held both hands up, palms towards him, in a gesture of apology. "No offense meant," I said.

He gave me the usual sardonic smile. "I'm just giving you shit. It was two MiG-29's. I remember being surprised that the NKs had something that modern."

"If you call 1980's technology modern," I replied.

"As I recall, isn't your much-vaunted Viper of that same era?"

I nodded. "True. But the Viper was leading technology and the MiG-29 was catch-up technology. Although it could outmaneuver the Viper in a visual fight if it was flown by someone who knew what they were doing."

Wilson reached down to the weather radar control knob on his side of the center console and turned it to STBY. Then he reached over and repeated the action with the identical knob on my side.

"Part of the procedure," he said. "They don't want us emitting radar while we're on the track."

I nodded. "That's because if our antenna was tilted the right way, we might see them coming. But we'd have to be very lucky."

"If you were flying the intercept, how would you do it?" Wilson asked.

I shrugged and smiled. "It's been a while and with the new radars and jets, the tactics might have changed. But back in the day, I would have been 5,000 to 7,000 below the target's altitude so I could do a low to high conversion at the endgame. I'd start the intercept by keeping the target on the nose until about twenty miles range, then I'd offset left or right and hold the offset until about eight miles range while I maintained the altitude delta." I thought about making a sketch of the Viper's radar display to show him how you could gauge the offset by using the radar but decided against it. "At eight miles," I continued, "I'd pull the target to the nose and climb to his altitude. During the conversion turn, I'd probably ease up on the g a little and wind up in about a one to two-mile trail. Then I'd slowly move up to a place where the target could see me."

"Sounds like you're paralleling the target's flight path until you turn in on him."

I shook my head. "If you look at it from God's eye view, from above, it looks more like a button-hook pattern that you see wide-receivers run in football games. During the initial part of the intercept, you're trying to build separation or turning room for the conversion turn. But you're also checking for target awareness."

"Awareness?"

I nodded. "As you begin the turn to build separation, you check to see if the target is maintaining its original course or changing course to keep you on its nose. If it stays with the original course, it's unaware. If it changes course, it's aware – it knows you're there."

"What happens if it's aware?"

"Then you're probably dealing with another fighter with an air-to-air radar. You pull the target the nose, deploy your wingman, and hope like hell you get permission to shoot him pre-merge because if you don't, he might shoot you pre-merge or you might get anchored in a visual fight. The second situation is better than the first, but neither one of them is great."

"Why is that?" Wilson asked. "If you're fighting him, you

can kill him. Right?"

"Maybe," I said. "If I'm lucky. But I'll also be very predictable while I'm engaged with him and that makes me pretty easy to shoot if his wingman is hawking the fight."

"That makes sense," he said. He looked over at me. "That all sounds pretty cool. Did you enjoy it when you were in the service?"

I nodded at him and turned my head to look out of my side of the jet as memories came flooding back. I had performed several intercepts since I had left the service, nearly all of them resulting in turning visual fights and almost all of them culminating in the deaths of those I had fought. My thoughts raced back six years, and my mind's eye conjured up the vision of the four hostile F-16's racing across the brown earth of the high desert of California, far below me. I came down upon them and shot all four of them down in about ninety seconds. I had been lucky that day. Very lucky indeed.

"You ok?" Wilson asked.

"Yeah," I said. "I'm fine. Just...remembering." A flash of motion caught my eye as I looked through the 7X's side window. Below the horizon and to our left, I could see two fast-moving aircraft making a turn towards us.

"We're about to have company," I said.

Wilson sighed. "Great."

At that moment, my phone buzzed on the table in front of me. I was tempted to look down at it, but I couldn't take my eyes from the two jets as they converted on us, executing the same maneuver I had just described.

"Piss poor job," I said as I watched them. "Not nearly enough altitude delta. Either they're not terribly proficient or they don't care if we see them." I exhaled in silent frustration. "What I would give for a 9-g turn right about now."

"Falcon November 622 Charlie Bravo, Pyongyang Control." The controller's English was clear and unaccented.

"Proceed on track at flight level 200 and prepare for descent in ten minutes. You will be escorted by two fighters of the Korean People's Army Air Force. They will come alongside you when they are ready for you to see them. You will call visual contact."

I keyed the mic button before Wilson could respond. "November 622 Charlie Bravo tally two, left eight o'clock low." I opened my mouth to add a wisecrack about their pilots needing more practice at intercept geometry, but I thought better of it and clamped my jaw shut.

There was no response from the controller, and I heard Wilson chuckle softly through the intercom. "That's showing them," he said.

My phone buzzed again, and I reluctantly tore my eyes from the two fighters and looked down at the screen.

RANDOM EXPLOSION IN NW SEOUL, said the first text. It was from John Amrine, Smith and Sharona's boss. TEN MINUTES AGO, SAME TIME AS YOU CROSSED BORDER.

The second text had come a few moments later. This one from Dave Smith. 20 DEAD. 73 INJURED. NO RESPONSIBILITY CLAIMED. WITNESSES SAY THEY HEARD NOISE BEFORE EXPLOSION – LIKE JET FLYING BY.

I shook my head as I looked at the screen, my mind suddenly overrun with theories and possibilities. I suddenly remembered the numerous intelligence briefings I had long ago, when I was stationed at Kunsan, and one of the largest target sets we had been tasked to eliminate if we had gone to war. Then, even as I saw the two MiG's move into position alongside us in my peripheral vision, I felt a thought emerge deep inside my brain and develop rapidly, like a seedling growing into a mature tree under time-lapse photography.

My fingers moved rapidly across the virtual keypad on my phone.

YOU NEED TO CLEAR THE AREA AROUND THE EXPLOSION AREA, I typed. HAVE LOCALS DO IT ASAP.

WHY? Came the reply from Smith. ATTACK IS OVER.

"Jesus, Dave," I muttered to myself as I continued to type. "You guys are the CIA. You should be ahead of me on this." CHECK AREA FOR RADIATION, I typed. AREA WILL BE HOT.

DAMN! Came the quick reply. WILCO.

"What's going on?" Wilson asked. "You seem mighty preoccupied over there."

I raised my head from the iPhone and looked out the left side of the 7X to see the two North Korean MiGs in lose formation, about a hundred feet off our left wingtip. The jets were gray blue in color, not unlike the paint scheme favored by their adversaries south of the 38th parallel. But rather than a subdued national symbol as part of the paint scheme, these jets featured thick red stripes high on the vertical stabilizers, with a white star in the center of each. The sleek aircraft were armed to the teeth, with four air-to-air missiles each. From this distance, I couldn't tell what kind of missiles they carried, but I was betting they were a mixture of infrared and radar-guided weapons. Both pilots' heads were turned towards us, their eyes indiscernible behind their dark visors.

I had a distinct feeling of helplessness as I watched them. For the first time in my life, I was in a "target" aircraft in an air-to-air environment. There was nothing I could do to keep them at bay. I was at their mercy.

I sighed loudly into the intercom and answered Wilson, trying to keep my voice as emotionless as possible. "I think I just solved the puzzle," I said, still watching the MiGs as they shadowed us. "I think I know what the fuck is going on."

CHAPTER TWENTY

Friday, January 15th
1330 Hours Local Time
On Final Approach to Runway 35
Pyongyang Sunan International Airport (ZKPY)
Pyongyang, People's Republic of North Korea

The 7X's landing gear thumped into the down and locked position as we broke out of a low overcast and beheld the capital of the People's Republic of North Korea, directly below us. The city looked small, drab, and unimpressive, displaying none of the urban glitz of its counterpart on the other side of the border. Row after row of white buildings with brightly colored roofs extended in front of us, the color an obvious attempt to disguise the dreariness of the place.

"I'm not sure I've seen a more depressing city in my life," I said.

"It reminds me of a prison," Wilson said. "This is the first time I've seen it so close. We usually make the approach to the opposite runway. When we climb out, we get into the weather so quickly, I've never been able to see anything."

"SF3, before landing checks," I commanded.

Wilson nodded and moved the SLATS/FLAPS handle to the SF3 position. Then he called up the BEFORE LANDING checklist on the electronic checklist display.

"Landing gear?" he asked.

I glanced down at my PDU and confirmed that three green wheels appeared in the GEAR display.

"Down and locked," I said.

"Slats and flaps?"

I looked to the other side of the PDU and confirmed that the slat icon was green, and the flap indicator was green and aligned with the 3.

"SF3," I said.

"Before landing checklist complete."

I nodded. "Now, if they'd only clear us to land. I understand that's quite a process."

"We're about eight miles out," Wilson said. "They've got plenty of time, and they usually take every moment of it. We've had to ask for clearance multiple times in the past. And they wait until absolutely the last minute to give it." He glanced to his right, obviously looking down at the city below. "Damn," he said. "I think that's the USS Pueblo down there. Looks like some sort of tourist attraction."

"That was a shitty situation, and those crew members were brave men," I said. "And our country completely let them down."

Wilson nodded. "You know the Navy never decommissioned the ship, as a tribute to the crew. It's the only U.S. Navy ship in enemy captivity."

I glanced to our left and noticed that the fighter escort had vanished. "Our friends in the MiGs are gone. I guess they figure we can find the place by ourselves now," I said. "Either that or they couldn't hang on the wing in IMC."

Wilson leaned forward to look around me. "Yep," he said. "Looks like." Then he sighed and reached for the mic switch on his cursor control device. "Well, here goes the battle for landing clearance," he said. "You know with all the diplomatic mumbo-jumbo and preparation that goes into these flights, you'd think they'd be primed to let us land for God's sake."

But before he could speak, a very precise English-voice came through our headsets, startling both of us. "Falcon November 622 Charlie Bravo, the wind is 030 at ten knots, you are cleared to land, runway 35. Welcome to the glorious People's Republic of North Korea."

"Well, I'll be damned," Wilson said. "That's never happened before." He keyed the mic. "Falcon November 622 Charlie Bravo copies cleared to land." He released the mic button and looked over at me. "You must be a good luck charm or something."

"Yeah, or something," I replied absently. I could feel my gut tighten up as I spoke. "So, that's never happened before?"

Wilson shook his head. "Not on any flights I've been on and from what I've heard, not on any of the others either. It seems like they actually want us to land this time. Go figure."

"Yeah. Go figure."

***

We touched down a few moments later. I managed to roll the 7X onto Pyongyang International's runway 35 smoothly, without even the slightest bounce, which could be a surprisingly challenging feat in the jet sometimes.

"Nice," Wilson said. "Even better than the one at Anchorage the other day. I'm impressed against my will."

I nodded in acceptance of the compliment. "I've got a fair amount of experience in jets with digital flight control systems and highly efficient wings. But I also get lucky from time to time.

"This damn jet has no feel in the flare," he said. "No feel at all."

"That's because it's still flying," I said. "With the digital

FCS and that high-efficiency wing, it will fly in the landing attitude for a long time, especially in ground effect, before it runs out of airspeed. That's why you have to put it on the ground, unlike every other business jet I've flown."

Wilson nodded. "Yep. Which is why guys typically land fast and bounce."

As the nose began to de-rotate, I pulled the thrust reverser lever on the center throttle.

"Trans," Wilson said, looking down at the thrust reverser position indicator in the engine display on his PFD. "Deploy."

The 7X's center engine began to spool up and generating reverse thrust. Taking Wilson's earlier advice, I kept my feet off the brakes and relied on the thrust reverser alone to slow us down to about 50 knots.

"Interesting runway arrangement," Wilson said, looking out of windscreen at the airport's other runway, 01-19, which was well north of our runway and offset to the east. "Do you think they did it because of the terrain or for tactical reasons?"

I shrugged. "Both. There are a lot of rice paddies around here that they probably didn't want to disturb. But with the two runways spaced so far apart, they'd be difficult to knock out with multiple ballistic weapons, especially from a low-altitude delivery."

"God, this is a desolate place. I used to think parts of the Middle East were the end of the world, but this place puts the Middle East to shame."

I nodded. "I've been there too, and I agree with you."

"And there's our escort," Wilson said, looking out the right side of the aircraft. "He's abeam us on the parallel taxiway."

"I'll take the second to last taxiway," I replied. "The high-speed."

I applied the brakes gingerly and then pushed gently on the right rudder pedal to turn the nosewheel and steer the jet onto the high-speed taxiway.

"They don't have any of the usual runway taxiway dividing lines," I said. "How do you know when you're officially off the runway surface?"

"Good question," Wilson said. "It's obvious they don't get much traffic here or that lack of markings thing would be a real issue."

As soon as the main gear were off the runway, Wilson's hands ran the normal after-landing flow. He turned off the strobe and landing lights, activated the APU, changed the transponder mode, and called up the airfield diagram on the upper display between us.

"Falcon November 622 Charlie Bravo, you contact Ground Control on 121.9," the tower controller intoned.

Wilson acknowledged the controller, made the frequency change, and checked us in with Ground Control.

"Falcon November 622 Charlie Bravo, Ground, you have Follow-Me in sight?"

"Sounds like the same guy," I murmured.

Wilson nodded. "Probably is," he said. "We'll likely be the only plane moving on the airport while we're here. Not sure they could justify having two guys up there." Then he keyed the mic. "November 622 Charlie Bravo has Follow-Me in sight."

"Falcon November 622 Charlie Bravo, you follow Follow-Me to parking."

"Falcon November 622 Charlie Bravo, wilco," Wilson acknowledged. "Damn good English for the second time today," he said after he released the mic button. But it's been that way every time I've been here. Must be trying to put on a good front."

Ahead of us, at the intersection of the high-speed taxiway and the parallel taxiway, sat a green utility vehicle that looked like a miniature tractor from a tractor-trailer rig. The words FOLLOW ME were stenciled on a panel behind the driver's cab and below the rear window.

"Sure glad we won the war a long time ago and made English the international language of aviation," I said. "I'm not sure I could read that sign if it was in Korean."

Wilson grunted. "The North Koreans being the North Koreans, I'm a little shocked it's not in Korean anyway." He motioned towards the truck in front of us. "After Landing Checklist is complete," he said. "Just follow our friend here to parking, and we'll get unloaded and get the hell out of here."

"Sounds good to me."

***

The journey to the parking ramp took several minutes, even though the distance was less than a mile, mainly due to the snail-like pace of the escort vehicle. I didn't have to apply power to the 7X to follow him. Just leaving the big jet's throttles at idle power generated enough thrust to keep up. On a few occasions, I even had to tap the brakes to keep our distance. Finally, the vehicle turned into the parking ramp and led us to a marshaller awaiting us with two raised orange wands. It was then that I noticed that the marshaller and other ground personnel were all dressed in parkas, gloves, and boots.

"I guess I forgot it was winter here, too," I said to myself.

"Is it ever!" Wilson said. "It's minus twenty Celsius out there."

I stopped the jet on the marshaller's command a few moments later. Then I pulled the parking brake handle.

"Brake's set," I said.

Wilson pointed toward the electrical synoptic he had called up on the lower display unit between us. "APU's running," he said. "Busses are powered. You're cleared to shut down."

"Engines coming off," I said. I reached down to the FUEL

switches, just aft of the throttles, and pulled them to the OFF position. Then Wilson and I ran the AT RAMP checklist.

"You better get back there," he said. "They don't like it if the door doesn't come open right after we shut down."

I nodded and unstrapped myself. "Of course, they don't." I moved my seat to the outboard position and exited the cockpit. I grabbed my jacket from the forward closet and stepped through the galley and into the passenger area as I donned it. "Please have your passports ready. The door is coming open," I said. "I'd warn you about the Korean winter, but you're all from Chicago, so this should be old hat." I looked beyond the forward and center sections of the area and into the rear compartment where Marty Gordon, our spare pilot, and Jake Barnhouse, our technician, were standing. "You guys ready?" I asked.

They nodded.

"Here we go," I said.

As I turned to leave the passenger area, I noticed that none of them were looking at me. Instead, they were all staring out of the 7X's windows, seemly fascinated by the scene outside the aircraft.

Must be preoccupied, I thought. But then, as I reached the door and got my right hand on the handle, I glanced back into the cabin. Brenda Rowe, sitting in the powerchair, the first forward-facing seat on the right side of the aircraft, looked back at me. Her beady eyes fixed on me through a few strands of stringy hair, and she had a slight smile of anticipation on her wan face.

A familiar sensation of dread crept into the back of my brain. I was reminded, again, of the dogfight over the desert, years ago. But this time, instead of the triumph, I remembered the moment when I had almost been killed by an opponent who had maneuvered to a blind spot and who had remained concealed until the last minute before opening fire. I had been outmaneuvered and outthought, and I had barely recovered in time.

The hairs on the back of my neck began to slowly rise as I pulled up on the door handle. Then, as the door fell open, and I saw the personnel gathered at the base of the stairs, I realized I had been outmaneuvered and outthought once again.

At the base of the stairs stood two North Korean special forces soldiers, clad in full tactical gear and armed with AK-47 carbines. Their rifles were shouldered and trained on the center of my chest. Behind them stood a man in the traditional winter uniform of the North Korean Army, whom I presumed was their commander. He had his hands on his hips and a confident smile on his face.

"Mister Colin Pearce," he said with a mild accent. "Or should I say, Colonel Colin Pearce?" His voice was calm and almost conversational. "I am Captain Cho of the People's Army. We are glad to have you with us. It's not often we get to talk to someone from the American CIA." He smiled broadly. "As you can imagine, we have some questions for you. You will accompany us."

Outmaneuvered. Fuck.

I nodded in realization and raised my hands, very slowly. Then, I walked down the airstair towards them. As I descended to the tarmac, the two soldiers stepped backward, keeping their rifles trained on my chest and staying well clear of me. I didn't know whether my reputation had preceded me, or they were just being cautious. It didn't matter. The .45 Commander was zipped into a hidden compartment in my rollerboard, stowed in the 7X's baggage compartment. But even if it had been on my right hip, there was nothing I could have done.

I stepped onto the pavement in a daze, my mind pondering the surrealness of the situation. I felt like I was in a scene in a Cold War movie. A few words of bluster and bravado ran through my mind, but I didn't utter them. These men knew who I was and seemed to know what I was. Speeches wouldn't help my situation. I could only hope that the CIA would be tracking the iPhone in my pocket and would be able to find me. If they even decided to come after me.

Captain Cho stepped forward. He was tall for a Korean, probably about six feet. His complexion was flawless, and his eyes were crisp. His movements were precise and deliberate. There was none of the shouting or screaming I had seen in other depictions of North Korean behavior in the presence of supposed spies. Instead, there was coolness and confidence. He knew he had me. And he knew I was powerless.

"Your hands, Colonel Pearce," he said, gesturing for me to lower my hands and extend my arms in front of me.

I brought my arms down slowly, turned my palms up, and placed my lower arms perpendicular to my body.

"Very good," Cho said. He snapped a pair of handcuffs on me in a motion that was professional, but respectful. Then, he stepped alongside me, took my arm, and led me to a nearby vehicle that looked like a North Korean version of a Hyundai SUV. He opened the rear door for me and directed me to get inside. I did as I was instructed and pivoted to put my ass on the seat before drawing my legs into the vehicle. Cho assisted me by gently placing his right hand on my head and pushing down slightly to ensure that my head cleared the door opening. As the weight of my body hit the leather seat, I found myself marveling at my captors' courtesy and wondering when that politeness would deteriorate into brutality.

They didn't make me wait long.

Even as I got my legs into the vehicle, a syringe appeared in Cho's hand. He inserted the needle into my neck and pushed the plunger home in a movement that was impossibly quick and deft. I opened my mouth in protest even as my nervous system processed the sting of the needle penetrating my skin.

But I couldn't make my mouth work. My body collapsed into the seat like a deflating balloon. My eyelids began an inexorable, downward journey. I had the image of window blinds closing, not in a temporary way, for the day's journey into night, but in a permanent way, like when a house was closed down for good.

Then everything went black.

CHAPTER TWENTY-ONE

Unknown Date
Unknown Time
Unknown Facility
People's Republic of North Korea

Sometime later, I awoke. My head was still swimming from the effects of the sedative. As I tried to clear my mind, I realized that I was acutely uncomfortable. I struggled to process what my body was feeling even as I attempted to force my eyelids open.

The first thing I saw was a bare, cement floor, with a drain in the center of it, right beneath me. I was looking down at it, which didn't seem to make sense. The floor was a gloomy, gray color and appeared to be dingy, but clean, like it was well used, but meticulously scrubbed. Then my mind comprehended what I was seeing and put it into context. My feet were bare, and the floor was several inches below them.

I was hanging.

I looked above me and was rewarded with a view of my hands, tightly bound in leather straps attached to a chain, suspended from the ceiling that was several feet overhead. The discomfort I was feeling was due to the load placed on my shoulders and arms, as they bore the weight of my body.

As my brain processed the scene and sedative continued to wear off, the discomfort morphed into a dull, throbbing ache embedded deeply in my shoulder joints.

I brought my gaze downward, saw my bare chest, and then, as I looked lower, saw something that dismayed me, but somehow, didn't surprise me. It was the head of my penis protruding below.

I was naked, bound, and hanging. Utterly at the whim of my captors. A flash of hopelessness shot through me, and I swallowed hard as I forced it down. I looked around the room in a desperate attempt to distract myself, but what I saw was the opposite of encouraging. The walls around me were bare, cement cinderblock, and looked like they had been standing for decades. On the wall in front of me was a large, dark window, purposefully tinted so that the occupants of the room beyond would not be visible from my perspective. I imagined that I was being watched from behind the glass. I could have spit at the observers or uttered some curses at them, but I didn't see the point. It wouldn't change anything. Next to the window was a steel door that was currently closed, locking me into the prison room, if I somehow found a miraculous way to escape my bonds.

But then my eyes found the object they had meant for me to see. Halfway between me and the front wall was a metal table. It looked like it had been taken from either a kitchen or a surgical ward because it was highly polished stainless steel. And on top of the table lay an assortment of torture instruments: whips, batons, hand tools, knives, and various other implements.

My captors were giving my imagination time to create its own nightmares before they subjected me to the real pain. They wanted to give me time to obsess, to dread, to become hyper-sensitive in anticipation.

But they weren't getting a virgin in this sort of situation.

I had been tortured and threatened by the best of them in previous lives, and I knew how the game worked. I took a deep breath, lowered my head, and shut my eyes. Then, I closed the compartmentalization gates in my mind, carefully locking each mental door to ensure they wouldn't spring open during the stress that was sure to follow. I stored away my love for Sarah and the kids, the hope for my new life in Sedona, and the hopelessness that was stirring inside of me. In the final compartment and behind the final door, I stowed the terrible ache in my shoulders and girded myself for the pain that would ensue. Then, I allowed the dregs of sedative that were in my veins to lull me into sleep.

***

But there would be no rest allowed. Before I could completely relax, the door was flung open with a loud bang as the steel surface hit the concrete wall. The sudden intrusion and the noise were obviously meant to startle me, but I didn't allow myself to move or twitch. Instead, I slowly raised my eyes to watch my tormentors enter the room.

There were two of them, and they could have been brothers. Both were shorter in stature and had close-cropped black hair. They wore olive-colored, short-sleeved tee-shirts, and camouflage fatigue pants that were bloused into combat boots. Their arms were sinewy with muscle, and their faces were expressionless. The two men walked one behind the other. They carried themselves with military precision and seemed to march through the doorway. They stopped in the area between the window and the table. Then, like they had been given the command 'left face,' by a drill sergeant, they turned in unison.

Captain Cho's voice came over the intercom. "Glad to see you are awake, Colonel Pearce," he said. His tone was polite and businesslike. "These two men are lance corporals Park and Lee of the People's Army Special Operations Force. We work together to extract information from enemies of the state."

"Nice to meet you," I said, nodding at each of them.

The two men stood at attention and did not acknowledge my greeting.

"Do you have anything to say before we begin, Colonel Pearce?" Cho asked.

I shook my head and verified the compartment doors were still shut and locked in my brain. "Nothing that will matter," I said.

"Very well," Cho said. He gave some commands in Korean, and the two corporals went to the table and selected their tools.

The one on the left, Park, if he had been introduced in order, retrieved a wooden club that was about two feet long and about an inch in diameter. I was almost relieved when I saw it. I had been beaten before. I was prepared for that. But then, he spun the club around his wrist, and I saw the two silver electrodes extending out of the end of it. Lee stopped the rotation of the club and pressed a button on the handle. There was a sharp "snap" in the air, and a blue arc of electricity passed between the two electrodes.

The other tormentor, Lee, selected a wooden handle with several leather thongs dangling from it. He moved his wrist up and down in a well-practiced motion, and a 'crack' resounded in the chamber.

The two men came around opposite sides of the table and walked up to me, their implements at their sides. Cho gave another command over the intercom, and they went to work.

After being beaten, shot, stabbed, and ejected out of an aircraft at nearly 600 knots, I thought I knew the meaning of pain.

I was wrong.

The two corporals were artists. They alternated their timing and the places where they struck with vicious precision. Just when I thought I'd have a millisecond to recover from a blow, one or both would strike again. And when I was prepared for the reattack, they would wait for the extra second or two to catch me off guard. I writhed in response to the strikes and attempted to move my body to a place or a posture where the damage and pain would be less. But Park and Lee were always a step ahead of me, and as soon as my body tried to get to a place of less tension, the prod or the whip was there first.

The cattle prod felt less like a shock and more like a stream of fire passing through my flesh. The utter suddenness and intensity of the pain it generated was unlike anything I had ever felt.

But the whip was worse.

The multiple leather straps didn't hit me all at once. The impacts were separated by milliseconds, a salvo of acute, intense burns on my skin. Each blow was a demonstration in temporal distortion as my brain tried to deal with the impact of each strap in individual, excruciating events.

At first, I tried not to scream. Then, I found I couldn't scream. Screaming took energy, and it took extra air in the lungs. I didn't have either of those commodities as my body dealt with the continual, savage onslaught.

I tried to keep my brain parked in a place of detachment, of reflection, but it stubbornly refused to stay there. The meticulously timed blows pulled my consciousness front and center, forced it to stay in the moment, binding it to endure the misery.

But my brain did find one refuge. It counted. As each shock or blow landed, it tallied them, stubbornly, defiantly, etching a mental chalk mark on an imaginary blackboard deep under my gray matter. And as the tally increased, I became fascinated with the question of my own resilience. How many blows could I take? How long would I last?

As it turned out, I stayed conscious longer than I thought I would. The last shock I felt was number 38, and the last whip impact was number 35.

As my eyes closed, and I fell down the stairs of consciousness into blackness, one thought dug itself deeply into my mind. It had occurred to me repeatedly in the few periods of respite I had during the beating, but I wasn't able to dwell on it. Now, as I collapsed in exhaustion, it occurred to me again and was my last thought before I fell into mental relief.

They didn't ask me any questions.

***

I wasn't allowed to remain unconscious for long. The cattle prod was systematically applied to my body until I was jolted back into nightmare reality by a series of carefully timed and carefully placed strikes. Then, once I began to respond, Park and Lee went about their work, and my brain continued to count. The few times that I would open my eyes and catch them in my field of vision, I noticed there was no emotion in their eyes or on their faces. They were utterly detached and merciless. I was a job to perform, a task to complete. Nothing more. As I fell into unconsciousness again, I wondered if they ever took a lunch or dinner break.

***

I was jarred into consciousness five more times and endured a total of 187 shocks from the cattle prod and 201 strikes from the whip. Apart from my grunts, the snap of the prod, and the crack of the whip on my skin, no other sounds were made in the room. There were no questions asked, no taunts vocalized, no threats made. But, given Cho's initial comments to me when I had been taken, I had no doubt the questions were imminent. My captors seemed to be waiting for something. Or someone.

During my periods of semi-consciousness, I could hear a TV on in the background. Maybe Cho had left the mic button on in the observation chamber. The TV was tuned to a cable news channel, and the newscaster was speaking English with a British accent. I was so far down inside myself as I attempted to deal with the pain, that it was difficult for my brain to concentrate on the words. But I heard a repeated storyline about a series of mysterious explosions in Seoul and the high levels of radiation detected at each site. Apparently, the city was on the edge of widespread panic, and martial law had been declared.

As my muddled mind coped with the implications of the story, a thought crept up inside of me. It ripped my feeble, remaining resistance into shreds. I hung my head as two words dug into my hope and my will: *You failed.*

CHAPTER TWENTY-TWO

Unknown Date
Unknown Time
Unknown Facility
People's Republic of North Korea

I was at the bottom of a deep, dark body of water. Above me, the surface was visible. I could see a dim, flickering light in the distance, refracted by small waves. Consciousness was up there, and for some reason, there was where I wanted to go.

There were no cattle prods or whips to encourage me to come to the surface this time. It was up to me. I mentally willed myself upward, but it was slow going. My mind was sluggish, and my will was nearly gone. I didn't see the point in fighting any longer, even though I didn't know exactly what I was resisting.

Suddenly, I felt a surprising sensation that yanked me to the surface of the imaginary pool quickly, although I kept my eyes closed, and my posture limp. I could feel a hard stream of water directed between my buttocks and down my legs. It took me a moment to understand what was happening, but when the odor of my own shit hit my nostrils, I comprehended. Apparently, I had involuntarily defecated while I was unconscious this last time, and I was being cleaned. The process was a simple one since I was naked and hanging over a cement floor with a drain. In another lifetime, I might have been embarrassed at my predicament. But instead, I felt a tired smile etch its way onto my lips. It seemed that my tormentors didn't like the smell of shit while they were doing their work. I wondered if I could force myself to defecate a few more times while they were beating me.

"Not so fucking tough now, are you?"

The cold female voice violated my ears and invaded my brain. It took me a few moments to identify it, but when I did, I was more shocked than angry.

Rowe? My mind struggled to climb into a more coherent place and consider the reality of her presence in the room.

It doesn't make sense. Brenda, how could you still be here? How can the jet still be here?

"He's not coming around, Cho," she said. "It's time. We'll be leaving soon. I need him to answer some questions."

"He is conscious," Cho said. "He pretends not to be."

"How do you know that? You and your people have beaten the shit out of him. Our agreement was that I get what I need first, and you get to keep him. If you've left him unable to speak, I'll have words with your father, the Minister."

Suddenly, the reasons for the lack of questions before now became clear. They were softening me up. Getting me ready.

"He is conscious," Cho said, with a slight edge in his normally polite voice. "Lee!" he commanded.

A sharp blow landed on the right side of my lower back, and my right kidney erupted in a torrent of pain that ran through my body like 20,000 volts of electricity. I didn't know whether I wanted to scream or cry, but the pain was so intense I could do neither.

My eyes sprang open to see Brenda Rowe standing before me with a crooked smile of triumph on her ashen face. She was dressed in the ever-present black business suit, draped on her featureless frame like a dust blanket thrown over a piece of old furniture.

Captain Cho stood next to her, his uniform crisply pressed, his shoes brightly shined, and an inscrutable smile on his face. "Colonel Pearce," he said. "Good to have you with us again."

"Wish...I...could...say...the same, Captain," I replied between gasps as I tried to recover my breath.

He smiled at me and nodded slightly in acknowledgment. "It is good that you can remain polite in these circumstances," he said.

I nodded and coughed. A spasm of pain struck my body and brought tears to my eyes. I blinked hard and forced it down. Then I opened my eyes and looked at him.

"We're both soldiers, Captain," I said. "You're just doing your job here. Your duty to your country. I respect that." Then I inclined my head towards Rowe. "But that bitch is committing high treason. She won't get any respect from me at all."

Rowe's jaw dropped open, and she looked at Cho and then at me and then back to Cho. The unspoken outrage was palpable. Cho hesitated for a moment and then uttered a command to one of his men.

A millisecond later, the whip landed on my bare buttocks and upper legs, digging into nerves that were fresh and unjaded. My pain receptors went into overdrive with the sting of the whip's multiple thongs as they tore into my flesh and wrapped around my upper legs. It was everything I could do to keep my mouth shut. I knew that eventually, I'd reach a point where I'd scream or curse or maybe even cry. But I decided I would die before I allowed that to happen around Rowe.

As my eyes refocused, I looked at Rowe. Her eyes were distant and shiny, and her lips were slightly parted – like she was breathless. At that moment, all became clear.

You get off dominating men, don't you, Brenda? Why

doesn't that fucking surprise me?

Rowe pulled herself back into the moment and took a step forward. "I'm only going to ask you once," she said. "What does the CIA know?"

As the question came out of her mouth, a question of my own popped up in my brain – a question that should have occurred me long before this moment.

How do you know who I work for? How did Cho know who I work for?

I sighed in disappointment as the answer came to me. My mind went back to the feeling I had on Sarah's sofa, my realization that I had missed something when I had seen Lane and Rowe together that first time. I sighed in disappointment.

Damn, I thought. *Not him too.*

Cho must have given another command while I was contemplating Rowe's question. The cattle prod was jammed into my left armpit and actuated. I was taken unaware by the sudden attack and whistle of pain shot out from between my lips. I blinked back the sudden tears that welled up in my eyes. Then I raised my gaze to Rowe's face. Once again, she was looking at me, but her eyes weren't focused. Her step forward had turned her body to the right a bit, and she appeared in partial profile. I could see her blouse underneath the right lapel of her business jacket. Her right nipple was erect underneath the cotton material.

Jesus, I thought. *You are a sick bitch.*

I contemplated my options. Interrogations are tough to manage, particularly if you are on the receiving end and especially if you want to yield certain information. Years ago, as a cadet at the Air Force Academy, I had been taught how to endure and manipulate interrogations. That training had been reinforced by several real-world interrogations I had since then. The truth was, I wanted to tell Rowe everything I knew. I wanted her to know that the CIA was aware of her plans. I wanted to make her angry and force her hand.

But I had a problem. If I gave up the information too easily, if I didn't make them work for it, they wouldn't trust it. I would have to suffer some more.

Lucky. Fucking. Me.

I decided to start the proceedings at the logical place. "CIA?" I asked. "I don't know what you're talking about."

Rowe's eyes flashed with anger, but Cho nodded at my answer, and there might have been a slight smile on his inscrutable face. He nodded to his team of tormentors, and the interrogation began in earnest.

CHAPTER TWENTY-THREE

Unknown Date
Unknown Time
Unknown Facility
People's Republic of North Korea

I don't know how many hours it took them to get everything out of me that I wanted to give them. Time is difficult to judge when you're under constant assault. At one point, they tried to get me to provide the code to unlock my phone, and I gave it to them, but I didn't tell them about the pause that had to come between the third and fourth digits. After they tried to enter the code ten times, the phone went into a CIA-designed protection mode and appeared dead. That got me another beating, but it was worth it.

When it was over, I hung in my straps from the ceiling, naked, bruised, and bleeding, hoping I had given a decent performance of a man who told them everything he knew. It didn't require much acting on my part. There wasn't a nerve in my body that wasn't raw, and I ached in places I didn't even know existed.

I eyed Rowe through eyes that were half-open with fatigue and pain as she seemed to finalize her notes. Throughout the ordeal, she had prodded Cho with questions and had taken notes on her phone about every answer I had given. Some of the responses had taken longer than others.

Smart interrogators ask the same questions over and over, in different ways. Often, they'll change the line of questioning, dwell on a new topic for a bit, then rapidly circle back to previous topics to see if they can catch the respondent in a lie. Hence, to get trustworthy answers to questions, the process takes some time.

Rowe finished typing and put her phone in the side pocket of a business suit jacket. She lifted her eyes to mine and nodded in brutal satisfaction. Her lips were still parted, and her eyes were still shiny with arousal. I wondered if it had been an effort for her to concentrate on the answers I provided.

But there was something about the scenario that I told them about that didn't make sense. I needed an answer of my own.

When I flew the F-16 in Korea, many years ago, the war plan had called for us to spend the first several days of a no-notice war bombing the largest target set in North Korea, the hardened artillery sites or HARTs. The North Koreans had constructed an entire network of the sites, many of them built into the north side of mountains. The sites were constructed so that a gun or rocket launcher could be rolled out, fired, and rolled back into its refuge before counterbattery fire or air-strike missions could attack them. The largest weapons, the 170mm cannons and 240mm rocket launchers, could reach Seoul from their concealed positions and could put several projectiles on target with little or no warning. I knew that the NKs were using the radioactive waste Enteron was providing them to make some of the artillery shells 'dirty.' But I didn't understand why. And I didn't understand the timing.

I summoned the remaining energy I had in my body to ask the question. "I don't get it," I said. "Why would an American energy company want to start a war on the Korean Peninsula?

What do you possibly have to gain? I mean, sure they can pay you, but it's not like you can invest the money."

Rowe snorted and shook her head. "It's not about war," she said. "It's about business."

My hyper-fatigued mind didn't want to believe her, but there was something about the way she uttered the words that made me realize she was telling the truth.

Shit, I thought. *I've missed something.*

"Business?" I asked. "You're giving the North nuclear waste to put inside artillery shells to pummel Seoul with, and you're telling me it's about business?"

She nodded. "We haven't given them that much. Maybe a hundred and fifty pounds with the last shipment. Enough for..." She looked at Cho. "Thirty of the shells for that big gun? The 170 millimeter one?"

Cho nodded.

"And thirty shells in a campaign that will last a few weeks should do the trick."

"Trick?" I asked. "What trick?"

She paused for a moment, as if she was thinking about what to tell me, then shrugged. "I guess it doesn't matter," she said. "You won't live to tell anyone." She extended her neck forward, so she could watch me closely as she spoke.

"The North Koreans have already fired five radioactive artillery rounds on Seoul," she said. "Those in the South believe it is the work of a radical terrorist group, not the North."

I shook my head as she spoke. "But the South has radar. They can track the incoming shells with counterbattery radar. They'll know where the rounds are coming from."

Cho's mouth broadened into a Cheshire cat smile. "Not always. I have a brother in the South Korean Army. He works in the Joint Air Defense Command Center."

"Let me guess," I said tiredly. "That's the only place on

24/7 alert looking north."

Cho nodded. "We bought software from the Chinese that puts a virus into the system and allows my brother to blind it for brief periods while the rounds are in flight."

Cho's words were stirring memories from distant and deep portions of my brain. I had some knowledge of artillery from my days supporting the Army as a Forward Air Controller and flying the A-10. Artillery could be fired via high-angle or low-angle trajectories, depending on the distance from the gun to the target as well the obstacles in between.

"But that's high-angle fire," I said. "You'd have to keep the system down for several minutes."

Cho shrugged. "Only on certain azimuths and below certain altitudes. He doesn't have to blind the entire system. Just a portion of it."

"Jesus," I said. "The explosions just happen. And no one knows why. And no one can do anything about them."

"That's not the best part," Rowe said. "There is no team of operatives to be captured, and the explosions are happening randomly throughout the city with no warning. We're contaminating and isolating portions of the city, crippling infrastructure and transportation. And when they bring the experts in to do the analysis, they find a radioactive signature that is not North Korean. The areas that are rendered radioactive appear to have been contaminated by a terrorist group with access to western materials."

I nodded in comprehension. It was classic terrorism. "So, when is the uprising?" I asked.

"Already in progress," Rowe said. "By the opposition faction. The group that lost the last election. They're not only more friendly to the North, but will cede a controlling interest of South Korea's Hydro and Nuclear power company to Enteron as well as expand the role of nuclear power in South Korea over the next century." Her eyes took on a wistful look, and I could see the lust for power seep into them. "That will more than double our nuclear generation capacity and make us the second-largest nuclear operator in the world." She rubbed the palms of her hands across each other in anticipation. "Our stock will go crazy." She seemed to gather herself and looked at me with an expression of mock pity on her face. "Too bad you won't own any."

I allowed myself a tired smile. "Given what I've seen, I wouldn't buy any if I could."

Rowe's eyes twinkled, and she smiled back at me but said nothing in response. Instead, she walked up to me and reached down to cup my genitalia in her right hand. She looked over at Cho. "Any chance I can have these as a trophy?"

Cho's eyes flashed and he shook his head rapidly. "No," he said. "We must deliver him intact. Those were the conditions of the deal. Hopefully, they will not be too angry at what we have already done. My country can do much with the 15 million US dollars that the drug cartel will pay for his bounty."

Damn, I thought. *My latest exploits in Mexico must have pissed some people off.*

Rowe squeezed me gently and then released me. "Too bad," she said. "I'd get them bronzed and put them on my bookshelf as a warning to others."

Of course, you would.

Rowe stepped away and gathered her purse and coat off of the table. "Is the van waiting for me outside?" she asked Cho.

He nodded. "Just outside the door. Your aircraft just landed. The driver will take you down to the ramp where it is parked."

I was stunned. We had never left the airport. The thought that there was a U.S. jet, let alone a familiar one, so close by was almost more than I could take. I allowed my head to fall, and I contemplated the cement floor below my feet.

"Goodbye, Pearce," Rowe said as she opened the door.

"I'll give your regards to that back-stabbing bitch and her little brats."

Deep inside of me, the Darkness awoke and tried to energize me to action. Years ago, I had broken free of my bonds and killed a guard when it had been triggered at close range. But my body was too bruised; my will was too broken.

I managed to raise my head and look at her. "What goes around comes around," I said. "At some point, all of this shit will catch up with you, Brenda. And it will be your turn to suffer. When that time comes, remember this moment. And be glad you're not at my hands."

She shrugged and walked out of the door.

I turned my eyes to Cho. "How long until they get here?" I asked.

He looked down at his watch. "Their plane lands in thirty minutes," he said. "We must get you ready for them."

As Park and Lee lowered to me to the cement floor a few minutes later, I should have been grateful. But instead, all I felt was dread. I was leaving the room in which I had endured the most brutal torture of my life. But it would be nothing compared to what I would suffer at the hands of my new captors.

CHAPTER TWENTY-FOUR

Monday, January 18th
1330 Hours Local Time
Transient Ramp
Pyongyang Sunan International Airport (ZKPY)
Pyongyang, People's Republic of North Korea

It was another dark and gloomy day in North Korea. As I looked out of the SUV's windows, I felt like the dismal surroundings were a reflection of my soul.

To say my prospects were bleak was an understatement. I was on my way to a place on the other side of the world where I would be tied down, tortured, and abused to an extent far beyond what I had just experienced. I would be kept alive by artificial means for as long as my body would survive the brutality that could be inflicted upon it. I would be beaten, cut, burned, and maimed, and God knew what else. The work would be done slowly, excruciatingly, by someone who enjoyed their work and would be under strict orders to keep me alive and aware for as long as possible.

And throughout the ordeal, my captors would taunt me with the only release, the only freedom possible from my gruesome situation. Death.

They would make me bargain for it, plead for it, and even

beg for it. They would take joy in promising it to me, only to deny it.

I wasn't afraid of death. I had made my peace with it long ago. I had been living on borrowed time since I was shot down and captured in Iraq, over 25 years ago. It was the torture I feared, not for the pain alone, but for what I would reveal in the process. I didn't want to tell my captors about Sarah and my kids, because I knew what would happen to them if I did. But I would. Everyone breaks under torture. It's just a question of time.

I needed to find a way to kill myself. I had to die before I could betray the only thing in the world that mattered to me. Before I could compromise the only true innocence I had ever known or seen.

The SUV stopped mere feet from where it, or a clone of it, had picked me up before. I glanced down at the watch that had been replaced on my wrist. I stared at the time and date in disbelief as we drove. Barely three days had passed since I arrived. It had seemed like weeks.

I raised my eyes to look outside the vehicle. A low overcast of thick clouds darkened the sky and made the atmosphere feel like dusk, rather than early afternoon. The sound of a jet engine going into reverse thrust caught my attention, and I looked at the runway to my right. A Falcon 2000 with Mexican registration rolled past, decelerating to make the turnoff further down the runway.

My chariot to the underworld had arrived.

I hung my head and waited for it to arrive on the ramp, mentally tracking its progress toward me by the sound of the engines. I briefly considered making a break for it, but the driver and his colleague in the front seat were both armed, as was Cho, who was seated next to me. I looked over at him, and his normally inscrutable expression was gone. He was smiling and beaming. He had gotten everything he wanted.

He had spent several days torturing an American, and now he got to hand that American over for $15 million.

"Is it worth it?" The words popped out of my mouth without my willing them.

Cho's expression deteriorated into a half-smile. "I beg your pardon?"

I smiled tiredly. Always the gentlemen. Even when he was playing the role of Torquemada. "The 15 million. Is that worth not having an American around to continue the torture for the next several days or months?"

He shrugged. "I will not deny, torturing you would have been enjoyable to me, but trading you is much better for my country. We are in desperate need for hard currency. Besides," he turned to me as the full smile had returned to his face, "bringing in 15 million American dollars will probably result in my promotion in the Army and in the Party."

I nodded. "Everything has a price," I said.

The noise of the Falcon's jet engines was getting louder, an inexorable reminder of my fate and my doom. I never thought there would be a time in my life where I'd dread the sound of a jet engine or the sight of an approaching aircraft, but that day had arrived.

But then, the oddest thing happened.

The jet engine noise was eclipsed by the noise of another Army SUV. It roared across the ramp and came to a sudden stop to our left. As soon as it halted, both front doors opened, and the soldier in the passenger seat jumped out. He pulled the rear door open on his side and stood stiffly at attention.

Cho's head snapped to the left, and even from my limited viewing angle, I could see his eyes widen. He snapped a question at the men in the front seat. From their response, I could tell they answered negatively. It seemed the visitor was unexpected. Cho uttered something under his breath.

As I watched, an older man exited the rear seat of the other

SUV and made his way towards us. I wasn't familiar with North Korean Army rank insignia, but the man's shoulder boards had stars on them. I nodded in comprehension. He was a general.

What the fuck? I thought to myself.

As the General approached the side of the vehicle, he motioned to Cho impatiently. Cho glanced back at me. Then he opened his door and exited the car. A rapid-fire exchange in Korean occurred between him and the General. Cho stiffened like he was being scolded.

The General motioned again. The driver and his colleague jumped out of the front seat like their seats had been electrified. I grinned in spite of myself as I remembered the cattle prod's effect on me. But then I grimaced involuntarily as I remembered the pain. The two soldiers swiftly moved to stand alongside Cho, and they assumed the position of attention. The General nodded at them and returned his gaze to Cho. He asked Cho a series of questions and Cho answered, nodding to the back of our vehicle as he spoke. The General then issued a command to one of the soldiers. The soldier practically ran to the rear of our SUV and opened the hatchback. I glanced behind me and saw that he was digging into a suitcase. My suitcase.

As the questions started flooding into my mind, I felt a weight on the seat next to me and saw that the General had joined me in the back of the vehicle. He had closely cropped gray hair and a tired expression on his face, but he seemed fit and aware.

He nodded at me. "You are Colonel Colin Pearce," he said in heavily accented English.

I nodded back. "Yes, I am General."

He produced a small knife and reached across to my hands and cut the flex tie binding my wrists together. I looked down at my wrists, then I looked across at him. My mouth dropped open in disbelief.

Before I could utter a word, he spoke. "Tomorrow evening at 2000 hours local time, the final shipment of material from will be moved from here to the artillery batteries north of Kaesong," the General said. "Your phone will be on that truck. The truck must be destroyed before it reaches its destination."

I stared at him and remained silent.

"You must destroy it." He spoke slowly, like he was explaining things to a child. "You must bomb it. But you must use something that cannot be traced back to America or the West."

I nodded at him in comprehension of what he was saying, but my mind was too tired and too cluttered to understand how it could be done.

The General shook his head impatiently. "Go to Osan. Go to Kunsan. Use one of your F-16 fighters. You fly the F-16, yes?"

I nodded at him again, my head moving languidly as my mind considered his words. "But...how?"

"If you were attacking a target in the southwest side of my country, what direction would you attack from?"

For a fleeting moment, I wondered whether the General might be using the conversation to probe the weaknesses in American air defense or to reveal the secrets of the war plan against his own country. But his eyes were earnest and his expression intense.

I spoke without willing my mouth to operate. "From the southwest. From over the Yellow Sea."

The General nodded. "Not from the direction of Inchon Airport. We watch airport very close."

"Makes sense," I said.

"I come from infantry," the General continued, "so I do not know air defense. But I know our radar is not good for low altitude. We do not see things sometimes. Even over the sea."

I nodded as my knowledge of basic radar detection emerged in my mind. Even in my fatigued state, given the era of most of North Korea's military apparatus, I could see a few reasons why that could be true.

The General was watching me closely as I processed what he had said.

"Low altitude?" I asked at last. "How low?"

The General shrugged. "Very low."

"Okay," I said. "I think I can do that."

The General nodded slowly in response. "Johseubnida," he said with an audible sigh of relief. "Aju joh-a."

I looked at him with an expression of non-comprehension.

"All is good," he said. "Very good." Then he turned his gaze to me, and his eyes took on the look of a commander who is about to order his troops into battle. "You must succeed," he said. "For both of our countries."

I shook my head at him. "I don't understand. Why don't you want this?" I asked. "If an opposition faction that is friendly to the North assumes power in the South, your two countries would finally have peace."

The general smiled sadly. "There can be no peace. With peace, our people would become aware of the prosperity in the south. There would be a national outcry. There would be a mass revolt. Our country would tear itself apart. Do you not see that?"

I nodded, but I was still lost about the current circumstances. The Falcon's jet engine was getting louder. I didn't have much time for increased understanding.

"But why are we here? How did all of this happen?" I asked.

The General shrugged. "Cho's father is a powerful minister. He has many with him. It was he who invited the American company into our country and convinced the Young Leader to allow it. But the Young Leader can be naïve sometimes. He did not understand the minister's full intentions."

Some of the pieces of the puzzle began assembling in my mind. "It's a coup attempt," I said as I shook my head in realization. "It's subtle. It's brilliant. Cho's group takes credit for harassing the South and embarrassing the West. And in the process, they set themselves up to depose your Leader, put themselves into power, and get rich."

The General nodded. "Even now, they are positioning to do that. But the Young Leader and we who support him are now aware of the ultimate plan and will not allow it. If you do not succeed, there will be civil war. There will be uncertainty. Control of our weapons of mass destruction could be lost. And," he looked at me with a grave expression on his face, "if control is lost, those weapons could be launched by those who are no longer held accountable. Many may die. On both sides and even in areas of your country." He leaned forward in earnest. "That is why you must succeed. Cho's father will lose face. He will be vulnerable. We can deal with him. Only then will the random artillery attacks against the South cease."

I nodded and looked hard at him. "If I hit a truck full of nuclear waste, it will have consequences. I'm not an expert, but it will be very dirty. Very radioactive. And it might stay that way for a long time."

The General shrugged. "We will send the truck on the coastal road. It is not very populated there." He looked back at me. "It must be done."

I nodded again and turned my head to watch the Falcon 2000LXS as it pulled up next to the car, marshaled into position by an airport worker in a green vest. It was white with green and blue stripes. The registration was XB-LDC.

"Mexican," I said under my breath. "Los Diablos Cartel. Jesus." I looked at the General. "I'm with you," I said. I inclined my head towards the jet. "But what about them?"

The General smiled. "We will take their money, of course.

And then we will send you upon them."

I shook my head. "General, after what Cho's boys did to me, I'm not in shape to do much of anything."

He nodded, and his mouth turned down. "You have my apology and the apology of my country for your ordeal. If we had been aware of it earlier, we would have stopped it. But we have some...expertise at returning people to duty after they have been...treated harshly. One of my men is a medic. He has medicines with him that will help you."

I smiled at him and nodded. "I have some experience engaging the bad guys with performance-enhancing drugs in my system," I said. "Let's do this."

CHAPTER TWENTY-FIVE

Monday, January 18th
1400 Hours Local Time
Transient Ramp
Pyongyang Sunan International Airport (ZKPY)
Pyongyang, People's Republic of North Korea

I ascended the Falcon's airstair with my head hung in resignation, and my hands bound behind my back. Thanks to the injection I had been given in the car, the climb was easier than I was making it look.

I had no idea what drug the North Korean medic had given me, but the effect was exquisite. It was like the damage that had been done to my body was detached from me somehow. It was still there. I was conscious of it. I just didn't feel it. There was a stimulant effect as well. I could feel my heart beating faster, and the blood coursing through my veins. The lack of pain and renewed energy had an additional effect. The Darkness had awakened, and after being beaten into submission by the torture session we had endured, it was ready to exact vengeance.

As I slowly made my way up into the airplane, I raised my head and saw a burly Mexican guard standing just inside the aircraft door, in the galley. He had a swarthy complexion and greasy black hair. Like many of his kind whom I had encountered, he had a visage from Mexican gangster central casting, with sharp features, and intense dark eyes with teardrop tattoos next to them.

"Buenos Dias Senor Pearce," he said as I approached him. "The Boss, he will be expecting you."

"He flew all this way just to pick me up?" I asked.

The guard shook his head. "No, the Boss, he will be waiting when we land. He inclined his head to the left. "Pedro and I, we will keep you company until we get there."

"It's a long flight back to Mexico," I said. "And there's got to be at least one fuel stop. "So, I guess it's you, me, Pedro, and the two pilots in the jet for what, sixteen hours?"

The guard nodded. "Si," he said. "And we will get to know each other very well."

I shook my head. "I don't think so," I said. My left foot reached the top of the airstair, and I freed my hands from the fake bindings behind my back, raising the Colt .45 commander to eye level.

It took the Mexican a moment to process what was happening. That hesitation cost him his life. The Darkness pulled the trigger twice and put two bullets into the center of his forehead, the twin "pops" of the suppressed weapon barely audible over the loud whine of the Falcon's APU. He fell back against the wooden cabinetry of the jet's galley and slowly slid down to the vestibule floor.

I stepped inside the jet quickly, pushing him aside as I went back into the passenger cabin.

It was empty. As I looked to the rear of the cabin, I could see the lavatory door was closed. I nodded to myself. Apparently, Pedro had some physiological needs to deal with.

I turned and stepped forward to the cockpit. The two pilots were still busy reprogramming the jet for the next leg and had not noticed the dead man lying just aft of them. Using my left hand, I hit the switch on the left panel just aft of the cockpit to raise the passenger door. The hydraulic pump whined, and the door climbed upward. As soon as it reached the top position, I pulled it closed and lowered the handle to lock it into place.

The pilots were still engrossed in their duties. I glanced aft. Pedro was still in the lavatory. I ejected the magazine from my weapon and checked it. Five rounds remaining, plus one in the chamber. The General or his men had been nice enough to ensure my weapon was fully charged.

I had three people left to deal with. At the moment, none of them was a threat. But I had to commandeer the jet and fly it to South Korea, and I couldn't do that with a non-cooperative crew. A flash of guilt went through me. These guys were pilots, crew members, just like I was. It didn't seem fair that they might have to pay with their lives for being at the wrong place at the wrong time.

They made their choice, the Darkness said. And I found that I agreed. They had joined the employ of a ruthless drug lord. It seemed a good bet that I wasn't the first 'prisoner' they had transported to their boss for torture or even death. Regardless, they had to be aware of the cartel's brutality.

Oh well, I thought.

I raised the .45 and shot the pilot in the left seat twice in the back of the head. The impacts drove his body outboard, and he collapsed against the left side window. With the external door closed and the whine of the APU isolated outside the jet, the two reports of the suppressed .45 were clearly audible in the enclosed space. The pilot in the right seat startled at the sound. He turned and looked up at me, raising his hands in surrender. But then he saw my face, and I saw an angry sneer form on his lips.

"Thanks," I said, and the Darkness shot him twice in the face. His head snapped back with the impacts, but then as life left his body, he slumped towards me. I knelt down to catch him before he fell onto the pedestal.

That action saved me.

As I knelt, I heard two pistol shots and two bullets smacked into the wood veneer just above my head.

Pedro, I thought. *Goddamn it!*

I let the co-pilot's body fall and pushed myself backward, into the alcove with the external door. As I fell, I fired my remaining two shots down the Falcon's aisle, hoping I'd catch Pedro with at least one of the bullets. The .45's slide locked open, a clearly visible indication that I was out of ammunition.

"Fuck!" I said under my breath. The General's men had retrieved my pistol from my luggage before my bag had been stowed aboard the Falcon, but they had only provided me with the one magazine in the weapon. I glanced across the vestibule at the dead guard. His outer shirt had fallen open as he had slid to the floor and I could see the dark shape of a weapon on his right hip – about 18 inches out of my reach.

In the cabin, to my right, there was silence. I could hear the faint whine of the APU through the external door behind me, but I could hear nothing in the cabin. More importantly, I couldn't feel the movement of the jet on its landing gear when a person walked around in the back of the aircraft. For the moment, Pedro seemed to be still. Waiting.

The dead guard's legs were alongside me. I looked down at his shoe and had a flash of inspiration. I gently removed the shoes, pulling them off the inert feet one at a time and setting them on my lap. The leather from the shoes felt soft and rich in my hands. I glanced down to see the label - Ferragamo.

Why am I not surprised? I thought.

I listened again for any movement in the cabin and was rewarded with continued silence.

Now or never.

I cocked my left arm and threw one shoe down the aisle. I waited for a fraction of a second, launched the second one down the aisle, and catapulted myself across the narrow space. My left hand found the guard's pistol and yanked it from its holster. The width and texture of the grip made me think it was a Glock of some sort. I pulled it out from under the guard's shirt and verified the make and model. It was a Glock 21, full-sized .45 ACP. The weapon's weight told me it was loaded, probably with a full magazine of 13 rounds. I didn't like Glocks, but I knew them well. I tossed the gun to my right hand and pivoted the barrel down the aisle of the passenger cabin, turning my head to follow the weapon.

But I was too late.

"Detener!" A voice commanded in Spanish. "Ne te meuvas!"

My Spanish was rusty, but the intent of the commands was clear enough. I was being commanded to freeze. I looked down the aisle to see a man concealed behind the lavatory door, just over twenty feet away, with another Glock pistol in his hand. The gun was trained on me, and the hand was steady. I gave some thought to firing a few rounds through the door at him. Still, I wasn't sure that my rounds would penetrate the door, and my shots would only invite return fire which would either hit me or cockpit instrumentation behind me. Neither was a desirable option. Then I noticed the red glow of a laser coming from just beneath the barrel of his weapon and glanced down at my chest to see the telltale red dot of the designated impact point on the center of my chest.

He had me. For the moment, at least. I wondered why hadn't he fired? But I knew the answer to that question. Someone had to fly the plane. I did my best to keep a smile off my face as I realized the possibilities.

I put my index finger on the outside of the Glock's trigger guard, turned the weapon sideways to my assailant, and carefully placed it on the floor in front of me. Then I put my hands on my head and interlaced my fingers.

Pedro emerged from the lavatory immediately, a triumphant smile on his swarthy features. He was a big man, well over six feet tall with broad shoulders. He wore a tight polo shirt that could barely contain his sinewy upper body; a body that was clearly the product of many hours spent in the gym pushing heavy iron. He advanced towards me with his gun still trained on my chest, crossing the twenty feet between us in seconds, moving very nimbly despite his size.

He squatted down in front of me and retrieved his comrade's weapon, keeping his eyes and pistol focused on me as he performed the task. Then he uttered two words in barely understandable English.

"You!" he said. "Cockpit!"

Moments later, the bodies had been dragged through the cabin to the baggage area, and I was ensconced in the cockpit. I strapped into the left seat. Pedro kept his distance and stood in the vestibule behind me.

All the better, I thought.

I had received a type-rating in the new generation Falcon 2000 several years ago but had never flown an aircraft requiring that qualification. My rusty knowledge of the jet was mitigated by the fact that the 2000 LXS and the 7X shared the same cockpit layout, Dassault's Enhanced Avionics System or EASy. All the displays, controls, and menus were almost identical between the two jets. I had the flight plan loaded in five minutes, and the preflight checks accomplished in another five. Shortly after that, I was taxing for takeoff.

It was only about half a mile to the approach end of the runway, and it was everything I could do to keep the Falcon's taxi speed under 25 knots. I couldn't get out of here fast enough. I ran the taxi checklist, confirmed the departure procedure and subsequent routing. Then, I checked my progress to the end of the runway, and once again took in my dismal surroundings. The cloud layer had thinned and allowed more of the sun's rays to penetrate it, casting indirect illumination on the dreary features around the airport. The rice patties in front of me looked dull and deserted. The buildings down the left side of the taxiway, outside of the airfield fence, appeared abused, abandoned, and beaten up.

The state of the buildings reminded me of the state of my body. It too had been abused and beaten up, although I didn't feel it at the moment. I wondered how I'd feel when the drugs wore off and how I'd be able to finish the chores in front of me.

The to-do list was intimidating. My mind was churning with options to accomplish the task the General had given me. He was right. I'd have to use a Viper. The USAF had more of them in Korea than any other type of aircraft. They were stationed at two bases, Osan, about 25 miles south of Seoul, and Kunsan, which was another 75 miles south. I'd have to get the jet from Kunsan. Osan had too much visibility, especially with the 7th Air Force, the Korean USAF headquarters there. Kunsan was more remote and isolated. There was a time when I had known the base well. I had spent 19 months of my life there from late 1995 to mid-1997. I wondered how much the place had changed.

"Xray Bravo Lima Delta Charlie," said a heavily accented voice in my headset. "You cleared for takeoff. You fly runway heading to ten-thousand."

"Xray Bravo Lima Delta Charlie copies cleared for takeoff," I acknowledged. "Runway heading to ten thousand." It seemed they only used the first team of English-speaking controllers for the important American visitors.

I ran the before-takeoff checklist and ensured the Falcon was appropriately configured for takeoff as I taxied us onto runway 35. Then, without stopping the jet, I smoothly pushed the throttles forward about two-thirds of the way to max thrust and waited for the engines to stabilize. The turbine or N1 RPM indicators smartly rotated to the 11 o'clock position on the virtual gauges and stopped. I nodded to myself and advanced the throttles all the way forward. The Falcon accelerated forward like a thoroughbred horse that had been nudged in the ribs.

I nodded to myself and ensured my left hand was on the tiller as we moved down the runway. Unlike the 7X, the 2000 had a tiller, a smaller circular control wheel on the left console, to steer the nosewheel during the takeoff roll. I kept my left hand on the tiller until the jet reached 80 knots. Then I put my hand on the yoke and waited for the airspeed to increase. The thrust from the two Pratt and Whitney 308C engines pushed us forward rapidly. I glanced in the jet's Head-up Display and saw the airspeed karat pass 123 knots.

"V1," I said to myself as I removed my right hand from the throttles and placed it on the yoke.

We reached rotation speed a few moments later, and I gently pulled the yoke towards me, using the pull-up cue in the HUD at my guide. The Falcon's nose pitched crisply. For a second or two, the jet maintained the takeoff attitude as it continued to accelerate. I continued the backpressure on the yoke until the bottom end of the pull-up cue, a horizontal line, was superimposed on the zero-pitch reference on the HUD. Almost as soon as the nose stabilized, the jet's main gear left the runway, and we flew into the dismal gray sky.

I verified that the altimeter was increasing and that the vertical velocity indication was positive.

"Positive rate," I said to myself. "Gear up."

I reached across the cockpit with my right hand and raised the landing gear handle. The gear came up normally, thumping into the retracted position. The cockpit quieted as the nose gear doors closed and the air-noise of three vertical drag-inducing landing gear struts was removed from the airstream. I superimposed the flight path marker in the HUD over the steering cue and monitored the airspeed while the jet climbed above the pre-preprogrammed takeoff safety altitude. Once we were 400 feet above ground level (AGL) and had accelerated past the minimum airspeed for flap retraction, I moved the flap lever to the retracted position.

It was then that the fact that I was alone in the cockpit struck me. Until that moment, I had been so engrossed in my tasks and so intent on getting off the ground that it had not occurred to me that I was operating a two-person aircraft by myself. In the last five years, nearly all of my flying had been single pilot. It seemed I was more used to flying an aircraft solo than with another crew member. I had barely noticed my lack of company.

Get used to it, I thought. *There's a hell of a single-ship, single-pilot mission in front of you.*

Ten minutes later, after a frequency change and a series of radar vectors, we were level at 15,000 feet and headed due west over the Yellow Sea. The autopilot was holding heading and altitude, and the autothrottle system was maintaining the commanded airspeed of 250 knots.

"Xray Bravo Lima Delta Charlie," said another heavily accented voice, "You contact Beijing on 128.9."

"Xray Bravo Lima Delta Charlie copies Beijing on 128.9," I replied.

I had no intention of talking to Beijing. We were going south.

I rotated the heading bug to 130 degrees, and the jet began a gentle turn to the left. My plan was to split the Yellow Sea between China and North Korea and continue south to Kunsan Airbase, which lay on the western coast of South Korea. I set 320 knots as the airspeed target for the autothrottle system. The jet accelerated rapidly, seemingly eager to stretch its legs at this altitude. I entered 121.5, the international emergency frequency, into the radio and waited. I needed to put some distance between us and North Korea before I contacted the

South, and I had another task to take care of in the interim.

I felt the jet shift a bit as Pedro left his seat in the rear of the jet and began to move forward. He wasn't a pilot, but he knew that south was the wrong direction. I nodded to myself. The time had come. I tightened my shoulder harness straps and seat belts down as far as they would go and waited to for him to come up behind me.

Most air travelers are naïve about the physics of an aircraft in flight. Aircraft are bodies in motion, like cars, but whereas cars only move in two-dimensional space, airplanes move in three. Yet, the same people who won't leave their driveways without buckling their seatbelts in their vehicles will routinely roam the cabin of an airliner in flight, blissfully unaware that they could be suddenly and violently thrown about in the cabin of the aircraft. Pedro was about to get a fatal lesson in three-dimensional physics.

As I sensed him move up behind me, I clicked off the autopilot and waited for him to get closer. He didn't keep me waiting.

"No go this way," he began. "We go…"

I didn't let him finish his sentence. I pushed forward on the yoke once, hard, taking the Falcon from +1 positive g to -1 negative g in a fraction of second. Then I eased the yoke back a bit to put the jet into zero-g flight for a just a moment before I pulled back on the yoke and took us from -1 g to +2.5 g's in another fraction of a second.

Pedro, all two-hundred-plus pounds of him, was flung against the ceiling in the vestibule like an oversized ragdoll. Then, after hanging in the air at zero-g for a moment, he was slammed into the floor of the vestibule like he had been slapped down by a giant hand.

I glanced behind me. He lay motionless on the vestibule floor. He was on his right side, facing the airstair door, but his face was turned towards me, demonstrating that his neck was at an impossible angle. The dark eyes were sightless.

"All too easy," I said to myself. I reached down to the control pad next to my knee and entered 7700, the international emergency code, into the transponder. Then I keyed the mic. "Any United States control agency, this is Tango-Charlie. I'm squawking emergency and need vectors into South Korean airspace."

The response came faster than I had anticipated.

"Tango-Charlie, Dragnet, radar contact. Contact Dragnet on 127.5 and squawk 3454."

Dragnet? I asked myself. *AWACS? Here? Now? Why?*

But I knew the answer. The explosions in the South had put the country into turmoil. The U.S military there was in high alert. Deploying an AWACS, the USAF's airborne warning and control system, a flying radar platform, to the region would have been a standard move. If the North came south, U.S. jets would be vectored to intercept by U.S. controllers. Little did they know the degree to which the North had problems of its own.

I entered the new code in the transponder and the new frequency into the radio. "Dragnet, Tango-Charlie on 127.5, squawking 3454."

"Tango Charlie, Dragnet, radar-contact. Turn left heading 180. Maintain one-five thousand."

"Left to 180, one-five, fifteen thousand, Tango-Charlie copies."

I set the heading bug to 180 degrees and began a gentle turn to the left as I leveled the jet back at 15,000 feet. Then, I engaged the autopilot and sat back in my seat.

"Tango-Charlie, this is Delta Sierra." The voice was new on the frequency, but it wasn't new to me. I knew it well, and I felt a lump occur in my throat for no particular reason.

"Delta-Sierra, Tango-Charlie. Good to hear your voice," I replied.

There was a pause for a moment, and then came the response. "Yours also Tango-Charlie," Dave Smith said. "We thought we had lost you."

I nodded, even though I knew he couldn't see me. "Makes two of us," I said.

There was another momentary pause, and then I heard Smith's voice again. "What do you need, T.C.?" he asked.

I keyed my mic. "How about a vector to Kunsan and I'll explain it there."

"Copy that, I'll meet you there myself. Handing you over now."

"Delta-Sierra, I need one more thing before you go."

"Copy T.C.," Smith said. "What's that?"

"I don't suppose you have a sanitation crew in-country?"

There was a quiet laugh across the airwaves.

"We never go anywhere without one," Smith said after a moment. "Especially with you around."

CHAPTER TWENTY-SIX

Monday, January 18th
1730 Hours Local Time
8th Fighter Wing Headquarters
Kunsan Air Base (RKJK), Republic of South Korea

I was standing in the lobby of the 8th Fighter Wing headquarters building looking at the rows of unit citations and patches. As I looked at the wall and re-read some of the unit's history, the memories from over 20 years ago came rushing back.

The 8th Fighter Wing, nicknamed the "Wolf Pack," had a storied history in the United States Air Force, beginning from before World War II. The wing was probably best known for its exploits in the skies over North Vietnam under its then Commander, Colonel Robin Olds, where it accumulated 38.5 MiG kills, more than any other wing in the Air Force. It was the charismatic Olds who first coined the "Wolf Pack" moniker during the Vietnam war, likening his fighter pilots to wolves because of their aggressiveness and teamwork. In 1974, the 8th Fighter Wing was transferred from Thailand to South Korea and had been there ever since.

Kunsan had been one of my best tours in the USAF. With the bad guys only 100 miles north, the teamwork and focus on the base was a refreshing break from the political correctness that had come to characterize the stateside USAF. I had enjoyed my time here, extending my one-year tour by seven months. I had been saddened to leave and had missed the place.

Smith stood in the lobby with me, but he wasn't looking at the unit memorabilia. Instead, he was looking at me. Regarding me. Assessing me. Finally, I turned to him.

"What?" I demanded.

"I talked to the doc about you after he did your exam, and you were getting a shower," he said. "You shouldn't be walking, let alone contemplating a flight in an F-16. The only thing keeping you going is the drugs. This is nuts. You need some rest, and we need to figure out another way to do this."

I shrugged. "We've been through this. There has to be plausible deniability for the U.S. and for the Air Force. It has to look like a rogue pilot thing, or it won't sell. Besides," I said, shaking my head and looking away from him, "I can sleep when I'm dead."

"That may come sooner than you want it to," Smith said.

"Thanks for that vote of confidence," I muttered.

"And speaking of death, why didn't they just kill you after you told them what they wanted to know?"

I laughed humorlessly. "In what has to be the height of irony, I actually owe my life to the contract on my head. It hasn't gone away and apparently is up to fifteen million U.S. dollars. The North Koreans, and in particular young Captain Cho, wanted to sell me to the Mexicans for the reward. They were under strict orders that I not be damaged 'too much' – whatever the fuck that means." I turned back to him. "That plane I flew in here, the one your crew took the bodies off of, was Mexican-registered and the markings were XB-LDC, the LDC standing for Los Diablos Cartel, of course."

"Jesus," Smith said. "I can't believe they're not all dead after what you did to them with that A-10 a few weeks ago.

You killed hundreds of them."

I nodded. "Which is probably why the contract went up another five million. It was ten when I was ambushed in Sedona."

"Who in the hell is calling the shots now?"

"Maybe it's Miguel's son, Mariano. I thought he was in the convoy I strafed. Maybe he survived somehow."

"Who knows."

"At some point, we're going to have to take direct action against those idiots. I can't keep looking over my shoulder for the rest of my life, and I can't keep risking the lives of Sarah and the kids."

My heart sank as I was reminded, again, that they were still missing. I had questioned Smith intently when he had met me in the clinic an hour ago, but he had no news.

"What's the status on the search warrant for Enteron's nuke plants?" I asked him.

Smith shrugged. "It's in front of a federal judge now," he said. "The trouble is we don't have much evidence other than you."

I nodded slowly. "Damn," I said.

"Gentlemen!" said a pert female voice. "I'm Colonel Jessica Tate. I'm the vice wing commander."

Smith and I turned to see a female colonel in crisply starched fatigues. She had blonde hair that was professionally pulled back behind her head and piercing blue eyes. She shook our hands, and we introduced ourselves. As my eyes met hers, I had a striking sense of familiarity about her, but I couldn't quite place it.

"The battle staff has been assembled," she said. "Please follow me."

Every front-line, combat-coded USAF wing had a "battle-staff," which consisted of the senior leadership needed to run the wing when it transitioned to a wartime footing. During my time in the USAF, I had seen them in Europe during the Cold War, and of course, here in Korea. Given the geopolitical nature of modern conflict, I wondered if Osan and Kunsan were the last two bases in the USAF where the term was used.

Tate turned and led us into a hallway to the right of the lobby and then up a flight of stairs. Even as pre-occupied and tired as I was, I couldn't help but notice the superb proportions of her body as she climbed in front of us. I glanced over at Smith and caught him watching me with a wry smile on his face and shaking his head.

We reached the top of the stairs, and she led us to the right, down a hallway with rows of photographs featuring the men and women of the 8th Fighter Wing as well as several of the standard USAF propaganda pictures. As we reached the end of the hallway, Tate motioned us through a door on the left side. We entered a large conference room, with a long, rectangular wooden table in the center, three rows of stadium seating surrounding three sides of the table, and an impressive presentation screen on the front wall. The room was nearly full to capacity. There were colonels seated at the table. Various other ranks were seated in the chairs around the room. All eyes were on Smith and me as we entered.

Tate closed the door behind us and hit a switch on a panel next to the viewing screen. A sign above the screen illuminated. TOP SECRET it said, in bold red letters.

"I hope that will suffice for the classification level?" she asked.

Smith nodded. "Close enough," he said.

A gray-haired colonel, seated at the head of the table, rose to his feet. "Gentlemen, I'm Dave Moody, the wing commander here. In a strange series of events, I get a call from the commander of PACAF, have a civilian aircraft land on my base that's full of dead people, and you two at my doorstep asking for an audience with me and my entire staff. To say that you have my attention would be putting it mildly." He sat down and looked at Smith and me intently.

Smith stepped forward. "Ladies and Gentlemen, my name is David Smith. I'm an operations officer with the CIA." I could see eyes widen throughout the room, and a rustle of curiosity went through the officers assembled. People leaned forward to look at Smith more closely. He nodded and gestured to me. "The gentleman accompanying me in the borrowed fatigues is Colin Pearce. He's a retired Air Force officer who works for us from time to time. He has an interesting story to tell you. He motioned for me to come forward. I walked to where he was, stood in front of the screen, and began to speak.

It took me about forty-five minutes to convey everything. I spent most of the time telling them what I had learned about the covert artillery bombardment and the intent behind it. I minimized details about the torture session, but when follow-up questions were asked about what the enemy might know, I had to tell the gathering about how I had provided that information deliberately to force the bad guys' hand. And how I had apparently failed because they didn't seem to care. There were several gasps around the room as I discussed some of the more gruesome highlights. Several times, as I spoke and looked about the room, I could feel Tate's gaze on me. Once or twice, I could see empathy in those piercing blue eyes.

When I related my interaction with the North Korean General, Moody perked up, as did the major in charge of Wing Intelligence. The major, a shorter man with a shiny bald head, asked me for a description of the General, which I provided. Then the major did something on an iPad in front of him and showed me a photograph.

"Is that the man you spoke with?"

I nodded. "That's him. He was fairly literate in English, but his accent made him difficult to understand."

The major sat back in his chair and nodded in return. He

looked down the table at Moody. "That's General Hur Myung-Dae," he said. "He went to college in the U.S., that's why he had the vocabulary. He's probably out of practice speaking English. He's the equivalent of our Chairman of the Joint Chiefs of Staff. If someone at that level says there's a power struggle going on in the North Korean upper echelons, the country could be in big trouble. We should alert 7th Air Force and PACAF. This is a big deal."

Moody nodded and looked at me. "What do you need from the Wolf Pack?" he asked.

Every eye in the room was on me, but I kept my gaze fixed on him. I could see the weight of the knowledge I provided on his shoulders. Every U.S. service member who is assigned for duty on the Korean Peninsula knows they might have to fight the ultimate battle there, but no one is eager for it because all are keenly aware of the potential cost. Especially those in command.

"I need to borrow one of your jets, Colonel," I said. "And there's a damn good chance I won't be bringing it back."

CHAPTER TWENTY-SEVEN

Monday, January 18th
2000 Hours Local Time
The Loring Club
Kunsan Air Base (RKJK), Republic of South Korea

I was seated at the bar in the all ranks club at Kunsan, finishing my first sit-down meal since the dinner in Alaska, which seemed like a million years ago. The Caesar salad was too creamy, like most of them are these days, but the New York Strip steak was well prepared, and the accompanying baked potato and sautéed asparagus were adequate. I found that I was impressed against my will. Not that the quality of the meal would have mattered much. I devoured it so quickly I had barely tasted it.

"Another martini, sir?" The Korean bartender was soft-spoken, polite, and proficient.

I pushed my empty glass towards him and nodded. "Just like the last one, please. It was excellent."

He nodded in modest acknowledgment and set about his task.

"Make that two, Kwan," said a voice to my left.

I turned toward the voice to see Colonel Dave Moody taking the seat next to me.

"Where's your friend from the Agency?" he asked as he settled himself.

I shrugged. "Off doing Agency things, I suppose," I said. "Seems like he had some weapons to order."

Moody nodded and leaned towards me, a conspiratorial smirk on his face. "Do you think they have a secret stash of those Russian bombs he mentioned nearby?"

I smiled tiredly and shook my head. "I don't know," I replied. "But after some of the shit I've seen since I started working with them, I'd believe anything."

There was silence for a few moments as Kwan made our martinis. I had to resort to Bombay Sapphire instead of my usual Plymouth tonight, but desperate times call for desperate measures. It was highly probable that tonight's drinks would be the last ones I'd ever have. Kwan poured the two martinis, pushed them across the surface of the bar to us, cleared my dinner dishes, and made himself scarce.

Moody and I lifted our martinis, clinked glasses, and took our first sips. It was he who spoke first.

"That's outstanding," he said. "And I'm not really a martini drinker."

"You should taste it with Plymouth gin," I said. "Particularly after it's spent a few hours in the freezer, and you don't have to shake it. It's even better."

Moody nodded and gazed into his martini for a few seconds. I took the time to get a good look at him, something I hadn't been able to do in the wing conference room with all of the people and questions. Moody was an inch or two shorter than I was and stocky in a muscular way. He had a boyish face, brown hair that was mostly gray and intense brown eyes. I knew that he was a pilot and had extensive time in the F-16, but rather than wear the typical flight suit, like most pilots, he wore fatigues, like the non-flying personnel. I liked that about him.

He caught me watching him and seemed to nod to himself. "I looked you up," he said.

I raised my eyebrows at him and said nothing.

"Not only your active duty file, although that was interesting reading in itself, but also the file you've accumulated since you retired."

I nodded, took a sip of my martini, and turned back to the bar. "I guess I didn't know I had another 'file' in the works."

"I'm not sure how official it is. There are a few offices in the Pentagon keeping track of you. One of them is the Joint Staff, where I used to work."

"Interesting," I said. "I wonder why."

Moody chuckled. "Well, if for no other reason, because you've becoming one of the highest-scoring jet aces in Air Force history!"

I turned to look at him. "What?" I asked.

Moody lifted his hands and began to count on his fingers. "Five F-16s back in 2009. Two F-35s, two Mig-31s, and two SU-27s in 2010. That's a total of eleven." He stopped counting on his fingers and looked at me intently.

I looked back at him blankly. I remembered every engagement and could still recall the details of each one. It had never occurred to me to count them.

Moody slapped his hands on his thighs and shook his head in disbelief. "You never did the math?" he asked.

I shrugged. "Never took the time to think about it."

He grinned at me and leaned back on his barstool. "Dude, you've got more jet kills than any modern ace in US history, and you're not too far away from the all-time total!"

I raised my glass in acknowledgment and turned back to the bar. Then, I took a long sip of my martini and let the icy gin dance across my tongue and ease its way down my throat as I pondered Moody's words. I was reminded of the discussion I had with Sarah on her sofa another million years ago. I hadn't counted the engagements for the same reason I hadn't counted the other deaths I had caused. I didn't want to know the total.

"I never thought about counting them because they didn't seem like events that should be quantified," I said. "Nearly all of them involved the death of another human being. And while some of them deserved to die more than others," I glanced over at Moody, "they all died at my hands. It doesn't seem like something to celebrate." I took another long sip of my drink and contemplated the next 24 hours. "Besides, it's probably not going to matter after tomorrow anyway."

Moody turned to the bar, and we sat in silence for a few moments, nursing our drinks. I glanced at our reflections in the mirror behind the bar. The place seemed to be empty except for the two of us. Moody was hunched over his drink and seemed to be lost in thought. I could see the tension in his shoulders. There was something else he needed to say. I wondered how long it would take him to get it out.

"Do you remember the Pueblo incident?" he asked at last.

I nodded. "I remember seeing reports about it on TV when it was happening," I said. "Since that time, I've read about it." I didn't mention that we'd seen the ship on our way into Pyongyang a few days ago.

"My dad was here then," Moody said, pointing down at the bar as he spoke. "Here at Kunsan. He was deployed here along with four other pilots and a four-ship of Thuds. They sat nuke alert at the facilities at the end of the runway."

I nodded. Thud was the nickname for the F-105 Thunderchief, a jet that was a legend during the Vietnam War. A huge single-engine jet designed for low-altitude nuclear bombing, it was one of the fastest aircraft the Air Force had ever operated.

"After the Pueblo was taken, it was moored in the harbor at Wonsan, on the northeast coast. Apparently, Johnson and

McNamara were considering a bombing raid on the harbor to destroy the boat. The jets they were going to use were the ones deployed here. My dad was in charge of the detachment and led the strike planning. The raid was a suicide mission. As the commander, my dad could have ordered the other four pilots to fly the mission and sat the strike out, but that's not who he was. He insisted on leading the strike and asked only for volunteers to go with him. All of the pilots volunteered to fly in the three remaining aircraft, one of which was a two-seater. They all signed up for a mission that they knew would get them captured or killed. Maybe both."

Moody shook his head in amazement and admiration. "It wasn't about the glory for them. It was about duty. It was about getting the job done." He looked over at me. "You remind me of them," he said.

I looked back at him and gave him a sardonic smile. "I hope you're not saying I'm old enough to be your dad," I said.

He laughed and shook his head again. "No," he said. "It's not about the vintage. It's about the attitude. You didn't ask about the cost or the odds of your mission. You just signed up to do what had to be done."

I nodded and exhaled softly. I could have told him about the $15 million price tag on my head and how I seemed to get everyone around me hurt or killed. I could have told him that I didn't particularly care about my own life. Instead, I raised my glass to his in grateful acknowledgment. "It's what I do," I said after we clinked glasses. "And I'm not sure why."

CHAPTER TWENTY-EIGHT

Monday, January 18th
2100 Hours Local Time
The Loring Club
Kunsan Air Base (RKJK), Republic of South Korea

Moody had left to attend to his wing commander duties, and I was left alone in the empty room. I was eying the row of bottles behind the bar and looking for a single-malt or five to finish the evening. As my eyes found the right place on the shelves, I regarded the selection and was impressed yet again. There were the requisite bottles of Glenlivet and Glenfiddich, of course, but there were also bottles of Macallan 12, Macallan 18, Glenmorangie 10, Glenmorangie 12 Lasanta, Dalwhinnie 15 and the Lagavulin 16. I had some good choices for what was likely to be my last taste of scotch whiskey on earth.

Like he had been summoned by my musings, Kwan appeared on the other side of the bar and looked at me with raised eyebrows.

"A scotch, sir?"

I nodded. "Lagavulin. A double. Neat, please."

Kwan poured a generous portion of the luscious stuff into a brandy sniffer and slid it across the bar's wooden surface to me.

"That's a nice pour. Thanks, Kwan."

He nodded in acknowledgment and replaced the bottle on the shelf. Then he discretely disappeared to wherever he had come from.

I lifted the glass and stuck my nose down inside the opening. Peaty single malts are definitely an acquired taste, but of all of them, Lagavulin is probably the most subtle and complex. While the nose is undeniably smoky, it's also redolent of sherry, creamy vanilla, and sweet spices. I took a long sip of the whiskey and let it slide across my tongue, relishing the multitude of flavors as the liquid flowed through my mouth. The palate was a massive mouthful of malt and sherry with a lot of sweetness, as well as the powerful taste of peat and oak. As I swallowed the whiskey, I marveled at its long, spicy finish, with flavors of figs, dates, vanilla, and the inevitable peat smoke.

I lowered the glass to the bar and stared into the dark amber depths, thankful for the passionate craftsmanship of those who had made the luscious stuff. I also found that I felt a bit melancholy at the thought that I might not be around to enjoy it after tomorrow night.

"May I join you?"

I started at the female voice and turned to my left to see a gorgeous blonde in a simple black dress seated on the next barstool, where Moody had sat previously. She had wavy hair that cascaded to her shoulders and piercing blue eyes. The dress looked like it could have been painted on her, and it showcased her figure in a way that would have increased the morale of the male service members on the base if she had appeared in public. It took me about a second too long to realize who she was. Colonel Jessica Tate, the vice wing commander.

She smiled as she saw the eventual recognition on my face.

"Surprised?" she asked.

The appearance of a beautiful woman lightens the heart of any man with an ounce of testosterone in his blood, and I was no exception. I smiled and nodded. "In a couple of ways," I said after a long moment. "You clean up pretty good."

She shrugged in response. "It's boring to be professional all the time. Sometimes, I just want to be a woman."

"Well, as a representative of the male gender, I can tell you that you've got that pretty well covered," I said.

Kwan magically reappeared on the other side of the bar. I was tempted to look for a teleportation device.

"Good evening, Colonel," he said. "What may I get you?"

"Glenmorangie 10, neat please," she said.

I nodded at her selection. "Colonel Tate, you are a woman who knows her single malt," I said. "I appreciate that."

Kwan rendered another generous pour for the colonel, replaced the bottle, and made himself scarce.

Tate took her glass and raised it as she turned to me. "My name is Jess. What would you like to drink to?"

I raised my own glass and shrugged. "I don't know, Jess," I replied. "Maybe something corny? Maybe to something like life and the joy of it?"

She smiled in response, but I saw a trace of sadness in her eyes. "I don't think that's corny at all," she said.

We clinked glasses and drank silently. As I put my glass back on the bar, I could feel her eyes on me, watching me closely. I turned back to her and searched her face. Her eyes retained the same hint of sadness, but they also seemed intensely curious. I was about to ask her what was on her mind, but she spoke first.

"I can see what she saw in you," Jess said, nodding to herself and taking another sip of her whiskey.

"I'm sorry?" I asked, my confusion evident. "What who saw in me?"

"When I met you in the hallway earlier, I knew you looked damn familiar, but when I heard your name, upstairs, in the conference room, I remembered who you were."

I looked back at her with a blank expression on my face.

"We've met before," Tate said. "But you probably don't remember. It was at a funeral. In Colorado. A little over five years ago."

My heart sank. I knew exactly what she was talking about. "Gail's funeral," I said, exhaling and shaking my head.

Gail Petersen, a USAF two-star general, had been the last relationship in my life. It had ended with her death on a chartered boat in Lake Tahoe, California, at the hands of a maniacal sniper. The time we had spent together had been light and fun. She had touched a place inside of me that I hadn't known was there. I still missed her.

"She was an amazing woman," I said. "I was lucky to know her." I retrieved my glass from the bar and took a long, slow slug of the Lagavulin, savoring the fire of the liquid as it went down inside of me. I averted my gaze from Tate and stared down into the glass that I held in my two hands. "And I got her killed," I said, barely able to keep the sudden emotion out of my voice.

Tate reached over and placed one of her hands on my forearm. I raised my eyes to hers and saw a compassionate expression on her face.

"You didn't kill her," she said. "The damn sniper did. And you took care of the sniper. Gail died serving her country. She would have wanted it that way."

"How do you..."

"I'm her cousin," Jess said, interrupting me. "We were both only children and our mothers were only a year apart, so we were like sisters and best friends combined. When she died, I was working at the DIA. I read all the reports."

I shook my head in amazement at her. "How is it that you don't hate me?"

Jess smiled. "Because I read the reports! And because of

the way Gail talked about you," she said. "She was completely smitten with you."

I nodded as I felt the sting of an expected tear in my right eye. "We were good together," I said. "I thought we could have made a go of it. But she was so damn focused on her job that she couldn't make time for us."

Jess nodded. "I told her she was screwing up. And I think she knew it. But I think her job so defined her that she couldn't remove herself from it. Not even enough to have a normal relationship."

I looked down at my glass. "The irony is that we had decided to call it quits when she came to Lake Tahoe," I said. "That was going to be our last time together."

"And that was why she came," Jess said, with an affectionate tone in her voice. "She wanted to be there with you."

I nodded slowly. "And it ended up getting her killed." I raised my eyes to hers. "Without trying to be impolite, can I ask why you're here?"

Jess put her glass on the bar and took the glass from my hands. Then, she rose from her stool and stepped across the narrow gap between us and encircled me with her arms, pressing herself against me. I could feel firm breasts and a highly toned body through the flimsy cloth of her dress. The intimate human contact was intoxicating after the days of torture. A sudden, powerful craving awoke within me. I reflexively wrapped my arms around her and pulled her to me more tightly, burying my face in her shoulder. We held each other for a long moment, and I felt some of the tension that had been living inside of me begin to slip away.

"I'm here to give you something I think you need," she whispered after several seconds, her mouth mere inches from my ear. "Something I think you need very badly."

"And what's that?" I asked. "Besides the obvious."

Jess gently moved her head back, raised my chin with her

left hand, and tenderly turned my face to hers so she could look directly into my eyes.

"What I think you need the most," she said with a soft voice. "Forgiveness."

***

About ten minutes later, we were in the foyer of her private quarters, locked in a passionate embrace. I tore at the buttons of my borrowed fatigue jacket, and she nearly ripped it from my body. The t-shirt came off next. I heard her gasp as the numerous bruises, scars and burn marks became visible.

"Sorry," I said. "They worked on me a little bit."

She nodded but said nothing. Then she lowered her head and began to gently kiss every mark on me, working her way down my torso, across it, and around it. She was slow, methodical, and impossibly tender. When she came to my beltline, she slowly unbuttoned my fatigue pants and pulled them down, along with my underwear. She continued kissing the scars and marks that she found, all the way down to my feet, which she revealed after pulling my boots off, one at a time. Then, she pushed my clothes away, and I stood naked before her.

I was struck by the contrast of the current moment and the moments of the last few days. When I was stripped before, I was powerless and helpless, an impersonal object of pain and torment. Now, it was like I had been re-endowed with my masculinity. I was naked in front of a beautiful woman who seemed to be healing my body, even worshipping it. The injection of testosterone into my blood was mind-altering. I felt powerful, invincible, and totally male. My penis was so hard it was throbbing.

Mere moments later, she pushed me onto her sofa, shed her dress, and straddled me. Then we were joined. At first, we moved slowly together, tentatively together, watching each other, looking into one another's eyes, searching for the corresponding fire we both knew was there. There were passionate kisses and long, soulful gazes, interspersed with ardent sighs, as our bodies discovered how to move as one. Soon, however, the sensation and desire began to build toward the inexorable climax.

Without warning, the orgasm brewing inside of me tore its way to the surface. I felt an overwhelming surge of excruciating pleasure and relief free me of the trouble, sadness, and apprehension circling within me. I erupted inside of her with repeated spasms that seemed to go on and on.

"Oh my God," Jess breathed. "I can feel you…" She pushed herself down onto me one last time. I felt her body shudder around me, even as she gripped my biceps tightly, almost painfully. She held herself there as the waves of pleasure passed through her body.

After a few moments, she threw her arms around me and buried her face in my shoulder as the tremors of passion slowly ebbed. We held each other like that for a long while, basking in the aftermath of the desire and the need and the union.

I wasn't sure where she was in the mental/ spiritual/ emotional/physical aspect of our union. For my own part, I felt that for once in my miserable life, the universe had blessed Colin Pearce. I felt my heart lighten about what lay ahead, and I smiled to myself as I felt Jess's breasts heaving against my chest.

I had always believed in the tag line that 'I'd rather be lucky than good.' Well, the universe had given me luck this night. And it felt liberating and wonderful.

It turned out that I would feel lucky a few more times that night. Sometimes, the universe can be quite generous.

Even to a condemned man.

CHAPTER TWENTY-NINE

Tuesday, January 19th
0630 Hours Local Time
Colonel Jessica Tate's Quarters
Kunsan Air Base (RKJK), Republic of South Korea

The buzzing of my newly-provided CIA iPhone aroused me from a pleasantly dreamless sleep. I slowly climbed the ladder back to consciousness, annoyed at the disturbance. I became aware of the feeling of Jessica Tate's body next to mine. She was sleeping on her right side, her left leg intertwined between mine, her left hand on my chest and her head on my shoulder. I smiled as I felt the gentle wind of her breath on my skin. It was a moment to relish and enjoy.

But the damn phone wouldn't stop buzzing.

Goddamn it! I thought. *Why the hell did I ever even bring it in here last night?*

Then I remembered getting up to pee in the wee hours of the morning and retrieving it from the pile of clothes in the foyer just in case.

And it seemed 'just in case' had occurred.

I reached over to the nightstand with my free hand and retrieved the phone. Then I moved the slide on the screen and raised the phone to my ear.

"Where are you?" Smith's voice was harsh and urgent in my ear.

I thought for a moment before I answered. Apparently, a moment was too long.

"You're not in your quarters," Smith said. "So, where the fuck are you?"

"Good morning to you too, Dave," I said. I looked over at the bedside clock, a small black box with large white characters. "Jesus, it's only six-thirty, Dave. What's going on?"

"The bombs are coming via a C-17 out of Guam," Smith said. "They'll be here in the early afternoon. In the meantime, Moody has called a planning meeting in the wing conference room at 0800. The 7th Air Force and PACAF staffs are going to attend via teleconference. You need to be there."

"Well, shit," I said. "Okay. I'll be there."

"So, you are on base. Somewhere."

"Yes, I am," I answered. I looked over at Jess's face as she blinked the sleep from her eyes. "And I even have transportation." I ended the call and replaced the phone on the nightstand.

"Wing HQ at eight?" Jess asked. Her voice was groggy, and she hadn't moved.

"Unfortunately, yes," I said.

Jess stroked my chest with her hand and nuzzled my neck with her face. Then, her hand proceeded down my abdomen. My body began to respond in typical fashion.

"That's a while from now, right?"

"Ninety minutes or so," I said.

"Then we have time," she said. Jess swung her leg over my hips and straddled me. Then her mouth came down on mine.

***

Jess and I walked into the wing conference room just

before the appointed time, freshly showered and probably still flushed from our encounter earlier that morning. The room was nearly full of senior officers and support staff. Moody was seated at the head of the table, with the chair designated for Jessica, as the vice wing commander, blatantly empty next to him. Smith was standing at the head of the table talking to Moody as we entered, explaining something to him as they looked at a piece of paper on the table in front of them. Smith raised his gaze from the paper as Jess and I entered. He looked at the two of us for a moment. Then, a droll smile etched its way onto his features. He caught my eye and shook his head in disbelief or amazement. It was hard to tell which.

"I'm here," I said as I approached him and Moody. "Where do you want me to sit?"

"You don't get to sit," Moody said. "You're leading the briefing."

I felt my eyebrows raise involuntarily. "Am I now?"

Moody nodded and gestured to Smith. "In about five hours, a C-17 will land with six Russian 500-pound incendiary bombs on it, courtesy of our friend here. You need to tell us how you're going to deliver them and accomplish your mission without starting a war."

"Who will be in attendance?" I asked.

"All of my senior staff, the battle-staff from 7th Air Force and the senior staff at PACAF Headquarters at Hickam."

I looked at Smith. "Isn't that a lot of people to get briefed on a need-to-know, top-secret mission?"

Smith shrugged. "I discussed that with Amrine and my superiors at the Agency. Given what could happen as a result of the strike, they decided all of the involved air commanders should be part of the brief and decision process."

"Decision process?" I asked. "What's to decide? If this doesn't happen, the bad guys win." I looked between Smith and Moody. "Weren't you two paying attention yesterday?"

They both nodded, but it was Smith who spoke. "We were. But this is big. Very big. And it could have worldwide consequences. We had to take this outside of black channels and go for approval from the Joint Chiefs and the President."

I thought for a moment and then nodded slowly. "Yeah," I said. "I guess that makes sense."

I heard the conference room door shut behind me. I turned to the main screen and saw two other conference rooms displayed, one at 7th Air Force Headquarters in Osan, about 75 miles to the north, and the other at Pacific Air Force Headquarters at Hickam Air Force Base in Hawaii, about 4,200 miles away. A banner appeared at the top of both screens, TOP SECRET.

"Connection is secure and good to go at all locations, Colonel Moody," said a voice over the room's intercom system. "We're ready."

"Ladies and gentlemen," Moody said. "Good morning or afternoon, depending on your location. Yesterday, we had a man land here in a hijacked business jet with," he glanced at me," four dead bodies on it?"

I shrugged in response.

"Since then, he's told us a fantastic story about a possible upheaval in the north, and how he thinks we can stop it. Given the possible implications, we felt it best that he relays the story himself." Moody gestured to me. "May I present retired Air Force Colonel Colin 'T.C.' Pearce."

Even across the encrypted airwaves from Osan and Hickam, the response from those gathered was obvious. There was an instant undercurrent of conversation at both locations and plenty of raised eyebrows to go along. I heard at least one exclamation of "*The* Colin Pearce?" Apparently, my reputation had proceeded me.

Great, I thought.

"Ladies and gentlemen," I began. "Yesterday, after a

weekend that was somewhat…eventful…I had a conversation with General Hur Myung-Dae, on the tarmac of the Pyongyang International Airport. He told me there was a significant internal struggle happening within the People's Republic. Specifically, a faction loyal to a powerful minister in the country named Cho is trying to incite unrest in the South so that the two countries might seek reunification. The faction is creating that unrest by anonymously lobbing artillery shells into Seoul that have been filled with nuclear waste provided by an American company named Enteron. Since the shells are detonating randomly and with no warning, the perception is that the government is not in control of the city. This is the scenario that has been unfolding over the last week or so. You probably thought it was some terrorist group. But it's been North Korea all along."

"That's impossible!" said a deep voice from Hickam. I looked at the screen. The camera had focused on a man with gray hair and two stars on each shoulder. "The back-azimuth radar would see it! I used to be in charge of those sites. Nothing would get past them. We would have known it was North Korea from the very beginning."

"Sadly, General," said a female voice from 7th Air Force, "it is possible." This speaker was a lieutenant colonel wearing a communications badge on the left breast of her fatigues. "The NKs were able to infect our consolidation and display software with a virus that can keep the computers from displaying certain inbound azimuth and altitudes for finite periods of time. Definitely long enough for the time-of-flight of an artillery shell, even in a high-angle trajectory."

"You mean the radar isn't seeing it? the two-star asked.

The female Lieutenant Colonel shook her head. "Not exactly, General," she said. "The radar sees it just fine. But the system isn't displaying it. So, no warnings or alerts are issued."

"Have you been able to get the virus out of the system?"

"Not yet, Bill," said a male voice from Osan. The camera focused on a three-star General with dark hair and dark eyes. There was only one three-star Air Force General on the Korean Peninsula – the 7th Air Force Commander. "The virus is pretty tenacious. It's got Chinese fingerprints all over it. The only good news is that we think it has to be locally activated. We've swapped out any radar surveillance staff who were on duty during the explosions as a precaution. Our cyber folks are continuing to work on it, but to scrub it might require us to shut the whole system down and re-boot it, which we obviously don't want to do given the circumstances."

"But we're good for the moment, right?" Another voice from Hickam. The camera pivoted to a man with four stars on each shoulder and the weight of responsibility on his face. He had brown hair streaked with gray and bright green eyes. "We don't need to mount any operation against the north. Especially something as foolhardy and what has been proposed."

"I don't know, General," said a female voice from Osan. This time, the camera there pivoted to a major with red hair and freckles. The name 'Brown' appeared on her nametag. "The unrest continues to grow in the South. There are riots in the streets in Seoul. The opposition faction is calling for a vote of no-confidence in the government. If that vote occurs, and the opposition wins, they'll immediately open arms to North Korea, and the scenario described by Colonel Pearce in the briefing material could come to pass."

"And that means the faction in the North that wants to depose Kim Jung Un would take over the NK government," I continued. "And the loyal faction will never allow that. That will bring civil war to the country along with the possibility that weapons could be launched as a result in the upheaval. If they launch weapons, we respond. If we respond, the Chinese and the Russians could get involved. You know where that story goes."

There was a moment of silence in both Osan and Hickam. After a long moment, the PACAF commander asked the obvious question. "Why do you think this information was is credible?"

I shrugged. "General, I was tortured for three days at the hands of Cho's son. I saw, firsthand, the involvement of an American Fortune 100 company. One of its senior executives, who was convinced I was going to die, verified the plan. If nothing else, Enteron's behavior over the last few months validates one side of the argument. And the bad news is that it would seem to be a perfect scenario," I concluded. "The faction in the North gets what they want, money and power, the two Koreas are reunified, the world is a happier, better place. In the meantime, a major U.S. corporation makes out like a bandit. There's only one problem with it."

The four-star was quick. I had to give him that. The follow-up was instantaneous. "It won't fucking work," he said. "Because the loyalists won't allow it to. Damn."

"And your plan to stop it, Colonel Pearce?" This from the 7th Air Force Commander. "A single ship raid against a truck carrying the final load of material?"

"Not my plan, General. It was General Myung-Dae's plan. He practically begged for it. He said that the truck carried the final installment of material and was crucial for the overthrow plan to succeed. If the truck was stopped, Cho's faction would lose face, and they could be taken down."

"You're going to find and bomb a truck inside the densest air defense environment in the world?" The camera panned to a female one-star at Hickam. She had an intelligence badge above her left pocket. "How are you planning to get through the SAM and AAA cordon at the border?"

"General Myung-Dae indicated the truck would travel

a road on or near the southwestern coast of the country, General," I said. "He also indicated that if I ingressed from over the Yellow Sea, at very low altitude, their acquisition radars would have a difficult time detecting me."

There was a stunned silence. The United States had been provided a crucial piece of intelligence about a possible chink in the North Korean armor. The value of the knowledge was inestimable. If it was valid, of course.

"Assuming the radar doesn't see you, how will you find the truck?" the General from Intelligence asked.

"They took my old CIA iPhone," I said. "It can be interrogated for position and will provide it within ten meters. General Hur insisted the phone would be on the truck.

"Agent Smith?" the PACAF Commander asked. "Is the phone really that accurate?"

Smith thought for a moment and then spoke. "Let's just say we've used similar devices as beacons for precision bombing strikes," he said.

The PACAF Commander turned his gaze to me. Even though he was 4,200 miles away, I could feel the intensity of his eyes. "So, Colonel Pearce, you're volunteering to fly what could be a suicide mission into the most heavily defended airspace in the world on the word of a North Korean General whose motives are questionable at best?"

I thought for a moment and remembered the relief on Myung-Dae's face when I told him I thought I could do what he needed me to do. Then I looked back at the PACAF commander and nodded. "Yes, General," I said. "I guess I am."

"You're either incredibly brave or incredibly stupid, Colonel," he said.

I smiled at him. "Let's not flip a coin on that, General," I said. "I'd prefer not to know."

"Colonel Pearce," said the female intel general in the same room as the PACAF commander, "you do realize that this whole scheme could be some sort of elaborate trap, don't you?"

I thought for a moment and then shrugged. "I guess I do, General," I said.

"Then why are you doing it?" she asked. "Why are you volunteering?"

I glanced down at the end of the table. Jessica Tate was watching me closely. I could see a thin sheen of moisture on the surface of her eyes, barely visible in the darkened room. I looked back at her and briefly raised my eyebrows, giving her a non-verbal apology for what I was about to say.

"It feels right to me, General," I said after a moment. I shrugged. "Apart from that, I'm not sure I have a good explanation. It just seems to be what I do."

"We're going to go silent for a few, ladies and gentlemen," the PACAF Commander said. "To make a decision. We'll be back in five. John, I'll need Seventh Air Force's decision."

"You got it, boss," the 7th Air Force Commander said.

"Dave," the PACAF Commander said, "I'll need the Wolf Pack's answer as well."

"We'll have it, General," Moody said.

The audio feed from both screens went silent. Moody motioned for Smith and me to leave the room as he conferred with his staff.

Smith and I left the chamber and made our way down the hallway to a break room between the stairs and the conference room. We helped ourselves to coffee from the standard glass Bundt pots that were Air Force staples. Smith had his black, which didn't surprise me a bit. I, on the other hand, doctored mine with plenty of cream and sugar. We leaned against the wall of the small space and drank in silence.

After a night of sex and intermittent sleep, I desperately needed the caffeine and sugar energy. I drank my cup greedily, ignoring the slightly burnt taste of coffee left on the burner too long. As I returned to the pot for another dose of the stuff, I saw Smith leaning against the wall of the room and looking down into his cup with a glum expression on his features.

"What's on your mind, Dave?" I asked.

He raised his eyes to mine. "Have you even taken the time to think this through?" he asked.

I shrugged. "Do I ever?"

He shook his head in frustration. "This time is different," he said. "You're going up against an entire country. And they could actually know you're coming."

I nodded. "Yes, they could." I looked down into the depths of my coffee and pondered the brown liquid. He was right, of course. The odds were against me. But then, they nearly always had been. It wasn't a new feeling. Yet, this time, the sensation was different. I had Sarah and the kids to think about. As well as settling the score with Rowe and Enteron. I didn't have the usual ambivalence about living through the upcoming ordeal that I normally did. I wanted to survive. I wanted to make things right for those who were depending on me. I wanted to watch Rowe's eyes turn into limpid pools of blackness as the life left her body.

But I still wanted to do this mission. I still wanted to fly into North Korea and bomb a truck and get out of there. I still wanted to clean up the mess.

The two objectives seemed to be incompatible. Yet a part of me told me they could both be done.

Moody appeared in the door of the breakroom with Jessica Tate at his side. Moody's face was grim, and Jess's face was ashen, like she had suffered some sort of severe loss.

I looked up at them. "You two don't look happy," I said. "I take it they told us to stand down."

Moody shook his head slowly. "Just the opposite, T.C.," he said. "It's a go. We're still waiting on JCS and presidential approval, but you need to get down to the vault and do some mission planning."

I nodded. "I think I still remember where the vault is," I said. "But someone will have to let me in."

"I'll do it," Jess said.

I left the room with Jess at my side, leaving Moody and Smith behind me. We walked down the hall and down the stairs without speaking, the clacking of our boots on the vinyl flooring of the stairs breaking the silence as we descended. Once we made it to the first floor, we turned a few corners and found ourselves in an alcove, facing a large, metal safe door, the entrance to the secure sensitive compartmented information facility, or SCIF. Jess turned to the keypad to input the entry code, but she stopped and turned to me. She looked down and took my hands in both of hers and raised her eyes to mine.

"Why are you doing this?" she asked. "And don't give me that bullshit you said in the conference room. You'll be killed. You can't not care that much. Why are you so willing to throw your life away?"

I squeezed her hands gently and lowered my lips to hers for a quick, but soulful kiss.

"I don't see it as throwing my life away, I guess," I said as I raised my head. "I see it as one man maybe making a difference. One man maybe making the world a little better. Somebody has to do this. It might as well be me."

"But, it's one of you against all of North Korea!" Jess said. "How can you possibly think you'll come out of this alive?"

I shrugged. "Because somehow, I always do."

CHAPTER THIRTY

Tuesday, January 19th
2030 Hours Local Time
FL 160 and 250 KIAS
On the Moorey 1A Arrival into Incheon Airport
Over the Yellow Sea

The dark belly of the KC-10A floated over me as I moved to the contact position for air refueling. I craned my neck forward in the cockpit to see the receiver director lighting panels on the bottom of the massive jet. Located closer to its nose, the panels were designed to give the refueling pilot a direction of where he or she should maneuver their aircraft to center the refueling boom in its limited envelope. One panel was for vertical position and had the letters D and U at either end for Down and Up. The other panel was labeled F and A at opposite ends for Fore and Aft.

I smiled as the letters came into focus. "Down you fucking asshole," I said to myself in the intercom,

I couldn't remember the last time I had air refueled. The conditions tonight wouldn't have been easy, even if I had been more current. The refueling had been arranged for me to get as much gas as I could before I began the mission into the North. Rather than intercept the tanker in a standard air refueling track, we had decided I'd refuel while the tanker flew one of the arrivals into Incheon airport, which would get me much closer to the border and keep my presence from being noticed until the last possible moment. The plan was that as the tanker made its turn south, to intercept the extended final for runway 15L or 15R, I'd break away, dive for the surface, and head into the North.

But in addition to the challenging weather, there was a significant issue with that plan. The typical refueling speed for the Viper was 310 knots. On this segment of the arrival procedure, the tanker was speed restricted to 250 knots. The heavily loaded Viper wasn't happy. Even with its digital flight control system in Takeoff and Landing Gains, which was a pitch command mode of the system, its normally responsive flight controls felt sloppy and heavy.

"Cleared to contact, sir," the boom operator said over the discrete refueling frequency.

"Tango Charlie cleared to contact," I replied.

As the winds and rain buffeted my aircraft, I tried to ease the stubborn Viper forward. I managed to stop it a few feet short of the extended boom, in approximately the right vertical position.

"Forward five," came the voice of the boom operator in my headset.

"Okay," I said to myself.

I eased the Viper's throttle forward a hair and let the aircraft begin to creep towards the boom. As soon as the jet began to move, I returned the throttle to its original position. The jet stopped its movement.

And then we flew through a pocket of turbulence, and my jet was driven upward, towards the tanker.

"Jesus!" I said into my oxygen mask.

I pushed forward on the sidestick reflexively and drove my jet down and away from the larger aircraft. When I looked up to check my position, I could barely see the KC-10 through the clouds.

"Nicely done, idiot," I said to myself.

But the boom operator was a cool customer. "A little bump there, sir," he said. "Why don't you go back out to pre-contact and try it again?"

I keyed the UHF mic switch and replied. "Wilco."

I reduced power slightly to move the Viper aft. Then, I gently increased backpressure on the sidestick to ease the Viper back up to the pre-contact position, level with the boom and about one aircraft length back. The jet slowly floated upward, through the mist and the rain, the streams of cloud and moisture swirling by the canopy as it climbed. I watched the gray outline of the tanker turn in to a dark silhouette. Then the detail on the belly of the aircraft became visible again. I stopped the jet's movement in an approximation of the pre-contact position and waited.

"Cleared to contact," said the operator.

"Tango Charlie cleared to contact," I replied.

Once again, I eased the Viper's throttle forward to move the jet into the contact position. It was a delicate maneuver, one that had to be performed decisively and expeditiously, but not so aggressively that the boom operator thought you were going to run into the boom.

I closed the 50-foot space in about five seconds and stopped the jet a foot short of the boom, the metal nozzle clearly visible above and slightly in front of my canopy.

"Forward three and down two," the boom operator said.

I squeezed the throttle with my left hand and coaxed it forward slightly. Rather than push the sidestick controller forward to descend, I gently pushed the trim button forward one click and waited for my inputs to take effect.

But the boom operator wasn't waiting for me. I watched the boom retract slightly and then go over my head as the operator moved it to the air refueling port on the top of the jet, about five feet behind the cockpit. Before I had stopped the motion of my aircraft, I felt the dull thud of the boom engaging the receptacle, and I heard the boom operator's voice through the jet's intercom, a feature unique to the KC-10.

"Contact, sir," the boom operator said.

"Contact it is," I said. I glanced down at the fuel totalizer just outboard of my right knee and saw that the numbers were increasing rapidly. The flow rate of aerial tankers was impressive. "Taking gas," I said.

"Copy that, sir," the operator replied.

I took a mental snapshot of how the tanker looked in relation to my aircraft and tried to maintain the picture. Maintaining the correct position for air refueling is similar to flying formation, but that was another task I hadn't performed in years, so I wasn't sure how useful the skill set would be.

A few seconds passed. I flexed my fingers on the throttle and sidestick and did my best to be as subtle as possible with my control movements. There was a pregnant silence over the intercom. I got the notion that the boomer wanted to ask me a question but didn't know how to phrase it.

"Sorry to bring you guys out on a night like this," I said. "I'm sure you'd rather be back at the club drinking a cold one."

"Happy to do it, sir," the boomer said. "We'll be hanging out waiting to catch you on the far side if you need the gas."

I nodded to myself. That had also been part of the plan. If I needed to tap the afterburner a lot across the border, it would be useful to have a tanker waiting for me to get the gas I needed to get back to Kunsan. "We'll see," I answered. "Depends on what happens."

A few more seconds passed. "Sir," the boom operator said at last, "the crew has a question for you, and they're all listening."

I felt my eyebrows raise. "Okay," I said. "Fire away."

"There are a lot of rumors floating around about who you are," the boomer said. "And we know we're not allowed to ask your name, but I think we can ask you this. Are you the real Tango Charlie? The real T.C.?"

I smiled to myself under the oxygen mask. I nodded unconsciously and replied. "Unless there is more than one of us, then yes," I said. "I guess I am."

"We've heard about you," Another voice said. Female and authoritative. Probably the aircraft commander. "You've shot down a lot of bad guys. Any idea how many?"

"I haven't kept track," I said. "But a guy I know and respect a lot says the number is 11."

"Maybe you'll add to that number tonight," the voice said. "While you're doing whatever it is you'll be doing."

I shook my head slightly as I continued to hold the Viper in position while the wind and rain pelted our two aircraft. "Honestly, I'd be happy to get in and out undetected," I said. "Without even seeing another jet. But unfortunately, that isn't likely."

"Well Godspeed and good hunting, T.C.," the voice said. "We'll be waiting for you."

I nodded, but before I could reply, the nozzle disconnected from my jet and retracted. I keyed my mic. "Pressure disconnect?" I asked.

"Affirmative, sir," the boom operator replied over the refueling frequency. "Offload is complete."

"Roger that," I said. "Appreciate the gas and the support. Hope to see you on the far side."

Without waiting for a response, I rolled the Viper on its back and dove for the dark expanse of the Yellow Sea, through the clouds and far below.

CHAPTER THIRTY-ONE

Tuesday, January 19th
2100 Hours Local Time
300 feet AGL and 480 KIAS
Over the Yellow Sea

I had forgotten how noisy the cockpit of a Viper can be at low altitude and high speed. Even with plugs in my ears and a helmet on my head, I could clearly hear the deafening sound of the air rushing by the canopy, the molecules brutally shoved aside by the Viper as it forced its way through the dense sea-level atmosphere, powered by the massive GE engine.

But even with all the noise outside the jet, the lack of noise inside of it was more disturbing. Any other time in my life when I had ingressed real or simulated hostile territory in a jet, the noise inside the cockpit had been so intense that the outside noise was all but forgotten. The UHF and VHF radios were usually teeming with chatter from air traffic controllers, AWACs controllers, ground coordinating agencies, squadron or wing supervisors, and flight members.

But not tonight. The need for secrecy and plausible deniability was too great. Even with frequency-hopping radios and encrypted communications, the radios were utterly silent. There wasn't even an audio alert from the datalink system. I seemed to be on my own.

"Par for the course," I said to myself over the intercom.

I was heading south, southwest, away from my tanker rendezvous, and further out over the Yellow Sea before I made the turn inbound to the target area. Even though General Myung-Dae had assured me the radars in the North weren't good at low altitude, I wasn't taking any chances. The plan was to give the NK radars a last look at an aircraft proceeding on a non-threatening course as it descended to low altitude. Assuming the radar could even see me.

I turned my head to the right, to the north, and gazed out over the dark waters. I was grateful for the symbology and imagery of the digital Joint Helmet Mounted Curing System (JHMCS) I was wearing. I could turn my head nearly anywhere in the cockpit and still see some of the symbology of a HUD through my visor, including airspeed, altitude, angle of attack, g-loading and distance to target, presented on top of a night display that featured both light-enhanced and infrared imagery of the surface. I could tell that my speed, altitude, and attitude were constant while I was looking away from the HUD and flight instruments and make sure that I wasn't on a downward vector into the sea or an upward one into NK radar coverage. I moved my eyes to the navigation display in my visor and nodded unconsciously as I saw the distance to the displacement waypoint was decrementing to zero.

Now it was a waiting game.

My target was a "kill box" on Highway AH1, six miles south of the town of Sinmak, and about two-thirds of the way between Pyongyang and the DMZ. The kill box was a three-mile stretch of road between two tunnels and was deemed the best spot for me to lay down six 250-kilo incendiary bombs, minimize collateral damage on the nearby town and surrounding countryside, and possibly mitigate the nuclear contamination that was sure to follow. I had two options for the attack depending on the ceiling and visibility in the target area. If the weather gods were kind, I'd be able to pop-up to a 10-degree low angle attack, have more time to acquire the target, and put the bombs very precisely on it. If the weather gods were pissed, as they seemed to be tonight, I'd be limited to a level delivery. Given the rugged terrain in the vicinity of the target, that would be very challenging indeed.

"Guess I should have made a sacrifice or something," I muttered to myself.

The timing would have to be very precise. The truck would only be in between the tunnels for a little over three minutes, and a level delivery at 540 knots calibrated airspeed would not allow for a correction maneuver. I couldn't begin my turn in to the target until we had verification that the convoy was the appropriate distance from the kill box, about ten miles or so.

I began an easy turn to the left, in the pre-briefed orbit pattern, just south of North Korean airspace. Keeping my focus on maintaining level flight and stealing glances at my right multi-function display or MFD, awaiting the datalink message that would provide my signal for action. The CIA was monitoring the GPS in my phone, and theoretically, my phone was on the target truck. They would ping me when the time was right.

It's strange what you think about when your mind is engaged in an activity that requires technical precision but little mental effort. I was in a gentle 360-degree turn at 480 knots and 300 feet over the Yellow Sea. In moments, I would turn inbound to North Korea, penetrate one of the most lethal air defense networks in the world and attempt to hit a target provided by a North Korean general whose objectives could be suspect. At that time, my mind would go into high workload. But for the moment, it was free to wander a bit. I thought about Sarah and the kids and hoped like hell that the CIA had managed to find them. I thought about last night, with

Jess, and the small piece of heaven and respite that interlude had provided. I thought about my "real job" in Sedona, flying tourists and photographers around in the OV-10, and how much I liked it. And I realized, much to my amazement, that assuming we could get Sarah the kids out of their predicament, I had many of the conditions for a happy life.

"Damn," I said to myself in the intercom. "Imagine that."

An audible cue pulled me from my reverie. I glanced down at the right MFD and saw the new text message on the datalink Screen.

ABOUT TEN MINUTES OUT, it said.

"It's showtime," I said into the intercom.

I toggled the navigation system to the target coordinates. I had completed about 180 degrees of turn in the orbit, so my distance to the target was about 95 miles. I had work to do. I pushed the throttle forward and over the detent into minimum afterburner and felt the small kick in the back as the burner lit. Then I increased the bank to nearly ninety degrees and pulled the Viper's nose around to the northeast, to North Korea.

When you're making a turn a low altitude, it's tempting to look at the surface or to the inside of the turn as the nose tracks. Either would be a deadly mistake. The place you look is out of the front of the jet, carefully watching the nose and making sure the turn is absolutely level. A slight overbank and small descent can result in a ground impact in just a few seconds. Even with the symbology built into the helmet, I was old school, and I wanted the precise pitch display built into the HUD. So, I turned my head forward and looked directly through the glass as I continued the turn, making gentle adjustments in roll as I pulled the nose to the target and allowed the jet to accelerate to the ingress speed of 540 knots.

I rolled out with the steering cue centered, inbound to North Korea. I checked my time on target or TOT in the HUD.

1215 Zulu time. About 10 minutes from now.

I typed "TOT 1215" using the keyboard on the upfront control or UFC. Then I hit the send button and concentrated on the view in front of me.

My ingress was to take me between a small peninsula on the southern coast of western North Korea and an island that lay just inside the South Korean border, about 40 nautical miles west, northwest of the Inchon Airport. The rain had lightened a bit, and thanks to the light enhancing and infrared imaging capability of my helmet display, I could see outlines of both geologic structures in the distance, about forty miles off the nose. As I approached them at nine miles per minute and began to discern some detail, I amazed by the differences in activity between the two. The South Korean side teamed with light and movement, while the North Korean side seemed dark and lifeless.

I glanced down at my radar warning receiver display. It too seemed dark and lifeless, and there was silence in my headset. So far, nothing was looking for me or at me.

I nodded to myself as the terrain features in front of me grew in the display. I reached to the left side of the instrument panel with my left hand and moved the MASTER ARM switch to the upper/on position. All the required modes and sub-modes had been programmed into it when I loaded the data-transfer cartridge earlier. My jet was ready to deal death.

"So be it," I said into the dark.

I shot between the peninsula and the island a few moments later and crossed into North Korean airspace. In front of me was a bay area that would lead me to the coast, about six miles in front of my jet's nose. The rain had lessened somewhat, and the visibility was such that I could see where the water met the land. Apart from an occasional light that was visible on the land, the coast seemed devoid of life and activity.

Something isn't right.

I was now inside of North Korean Airspace at low altitude and on a course that would take me over land in less than a minute. And not only was I not being tracked, there were no spurious radar hits on my jet.

"I come from infantry," General Myung-Dae had said, "so I do not know air defense. But I know our radar is not good for low altitude. We do not see things sometimes. Even over the sea."

I wanted to believe it, but he was part of one faction of the torn NK government. He didn't control everything. And the other faction, the one personified by the vicious Captain Cho, was methodical and patient.

"This is bullshit," I said to myself. "Something has to be looking at me. The long-range acquisition radars might not see me, but there has to be some kind of coastal warning radar that would pick me up. I should be hearing and seeing something."

I heard the audible ping of an incoming datalink message in my headset, followed by the words "LOOK HIGH" appearing on the screen.

"Fuck," I said. "I knew it."

My headset came alive with the sound of multiple air-to-air radars locked onto my jet. Then, two symbols appeared in my RWR display at 12 o'clock, directly in front of my aircraft, symbols that translated to third-generation Russian-made fighters, like the Mig-29.

I had been lured into a trap.

Conventional air-to-air radars, like the APG-68 installed in my jet, are limited in their vertical scan pattern. Essentially, the vertical scan pattern resembles a funnel if viewed from the side of the aircraft. The amount of airspace it can see is dependent on the range to a potential target. I had set the upper scan limit on my radar at 20,000 feet and the lower level on the ground, so I could see anything that would be an immediate threat to my low-altitude ingress.

But the text message said LOOK HIGH. HIGH was a brevity term that indicated a radar contact was between 25,000 and 40,000 feet. I rotated the EL STROBE knob on the throttle with my left thumb, oriented the funnel of my scan upward.

"And there you are," I said.

My radar MFD showed two squares of video in the display. They were line abreast and moving directly towards me at 35,000 feet altitude. I couldn't tell if they had fired a radar missile at me yet, but their current orientation indicated they might not have.

I wasn't going to give them the chance.

Using my left thumb on the throttle, I slewed my radar cursor to the left contact and designated it with my right thumb on the stick-mounted target management switch. I did the same with the right contact.

Then I pushed the DOG-FIGHT switch on the throttle down, into the inboard position, and called up the mighty AIM-120 AMRAAM missiles. In seconds, a designated launch zone display appeared in my HUD and in the radar, and I could see that both targets were well within it.

"Might be a bad night for you, boys," I said and pressed the weapons release or "pickle" button on the sidestick. There was a slight delay, but then I heard a roar as the AIM-120 on the left wingtip departed the aircraft, leaving a trail of thin smoke behind it. It immediately disappeared into the clouds above me. I stepped the primary target indicator from the left bandit to the right and fired AMRAAM number two. It roared off the right wingtip a few milliseconds later.

Now I had a dilemma to resolve. Typically, when you fire an AMRAAM at a long-range adversary, you turn left or right of the target and keep the target on the edge of the radar to provide guidance data to the missile(s) fired until the missile goes into the terminal mode, about 15-20 seconds from impact. This maneuver, called a crank, is designed to maximize range from the target aircraft while providing guidance to the missile in flight. When the missile went into terminal guidance mode, the next maneuver on the agenda was called a drag, where I'd turn tail to the bad guys and run away, hopefully defeating any missiles inflight towards me in the process.

But I didn't have the option for either. I was on a tight time schedule to the target, and I couldn't afford any delays. I had to maintain my course, keep the bad guys on the nose, and hope for the best.

I kept my eyes on the time of flight or TOF indicator in my HUD and held my breath as I went feet dry on the southwest coast of North Korea. In my peripheral vision, I saw the dim lights of the village of Haeju go by on the left side.

I couldn't remember what kind of radar-guided air-to-air missiles the NKs had and whether I'd get a subsequent launch warning from my RWR system.

"A little threat study might have been nice, Pearce," I muttered to myself.

The flat terrain of the shore transitioned into more rugged topography, and I could make out the cragged outlines of some rocky hills in front of me. I knew the orientation from the map study I had done. There were three rows of hills that came from the left and merged into one low ridgeline in front of me. Then, there was a small gap or valley and another ridgeline beyond. The target was in the valley north of the second ridge – four minutes away.

I glanced down at my radar display and noticed the two squares of video were no longer there. I double-checked my EL STROBE to make sure the altitude coverage encompassed the bandits' former altitude. It did.

I looked through the HUD and saw the navigation display

decrementing in both miles and time to target. As the imagery in my helmet visor revealed more details of the terrain in front of me, I applied slight backpressure on the sidestick to lift the Viper's nose just enough to clear the hills ahead.

An audible ding sounded in my headset. I looked down at the datalink display.

SPLASH TWO, it said. NICE JOB. TARGET STILL MOVING. ABOUT THREE MIN OUT.

I nodded as I guided the jet over the first set of hills and ensured that my altitude didn't increase any more than that required to clear the terrain. The cragged rocks passed underneath me, seemingly reaching for the belly of my aircraft through the rain. I fought the urge to climb and kept my steering cue centered, watching the time to target and distance continuing to shrink.

Two minutes and 18 miles to the target.

I came over the first hills and descended into the valley in front of me. I glanced at my map to verify my position. Then I looked back up to the HUD. I nodded to myself. It was time for the action.

"Here goes nothing," I muttered.

I rolled the Viper up on its right wing and pulled the nose into a 90-degree turn, grunting slightly as my g-suit inflated against my gut and the force of four gs came upon me, pushing me deeper into the seat. A crooked smile crept onto my lips underneath the oxygen mask. I loved the feeling of g on my body. Even now, in my mid-fifties, I still relished it. Then, I saw something flash by in my peripheral vision that wiped the smile off my face.

"No fucking way," I said.

When flying at low altitude and high speed, it's easy to see things that are a few miles in front of you or a few miles off to the sides of the jet, but it is challenging to see what's near or directly underneath you. What I had seen in my peripheral vision was pretty big, and if it was what I thought it was, I should be able to get some confirmation even as I flew over it.

A glance out of the right side of the jet made it certain. I saw a long taxiway, disappearing into the trees, with several hardened aircraft shelters on the east side of it.

I had just executed a low altitude turn over a military airbase.

"What the fuck!" I screamed into the intercom. "That wasn't part of the intel brief!"

A part of my brain wanted to dwell on the event and contemplate whether it had been caused by a lack of knowledge on the intel staff's part, or a navigational error on mine, but there wasn't time. The geographic references that I had committed to memory were coming into view, thankfully visible through the lessening rain. I had to fly the Viper to a specific point in space just a few miles in front of me.

Typically, low-altitude attacks in the Viper were executed very mechanically. The pilot flew directly towards the target until the designated action point, executed a 4-g turn 30-45 degrees to the left or right of the original course, maintained the new heading for a set amount of seconds, then aggressively climbed to a pulldown altitude if he was performing a diving attack or to a delivery altitude for a level attack. At the moment, I didn't know which of the two I was going to execute. Still, I did know that given the terrain, weather conditions, and threat environment, randomly flying for a few seconds without reference to the terrain could end in disaster.

I peered through the display in my visor to see a long, triangularly shaped lake ahead. I applied scant pressure to the sidestick and nudged the Viper a few degrees to the right so that I was flying over the center of the lake. Ahead of me, I could see the damn at the end of the lake and the riverbed beyond, stretching a few miles to the southeast.

I nodded to myself as I remembered the words of the intel

briefer. "Don't hold down for a period of time like you guys normally do," he had said. "After your action, fly down this river and pop up when it turns right."

The dam went under the nose, and a line of low hills flashed by me on the left, clearly visible in the low-light display built into my helmet. Just off the nose, the riverbed cut through the land in front of me, its crooked path etched into the terrain, dividing farm fields and rice paddies. I glanced out of the top of my canopy and tried to gauge the height of the clouds above me, my mind wrestling with the question of whether to pop-up to a low-angle bomb attack or stay low and try a level attack.

The ping of an incoming text message interrupted my thoughts.

THIRTY SECONDS OUT. JUST ENTERING NORTHERN TUNNEL.

The bend of the river shot under the Viper's nose, and I flipped a mental coin.

"Pop-up it is," I said to myself. I pulled the jet upward into a 15-degree climb. In front of me, I could see the straight pavement line of the Pyongyang-Kaesong Motorway, Highway AH-1, to my left. It seemed deserted at this time in the evening. I ran my eyes up the road to the north, peering through the left side of my canopy to gain sight of the tunnel exit on the south side of the northern mountain. Fortunately, the infrared feature built into my helmet display picked up the heat radiating from the road as a result of the traffic that had been upon it earlier. I could readily see where the highway entered the mountain.

But the target vehicle wasn't visible yet. It was still in the tunnel.

"Come on, guys," I whispered into the intercom, "I've got something for you."

At that point, the right thing to do, the predictive thing to do, would have been to roll the jet to the left, put the lift vector on the entrance of the tunnel, and pull the jet down into the bombing run, betting that the truck would exit before I reached release altitude.

But like an idiot, I didn't do that. Instead, I waited, and floated the climb upward, keeping my eyes on the tunnel entrance and not paying attention to how high I was climbing. A second passed. Another second passed. Suddenly, two round orbs of light appeared in the helmet's low light display – the headlights of the truck as it exited the tunnel.

"Yes!" I said.

And then the headlights disappeared as I flew into the clouds.

"Son of a bitch!" I spat into the intercom.

I instinctively rolled the jet to a nearly inverted attitude and applied backpressure to the sidestick to stop the climb, but I didn't pull the nose down hard. I had read too many accident reports about people killing themselves when they exited a low overcast with a severe nose-down attitude. I had to do a shallow, descending turn to get around to the truck. A right turn would take less time and improve my odds of getting ordnance on it before it entered the southern tunnel. A left turn would take longer and give me less time to get ordnance on the truck but would allow me a longer time to find it. I shrugged and pulled the jet into a gently descending turn to the left.

The seconds ticked by. I held my breath as the clouds seemed determined to remain between my jet and the ground. I resisted the urge to increase the backpressure on the sidestick and forced myself to take a few deep breaths as the descending turn continued.

"You'll have more time," I said to myself. "You'll have more time. It will work out."

A few more seconds went by. I found myself wondering if I had climbed further than I thought, or the clouds had lowered.

With the jet in a bank, the radar altimeter couldn't see the ground, and I was betting my life as well as the mission, that I'd have time to stop the turn and descent before I slammed into the rocks that surrounded the road.

Suddenly, the terrain became visible around me, and I shot my gaze southward along the road. The truck was clearly visible, about a mile south of me.

But it was approaching the southern tunnel. I had only a few seconds to catch it.

I pushed the throttle over the detent into MAX AB and pulled the Viper's nose around at about 5gs, hoping I wasn't over g-ing the Russian-made bombs in the process. I reached up to the up-front control, just under the HUD, and actuated the air-to-ground master mode. Then, as I returned my left hand to the throttle, I moved the DOGFIGHT switch to the center position. In the HUD, I was rewarded with the sight of a bomb fall line or BFL in the display. At the end of the BFL, near the bottom of the HUD was the pipper, a round circle with a dot in the center of it. Due to the accuracy of the Viper's computerized weapons delivery system, that two-mil point of light was often referred to as the "death dot."

The Viper was ready to rain hellfire and destruction from above, but the time was growing short for that capability to be used.

The truck was nearing the southern tunnel entrance, but I was moving at more than ten times its speed and closing the distance between it and me rapidly. I eased the Viper's nose to the right slightly and superimposed the BFL directly on the truck as the vehicle continued up the road. The pipper chased the truck up the pavement, the death dot seemingly eager to consume its target. I nodded to myself as I noted how far down the pipper was in the HUD.

"High drag weapon," I said to myself. "Longer time of fall. Have to put the pipper in front of the truck to allow for his speed."

I looked ahead. The truck was about a half-mile from the entrance. But my realization about the bombs' ballistics helped my situation. The road was curving to the right slightly. I didn't need to bomb the truck. I could aim for the entrance to the tunnel. The bombs would impact and detonate in front of the truck and it would drive right into the explosions. I disregarded the vehicle, pulled the nose to the right about five degrees, and ran the BFL through the tunnel entrance.

Suddenly, my eyes focused on the airspeed in the HUD. I saw it accelerating through 600 knots, probably well above the release envelope for the clumsy weapons I was carrying. I yanked the throttle back to idle just as the top of the pipper circle touched the entrance to the tunnel.

A loud cacophony of synthetic audio blared in my headset. Even as I stared at the HUD, waiting for the eternal microsecond as the pipper tracked to the target, at the bottom of my gaze, I saw two wingform shapes appear at the six o'clock position on my RWR scope. I had two more NK fighters on my tail. And the strength of the signals meant they were close. Very close.

I've experienced the phenomenon of temporal distortion many times in my life. It always amazes me when it occurs. At times of high stress and high workload, time seems to slow down; multiple tasks can be accomplished nearly simultaneously, but they seem sequential in the prolonged reality of the moment.

The pipper hit the entrance, and my right thumb came down on the pickle button. I felt the rapid sequence of thumps as the six bombs separated from my jet, each one pushed away from its slot on the bomb rack by an explosive impulse cartridge in the rack. I counted all six thumps, nodding to myself as I confirmed their departure from the aircraft. I reached down to the right MFD, called up the stores management system, actuated the buttons to arm the external fuel tanks for jettison, and punched them off with the pickle button. As the tanks tumbled to earth, I rolled the Viper up on its left wing, used my right thumb to dispense flares with the countermeasures management switch on the sidestick, and used my left thumb on the throttle to slide the DOGFIGHT switch to the outboard or DOGFIGHT position. Then, I got into my straining maneuver and pulled the Viper's nose around to the left, as hard as I could, grunting with the heavy g and forcing my eyes to the inside of the turn to find my attackers.

"Okay, you commie fuckers," I spat into the intercom, "Let's dance."

CHAPTER THIRTY-TWO

Tuesday, January 19th
2115 Hours Local Time
500 feet AGL, 450 KIAS and 9Gs
6 Miles South of Pyongsan, North Korea

The combined actions of pulling my throttle to idle for the bombing attack, dispensing flares, and executing the high-g defensive turn, saved my life. The strength and proximity of the radar signals in my headset and RWR scope told me the attacking fighters were close. Still, it wasn't until I was in the defensive turn that I knew how close.

In about four seconds, I was through 90 degrees of turn, and as I looked to the inside of my circle, I saw two fiery objects pass behind my jet, each with its own wispy trail of smoke. Two heat-seeking air-to-air missiles, fired at where I was seconds ago, had been successfully decoyed by the flares I had released behind my jet.

A second or two later, as I pulled the nose through another 30 degrees of turn, I saw the flashes as the two warheads exploded harmlessly when they contacted the flares that were still hanging in the air. If I hadn't turned when I did, as hard as I did, I would have been toast. Literally.

"Thank God for older technology," I grunted to myself.

The North Koreans wouldn't have the latest infrared-seeking air-to-air missiles with modern flare rejection technology. Instead, they'd have the older stuff, like Russian-made AA-8 or AA-11 missiles, which were easily decoyed by the infrared spectrum displayed by the flares loaded into my jet. But surviving the initial turn was the easy part of the engagement. Now I had to find my attackers. And kill them.

As I continued my turn, I peered out through the canopy, desperately trying to get my eyes onto them, even as I commanded the radar to look to the inside of the circle.

In my peripheral vision, I saw my bombs explode as they made contact with the entrance of the tunnel, generating a series of fiery plumes as they impacted and detonated. There was no time for me to appreciate my handiwork though. I had work to do.

LOCK, LOCK, said the sensual female voice in my headset. The Viper's APG-68 radar had found one of the bad guys. I followed the line from the gun cross to the target ID box in my helmet display and saw a fighter-shaped silhouette in the center of the box. I checked the DLZ display in the HUD, verified that the range made sense, and uncaged the AIM-9X on my left wing. I was rewarded with a strong tone in my headset. I pressed the pickle button on the sidestick and the infrared-seeking missile was gone in an instant, like a bottle-rocket leaving the ground, only with a far more deadly payload. The missile raced across the rainy sky. My eyes followed the small flame of its motor as it sought its prey. A few seconds later, there was a fiery explosion as the projectile found its target, a MiG-29, and blasted it into the atmosphere. Even in the light rain and darkness, I could see large pieces of the aircraft falling to the ground. I had no doubt that the pilot had been killed. When the AIM-9X was used in a forward aspect attack, the warhead typically detonated as soon as the missile's laser detector sensed the missile had reached the target – which usually meant the warhead detonated abeam the cockpit of the target aircraft. The warhead's expanding titanium rods would rip the front of the aircraft and the pilot apart in milliseconds.

"One down, one to go," I said to myself. "Time to get some energy back."

I flew past the wreckage of the fallen jet and scanned the sky in front of me for the other aircraft as I eased the throttle forward to accelerate back to fighting speed.

For the second time that night, my headset was eerily quiet. The radar tones had gone away shortly after I had executed my defensive turn, and my RWR had definitely displayed the radars of two aircraft locked onto my jet. There had to be another bandit out here somewhere.

"Where the fuck are you?" I asked the night around me. "And why aren't you looking for me with your radar?"

But then my mind began putting together the geometry of the bandits' initial attack. When I had made my turn, the smoke trails had been close to me, but by the time I got my nose around to kill the aircraft I had fired upon, he had been nearly two miles in trail. That meant the leader had been the one who fired the missiles and he had flown past me as I had turned.

"Damn," I said to myself as the realization hit me, "He's fucking behind me."

That was when I remembered that the MiG-29 came with an earlier version of the helmet-mounted sight that I was wearing. A sight that enabled the pilot to aim and shoot infrared-guided missiles without a radar lock.

I yanked the throttle to idle and pulled the Viper into a hard right turn as I dispensed a few more flares. I threw my gaze to the inside of the turn to find the bandit that I knew had to be attacking me. The Viper's nose came around eagerly and quickly, but the seconds seemed to crawl by as I held my breath and waited for the inevitable missile or gun shot that had to be coming my way. 120 degrees of turn, then 150 degrees. I searched the usual avenues of attack. Inside the turn, level, and high, but I couldn't see anything in front of me or around me in my helmet's low-light and infrared display. I commanded my radar to search the inside of the turn, both low and high, but it found nothing.

"Well, shit," I said to myself. "This is damn peculiar."

My headset pinged with the tone of an incoming text message. I had been so engrossed in my target search that the sudden noise startled me. I glanced down at the right MFD.

EGRESS NOW. NKS SCRAMBLING FOUR MORE MIGS.

"Great," I said in response. "I haven't even found the other guy around here yet."

I called up the exit steerpoint in the display and pulled the nose of the jet to superimpose the Viper's flight path marker over the steering cue.

"You're right, Dave," I said. "It's high time to get the fuck out here."

I eased the throttle forward to 7500 pounds per hour of fuel flow to give the Viper the thrust needed to accelerate to a comfortable 520 knots indicated, about 540 knots ground speed. As the airspeed increased, I applied slight forward pressure on the sidestick to get back to the comfort of low altitude. As I descended, I could see the cold, black mass of the Yellow Sea in the distance, only about five minutes flying time away.

The rugged terrain I had crossed and fought over earlier rose to meet me as I leveled off at 300 feet AGL and settled into my exit route. I glanced at the map on my right knee and verified my position. In less than five minutes, I'd be over the water. In another two minutes, I'd be out of North Korean airspace.

The mission was almost over.

The Russian bombs had worked as advertised and generated a maelstrom of fire that would have consumed the truck carrying the nuclear material, assuming the bombs had detonated before the vehicle made it to the tunnel. There hadn't been time to verify that. I wondered if the strike would generate the chain of events that General Myung-Dae had predicted. I wondered if the machinations of Rowe and Enteron would be foiled. And I wondered if the CIA had been able to find Sarah and the kids and what would be done to rescue them.

A line of hills loomed in front of me. I raised the Viper's nose slightly to clear it. As I flew across the top of the ridge, I could see the bay I had crossed earlier a few miles off the nose. I was almost home.

And that's when the other MiG appeared.

He materialized on my nose, out over the bay, like he had been teleported there. But I knew what had happened. He had been vectored to the intercept by North Korean ground control. He was the goalie, the gatekeeper, the one who was to keep me from leaving NK airspace since his wingman hadn't been successful in stopping me.

The synthetic radar tone ripped into my ears as he locked me up. I pushed forward on the target management switch on the stick and did the same to him. We were two miles apart, and the closure was nearly 1200 knots. Instinctively, I pulled my throttle back to idle as I uncaged my remaining AIM-9X. The missile's tone was weak and wavering, and the circle in the HUD that represented the missile's field of view refused to lock onto the MiG's exhaust. The MiG pilot had retarded his power to idle as well.

I nodded to myself. The MiG pilot obviously knew what he was doing. At least pre-merge anyway. "Okay, buddy," I said. "Let's see what's on your mind."

Like knights in a medieval joust, we were charging each other, poised for the classic geometry of a high-aspect engagement, an encounter I had practiced more times than I could count. We were neutral in position and co-energy. The winner would be the one who could maintain his energy while looking for a way to cash that energy in for positional advantage. It would be a battle of patience, skill, and subtlety.

A smart man would blow through the merge, select MAX AB, and race for the edge of North Korean Airspace, forcing the MiG to chase him into international airspace. The North Koreans must have thought that my American arrogance would compel me to stay and fight. Or maybe, thanks to Cho, Rowe, or even Myung-Dae, they knew who I was and were counting on my personal ego to do the trick. By now, I knew my jet was visible on radar screens both in the South and the North. I imagined that many on both sides of the border would be watching me intently, anxious to see what I would do.

"Just blow through," I said to myself. "Blow through, light the wick, and find that fucking tanker."

The MiG was 3000 feet away. We'd merge in less than two seconds. Through the display in my helmet, I could see the alternating colors of the North Korean paint pattern, rendered in grayscale by the low-light and infrared scheme. I could see the outline of the pilot's head behind the HUD in his own aircraft. He seemed poised for action. Waiting to base his own actions on what he saw me do.

"He'll turn first," I said to myself. "He has to turn first to get me to turn."

Our two jets merged, right side to right side and about 100 feet apart. I threw my head over my right shoulder and watched the MiG.

The yellow flame of his afterburner ignited and he turned to his right, across my tail.

And in the moment, I made the decision to turn and burn with him. I shoved my throttle into MAX AB. I didn't have the altitude to do a 9-g duck-under. Since I was limited to a flat fight, I should have replicated the MiG's action and turned across his tail and into the standard two-circle fight, which would have let me capitalize on the Viper's superior performance at high speed.

But, instead, I did the one thing Viper pilots should never do when they fight an adversary who has superior turn performance at low speed and high angle of attack – I turned left, into the MiG, into his circle, and into his phone booth.

It was a spontaneous decision but not a rash one. I presumed that the guy I was fighting was probably one of the best the NKs had. He would have studied all of the standard intel about the F-16 versus the MiG-29 in close combat. He would have expected me to go for the two-circle fight. Which was precisely why I didn't. In all the air-to-air engagements in my career, mock ones or real ones, my ability to prevail had been based on one primary tactic – show my adversary something he or she didn't expect.

I pulled through about 45 degrees of turn and looked through the top of my canopy, across the circle at the MiG. He was about 4000 feet away and clearly visible in my helmet's low light/infrared display. I could see the water vapor generated by the condensing air at high g-loading streaming from his wingtips as he pulled into me. I could almost sense a question mark emanating from his cockpit. This scenario wasn't the one he was anticipating.

I was about to make it more challenging. A MiG-29 with a helmet-mounted sight and AA-11 air-to-air missiles aboard was not something to be trifled with in a close visual fight. Odds were that in a few more degrees of turn, the NK pilot would be able to put his head into a place where he could look through his visor display, get the visual depiction of a reticle on my jet, and fire a missile across the circle at me.

But I wasn't going to give him that chance.

We were currently in a flat orientation, about 500 feet above the bay, tracing our way along opposite sides of the same circle in a fight that was two-dimensional. It was time to change that. I looked at the clouds above me, tried to gauge their height, unloaded a bit, rolled the Viper slightly to the right to re-orient my lift vector above the MiG, and I re-applied backpressure to the sidestick.

My flight path changed.

My plane of motion was now oriented above the MiG's. The NK pilot had a choice to make. He could stay in his current plane of motion and allow me to build turning room above him or come up into me and take that turning room away.

He did what I expected him to do. He reoriented his lift vector and came up into me.

"Perfect," I said to the intercom.

As I encountered the first wisps of the overcast clouds, I overbanked to stop my ascent and waited for the MiG to climb into my plane of motion as we continued along the outside of the circle. While initially, the noses and flight paths of our jets had been approaching diverging, now our courses were beginning to align, and our respective infrared signatures were becoming increasingly visible to each other.

I eased my throttle back to idle and hoped that the small trace of my exhaust plume would not be easy for his missile seeker head to track against the background of the moisture-laden clouds. I threw my helmet back, against the seat, peered out through the display on my visor, and tried to move my head to a position where the circle of the remaining AIM-9's seeker head would overlay the MiG as he continued to turn.

"Uhhhh," I grunted. The air came out of me involuntarily as I fought to stay conscious and rotate my head under the punishing load of nearly 9 gs. I could feel the rivulets of perspiration running down the side of my face as the missile reticle slowly traversed the distance and made its way onto his jet. I instantly hit the missile uncage button on the throttle and was rewarded with aimless static in my headset. The AIM-9's seeker head didn't see enough IR energy to track. I wasn't surprised. The MiG pilot was experienced, and he wouldn't have committed the rookie error of leaving his power up.

In a few more seconds, we would merge again, reverse the direction our turns to transcribe another single circle, this time on opposite sides, and the sequence of events would be repeated. As long as we kept our power in idle for each merge, no missile shots would be possible. We would eventually wind up in a dogfighting scenario called a flat scissors where we would maneuver and counter maneuver across each other's flight path at slow speed and high angle of attack.

It wasn't a game I could win.

Once my Viper slowed, its flight control limiters would kick in, and my ability to move the nose of the aircraft would become restricted. The MiG-29 had a conventional flight control system and superb maneuverability at high angles of attack. He would eventually get his nose on me and that would be that. While he probably wouldn't have the minimum range necessary for a missile shot, I'd be a sitting duck for the MiG's internal 30mm cannon, even though the jet carried a mere 150 rounds.

But I had a plan.

In the process of the upcoming merge, there would be a narrow window where a gunshot could be possible. If I could get a few 20mm rounds into his jet, and avoid colliding with his aircraft, I might be able to change the game.

We were about 2,000 feet apart, and we had about another 45 degrees of turn to negotiate before we'd be pointing at each other. I toggled my radar into the 10 x 60 mode, where it looks to the inside of the turn, increased my bank angle, and shoved the throttle into MAX AB. Then, I pulled aft on the sidestick as hard as I could.

Once again, the phenomenon of temporal distortion kicked in, and the milliseconds seemed to turn into long moments.

LOCK! LOCK! said the luscious voice in my headset.

In my HUD, a line of video appeared. It led from the gun cross at the top of the display to the target ID box that was now superimposed on the MiG, a function of the radar lock. Next to the gun cross, the number 25 materialized. The MiG was 25 degrees off my nose.

My nose began tracking toward the MiG. The number next to the gun cross decreased rapidly. I adjusted my bank angle so that the funnel of the gunsight was oriented in the MiG's plane of motion and continued to apply backpressure to the sidestick. There wouldn't be time for a stabilized gunshot because if I stopped my turn to point at his aircraft, I'd collide with him. I'd have to drag the pipper or "death dot" though his aircraft and hope I got some rounds into him as I continued the turn to pass next to him.

For a moment or two, the MiG continued his turn in a level plane. But then, the NK pilot seemed to guess my game plan. He executed the standard maneuver that every fighter pilot is trained to perform when an air-to-air gunshot was imminent: a jink. The jink was an aggressive out of plane maneuver designed to foil the tracking solution of an opponent. The MiG pilot executed it perfectly. He unloaded for a microsecond, rotated his lift vector out of our plane of motion, and reapplied backpressure. His nimble jet went vertical, completely spoiling the opportunity for my gunshot.

Which was exactly what I wanted him to do.

Before he had a chance to realize what he was doing or correct his maneuver, he vanished into the clouds above us.

I didn't have much time. The NK pilot would find his way out of the clouds in mere seconds. I needed to be in a better position when he did. But which way to turn? And how quickly to do it. What would the MiG driver expect?

I processed a few options and then rolled to the right, continuing my direction of turn but relaxing the backpressure on the sidestick. I kept the jet level just below the clouds. I pulled the throttle out of AB and glanced down at my fuel totalizer.

"4100 pounds, Pearce," I muttered into the intercom. "Not a lot of fucking gas to fight with and then get the fuck out here."

The right thing to do would have been to leave the area. Pull my nose toward the exit point, light the wick and depart NK airspace as quickly as 28,000 pounds of thrust could make it happen. A smart man would have done just that.

But my anger and my frustration wouldn't let me leave. Someone had to pay for what had happened to Mark Hill. And someone had to pay for the terror that Sarah and the kids were enduring. Maybe, in the next few moments, that someone would be the nameless North Korean pilot in the MiG. Maybe, in the next few days, that someone would be Brenda Rowe and her crew. But I had an idea who the someone would be. Sooner or later, it would be me. I was the one who needed to pay.

"Come on, commie," I said to my nameless adversary who was still trapped in the clouds above me, "Get your ass down here. I'm not done with you yet."

It is dangerous to stay in a constant turn in a combat environment. It makes your flight path predictable to those above and those below. It also creates a huge blind spot on the outside of the turn. A memory from several years ago flashed through my consciousness. I had been in a defensive turn, and a crafty opponent had almost killed me by entering the fight from the outside of the turn. Reflexively, I rolled out to scan the area to my left.

For the second time that night, instinctive action saved my life. I had no sooner become wings level when the MiG came through the clouds directly in front of me, in a gradual descending turn, so close that I could see individual feathers of the engine nozzles as it moved down and to my right. If I had continued my own turn, we would have collided.

I watched him with rapt curiosity as he continued his turn. I could almost feel the intensity of his thoughts as he searched the airspace around his aircraft, searching for me, looking for the slightest trace of where I had gone.

"This isn't even going to be fair," I said to myself.

I was behind him and on the outside of his turn. He didn't even know I was there. The prudent thing to do would have been to float further outside the turn, put the missile reticle on him with my helmet and not lock him up with the radar, shove the remaining AIM-9 up his ass and blow him out of the sky.

I suddenly found that I didn't have the appetite for any more killing tonight. I pulled my nose to his jet and settled the gun cross just above his left wing. My plan was to lock him up, put the death dot on his left wing, and saw the wing off with 20mm bullets. Then, he'd have the opportunity to bail out of his crippled jet and live to fight another day.

But the MiG driver's quick reactions took that option away from me and ended his life. The moment I pushed the target management switch forward to lock him up, he instinctively reversed his turn into me. I didn't have much time to react.

LOCK! LOCK!

The death dot ranged in and settled on the canopy of the MiG-29, and I squeezed the trigger. The M-61A1 Gatling gun spewed 20mm death across the sky at 6,000 rounds per minute and over 3,000 feet per second. The stream of high explosive incendiary bullets shattered the cockpit and cut through the center of the MiG's fuselage, igniting the fuel tanks and generating a nearly instantaneous fireball.

"Fuck!" I spat into my oxygen mask.

I unloaded, rolled to the right and pulled my nose away from the carnage, but once I was clear of the potential impact, I rolled back to the left and watched as the fiery wreckage slowly fell to the waters of the bay below in an odd, protracted trajectory, almost as if it was trying to extend its time in the air.

I heard the ping of an incoming text message in my headset, but I didn't look at it. Instead, my eyes continued to follow the remains of the MiG as it floated downward.

"Poor bastard," I murmured. "You were too proficient for your own good."

Another ping resounded in my ear.

"Yeah, yeah, Dave," I said. I centered the DOGFIGHT switch on the throttle and called up the navigation master mode in the jet. Then, I pulled the nose to center the steering cue in the flight path marker and pushed the throttle up to MIL power. Once I was on course, I glanced down at the right MFD to see the messages.

GET YOUR ASS OUT OF THERE, the first message said. FOUR MORE MIGS INBOUND. F-22S IN PLACE TO COVER YOUR EGRESS.

I raised my eyebrows as I read. "F-22s?" I asked myself. "Where the hell did they come from?" My eyes moved to the next message.

TANKER WAITING FOR YOU. SENDING YOU RENDEZVOUS POINT COORDINATES.

I nodded as I looked down at my fuel totalizer. I had 3000 pounds of fuel remaining, not enough to get back to Kunsan with any reserve.

"Good thing," I laughed tiredly into the intercom. "After all this shit, the last thing I want to do now is end up swimming because I ran out of gas."

CHAPTER THIRTY-THREE

Tuesday, January 19th
2230 Hours Local Time
Hardened Aircraft Shelter 22
Kunsan Air Base (RKJK), Republic of South Korea

"Take your stuff, sir?"

I looked up to see my crew chief standing next to my cockpit. He was patiently waiting for me to hand him the nylon bag in my lap with the helmet, data transfer cartridge, and target materials. The expression on his young face was an odd mixture of awe and disbelief.

I nodded dumbly and handed him the bag. Then I went about the chores of unfastening myself from the Viper, glad that the rain had abated, and I could take my time with the tasks in the open cockpit. As I released the survival kit straps, Koch parachute fittings, g-suit hose, and oxygen hose, it occurred to me that I didn't recall much about the flight back. I remembered that there had been some commotion on the radio as I had flown to the tanker, but I had been too exhausted to process it. Thanks to the long day and the effort required to fly the mission, all of the elements of my return to base, the air refueling, the approach, landing, and taxi back, were blurred memories.

I extracted myself from the Viper's cockpit. I made my way down the boarding ladder, pausing at the bottom to unbuckle the leg straps of the parachute harness and fasten them outside my legs. Then, I turned around to find a reception committee waiting for me, lined up in a row in front of the crew van. There was a three-star general that I recognized from the teleconference earlier. He appeared younger in person than he had on the screen, and he looked trim and fit in the standard olive green flightsuit and A-2 leather jacket. The leather name tag said: John Weeks, Lieutenant General, USAF. The wing commander, Dave Moody was next in line. Then there was the lovely Colonel Jess Tate. Jay Lindell, the squadron commander who I had borrowed the jet from, stood next to her. At the end of the line, stood the man who hadn't expected to see me alive again, CIA Operations Officer Dave Smith. I could see him shaking his head with a disbelieving smile on his face.

The general stepped forward first and extended his hand. "Damn fine work out there," he said. "The North is in an uproar about it. Normally, we'd be worried about that, but we're getting a lot of chatter indicating that a huge power struggle is in progress, and that is distracting the hell out of them."

I nodded as I shook his hand. "That was quick," I said. "So, General Myung-Dae was right?"

Weeks nodded in return. "It would seem so."

"Glad it wasn't all for naught," I said, releasing his hand.

"You've done your country a huge service, Colonel Pearce."

"Which no one will ever know about," I replied tiredly. "But that's the world I live in these days. I'm okay with that."

Weeks nodded at Moody. "I'm going to get back on the helo and get back to Osan, Dave. I think this man has earned a drink. Maybe you can have something set up for him during the debrief."

"Already happening, General," Moody answered.

"Take care of yourself, Colonel Pearce," the general said. Then he allowed himself a wry smile. "I'd tell you to stay out of trouble, but something tells me you won't."

I nodded at him as I raised my arm in a salute. "It does seem to find me, sir." He smartly returned the salute and walked to a staff car waiting for him beyond the van.

Moody stepped forward next and extended his hand. "Great work, hero," he said. "I guess you impressed somebody if the three-star flies down from Osan for the sole purpose of shaking your hand."

I shrugged as I shook Moody's hand. "Just glad to be here. And alive."

"We won't keep you too long for the debrief," he said. "In spite of the covert nature of your mission, it was under super-surveillance by every intelligence asset we could spare..."

"That's for sure," Smith said, nodding his head in agreement as he looked down at the cement.

"We have most of the picture," Moody continued. "We just need you to fill in a few details."

"Here to help," I said.

Moody motioned to the van behind him. I picked up my helmet bag and moved to enter it. But before my foot hit the ground, Jessica Tate stepped towards me quickly, threw her arms around me, and pulled me to her.

"I'm so glad you're okay," she said, her breath warm in my ear.

I closed my eyes and reveled in the feeling of her body next to mine. "Me too," I said.

We held each other for probably a moment or two longer than a friendly hug would have lasted. As we separated, I could see both Moody and Smith eyeing us. Both were shaking their heads and had smiles on their faces.

"Barely here a day, and you've already corrupted my vice-commander," Moody said under his breath.

Jess winked at him. "But what a way to go," she said. Then she unabashedly took me by the hand and led me into the van. We climbed into the rearmost row and sat down. Smith and Moody got into the row in front of us, and Lindell got into the driver's seat. Moments later, we pulled out of the parking spot and headed down the taxiway towards wing headquarters.

As we drove, I leaned my head back against the seat's headrest and shut my eyes, enjoying the warm and human touch of Jess's hand in mine. I let my mind wander, and it ventured to the same place it had gone numerous other times tonight, to the odd coincidence of being back at Kunsan all these years later and flying a sortie in the Viper from the base's 8,000-foot runway. Imitating the past, but not imitating the past. Performing a version of the mission in the present that I had trained for two decades ago. It all seemed so damn surreal.

"Thanks for bringing my jet back," Lindell said from the driver's seat. "They're not making Block 40s anymore, and we wouldn't have been able to replace it."

"You're welcome, Jay," I said without opening my eyes, "but that was pure luck. Four other MiGs were hunting me, and they probably would have killed me if they had shown up. I only had one AIM-9 and about 200 rounds of gun left."

"They did show up," Moody said. "They were being vectored to intercept you from the North. "But we had a pair of F-22s on CAP duty over the Yellow Sea backing you up. They saw the four MiGs before AWACs did. They supercruised in, knocked the MiGs down, and supercruised out. I don't think the NKs ever saw them."

I nodded. "That's all the traffic I heard on the radio on my way to the tanker."

"Some of it," Moody said. "There was also a whole discussion with the SK Air Force about whether you were friendly or hostile since they weren't expecting you. All the exploding jets on the north side of the border drew their attention. Fortunately, we got that situation resolved."

"Yes," I said. "I can't believe this nutty plan worked."

"We'll have to wait until the dust clears to see if your airstrike will have the far-reaching effects that the North Korean General said it would," Jess said from beside me. "But the initial indications are excellent. The intel folks are being inundated with imagery and signals data. So far, it points to a massive power struggle underway. It looks like the folks from that energy company are going to get some serious scrutiny. What was the name of it, Enter-something?'

"Enteron," I said, snapping my head up and opening my eyes. I found myself looking directly at Dave Smith's face. He had pivoted in his seat and was looking back at Jess and I. "Where's Rowe and the 7X?" I asked him.

"I wondered when we'd get around to that," he said. He glanced down at something in his lap. I presumed it was his phone. "At the moment, they're over the Sea of Japan, on their way back to Chicago via Anchorage."

"Damn," I said. "When did they take off?"

"About fifteen minutes after you left North Korean airspace."

"So, they knew, she knew, what happened. And what it meant."

Smith nodded. "Looks like."

"You know she's on her way back to deal with Sarah and the kids, Dave. Have your people found them yet?"

He shook his head. "We couldn't get a warrant because we couldn't narrow it down to one specific plant. Enteron has so damn many of them we didn't know which ones to specify. We tried to get a blanket warrant, but the federal judge wouldn't go for it. Then, we tried limiting the warrant to the plants Enteron has in Illinois, but the judge wouldn't go for that either."

"Damn," I said.

He nodded and looked up at the ceiling of the van for a few seconds as he exhaled in frustration. Then he looked back at me. "If we knew the exact plant, I think our guys in Washington could rush the warrant through and get approval for an Ops Team strike," he said. "But we'd have to be pretty certain. Until then, we can't do shit."

I put my head back on the headrest and shook it from side to side as I thought. I felt Jess give my hand a reassuring squeeze. She had obviously been briefed on the situation.

"Well, they'd have to be in Illinois somewhere," I said. "Driving them out of the state wouldn't make sense."

"We agree."

"What are the locations in Illinois?"

Smith took a moment as he consulted something on his phone. "Well, it's like I told you. There are seven and they're all in or near small towns. One in Brakeville, one in Bisone, one in Clinton, one in Manion, one in Versailles," he paused for a second, "how in the hell is there a Versailles in Illinois?" he asked. "Then there is one near Davenport, Iowa, but on the Illinois side of the Mississippi River and finally one in Zeebree, Illinois."

As he read the list, I felt something pulling at my brain. "Where are you, Sarah?" I whispered to myself.

"I told you where," a voice that sounded like hers said from somewhere inside my head. "I showed you where."

"Read the list again, please."

Smith began to go through the list again, but I stopped him as he got to the third name.

"She told us where she is, Dave," I said, sitting up and looking at him. "She showed us where. They told her where and she told us."

"What are you talking about?"

"The picture," I said. "Remember the one picture that was broken when they took her. The picture that the kidnappers obviously put back on the shelf?"

"What picture?"

"Remember? Your team saw it. It was the picture of her and a very important passenger she flew once upon a time. A former president?"

Smith's eyes widened as the knowledge came to him. He opened his mouth to speak, but I finished my thought before he could.

"Clinton," I said. "Bill Clinton. She's at the Clinton Plant, Dave. And that's where we'll go get her."

He nodded. "I'll let Amrine know," he said. "He'll get the warrant paperwork rolling and get a team tasked for the ingress."

"I want to be on that team."

"How do you propose to get there at or before Rowe does?" he asked. "She's got a pretty good head start."

"Oh, I don't know," I said, shrugging. "Given that the life on an innocent woman and two small kids is hanging in the balance, I'm betting these fine officers here would be willing to lend me a jet for a mere milk run from here to the U.S. I'd need tanker support of course."

"You can use the same one you just flew, T.C.," Jay Lindell said from the front seat. He inclined his head towards Moody. "If the Wolf there is okay with it. It was headed to the depot in a few months anyway. I'll have the racks pulled off and new wing tanks installed. It will be fueled and preflighted within the hour."

He brought the van to a stop in front of the Wing Headquarters. Moody turned around in his seat.

"Approved," he said. "But you won't be able to leave that soon. It will take us five to six hours to coordinate the tanker support."

I could see Smith doing some math in his head. After a moment, he nodded and looked at me. "The timing should work," he said. "The 7X will have to stop in Anchorage for gas and land at Chicago. You can make the time up by going direct at a faster speed, hitting the tankers enroute, and landing at an airport closer to the plant."

"It's settled then," Moody said. He looked at me. "And you've got to be exhausted," he said. "After the debrief, I think you should use that time to get some rest. Do I need to get you someplace to stay?"

As I was beginning to reply, Jess squeezed my hand to stop me from speaking. "I'll handle that, Dave," she said. "I've got the perfect place in mind."

CHAPTER THIRTY-FOUR

Wednesday, January 20th
1130 Hours Local Time
FL 290 and 310 knots
Air Refueling Track 508E
West of Alaska, USA

After averaging Mach 1.25 crossing the northern Pacific Ocean, I had joined the air refueling track off the coast of Alaska with a thirsty Viper. I was catching up with Rowe and crew, but I was killing a lot of dinosaurs in the process. Thank God for tanker support.

"Contact, sir," the boomer said over the intercom.

"Contact here also," I replied. I glanced down at my fuel totalizer and saw the numbers increasing. "Taking gas," I said.

"Copy that, sir."

Unlike the boomer in my last refueling, over Northern Japan, who spent the entire engagement telling me how much he loved the Air Force, this gentleman was thankfully silent. I was grateful for the lack of conversation as I reviewed the scenario yet again.

It sucked that Rowe and crew had about a six-hour head start, but that reality was unavoidable. For non-wartime operations, aerial tankers are extremely difficult to schedule without substantial notice. Most tanker units are committed months in advance to support deployments, exercises, or regularly scheduled refueling practice. Scrambling four of them on short notice and having them deploy to specific geographic orbits to support my journey was no small feat. Yet somehow, in a few hours, Moody and Smith, working with the powers that be in the Pacific Theater, and in the U.S., had made it happen. I couldn't imagine the strings they had to have pulled.

I tried to put the time I had been given to good use. After a quick debrief at the 8th Fighter Wing Headquarters, Jess took me back to her quarters, let me use her shower, and put me to bed. I was asleep seconds after my head hit the pillow.

After four hours of dreamless sleep, my phone rang.

"We've got three coordinated, and we're waiting for confirmation on the fourth," Smith had said without preamble. "Sadly, the one we're waiting on is the first one over northern Japan, so you can't leave yet. Still the middle of the night here, obviously, which comes with its own set of problems. We think we're close, though. You better get up and about and be ready for the call."

"Roger that," I had said. "By the way, do you have some of those CIA performance-enhancing drugs available? It's going to be a long flight, and I'll need to have the strength to be part of the entry team when I get there."

Smith had chuckled. "I'll see what I can do." He rang off.

Jess had stirred next to me when I answered the phone and had nestled herself next to me as Smith had talked. Now, her hand was caressing my torso, and her warm breath was in my ear.

"How much time do we have?" she had whispered.

"No idea," I had replied as I rolled towards her. Hopefully enough."

We received notice that the first tanker would be on station about thirty minutes later. Fifteen minutes after that, I arrived at the jet in Jess's staff car. Lindell was waiting for me with a life support technician, flight gear, a data transfer cartridge, and a navigation package. He had arranged the rendezvous to save me a trip to the squadron building.

Smith had been there too, along with a female flight surgeon who looked young enough to be my granddaughter. I dutifully offered my arm to her. She produced a hypodermic needle and injected me.

"I probably don't want to know the answer, but what's in that stuff?" I had asked.

"I got the compound formula from your buddy there," she had said, nodding. "And you're right. You don't want to know. I'm not sure I did."

"What will it do?"

"Relieve your pain, enhance your mood, and increase your energy. For about 24 hours. But after that..."

"After that, what?" I demanded.

She gave me a doctor's knowing smile. "You're going to crash and burn. You'll need to sleep for about a day."

"I'll keep that in mind," I had said.

I had suited up and shaken Smith's and Lindell's hands. Then, Jess and I had a quick but soulful embrace, offering promises to see each other again while knowing that the possibility was doubtful.

I was airborne ten minutes later.

***

Now, over the cold waters of the northern Pacific, I pondered my time with Jess again. We had only been together for a short interval, but there was a timeless element to us that seemed new and unique. I was also aware that it dulled the pain of my eventual release of Sarah and the kids to a life without me.

That thought brought me back into the moment. "Assuming they're still alive," I said to myself.

"Pardon me, sir?" the boomer asked.

"Nothing," I answered, bringing myself back into the moment. "Just thinking out loud."

I put my mind on the math. Smith's calculations seemed to be holding. Given typical travel times, Rowe and crew would arrive back at Chicago's Midway Airport at about 1230 AM local time. From there, it was about a two hour and fifteen-minute drive to the plant at Clinton, located approximately 150 miles south, southwest of Chicago off of Interstate 55. Assuming they actually landed at Chicago and didn't divert to somewhere further south. Even though I had left Korea six hours after they did, I was flying much faster, Mach 1.25 as I crossed the northern pacific and .99 Mach across the land. I was also flying a more direct route, and I wouldn't have to spend an hour on the ground in Anchorage, clearing customs and getting refueled. With any luck and two more expeditious air refuelings, I'd be on the ground at Springfield, Illinois, the airport at the state's capital city at about 0100 hours. Springfield was home to the Air National Guard's 183rd wing, which until recently had operated F-16s. They would be very familiar with my jet. The CIA Ops Team would be waiting for me in a C-130, and we'd be airborne and off to Clinton in moments, hopefully beating Rowe and crew to the destination.

I clenched my jaw as I considered the timing. It was possible that Rowe would order Sarah and the kids killed before she got there. It was also possible they were already dead. But I was betting neither would be the case. Rowe would want to be there and look Sarah and the kids in the eye and tell them how I failed to save them. She'd want to see the disappointment and fear on their faces. And she'd want to enjoy their deaths. Personally.

I glanced down at the fuel totalizer. It was approaching the jet's maximum capacity. The boom separated from my jet, and I saw a small spray of fuel as the boomer retracted it upward.

"Pressure disconnect, sir," he said over the radio.

"Copy that," I answered. I reached down to the left side panel and hit the switch to close the air refueling door on the top of the jet, a standard procedure that allowed the boomer to see the door close.

"Cleared off, sir," he said.

"Leaving your frequency," I said. "Switching back to Anchorage Center."

I punched Anchorage's frequency into the Viper's upfront control panel and thought about my arrival in Springfield five hours from now. An image of Rowe's bony face popped into my head with the same maniacal expression she had when she held my genitals in her hand and asked my captor if she could take them for a souvenir.

"I'm coming for you, Brenda," I uttered into the intercom. "And I'm going to take everything you fucking have."

CHAPTER THIRTY-FIVE

Thursday, January 21th
0215 Hours Local Time
15,000 Feet and 220 knots
Over Central Illinois, USA

The loud, mechanical, whine of the C-130's cargo door roused me from a short nap that had lasted the fifteen minutes since we had taken off. I startled and tried to jump to my feet, only to be restrained by the seat belt, holding me to the canvas seats in the cargo bay of the aircraft. I impatiently released the belt and stood up, ensuring the muzzle of my M-4 remained pointed downward.

"Relax, T.C.," the squad leader said over the communications link in my helmet in his precise voice, "we weren't going to leave without you."

As I gained my footing in the darkened cargo hold, I lowered my NVGs into position over my eyes and powered them on. Per the standard procedure for night jumps, the bay was blacked out before the main door opened to avoid highlighting the aircraft to hostiles who might be looking for it. My newly acquired night vision came into focus, and I took in the group around me. There were ten of them, all dressed in black tactical gear with multiple weapons strapped onto them. When I met them at the airport earlier, they had known who I was but had not introduced themselves by name.

"Better that you don't know," the squad leader had said. "For all of us. We're Zulu Squad. I'm Zulu One, and the rest of the squad is two though ten. You can call us by our numbers. We'll call you T.C."

I had nodded, thinking of Sharona, whose real name I had never learned for the same reason. "Fair enough."

"Not sure I'm sorry you didn't leave without me," I said. "I can't even believe I'm going to jump out of a perfectly good airplane again."

"When was the last time you did it?" One of the other team members with a southern accent asked.

"About six years ago," I said. "And I ended up having to pull my reserve because my main canopy malfunctioned. We had a traitor on the crew who sabotaged it."

"No worries there," the squad leader said. "Bruiser and Bart seem to like you. And if they like you, that's good enough for us. We'll take good care of you. We'll also get your girl and her kids out of there without a scratch."

"Assuming we can find them," I said.

"We have pretty good intel on where they could be. There's a conference room that is down the hall from the reactor control room. It's just about the only place on the hard side of the plant where they can limit access to personnel, but also be close to restrooms. Apparently, they keep cots in the room for long shifts and contingencies."

I nodded. "That's pretty damn precise intel," I said. "Hopefully, we'll all survive long enough to use it. How good is the security force do you think?"

The squad leader shrugged. "They could be very good. Every nuclear power station in the US has its own security force to prevent exactly what we're trying to do, gain access to the main reactor building. Many of them are ex-policemen or armed forces. They train regularly and practice against several scenarios. But there has never been a ground assault on a nuclear plant in the U.S., and complacency can make even the best security forces sloppy. One thing we've got going for us is that these guys typically train for a ground ingress, not an aerial one. We're hoping that will give us the element of surprise. We also have two snipers in position to cover our landing. They'll deal with any ground troops that try to shoot at us while we're under-canopy."

I nodded again. "Not surprised you guys have got this doped out," I said. "And per our agreement, I'll do my best to stay out of the way while you do your thing. I just hope we get there in time."

"Me too," the squad leader replied.

Our elaborate timing had not worked out the way we had hoped. Rowe's 7X had landed early thanks to strong tailwinds and a 30-minute turn on the ground in Anchorage. She also had diverted the jet to Decatur, Illinois, which was just over 30 road miles from the Clinton Generating Station. Our C-130, on the other hand, had been late thanks to air traffic control restrictions into the Springfield Airport. Ground intel had told us that a small convoy of vehicles had entered the plant twenty minutes ago. We were already late.

A red light illuminated overhead the C-130's cargo door.

"Two minutes!" The squad leader said calmly. "Lock and load."

Like the rest of my team, I inserted a 30-round magazine into the well of my M-4 carbine and charged the weapon. I doubled-checked that the selector switch was in SAFE and tightened the straps to secure the weapon to my chest. I reached down to the quick access holster on my right leg, removed the 1911 .45 automatic, ensured it was charged, and replaced it.

"45 guy, eh?" the team member standing closest to me

asked.

I nodded. "I just want to make sure the bad guys go down if I actually hit them."

He removed his sidearm from his holster and offered it for inspection. "Me too," he said. "But you might think of looking at the Sig P220 instead of the 1911. It's got the same magazine capacity, but you lose the single-action trigger. It's easier to recover, and it points better."

I took the pistol from him and gripped it. Then I aimed it at a few of the rivets on the C-130's cargo deck. It felt good in my hands. I gave it back to him.

"Nice," I said. "I'll have to check it out."

"Stand-by," the squad leader said.

The team members lined up behind him. I took my place behind the last man. Like the rest of them, I verified that my parachute harness was secure and that my helmet strap was tight. Then, unlike the rest of them, I reacquainted myself with the exact position of the drogue chute compartment for the main chute and the ripcord for the reserve one. I closed my eyes and reached for both a few times to make sure I could find them.

"Okay, gang, remember," the squad leader said, "we're pulling at 2,000 feet on the altimeter. That's about 1,200 to 1,300 feet above the ground. You'll be under canopy for about a minute. The LZ is the parking lot inside the fence on the southwest side of the main reactor building. The snipers will be in concealed observation positions and deal with anyone who looks hostile."

The light over the door turned green. Without a further word, the squad leader turned around, ran down the ramp, and jumped off into the night. The other team members followed. Without allowing myself time for thought or consideration, I ran after them.

Moments later, I was in the air and falling towards the

Clinton generating station far below us. The detail provided by the NVGs was remarkable. I could clearly see the well-lit compound with its central reactor building, side buildings, and parking lots. The station was surrounded by a lake that reminded me of an octopus in orientation and form, with legs oriented to the northeast and a squiggly-shaped head to the southwest. The shoreline of the lake, with its accompanying details, was distinctly visible as well. The whole mosaic seemed to be slowly rising to meet me.

When you jump out of a forward-moving aircraft, there is virtually no sensation of falling. Instead, there is only the wind against your body, like you're in a wind tunnel with a gale-force air current pummeling your torso and limbs.

But you are falling, at about 200 feet per second. The time of fall from 15,000 to our opening altitude was just over a minute, which isn't a lot of time when your mind is active considering landing sites and possible hostiles on the ground.

I saw the first canopy open up beneath me as the squad leader activated his parachute and was amazed that an entire minute had gone by. The black rectangle of nylon appeared in the night almost instantaneously. The rest of the squad deployed their canopies straightaway. I reached back to my right hip, found the drogue chute compartment easily, ripped the Velcro open, and tossed the drogue into the airstream. Almost immediately, I felt the jerk of rapid deceleration as my fall was reduced to about 10% of its previous rate.

Where there had been intense wind noise and vibration, there was now utter, serene silence. That lasted for about five seconds.

I felt a vibration in the air near my face, and saw several holes appear in the canopy above me. A millisecond later, I heard the staccato sound of automatic rifle fire. One of the parachutes below me began to aimlessly wander out of our train of jumpers and head off to the right.

"Six appears to be down," one of the other team members said with a distinct Bronx accent.

"One copies," the squad leader replied. "Evasive action. You know where the LZ is." He laughed dryly. "T.C. you might just get a shooting role in this gig."

Assuming we all make it to the ground, I thought.

I didn't know what evasive action under a parachute canopy looked like, but I knew how to do it in a jet. I immediately began using the steering lines to make random turns with my canopy. Below me, the other squad members were doing the same thing. I nodded to myself. *Jinking is jinking*, I thought, *regardless of the platform.*

More volleys of automatic weapons fire came our way, but we were managing to avoid them. For the moment. The lower we descended, the closer we came to the shooter, and the less effective our maneuvers would become.

"Ground one and two why aren't you getting lead on this guy?" the squad leader demanded.

"Ground one negative contact," the first sniper replied.

"Ground two same," said the second one.

"He appears to be on the roof of the main reactor building, Zulu One," the first sniper said. "We can see the flash when he shoots, but we don't have an angle to get any ordnance on him. He's too well concealed."

They knew we were coming, I thought. *How in the hell did they know that?*

Our group was arcing north around the compound to make our landing approach to the parking lot on the southwest. To a shooter on the top of the large reactor building to our left, we were perfectly arranged to be picked off, one by one, despite our maneuvering.

Without thinking, I pulled my left steering toggle and turned towards the building. Then I loosened the straps on my M-4 and raised the carbine to my shoulder as I armed it.

The reactor building consisted of two sections. The bulbous reactor tower sat atop a square-shaped building to the southwest. The long rectangular building with the generating turbines was adjacent, oriented southwest-northeast. The roof on both buildings seemed to have cement walls on the edges, which was presenting barriers to the snipers.

But they were shooting from ground level. I wouldn't be.

I saw a flash of rifle fire come from the roof of the reactor building just as I heard another string of shots.

"Three is down," said a new team voice.

Son of a bitch, I thought. I raised my rifle, centered the crosshairs of my sight where I had seen the flash, and let go with two three-shot bursts.

"What are you doing, T.C.?" a voice asked. "You need to stay on course for the LZ."

I ignored it. I was waiting. I knew that I probably hadn't hit the rifle bearer. But I might have shaken him up a little. He'd have to deal with the new threat, me, before he could shoot at another one of our group. I was descending in a path that would force me to land on the same roof where the gunman was. If I maintained my current course, I'd land just to the left of the reactor tower itself. I had no idea what kind of surface was on the roof or if there were pipes or vents that I couldn't see behind the wall. But that was a future concern. For the moment, I was just trying to stay alive.

Through the NVGs and rifle sight, I watched the wall at the edge of the roof carefully, looking for the slightest movement. I could see the etches and defects in the concrete in clear detail, so I was confident I'd be able to see the gunman if he raised his head and his weapon. I fired another three-shot burst at the location where the shots came from.

It was then that the infrared feature of the NVGs proved to be particularly useful. I saw the movement of a heated human form to the left of where I had just fired. The figure appeared to be bent over, attempting to conceal himself behind the wall as he rapidly changed position to the northeast. I put the crosshairs on the form and fired three more shots. The form popped up, returned fire, and ducked back into concealment, but now that I was moving to his right and not directly at him, he didn't take the necessary lead into account, and his rounds missed me.

I glanced forward and noted that I was only about 100 feet from touchdown on the roof of the building, about 10 more seconds of flight time. I could see that I was going to pass directly across the axis of his movement, cutting off his escape or reposition route. But I had a severe tactical problem. I had to keep my path oriented directly ahead so that I could land safely, and he would be off my right side. I wouldn't be able to keep my rifle shouldered and engage him.

"Oh well," I said to myself.

I let the rifle fall against my chest and unholstered the .45, arming it with my right thumb as I raised it.

I was lower now, about 5 seconds from touchdown, and just above and outside the wall on the edge of the roof. In mere moments, I'd be passing directly in front of the shooter's position. I kept the .45 trained on where I'd last seen him and hoped he wasn't aware enough to understand what I was trying to do.

Two seconds later, I crossed over the wall and found myself pointing my weapon at no one. My assailant had vanished. I frantically searched for him for a few seconds, then realized I needed to land my canopy. I hurriedly shoved the .45 back into its holster, reached for the chute's steering toggles, and had just barely gotten my fingers into them when it was time to flare. I pulled down on both toggles as hard as I could. My descent and forward motion slowed simultaneously, and I landed very lightly on the cement roof of the reactor building.

I collapsed my canopy as quickly as I could and slid

out of my harness. Then I wrapped the harness around the canopy and stowed the rig behind some electro-mechanical equipment that was mounted in the corner of the roof area.

I had landed in the northeast corner of the roof area, where it abutted against a smaller structure. I could see a door directly to my left. It occurred to me that I'd have to find a way into the plant without forced entry tools of any kind. To make matters worse, if I got in, I had no map or directions to lead me to the conference room.

"Nice work, Pearce," I said to myself.

I raised my M-4 to the ready position and began to make my way around the reactor tower to ensure my stalker wasn't still lurking somewhere. Several volleys of automatic weapons fire cut through the night air. They sounded close but not nearby. The ground assault on the plant had begun. Then I realized I had heard no communications traffic since the radio call warning me about turning away from the landing zone. I began to feel a knot in my gut.

"This is T.C.," I said into my mic. "I'm on the roof where the reactor tower is. I've lost sight of the guy who is up here. Does anyone copy?"

Silence. *That can't be good.*

I continued around the reactor tower to the right, moving as swiftly as I could, the rubber soles of my boots quieting my steps. As I approached the southwest side of the reactor tower, overlooking the landing zone, I heard another burst of automatic weapons fire. Very close by. I instinctively crouched down and low walked, trying to make my way around the structure without becoming too exposed. A few feet further and I had eyes on the shooter. He was dressed in a kind of rent-a-cop uniform with a long-barreled automatic rifle, complete with a nightscope and bipod. The immediate implication was obvious. The CIA snipers were down.

Fuck.

He fired another long burst, apparently oblivious to my presence. He had to be shooting at the CIA entry team. I wondered if he had killed another one of them. I raised my rifle to take him down, my finger already taking in the slack on the trigger as I brought it up.

Then I felt a crushing blow on the back of my neck, the force of it driving me to my knees and causing the proverbial stars to appear in front of my eyes. Then another blow came, and I was forced to the pavement, barely able to turn my head in time to avoid face-planting into the cold, hard, surface.

"Why didn't you just kill him?" a voice asked.

"I think he's the one she wants," a second voice answered. "Only a fighter pilot would turn out of line to engage an unknown subject on a rooftop and try to land a parachute in a small area like that."

I smiled to myself as I drifted out of consciousness, but the next words kept me awake for a few more seconds.

"Why does she want him?" voice one asked.

"She knew he'd come," voice two said. "There's something she wants him to watch."

CHAPTER THIRTY-SIX

Thursday, January 21th
0300 Hours Local Time
Clinton Power Station
Near Clinton, Illinois, USA

I was ready when the Darkness finally spoke to me. I realized that I had been waiting for it. I needed it.

It's time, the Darkness said. Patiently, but insistently.

I mentally nodded to myself. *I know,* I replied.

Are you ready? it asked me.

Yes, I replied.

You need to stay out of the way.

I mentally nodded again. *I will.*

Here we fucking go.

I kept my head slumped on my chest as I became aware of my surroundings. I was seated in a wheeled office chair, with my hands zip-tied behind me. I subtly tested my bindings and discovered that the plastic band wasn't nearly as tight as it could or should have been. I could also feel the pressure of a knife scabbard against the inside of my left leg. Neither of these things made sense. The defenders we had encountered seemed to be disciplined and organized. Not securing my binding or overlooking a weapon should not have been mistakes they would make.

Idiots, said the Darkness.

No, they're not that stupid, I responded. Then, as my brain processed the anomaly, I felt my lips begin to break into a smile. I fought to control it. *She was here. Somehow, she was here.*

I felt a surge of optimism. If she was here, we could kick their asses. No matter how many there were.

"Bring him around," said the cold, familiar voice. "We don't have all night."

"You don't have to do that, Brenda," I said, opening my eyes and raising my head. "I'm here. No thanks to your boy with the rifle or whatever the fuck he hit me with."

My eyes zoomed into focus. It seemed the CIA had been right. I was seated at the end of a long table in a typical corporate conference room with the usual company propaganda photos on the walls. This room had seen better days, however. The furniture looked worn and shabby, and the paint on the walls was faded and stained. The atmosphere felt stuffy. I couldn't decide if that had to do with the number of people in the room or the lack of windows to the outside world. As predicted, there were a few cots against the walls, and through the main door, I could see a sign on the wall that indicated the direction to the reactor control room.

Damn precise intel, I thought. *Almost a little too precise.*

I gazed around the room. The table was surrounded mostly by people in business wear, presumably company executives or workers in the plant. I recognized a few familiar faces from the altercation in the lobby of the flight department the Monday that I had taken the reins of the organization. Their faces were masks of anger and hatred. But there were degrees of eagerness and excitement in their expressions as well. I had a mental image of a crowd assembling in the central square of a medieval town before criminals were executed.

There were four burly men clad in the rent-a-cop uniform of the station's security force. They wore body armor and had the usual M-4 carbines strapped to them. Their eyes were alert and attentive. I was a threat that had been temporarily neutralized, and they were there to ensure I remained that way.

"Do you have any idea how big a pain in the ass you are?" Brenda Rowe's grating voice broke the brief silence. She was seated immediately to my left, as she had been in the conference room back at Enteron's flight operations facility. She sat back in her chair with her arms crossed. Her expression appeared to be calm, but her eyes blazed with animosity.

I shrugged in response. "What I know is that you've committed both treason and kidnapping, Brenda," I said, "What are you planning for an encore? You can't hide inside a nuke plant forever. Sooner or later, the Feds will come back for you. And when that happens, your security folks won't be able to stop them."

"They did a pretty good job tonight," she snorted. "*My folks* made your CIA buddies look like amateurs and captured them or took them out."

I looked across the room at the uniformed men. "Former Delta or SEALs?" I asked.

"Neither," said a deep male voice from behind me, "we don't need no military types to tell us how to do our job. We're all former SWAT."

"Huh," I said.

I could feel the cogs turning inside my head. *A highly-trained CIA strike team captured by a group of urban SWAT graduates? Didn't seem likely. But if she was here, other things could be at work.*

"Impressive," I continued. "But you realize the only reason you knew when and where to look was because you had intel.

Someone tipped you off."

The lack of reply verified my suspicion.

"None of that matters," Rowe snapped. "That's not why you're here." Her face contorted into a crooked smile. "We have some business to take care of." She glanced to her right, behind me, presumably at the security force man who had spoken earlier and nodded at him.

My chair was abruptly spun around 180 degrees. I found myself facing a large man with a blond hair cut in close-cropped military fashion and cruel blue eyes. He had the same pants as the security force personnel, but he had removed his body armor, gear, and uniform blouse. He stood before me, eying me the way a wolf might eye its prey, flexing his muscular arms and letting the tension build between us.

Or so he thought.

I could feel the blood racing in my veins as the Darkness began to cock my body for action. *Let me have him*, it said.

He's yours, I replied.

I turned my chair to the right with my feet. "Seriously, Brenda?" I asked through clenched teeth in a voice I barely recognized. "This is what you're going with? Some clown in a tee-shirt and a public beating?"

"I'm going to hurt you like you've never been hurt before," muscle guy said in his best menacing tone.

"Quiet, sonny," I spat out of the side of my mouth. "The grown-ups are talking." I looked directly into Rowe's enraged face. "After what Cho did to me in that room in North Korea, do you think there is anything junior here can do that will faze me?"

Rowe didn't answer me, but her eyes were widening as she saw the Darkness twisting my face and hardening my eyes. She turned her head to muscle guy and gave him a panicked look.

He reacted just as I'd hoped he would. He reached forward,

grabbed the arm of my chair, and spun me back to face him.

It's time.

The Darkness used the momentum of my spin to launch me out of the chair. Muscle guy had been bent over slightly as he grabbed my chair and the Darkness took advantage of that vulnerability in his posture, driving the top of my head under his chin and standing him up like a right uppercut to the jaw. He was thrown backward against the wall of the room and hit the surface hard. There was a look of dazed confusion on his formerly arrogant face.

The Darkness didn't give him time to recover.

It broke my arms free of the zip ties, snatched the long-bladed knife from my boot, and savagely slashed the blade across his throat from left to right, reveling in the feel of the razor-sharp blade cutting through the tendons, arteries, and veins in the thick neck. The look on muscle guy's face changed from confusion to stunned terror in a microsecond. The Darkness smiled at him as his arterial spray hit the side of my face.

He was dead, but the Darkness wasn't through with him yet.

It made another vicious slash across the muscular throat, from right to left this time, severing anything left intact by the first stroke. His head rolled off his neck, and his body collapsed to the floor. Arterial spray shot into the air, raining a fine mist of carnage down on the walls and furniture.

There was a collective gasp in the room behind me. The Darkness remembered there were others left to deal with. It slowly turned me to face Rowe, ignoring the others around the table. I could feel the warmth of muscle guy's blood and the maniacal grin that the Darkness had etched into my face. I raised the blade and pointed it at her bony face, swirling the point in a slow circle as I held it, letting her see the tissue on the knife and the blood dripping from it.

"You're next," said the voice.

Rowe was frozen in her chair. Her once arrogant face wore several small droplets of muscle guy's blood that had rained down upon her after his decapitation. Her bony visage had taken on a look of abject horror, the formerly angry eyes transformed into pools of fear.

"And I'm going to love it," I continued.

We held each other's eyes for a moment. Then, I stepped forward. But the noise of shuffle and movement across the room distracted me. I looked across the table to see the business types pushing their way past the security guards to get through the door and out into the hallway. The guards were trying to raise their weapons, but the mass of humanity moving past them and around them was interfering.

There's time, the Darkness whispered to me. *Let's take her.*

THUMP! THUMP!

Two explosions suddenly rocked the building, and a mild shock wave passed through the air. A forced entry was in progress. It seemed the CIA was back for round two.

Shit hot! I thought.

Screams and panic erupted in the room and hallway. The remaining businesspeople nearly trampled the security guards as they fled. It suddenly became apparent that the security boys would have a clear field of fire to engage me in mere seconds. I pushed the Darkness aside, squatted down, ripped muscle guy's Glock from the quick-release holster on his right leg, and threw myself on the floor under the table. I spotted the legs of the security guys and opened fire on them. I kept firing when the bodies and heads attached to the legs appeared as the guards collapsed. In seconds, the Glock was empty, and the four guards were dead in front of me. I crawled out from under the table next to them. I stripped one of the guards of his harness and weapons, donned his gear, and ensured his M-4 was loaded and charged.

Then I remembered Rowe. I spun around to face that side of the room, shouldering my weapon as I turned.

She was gone. Of course.

"Fuck!" the Darkness screamed into the empty room. As I held the M-4 in the ready position, I could feel my limbs quiver as adrenaline and warm blood surged through my veins. The Darkness wasn't satisfied. It wanted more. But there was no more to be had. At least not at the moment. I took some deep breaths, trying to return my heart rate to normal.

"Well look who remembered his old tricks," said a familiar female voice from the door.

I lowered my weapon as I turned to the voice. There, standing in the door, resplendent in black tactical gear and assorted weaponry, was Sharona Brown, accompanied by a second CIA operations team.

"We need to find Sarah and the kids," I said, my voice barely under control.

"Easy, Tiger," she said, watching me closely. "Team one already found them, and they're being evacuated as we speak," she said.

"How? I thought the members of Team One were all captured or killed. That's what Rowe said."

Sharona shook her head. "The first team's attack was designed to make these security types show us their best moves so we could engage them. The team did a little playacting to provide a diversion for the second team and to make the security guys overconfident."

I breathed a sigh of relief and felt some of the tension ease out of me. "Seems to have worked," I said. "By the way, I thought you liked to work alone."

She shrugged. "I came in here alone. Just a few hours after you told Smith you knew where they were. I've been hanging out in various places, staying out of sight, and making a map of the interior."

"Probably not the first ultra-high security place you've broken into."

She smiled but didn't answer.

"And I couldn't know about any of that because if I did, I could be forced to say something about it if I was interrogated."

Sharona nodded. "You know the drill."

"By the way, thanks for cutting the zip ties and providing the knife. Not sure when you did that, but it obviously helped."

"They were so convinced they were in total control, they left you alone in here for several minutes before the meeting started. I slipped in, took care of you, and made my way out to be in position for the second entry team." She looked around the room with an appraising smile on her face. "And apparently, you made good use of what I gave you." Then she turned back to me. "But you didn't get Rowe?"

I shook my head. "I had to do something about the security boys first. "She's gone. No idea where she went."

'She won't get far," Sharona said. "We've got her name and picture on every most-wanted list out there. She won't be able to even buy gas without someone recognizing her."

"That's good."

"So, what are you going to do now that Sarah and the kids are safe, and Rowe and gang are out of the picture?"

I looked over at her. "I think you and I both know there are some loose ends at Enteron I need to deal with."

She nodded. "What are you going to do about that?" she asked.

"Well," I replied, "for starters, I think I'm going to go to the flight department and get back to work."

CHAPTER THIRTY-SEVEN

Monday, January 25th
1553 Hours Local Time
At FL330 and Mach .85
On the ANTHM THREE Arrival
Baltimore-Washington International Airport (KBWI),
Maryland, USA

"November 613 Charlie Bravo, Washington Center, cross Lundy at flight level 290, descend via the Anthem Three arrival, landing runway 10 at Baltimore-Washington International Airport."

Allen Macy keyed the mic button on his side of the 7X's cockpit. "November 613 Charlie Bravo will descend via the Anthem Three, landing runway 10," he replied. Then he reached up to the altitude selector knob on the guidance panel and looked over at me. "Down to four thousand, do you agree?"

I looked at the arrival depiction on the lower center display and verified that the lowest altitude on that path of the arrival was indeed 4,000 feet. It was. I nodded at him.

Macy dialed the selector down to 4,000 feet and pointed at it with his left index finger. "Four thousand is set," he said.

"I see 4,000," I replied. I punched the VNAV button on the guidance panel. "V-Nav is set," I said.

Macy nodded.

With the arrival track and altitude programmed into the 7X's flight management system, the jet would now automatically descend to make the altitude restrictions on the arrival as it followed the lateral path to the airport.

"Can you handle ATC while I go off freq?" Macy asked. "I'm going to call the FBO and check on the boss's transportation."

I nodded at him. "Go for it."

It was standard practice in business jets to call the executive terminal at the destination airport 20 to 30 minutes before arrival to verify that ground transportation was in place for passengers. For today's flight, there was only one to be concerned with, Enteron's President and CEO, Mark Lane.

I ensured that my audio panel was set so I could monitor Macy's communication. I listened to him verify that Lane's driver had arrived. He also placed a fuel order and requested a lavatory service for the aircraft. Nothing out of the ordinary.

At least not yet.

Macy reconfigured his audio panel so he could speak on the current air traffic control frequency, then resumed the tense, expectant posture he had maintained since we boarded the aircraft in Chicago. I watched him absentmindedly touch the helmet bag he had stashed on the right console as he had done numerous times throughout the flight.

It was obvious he was waiting for something.

Apart from the interaction required to prep the aircraft for flight and operate the jet, we had not spoken at all. No small talk, no niceties, no idle communication. I had no interaction with Mark Lane, either. I had been in the cockpit when he had boarded the jet. Macy had greeted him and shut the boarding door after Lane was seated. In most circumstances, a sole passenger on a flight would at least stick his head in the cockpit and render a greeting. But not this time.

I wasn't surprised. His avoidance of contact and communication confirmed what I already suspected.

The 7X reached the top of descent point on the arrival. The jet's nose lowered, and its throttles smoothly retarded.

"Do you have that package for me, Allen?" Mark Lane's voice asked from behind us.

Without speaking, Macy gingerly retrieved the helmet bag from the right console and handed it back to Lane. As I watched him handle the bag, it became instantly apparent what was inside of it.

I opened my mouth without looking back and spoke even as I heard Lane unzip the bag. "Not sure I'd use something like that at altitude, Mark," I said. "You never know what could happen."

I turned to look over my right shoulder to find Mark Lane in the entry vestibule, immediately behind the cockpit. He was pointing a Glock pistol at me. It was a perfect position of advantage for him. He was just out of reach, and I was strapped into my seat. He looked at me for a moment, then looked down at the gun, then back at me. The expression on his face was regretful. Even apologetic. But his hand was steady.

"What the hell happened to you?" I asked. "Where's the CEO who was brave enough to take a bullet five years ago? I guess that speech about the realignment of your priorities after your wound was total bullshit."

He shrugged. "Maybe," he said. Then his face turned reflective. "When did you know?" he asked.

"It came to me while I was hanging from the ceiling in North Korea and Rowe accused me of working with the CIA," I said. "There was only one person she could have gotten that information from. You.”

“You should have stayed away,” Lane said, shaking his head. “Why didn’t you?”

“Because you fucked over and killed a friend of mine,” I said.

“We would have offered him a piece of the pie,” Lane said, “but you Academy types are too strait-laced. We knew he wouldn’t take it.”

I nodded. “You were right. That honor code stuff tends to run deep. Especially when lives are at stake.”

“Well, it didn’t do him any good, and it won’t do you any good either.”

I looked directly into his eyes. “That remains to be seen,” I said. “So, what’s your next move? Your organization has been decimated, and Rowe is on the run. We’ll be on the ground at BWI in 20 minutes. I guarantee you that a full contingent of folks who work for three-letter agencies will be waiting for us.” I looked over at Macy and returned my gaze to Lane. “It’s over, Mark.”

Lane stiffened. “Aren’t you forgetting who has the gun, Pearce? We’re not going to BWI. We’re going to go to Salisbury, Maryland. Brenda has a helicopter waiting for us there. It will fly us to a yacht that’s waiting off the coast in international waters. Then we’re off to cruise the world. There are hundreds of ports of call worldwide where there is no extradition treaty. And we have the initial payment from the North Koreans in a numbered account in Switzerland. Enough money for several lifetimes.”

I felt my eyes widen. “You and Rowe? Seriously? Never saw that coming. You’re leaving your wife and kids for that bony bitch? What’s the allure? Can she suck a bowling ball through a garden hose or something?”

A sly smile crept onto Lane’s face, but he ignored the question. “That’s not going to matter to you. At least, not for long." Lane inclined his head toward Macy. "Allen is going to divert us to Salisbury, and you will have had a tragic cardiac incident on the way. We'll have a special ambulance there to remove you."

I smiled at him as I allowed my left hand to fall to the outboard side of my seat. I grasped the end of the left seatbelt strap and slowly pulled it as tight as I could.

"You're not a gun guy, are you Mark?" I looked over at Macy and then back to Lane. "And numbnuts over there probably isn't either. So, I'm betting that gun is probably loaded with stock nine-millimeter ammo, not the subsonic velocity stuff with frangible projectiles. That means when you shoot me with it, the bullet will go through my body and into something else, or maybe even through the hull of the aircraft. I'm not sure a rapid decompression is the way you want to end your day."

As I spoke, I moved my hand to the strap between my legs and pulled it tight. When I was finished, I put my left hand on the control stick and used my right to tighten my right seat belt. All the while, I kept my gaze fixed on Lane's face.

"Aren't you curious why I'm here, Mark?" I asked. "I didn't have to take this flight today to help you make your getaway, yet here I am."

"Well, you screwed up," he said with a sneer. "You put yourself at our mercy. And that was a mistake." He began to raise the gun.

I shook my head and smiled at him. "It wasn't a mistake at all, Mark," I said. "And I didn't put myself at your mercy. I put you at mine."

I punched the autopilot off and slammed the control stick forward. Even with the 7X's pitch limiters engaged, the jet still went from one positive g to one negative g in a little over a second. Lane had a mere moment to look above him before his forehead hit the ceiling of the vestibule, and his neck was pushed backward at an awkward angle. I heard the gun discharge twice as his neck popped. Then I pulled into full aft stick, throwing his body to the floor of the vestibule.

I looked over at Macy, who was still reeling from the rapid maneuvering. With my right hand, I reached over to the left console beside me and grabbed one of thinner volumes of the 7X quick response handbook, a checklist bound in a hard-plastic cover. I propelled the checklist in a wide arc and slammed the edge of it into Macy's exposed throat as hard as I could. I could feel his larynx and trachea collapse as the book impacted. He began gasping and immediately and reaching for his throat with his hands.

"It won't do you any good," I said to him as I tossed the checklist onto the floor of the cockpit behind the pedestal. "You've probably got a little less than a minute. Enjoy the trip to hell, you arrogant little shit."

I re-intercepted the lateral and vertical paths of the arrival and reengaged the autopilot. Then I sat back in my seat and exhaled. I glanced over at Macy. His eyes were wide and sightless.

"That didn't take long," I said to the empty cockpit.

"November 613 Charlie Bravo, Washington Center," the radio crackled in my headset. "Contact Potomac Approach on 133.85."

"November 913 Charlie Bravo copies 133 decimal 85," I responded. "Switching."

I entered the frequency into the VHF radio on my side of the jet and checked in with approach control. They issued me instructions to continue with the arrival and to expect runway 10 at BWI.

I glanced down at the navigation display on the upper center display to follow the jet's progress on the arrival route. We seemed to be on profile in both the lateral and vertical paths. For the moment, the situation seemed to be normal. Or as normal as it could be with me at the controls of a business jet alone with two dead bodies aboard.

"Par for the course," I muttered. "Par for the fucking course."

I gazed out of the windscreen through the 7X's HUD, watching the altitude decrease as the jet flew down the path towards the airport. We had passed north of Washington Dulles airport and were headed north of BWI to set us up for a right turn to a left base leg for runway 10. The jet was about ten minutes from touchdown. I was sure Smith and Amrine would have a full team awaiting our arrival. I suspected they would be disappointed Lane was dead, but those were the breaks.

I looked back at Lane, lying still and prostrate on the floor. "What the fuck happened to you?" I asked his inert form. "I thought you were a standup guy. What the hell did she do to corrupt you like that?"

As I returned my gaze to the front of the jet, I felt a pinch of pain on the upper right side, just under my armpit. I unconsciously put my hand there and felt the warm wetness of fresh blood.

"Well, shit," I said to myself. "I haven't been shot for at least six years or so. I must be due." Then the warning I had given Lane came back to me. "Uh oh," I said.

A few moments later, I located the exit wound just above my waist on the left side of my body. I could even see a dent in the sidewall of the aircraft where the bullet had lodged after it had exited my abdomen. Fortunately, my body seemed to have taken enough energy off the projectile that it didn't penetrate the hull of the aircraft. But it wasn't all good. As I took my hand away from the wound on my left side, I saw that the blood seeping out of me was dark, almost black red. I had seen enough gunshot wounds to know what that meant. The bullet had passed through some of my internal organs.

"Great," I said. "And gut-shot as well."

A sudden wave of dizziness passed through me. I shook my head to fight it off. In my headset, I heard the air traffic controller frantically issuing instructions to me and realized that he had been speaking to me for the last few moments. I hadn't heard him.

I keyed the mic. "This is 13 Charlie Bravo. Declaring an emergency. We've had an altercation on the aircraft. Shots have been fired. The assailants are dead, and I am the one remaining crew member. I am losing blood. Need immediate vectors for the ILS to runway 10 at BWI. I will need emergency vehicles and medical trauma personnel on-site."

Through an act of sheer determination, I found the button on the data entry panel to open the transponder window on the PDU and entered 7700 into the display.

"Charlie Bravo, Potomac Approach," said a new, authoritative voice. "Copy you're an emergency. Say fuel remaining and souls on board."

I glanced down at the PDU and found I couldn't focus on the numbers on the left side where the fuel quantity was displayed. I shook my head to clear it and then squinted as I tried to read the fuel remaining.

"Five thousand two hundred pounds and one soul remaining," I said after a long moment.

"Copy that," said the controller. "You're cleared direct to BWI, cleared ILS runway 10, cleared to land."

"13 Charlie Bravo copies cleared to land," I responded automatically. I released the mic button. Another round of dizziness passed through me. "Blood," I said to myself, "losing too much blood."

The 7Xs first aid kit was in the galley closet, about seven feet behind me. It might as well have been seven miles. I glanced over at the jump seat behind Macy's seat and saw his company-issued leather jacket there. I reached over to grab it and managed to retrieve it on the third try. It was heavy and high quality, but I wasn't interested in the jacket itself, I was interested in the liner. Using the little remaining dexterity I had, I half unzipped, half ripped the liner out of the jacket and threw the shell on the floor. Then I tied the liner around my torso, ensuring that both wounds were covered.

I hoped it would be enough.

I looked down at the navigation display and then out of the windscreen, scanning the terrain for the airport. BWI was at my right one o'clock, about nine miles away. And I was still at 11,000 feet. I would have been in great shape if I was flying the full arrival, which called for a much longer ground track, but I was far too high to be this close to the field for the straight-in approach.

I pulled the throttles to idle and punched off the autopilot. Then I deployed full speed brakes and turned the jet towards the airport, lowering the jet's nose as the field appeared in front of me. I slewed my cursor to the final approach fix for the ILS on the waypoint list and selected it. Then, I reengaged lateral guidance and centered the steering cue in the HUD. I was at 250 knots and had 9,000 feet and 100 knots to lose if I was going to get on any kind of profile that would allow me to land the aircraft.

My eyelids began to droop as my body began to succumb to unconsciousness and shut down. My extremities felt cold, and my hands were slick with blood and clammy with sweat. I couldn't imagine how much blood had seeped out of my body and onto the floor of the aircraft.

"Hell of a cleaning job someone is going to have," I muttered to myself.

I felt a wave of nausea pass through me, and I involuntarily coughed up bile. I forced it back down, hoping the burning in my throat might help to keep me conscious.

8,000 feet and 230 knots. About seven miles from the

field. Still far too hot on energy. The conservative thing to do would have been to make a 360-degree turn to lose altitude and bleed off the speed. I had an emergency clearance and could have performed the maneuver. There was only one problem with that plan. I wasn't sure I could stay conscious long enough to do it.

I pushed the nose further down, accepting the increase in airspeed to lose altitude more quickly, hoping I could then burn off the speed once I assumed a shallower descent or even leveled off. The airspeed crept up to 260 knots, but I was descending more rapidly now, about 3,000 feet per minute.

Five miles from the field now, passing through 4,000 feet at a place where I would have normally been about 1,500 feet above the ground for a standard approach. The airspeed had stabilized at 265 knots. The runway was rapidly growing larger in the windscreen in front of me. It became apparent that I was going to need to slow down more quickly than the speed brakes would allow. I knew what I had to do. I just didn't know quite when I'd do it.

3,000 feet at three miles, I began to shallow the descent slightly, hoping the six panels of speed brakes would get me below 245 knots, the maximum operating speed of the landing gear. The wind stream would probably rip the landing gear doors off the jet because their limit was 200 knots, and they retracted after the gear extended. But at this point, I didn't care.

Another wave of dizziness passed through me, and my eyelids closed. I fought them open with every ounce of strength I had. The first thing I saw as my eyes came back into focus was an airspeed of 240 knots in the HUD. I reached across the cockpit and tried to throw the gear handle down. But my right hand was too wet with blood, and it slid off the round plastic knob. I dried my hand off on Macy's left pant leg and tried again. This time the gear deployed, along with a stern warning from the 7X's crew alerting system.

GEAR! GEAR! GEAR!

I ignored the warning and took stock of my position. 1,500 feet and two miles. But the airspeed was now decreasing to less than 200 hundred knots. I shoved the slats and flaps handle all the way down to SF3, the approach setting. The CAS system expressed new disapproval.

FLAPS! FLAPS! FLAPS!

About a mile to go and I was slowing through 185 knots and descending through 900 feet. My approach angle was about six degrees, about twice as steep as it would have been for a standard approach. My mind flashed back to the approach into London City, five years ago, and the 5.5-degree path there. I was beginning to see a situation I recognized, and the landing problem was becoming solvable.

Half a mile to go, altitude descending through 500 feet and airspeed rolling back through 150 knots. I decided to hold the steeper path for a few moments longer, but I retracted the speed brakes from AB2 to AB1, leaving just two panels deployed to slow the aircraft.

"It'll be enough," I said to myself. "It'll have to be enough. Thank God the runway is 10,000 feet long."

I crossed the threshold of the runway at 250 feet and 140 knots. The flashing lights of the emergency vehicles on the parallel taxiway barely registered in my peripheral vision. I held the steeper glide path until the ground proximity warning system issued its 100-foot warning. Then, I checked the throttles in idle and rotated the jet's nose upward, as smoothly as I could, hoping to not float the 7X in ground effect by rounding out too aggressively. The jet touched down a few seconds later. I deployed the thrust reverser and stepped on the toe brakes, trying to slow the aircraft as rapidly as I could, before my last few seconds of consciousness expired.

But my body had endured enough. Even as I saw the

airspeed slow through 70 knots on the HUD, my eyelids began to move downward, in a final, inexorable descent. I felt my limbs start to go slack.

Jesus, I thought. *To have made it this far only to die in a ground accident. What a fucking way to go.*

"Two things to do," I said to myself as my consciousness began to fade.

I reached for the engine fuel switches behind the throttles, located them by feel, and moved all three of them to aft position, my fingers barely able to grasp the slick metal. Then I found the emergency brake handle on the panel in front of me, fumbled with it for a second or two, and then pulled it all the way to the aft position.

The jet abruptly stopped, and I was thrown forward against the glare shield and the HUD. But I didn't feel the impact. The blackness had already taken me. And I found I was grateful for that.

CHAPTER THIRTY-EIGHT

Thursday, January 28th
2143 Hours Local Time
Intensive Care Unit
Johns-Hopkins Hospital
Baltimore, Maryland USA

There were several awakenings on my way back to the real world. But it was the final one that scared me.

***

The first time I had awakened, I was on a gurney being wheeled down a hallway. My eyes were barely able to stay open. I felt the déjà vu of a similar situation, many years ago, when a crazy Mexican assassin had embedded a huge knife in my shoulder. The eyes that looked down at me were concerned but distant.

Through the daze in my head, I heard a voice say: "He's lost a lot of blood. The bullet must have clipped the illiac artery."

I remembered thinking: "where the fuck is that?" and then drifting off with a slight smile on my face.

***

There had been a brief interlude where I was in a very bright place. I remembered being surrounded by familiar yet unidentifiable faces. I was comfortable and warm, and for some reason, I felt incredibly at home and at peace.

There was one face that became prominent. It radiated a depth of sincerity and kindness that was impossible for me to comprehend. He issued a command in a soft voice to the group around me. Suddenly four faces that I recognized appeared, Samantha Everheart, Susan Turner, Christine Billings, and last but not least, Gail Petersen, the four women who had been killed because of me. I almost recoiled when I saw them, awaiting the stream of accusations and recriminations that were sure to come. But they looked down at me with patience, understanding, and affection.

"It wasn't your fault," they said without moving their mouths, "we forgive you."

I remembered feeling the sting of moisture in my eyes and the warm wetness of tears rolling down my cheeks.

"I don't deserve to be forgiven," I said, unable to control the waver in my voice. "I've done so many horrible things."

"You've done your duty," the prominent face said. "That is who you are. And who you will continue to be for the rest of your days."

In that moment, I realized that I wasn't lying in a hospital somewhere. I was somewhere...else. And I wanted to stay there.

"I don't want to go back," I had said, my voice cracking. "I want to stay here with you."

The kind face had smiled at me. "It is not yet your time, Colin Pearce," He said.

***

A millisecond later, I awoke abruptly, pulled from the bright place with a painful thump to my chest. My eyes flew open. I found myself naked and lying on a hard table, barely covered by a paper blanket. I was surrounded by personnel and equipment and had a tube of some sort that had been inserted in my throat. I remembered reaching for it to tear it out of me.

"Restrain him!" an authoritative female voice commanded. "We just got him back, we can't lose him now."

"Colin, can you hear me?" Another female voice had asked. I looked up and saw a pair of dark brown eyes looking down at me over the top of a surgical mask. "Don't try to talk, just nod or blink your eyes."

I had blinked rapidly.

"We're trying to help you," she said. "We need to leave that tube in for your protection. I know its uncomfortable. We'll take it out as soon as we can."

"We need to put him under," a third voice, a man, had said. "I need to operate if we're going to stop the bleeding."

"Understood," the authoritative female voice said. "Once we get him stabilized, we'll anesthetize him, and you can go to work."

"You need to hurry," the man said. "He's gone through a lot of blood. I'm not sure how much of that type we have in the bank."

Oh yeah, I thought to myself. *I'm AB negative. Damn. That's fucking inconvenient.*

"The epinephrine seems to be keeping him with us," the authoritative voice said after a few moments. "John, you can start him on the propofol, the lowest dose possible to put him under."

"I'll push 50 micrograms per minute and see how he does," a new male voice answered.

In seconds, I could begin to feel my body relax. My eyelids

started to fall. I felt a smile creep onto my face. Maybe I was going back to the bright and warm place, where I would see the kind face again. But then I remembered his last words to me, and I knew that I wasn't going anywhere. At least not yet.

"Fuck," I tried to say with the tube down my throat.

The nurse who had spoken before stroked the sides of my head with her gloved hands.

"Try to relax, Colin," she said. "This will be over soon. We'll take good care of you. I promise. This team is the best there is. The folks at Langley insisted on it."

I looked up at her and nodded sleepily. Then my eyelids closed, and my brain began the slow descent into unconsciousness.

"He's under," John the anesthesiologist said.

"About time," the other male doctor, the surgeon, said. "Hopefully, we're not too late."

But my brain heard the words and processed them. I felt my relaxing mouth form another smile, and a prayer came to me, a heathen who had never prayed. *Please, God, let them be too late. Sarah and the kids are safe. No one I care about has been killed. Please do the world a favor, take me before I hurt anyone else.*

I didn't have any idea who or what I was praying to, but the kind face I had seen earlier filled my mind's eye as I went under. I didn't see his mouth move, but I heard something in my mind that embedded itself there.

Not yet, He said. *I have work for you to do.*

***

The next time I awoke, I had no tube in my throat. Sarah was holding my hand. As my eyes fluttered open, I felt her squeeze my hand, and I saw her wave someone over to my bedside.

"He's awake!" she exclaimed. "Oh my God, Colin! You're finally awake!"

I looked up to see Sarah's beautiful face looking down at me. Her makeup was minimal, and her thick red locks were pulled into a ponytail behind her head. But she still looked ravishing. I felt tears well in my eyes. It was one thing to be told she had been rescued, another thing to see her in the flesh.

"You're okay," I said, my voice hoarse from disuse. I tried to clear the cobwebs from my brain and force myself to speak coherently. "You're really okay."

She nodded and squeezed my hand again.

"And the kids?" I asked.

She nodded quickly and I could see the moisture in her eyes. "They're with Brett. They're great."

I had laid back in the bed as a grateful sigh came out of me.

A nurse materialized at my bedside. I looked over at her and was surprised to see the same pair of brown eyes I remembered from the operating room. She recorded my vital signs on an electronic tablet and then looked down at me. She noticed me staring back at her and nodded her head in acknowledgment of my gaze.

"I'm Nancy Travis," she said. "And yes, I was with you in the OR as well. You have a good memory for someone who was under that kind of sedation."

"Well, almost dying and getting shocked back into the present tends to make you remember things," I said.

She shook her head. "You didn't almost die," she replied. "You were clinically dead for fifteen minutes. Those bullets did a number on your insides. They hit several organs and nicked the major artery in your abdomen. You are fortunate to be alive." She looked at me with an expression of wonder on her face. "And how in the hell did you stay conscious long enough to land that airplane? You should have passed out from the blood loss in minutes."

I tried to shrug, but my shoulders barely moved. "No idea," I said after a moment.

"It was his duty," Sarah said. "It's what he does."

The nurse nodded. "I've heard that about you," she said. "I have a few colleagues who think very highly of you."

I smiled at her. "I wondered why an ER nurse would also be in the ICU. I assume you work for a certain three-letter agency we're familiar with?"

She nodded again. "I was part of the medical response team at the airport. I helped to get you out of the jet. Once we got you here, I was assigned to you to make sure you were properly taken care of."

"And the highly classified nature of what I was doing had nothing at all to do with that?"

She lifted her right hand and made a small gap between her thumb and index finger. "Maybe a little," she said.

I pushed my head back into my pillow. "Makes sense. So, now that I'm awake and coherent?"

"We'll keep you under observation here for 24 hours and then move you to another section of the hospital. Then you can probably expect about a week before you've healed enough that the doctors will feel comfortable discharging you."

"A week full of debriefings, no doubt."

She nodded. "You know the drill."

A wave of fatigue came over me. I felt my eyelids begin to droop.

"Sadly, I do," I said as I drifted off to sleep. "All too well."

"Sleep, Colin," Sarah's voice had said. "We're here for you."

***

I woke up the final time to find myself staring into Brenda Rowe's murderous eyes. At first, I thought it was some kind of nightmare, brought on by the cocktail of drugs coursing through my system.

I blinked my eyes several times and attempted to move my head from side to side in an effort to wake myself up. But each time I refocused, Rowe was still there, clad in the requisite medical scrubs and staring at me over the top of a surgical mask, the cold, hateful eyes looking nearly gleeful as they regarded me. I looked down at her hands and could see that she had a syringe attached to my IV unit and had her thumb on the plunger. In mere seconds, she would push the plunger home, and the vile stuff in the syringe would shoot into my veins, taking me away to whatever fate awaited me in the next life.

How could this happen? I wondered. *Where are the good guys?* But then, a thought occurred to me, and I found myself gently shaking my head in amazement. *Those bastards.* A smile found its way onto my lips.

"What are you so fucking happy about Pearce?" Rowe hissed through the surgeon's mask. "I'm about to put you out of my misery."

"For what, exactly?" I asked her. "Stopping your treasonous plot against our country? Keeping you from overthrowing a legitimate government in South Korea for the sake of increasing Enteron's stock price? Rescuing a mother and her kids that you had kidnapped so you could kill them? Maybe it was taking out your CEO boyfriend, or getting to the bottom of Mark Hill's murder and finding out that you killed him?"

Rowe snorted contemptuously. "I didn't kill him," she said. "I had Betty Jarvis do that. She used to work for me as an investigator when I was general counsel for the company. She's an evil little shit, and she owed me."

"But you ordered it," I said.

She shrugged. "Hill was figuring things out. He would have spoiled everything."

"And Jarvis found a way to make it look like a suicide."

"Everyone was buying it until you came along."

"It wasn't too hard to figure out. Besides, I knew Mark Hill. He was a good man. He was dedicated to doing the right thing. But he made the unforgivable mistake of actually standing up to you."

Rowe looked at me with a malicious smile.

"And you don't tolerate disagreement or dissension in your ranks," I continued.

She shook her head. "No, I don't," she said. "When you work for me, it's my way or the highway."

"Be glad I never worked for you. Mark Hill was a gentleman. I'm not. I would have taken your ass to task much earlier than he did."

Rowe sneered. "You're not going to be taking anyone's ass to task after I push about 50cc's of fentanyl into your IV here."

I laughed at her. "Brenda, you are so fucked, and you're too arrogant and stupid to realize it. Didn't you learn your lesson from that business at the Clinton Plant?"

The sneer ran away from her face, and a look of uncertainty came over her.

"I work with the pros. They had your game figured out at Clinton, and they have it figured out now. If you want to walk out of here alive, you'll back away from me and keep your hands in view."

For a mere few seconds, Rowe considered her options. Her eyes became contemplative, and I could almost hear the cogs turning in her brain. But her overconfidence, her arrogance, and her hate overcame her. Her eyes hardened, and she seated her thumb on the base of the syringe's plunger. She looked at me, malevolently. A maniacal smile etched itself into her features.

"Die, you fucker," she said.

"I don't think so," I replied.

And at that moment, a silver stiletto knife appeared in her neck, the point of it protruding from the middle of her throat. She dropped the syringe and did what they all do. She frantically reached for her throat as if somehow she could remove the silver projectile, and save her life. But she was already dead. She just didn't know it yet.

With all the strength I could muster, I pushed myself up on my elbows and looked her in the eyes as the terror began to take possession of her.

"You've been outclassed since the very beginning, you arrogant bitch," I said. "I hope there's a special place in hell for you."

Rowe's eyes glazed over, and she sank to the floor. There were two distinct cracks as her bony knees made contact with the tile, but her face remained impassive. She remained there, kneeling on the hard surface for a moment or two, and I watched her face process the prospect of her impending death. Where there should have been an expression of grief or sadness, or even regret, there was only anger and rage, like she had been cheated out of something she was entitled to. But then her eyes rolled back in her head. She collapsed onto the black and white tiles, her head making another distinct crack as it impacted the floor's cold surface. I looked over the side of my bed at her lifeless body. Robbed of its malicious energy, her skinny frame seemed very small and insignificant lying there. I found myself amazed that something so frail could generate so much fear and death.

I heard footsteps approaching and looked up to see Sharona Brown and Nancy Travis entering the room.

"Speaking of not losing your touch, Sharona," I said. "I haven't seen you and your stiletto in action for a while. Glad to see you've still got your magic there."

Sharona shrugged and smiled at me. "How did you know we were there?"

"It occurred to me that it would be damn difficult for someone to get into an ICU ward and make it past the CIA's finest unless they were allowed to. And I was the perfect bait to bring Rowe out of hiding. She would have had to come and get me to take her vengeance. She wouldn't have been able to let it go."

Sharona nodded. "That was our assessment as well. If it matters, we had the room and the approaching hallways under surveillance. We knew exactly when she entered and followed her every move."

"Good thing you got her before she pushed that plunger," I said. "Or your good aim might not have made a difference."

"It wouldn't have mattered," Nancy Travis said. "We re-routed your IV. The one that she attached the syringe to was a dummy."

"Huh," I said. "You didn't want her alive? For questioning?"

Sharona shook her head. "She's a lawyer. She would have engaged counsel, and the legal process would have taken years. We don't have that kind of patience, and she needed to die. We just wanted her to be in the process of committing a deadly act when we took her down. Looks better for all the bleeding hearts when they review the paperwork."

"I'm guessing the fact that IV valve was a dummy probably won't be in the report?" I asked.

Sharona shrugged, and Nancy Travis looked at the ceiling. Neither said a word.

Nice," I said. "I guess you guys had this all figured out. I'm not surprised." I looked down at Rowe's body and then back at the two CIA officers. "We got everyone except Jarvis, right? "

Sharona nodded. "We still have to arrest her."

I shook my head vehemently. "No," I said. "She's the one who killed Mark Hill. She's mine. You need to leave her alone until I get better."

"That's going to be several weeks," Nancy said. "You

realize that."

I nodded.

"She could run," Sharona said.

I shook my head again. "I don't think so. Once this story breaks and she finds out all the major players are either dead or in custody, she'll believe she's in the clear. She'll relax and go about her daily routine and get nice and comfortable in it. And that's when I'll go to her."

"The Klingon proverb?" Sharona asked.

I nodded. "Yes. Revenge is a dish best served cold. And Betty Jarvis is going to get hers right out of the fucking freezer."

EPILOGUE

Friday, March 4th
1800 Hours Local Time
Ian Brooks' House
Sedona, Arizona USA

"I hope you like my version of this," Patti Belmont said as she handed me the frosty martini glass. "I've tried to follow your recipe."

I accepted the glass from her gratefully. "You have no idea how much I need this," I said. "This is the first martini I've had since I was in the hospital. The doctors have had me on all these drugs, and no alcohol was part of the deal." I raised my glass. "Cheers to both of you," I said, including Patti's boyfriend and my business partner/boss, Ian Brooks, in the gesture. "Thank you for the dinner invitation."

"Cheers to you, Colin, and you're welcome," said Brooks. "Glad you're back."

"Me too," I said. We were enjoying our evening cocktail on the expansive back deck of Ian's house, gathered around a chiminea to ward off the chilly March air. The sun was setting and basking Bell Rock, Courthouse Butte and Cathedral Rock, down the valley from us, in a golden glow. Brooks' house was built into the side of the airport Mesa, about 300 feet above the valley floor, and the spectacular views from his deck encompassed the entire east side of Sedona.

I had introduced Patti and Ian at the end of my last adventure, in December, but hadn't seen the two of them together since the company Christmas party. Patti was a tall redhead with elegant features and sensual green eyes. Ian, well, was just Ian. He had black hair and sparkling blue eyes and carried himself in a mechanical fashion, a function of the multiple surgeries he had in the wake of a devastating plane crash at Edwards Air Force Base years before. The two of them looked to have come a long way since December. They seemed very comfortable with each other, and after observing them for just a few moments, I detected the unspoken shorthand between them that usually comes later in relationships. They were bonding, and I was happy for them. I was glad somebody was bonding somewhere.

I took a sip of the martini and closed my eyes as I let the icy Plymouth gin ease its way down my throat.

"Well done," I said, inclining my head to Patti.

"You hooked her on them after the two of you met back in December!" Brooks said. We go through a bottle of Plymouth every few days. She's addicted to it!"

Patti shrugged and smiled. "It's true," she said.

I smiled back at her. "There are worse things," I said.

I took another sip of my martini and looked across the valley at the Chapel of Holy Cross, just opposite us. The building was bathed in shadow, but the light from inside emphasized the huge cross that dominated the building's western wall. I found I took comfort in the shape and realized that after living in Sedona for over five years, I'd never been there. I made a mental note to visit the place soon.

"So, I guess the flight department folks at Enteron were sorry to see you go?" Ian asked.

I shrugged. "Not sure. While the place was certainly better

with the idiots removed, and everyone there seemed to be thankful I made that happen, I'm not sure they wanted me to stay on. I think I might have been a little intense for them."

Brooks grinned at me. "I can totally see that," he said. "Who will they bring in to replace you?"

"The guy I flew with, Rick Wilson, has been made interim director and I think he'll do a good job. I think they'll bring in a recruiter to formally advertise and interview for the position, though."

"They didn't make the Chief Pilot the interim director?"

I shook my head. "He was too interested in other things. I'm not sure he'll even remain Chief Pilot. I recommended they remove him."

Brooks nodded. "I see. So, I heard the CEO is going to stand trial for that whole business?"

"Yep. I'm surprised he lived through me bouncing off the ceiling of the jet. The 7X's digital FCS must have lessened the impact. But his wife and kids left him, and he'll never walk again. He'll probably spend the rest of his life in prison."

"How did all of that even happen?" Patti asked.

"The executives in the company got greedy," I said. "They saw a window of opportunity and took advantage of it."

"But how did it get from them helping the North Koreans with their nuclear power plants to them giving the NK's nuclear waste to put into artillery shells?" Brooks asked as he took a sip of his martini.

"I'm not sure we'll ever know," I said. "A lot of the main players are dead, and Lane is lawyered up."

"How fucking bizarre," Patti said.

"Agreed," I said, taking another sip of my drink.

There was another pause in the conversation, and I could sense Patti looking between Ian and me, obviously pressing him to continue the questioning. After a few moments, it became apparent that he wouldn't. Like me, he observed the fighter pilot emotional issue disclosure code: if you have emotional issues, you don't disclose them. At least not readily.

"Okay, you two can play the strong silent act, but Colin," Patti stepped forward and put her hand on my arm, "how are you doing?"

I felt a wave of emotion pass through me, and I looked at her with a helpless expression on my face. "I feel like shit. But I did what I had to do. I let them go. I had to let them go. Especially after what just happened. I know Sarah still loves me and probably always will, but she and Brett were perfect for each other. Besides, he'll be able to keep her and the kids a lot safer than I will."

"But your kids will grow up never knowing their father," Patti said. "That sucks."

I nodded. "It does. But at least they'll be alive. I'd like to participate in their lives somehow, but I don't know how I can without endangering them. I need to think about that."

Patti was shaking her head. "It's just not fair."

I sighed. "It never is. Story of my life."

"Well, Ian and I are here for you."

"I appreciate that," I said, looking between the two of them. "It means a lot."

"Well," Ian said, "now that all the serious shit is over, Patti and I will get about the dinner tasks. Steaks sound good to you, T.C.?"

I nodded. "Sounds great."

They turned to walk back into the house, but I stopped them.

"Hey, thanks for having me over," I said. "I could have been alone tonight. I can always be alone. But I'm glad I'm not tonight."

Patti reached over and kissed me lightly on the cheek. "You're always welcome here," she said. "You fixed me up with this lug over here and changed my life."

Ian shrugged and smiled. "Mine too," he said.

"One of the best things I've ever done," I said.

They turned back towards the kitchen, and I found my way to the rail of the deck and gazed out over the darkening Sedona landscape. Sunset was my favorite time of day here, no matter what the season. The interplay of the day's last rays of sun on the red rocks never failed to fascinate and inspire me. I took another sip of my martini and regarded the crimson hues of the sunlight on the sandstone of the massive edifices to the south. The upper levels of the monuments, particularly Cathedral Rock, looked almost blood-red in the dying sunlight. I stared at the rock and remembered my last errand in the Chicago area – the only one that had brought me any satisfaction.

***

The martini that night wasn't my first drink after being issued my new bill of health. The first drink had come the previous evening.

The CIA had provided me the intel and gear I needed. I had found Betty Jarvis' house easily and made my way in through an unobserved rear door, bypassing the alarm system in the process. Then, I had waited for her, seated in an easy chair in her sparsely decorated living room.

I had seen the signs of children in the place, toys strewn about, coloring books stacked on tables, and the inevitable kid videos piled up next to the DVD player. But the kids wouldn't be an issue tonight. They were spending the night at the ex-husband's house and would be out of the way.

She came through the garage door on cue at 2310 hours, just 10 minutes after her shift ended. She was dressed in black slacks, a white shirt, and a blue blazer, none of which complimented her corpulent figure. I let her get through the door, deactivate the bypassed alarm, and set her purse down in the kitchen before I announced my presence.

"Good evening, Betty," I said. "Please don't be stupid and go for your gun. I'll put two .45 slugs into you, and you'll be dead before you hit the ground."

She had raised her hands and slowly turned to face me. I was wearing a navy-blue suit and had a glass of Macallan 12 in my left hand. My Kimber 1911-style .45 commander was in my right hand, with a suppressor attached to the short barrel. As soon as she recognized me, her eyes grew very wide.

"My compliments on the scotch," I said, raising my glass to her. The Macallan 12 is excellent."

"What do you want?" she asked, her voice quavering.

"Why don't you come in here and have a seat?" I asked. "I think you need to explain a few things before I do what I came here to do."

She slowly walked into the living room, keeping her hands in view as she moved. She sat on the sofa, about ten feet away, facing me. She didn't sit back against the cushions. Instead, she sat on the edge of the couch, with her feet squarely on the floor. Her posture could have been one of preparation or nervousness. My money was on the latter.

"You've read my file, right?" I asked. "Maybe not before I visited you at the department headquarters, but since then, yes?"

She nodded slowly.

"Then you know you know what I am, yes?"

She nodded again.

"Is there any doubt in your mind that I'll kill you if I don't get the answers I want?"

Jarvis shook her head slowly and deliberately.

I nodded. "Good. Then we understand each other."

She nodded in response.

I removed my phone from a coat pocket with my left hand

and ensured she saw it. Then, I activated the recording feature on it.

"Tell me how you killed Mark Hill."

"Rowe made me do it!" she blurted out. "She was blackmailing me!"

"Not surprised about that," I said. "But I also don't really care. What I need to know is how you did it."

Jarvis' shoulders slumped forward like she had lost a battle of sorts. She shrugged and looked at me. "Scopolamine," she said.

I nodded. "Huh," I said. "The famous mind-control drug. How did you administer it?"

"I lined all of his coffee cups with it," Jarvis said. "I knew he had coffee every morning before he left for work."

"I see," I said. "Which is why all the cups were washed and put away when he was found by the patrol officer. So, after he had his coffee, you just broke in and told him to shoot himself?"

She shook her head. "It doesn't really work that way. A few minutes after he had his coffee, I knocked on the door and told him I was with the police and that he may have been poisoned, and I could help him. I showed him my badge, and he let me in."

"And then you told him to shoot himself."

She shook her head again. "No," she said. "I told you it doesn't really work like that. I just told him to sit in his chair. He was pretty drugged up."

"Then how did the gunshot wound get there?"

Jarvis swallowed hard.

"I knew he had guns," she said. "And I knew he always kept one in his car, so I knew it would be in his briefcase or nearby since he was getting ready to go to work."

"So, you retrieved the gun and..."

She opened her mouth to speak but hesitated. I knew what

she was going to say, but I needed her to utter the words. I needed her to hear her own voice saying them. I squeezed the grip on the Kimber and activated the laser sight, centering the red dot on her chest. She saw the laser emanating from the gun, looked down at her chest, and then back at me with a panicked expression on her face.

"I'm losing patience, Betty," I said. "You retrieved the gun and…"

"I put it into his hand, put it to his head, and forced his finger to pull the trigger! Okay? Is that what you wanted to hear?"

I took another sip of scotch. "No," I said. "It wasn't what I wanted to hear. But it ties up loose ends."

"But, I answered you, right?" There was a trace of hysteria in her tone. "What else do you want?"

"To give you a choice," I said, keeping the red dot of the laser on her. I reached into my jacket pocket with my left hand and removed a white envelope. Then, I showed it to her and placed it on the table next to me.

"What's that?" she asked, but her eyes told me she knew.

"A very touching suicide note," I said. "Similar to the one you, Rowe, and crew constructed for Mark Hill. It talks about how depressed you are, how you can't go on, how you regret hurting everyone, blah, blah, blah. And unlike the one you made for Hill, it actually looks like your handwriting, down to the signature. Good enough to fool a forensic detective."

"But…," Jarvis began to speak.

I held up my left hand to silence her. "There's no bargaining here, Betty. You killed a friend of mine. You die tonight. In this room. In the next few minutes. The only thing you have control over is how you die and the aftermath."

I gave her a few moments to process that while I took another sip of scotch.

"Do you want to hear your choices?" I asked after I put

my glass down.

She didn't respond. Instead, her gaze remained fixed on me, but her eyes didn't see me. She seemed to be retreating into herself.

"Earth to Betty," I said. "Do you want to hear your choices?"

Jarvis seemed to come back to herself.

"Here are the two ways this will go down," I continued. "In one scenario, you pull your service weapon out of its holster, put it in your mouth, and pull the trigger. The local cops will find the note, and everyone will believe it's a suicide. Your kids will be devastated, but they'll continue to believe their mom was a good person, but just suffered from depression.

"In the second scenario, I put two bullets into the center of your chest, and every news outlet in the Chicagoland area gets the story of a murderous small-town detective who killed a loving father, and manipulated the investigation because she was ordered to by a greedy executive from one of the largest companies in the area. Your kids will be shamed, and they'll probably despise you for the rest of their lives."

I reached over for the glass of scotch, raised it to my lips, and drained it. "What's it going to be?" I asked after a long moment.

Jarvis was shaking her head in disbelief. After she composed herself for a few moments, she spoke. "You can't do this," she said at last. "There are laws..."

"That's true. But this isn't about legalities, it's about justice," I said. "And tonight, Mark Hill gets justice." I sat back in my chair. "Now, make your choice before I make it for you."

"But, I have kids!"

"So did Mark Hill," I said. "Now, do the honorable thing for once in your fucked-up life."

I left the house a few moments later, slipping out the back door, after disposing of my glass and making sure my fingerprints weren't on the bottle of scotch I poured from. Jarvis' body remained on the sofa, the police-issued 9mm Glock in her hand. I had to retrieve it from the floor and put it back in her hand after she had used it to blow the back of her head off.

I put the suicide note on the table next to her. But I had lied about its contents. The note contained a full confession to Mark Hill's murder and Rowe's role in it. Jarvis's kids would have to grow up in the shadow of their mother, the murderer, but at least they would know the truth. They deserved that.

*****

I pulled myself back into the present and raised the martini glass to my lips, draining the last sip of the silky gin and lamenting that I would have to leave the scenic vista around me and retreat into the kitchen to get another one.

"Hey, Colin," Ian yelled from behind me. "You've got a visitor. She called earlier and wanted to surprise you."

I slowly turned around, and there, much to my surprise, clad in tight black jeans and a maroon sweater, stood Jessica Tate, holding two martinis. She offered one to me.

I accepted it and put my empty glass on a nearby table. We clinked glasses. I gave Ian an enthusiastic thumbs up. He smiled and retreated back into the kitchen.

"You're a long way from Kunsan, Colonel," I said after we had both sipped.

She nodded and joined me at the rail, looking out over the darkening landscape.

"I never came here when I was in the basic course at Luke," she said. "It's beautiful."

"You should see it in the daytime," I said.

Jess turned to me. "Well, maybe you can help me out with that," she said. "I don't have a hotel booked, but I heard a rumor you had a place here.”

I nodded. “But how...”

“We both have some friends in high places,” she said. “I was due for some leave and couldn’t think of anywhere I’d rather be than...”

“Sedona?” I interrupted. “Really?”

Jess put her glass on the railing and stepped closer to me, sliding her arms around my waist.

“No, you idiot,” she said. “Not Sedona. With you. I hope I’m not overstepping.”

I set my glass aside and put my arms around her. “Not a bit,” I said. “I’m really glad you’re here.”

“I found a conference to attend at Luke. I called your business here, and they gave me Ian’s number. I thought I might stop by and surprise you.”

I looked down into the deep blue eyes and smiled.

“Great thought,” I said. “How long can you stay?”

“I’m on my midtour break, and I have a whole month of leave I haven’t used. The conference is only the first two days of next week,” she said. “I can stay as long as you want me to.”

“I can’t think of a better way to pass the month,” I said.

Jess raised her lips to mine, and we lost ourselves in one another for a long moment. As the kiss ended, in my peripheral vision, I saw Ian and Patti watching us through the sliding glass door to the kitchen. Her head was on his shoulder, and they were smiling. They seemed to be so at peace with one another.

I stared down at Jess and looked into her eyes, taking in the radiance of her smile and the feeling of her body next to mine. I could feel the hope surging within me for the first time in a long while. Perhaps it was possible for me to finally find a person and a place where I could be at peace and feel at home. Perhaps that could even be with the remarkable woman in front of me. But in my heart, I knew that would never be my destiny. The words of the kind face in my vision from the operating room would make that impossible.

Not yet, He had said. *I have work for you to do.*

So be it, I said to myself as I held Jessica Tate in my arms. *So be it.*

But not for a while.

COLIN PEARCE WILL RETURN IN
THE LONE WOLF CONTRACT

ABOUT THE AUTHOR

Chris Broyhill is a retired U.S. Air Force fighter pilot who flew the OV-10, A-10, and F-16 while on active duty. He holds a bachelor's degree in Computer Science from the U.S. Air Force Academy, a master's degree in National Security Studies from California State University at San Bernardino and a Ph.D. in Aviation from Embry-Riddle Aeronautical University. Chris is an outstanding graduate of the U.S. Air Force Fighter Weapons School and is a National Business Aviation Association Certified Aviation Manager. He also sits on the NBAA Business Aviation Management Committee. Chris has flown multiple aircraft types and held several leadership positions in aviation organizations for over 30 years. He currently resides in the Dallas-Fort Worth area.